Through her marriage to Reggie Kray, Roberta Kray has a unique and authentic insight into London's East End. Roberta met Reggie in early 1996 and they married the following year; they were together until Reggie's death in 2000. Roberta is the author of many previous bestsellers including *Bad Girl*, *Streetwise*, *No Mercy* and *Dangerous Promises*.

ROBERTA
KRAY
SURVIVOR

sphere

SPHERE

First published in Great Britain in 2017 by Sphere
This paperback edition published in 2018 by Sphere

1 3 5 7 9 10 8 6 4 2

A CIP catalogue record for this book
is available from the British Library.

ISBN 978-0-7515-6105-0

Typeset in Garamond by M Rules
Printed and bound in Great Britain by
Clays Ltd, St Ives plc

Papers used by Sphere are from well-managed forests
and other responsible sources.

Sphere
An imprint of
Little, Brown Book Group
Carmelite House
50 Victoria Embankment
London EC4Y 0DZ

An Hachette UK Company
www.hachette.co.uk

www.littlebrown.co.uk

SURVIVOR

Prologue

1958

He watched the ground as he walked through the trees, careful not to make any noise. Every few yards he would stop and listen, his head cocked to one side. Over the last few weeks he had conducted a number of recces, got to know the lie of the land, but now it was for real everything felt different. He had a sense of anticipation, a surging energy that jangled his nerves and made his heart race.

He looked at his watch. There was still some time. Slowly he made his way down to the water's edge. The lake was calm, gunmetal grey and fringed with bulrushes. A fine, hazy mist hung over the surface but he could just make out the house across the other side, a substantial three-storey white building. His upper lip curled a little; other people's good fortune always filled him with resentment.

Glancing both ways along the path that circled the lake, he kept his eyes peeled for unwanted company. On all the occasions he'd been here before, he'd only ever seen one other person apart from the nanny, and that was the handyman walking the family's black retriever. The nanny was a slight girl who wouldn't put up much of a fight. No problem there. He could take her with one arm tied behind his back. What he didn't need was an interfering have-a-go hero or, come to that, some fucker of a dog trying to chew off his balls.

He stood for a while before retreating back into the shelter of the trees. Crouching down, he lit a fag, impatient now for it to begin. The waiting around was the hardest part. He went over the plan in his head, step by step, and automatically checked his pockets to make sure the coils of twine were still there.

The minutes dragged by and the chilly autumnal air began to seep into his bones. He needed a drink, a good strong shot of whisky. His tongue slid across his dry lips. He finished the cigarette, dug a small hole in the ground with the heel of his boot, dropped in the butt and covered it with soil and leaves. He stretched out one leg and then the other, and thought about what he'd do when it was all over. Go abroad, perhaps, and get some sun. He was tired of the cold, grey British weather, tired of everything about Britain.

And what about Hazel? If the truth were told he was sick of her as well. The things that had initially attracted him, her innocence and wide-eyed adulation, had long since lost their appeal. These days she just got on his nerves. Still, she had her uses. He'd need her over the next week or so, and after that she was history. He didn't have to worry about her grassing him up; she was in it up to her neck and if she went to the law she'd be sealing her own fate too.

It was a further five minutes before he heard the sound of the pram's wheels. Instantly he was alert, the adrenalin starting to flow. He pulled the scarf up over his nose and mouth. Then he got to his feet and began quietly to move down towards the lake. The girl came into view. She was dressed in a drab brown coat and her lips were moving slightly; she was talking to the baby or herself or maybe mouthing the words to a song.

He crept close to the path and waited for her to pass by before leaping from the bushes and pouncing from behind. She stiffened with fear and panic as his arm snaked around her neck and his gloved palm clamped hard against her mouth. With his body pressed against hers, he knew he had absolute power over her. It was a gratifying, almost sexual feeling – but he wasn't here for that.

'Don't try anything, love, or I'll snap your fuckin' neck in half!'

Paralysed with fright, she didn't dare move. He had her. Now all he had to do was make sure she stayed bound and hidden while he grabbed the baby and got the hell out of there. But then, as he tried to drag her towards the undergrowth, something unexpected happened. As if waking from a nightmare, she suddenly kicked out, catching him on the shin. He gasped in surprise, loosened his grip, and she twisted away from him. In the ensuing struggle, they grappled with each other, a messy desperate battle. She was small but she fought like a wildcat: bug-eyed, terrified, hysterical. As he tried to subdue her, he stumbled and barged into the pram.

There was a moment when time slowed and stretched, when seconds became interminable, when the wheels continued to turn and the pram lurched off the path, travelling down the bank towards the lake. There was a holding of breath, a terrible stillness in the air. He knew he had a choice: leave the girl and grab the baby or ... But he hesitated too long and the pram slipped into the water with a soft splash, tilted and turned over.

The girl let out a cry. 'Kay!' And then she started to scream.

He snapped into action. He had to silence her before she alerted the whole bloody world to what was going on. As he yanked her towards the lake, he covered her mouth with his hand. 'Shut up! Shut up, you stupid bitch!' And then, because he couldn't think what else to do, he shoved her hard and sent her flying into the water. It had the desired effect. The shock of the cold rendered her speechless and as she scrabbled around, arms flailing, he waded in to retrieve the child.

The pram was on its side, half submerged. He snatched up the soaking wet bundle but couldn't tell if the baby was alive or not. It had only been a short while, not long enough to drown, surely, but she was an odd colour and her eyes were closed. He started making his way towards the bank, but suddenly the girl was on him again, tugging at his coat, clawing at his arms, trying to snatch the kid off him.

'Give her to me!'

He pushed her away with his free hand but she kept

coming back. By now the scarf had slipped off and she could see him clearly. Fuck it! Damn! She wouldn't have a problem picking him out in a line-up. And suddenly he couldn't think straight. All kinds of shit was running through his head, including the prospect of a long stretch. He had a sudden flash forward to standing in the dock while a judge sent him down. Ten years? Twenty? Child abduction came with a heavy price. Rage and panic flowed through his body. No, he wasn't having it. He wasn't going to jail. He couldn't.

And meanwhile the stupid bitch was still clawing at him, still yelling, her cries echoing around the lake. Why wouldn't she just shut the fuck up? What he did next was impulsive, instinctive, a matter of self-preservation. He put his hand on the top of her head, grabbed her hair, pushed her under the water and leaned on her with all his weight. He just wanted her to be quiet. He counted off the seconds: one, two, three, four, five. He should have let go but he didn't. She struggled for a while, a futile thrashing of arms and legs – bubbles rose from her mouth to the surface – and then she went limp. He stared down through the grey water, knowing what he'd done but not wanting to acknowledge it.

Finally, he disentangled his fingers from her hair. She didn't move. And now what was done couldn't be undone. How had it happened? It shouldn't have happened. It was her fault, he told himself. If only she'd left well alone . . .

Quickly, with the baby in his arms, he scrambled out of the water and on to the bank. The kid wasn't crying, wasn't doing anything. The blanket was soaked through. Maybe the shock of the cold water had been too much. He didn't want to look too closely. He just wanted to get away. As he glanced back over his shoulder he saw the girl floating face down in the lake. And now he couldn't breathe properly. He felt cold, shivery, sick to the stomach. Shit, it had all gone wrong. It had all gone horribly wrong.

1

1971

By the age of thirteen, Lolly knew her mum was different. Unfortunately everyone on the Mansfield estate knew it too. Sometimes Angela Bruce was ill in a quiet sort of way, indoors with her face turned to the wall, but other times she roamed the walkways of the three tall towers shouting about God and sin, the Elgin Marbles, snakes, spiders, MI5 or whatever else had wormed its way into her head that day.

The flat, on the fourteenth floor of Haslow House, was cramped and damp. Often there was no electricity and no coins to feed the empty meter. Lolly, who was small and skinny and always hungry, had learned to scavenge. She would root through other people's bins for leftovers, or beg from the market stalls when they were packing up at the end of the day. Her clothes were old and ragged, cast-offs from the charity shops or from neighbours who felt sorry for her.

Today the sky was a clear solid blue. Summer was Lolly's favourite time of year, mainly because the days were longer and she didn't have to think about keeping warm. There were also six glorious weeks without school. She was glad to escape from the taunts of her classmates, the name-calling, the hair pulling, the relentless reminders that she was not one of them; she was odd, an outsider, an outcast. Sometimes she bunked off but she knew better than to do it too often. With frequent truancy came a visit from the Social, and that always meant trouble. Those busybodies were just looking for an excuse to take her away and dump her in a 'home'.

Lolly feared being taken away more than anything else. Well, no, perhaps not *anything* else. What she feared more was that one day her mum would leave the flat and never come back. This was why she felt uneasy as she gazed into the bedroom. It was seven o'clock in the morning and already the bed was empty. Perhaps it hadn't even been slept in. She stared at the rumpled blankets but was unable to remember what they'd looked like yesterday.

Last night her mum had been in one of her jumpy, anxious moods, unable to sit still, pacing back and forth across the living room. Every few minutes she'd stop the pacing and go to the window to stare down at the grim wasteland of the estate. Raising her hand to her mouth, she chewed on her bitten-down fingernails.

'He's been following me, Lolly. Why won't he leave me alone?'

'Who's been following you?'

'*He* has. You mustn't talk to him. You mustn't tell him anything. Promise me.'

'I won't. I swear.' Lolly had looked out of the window

too, but the only people she could see, apart from a few stragglers, was a gang of lads gathered by the main gate. This happened every evening at dusk. Like a pack of wolves, they came together to hunt down anyone stupid enough to be walking the streets of Kellston alone.

'We've got to be careful. He could be on to us.'

And Lolly had nodded because she'd learnt through the years that agreeing was the only way to keep her mum calm.

'I think he may be next door. He's trying to listen. We have to stay very quiet.'

'Why is he following you, Mum?'

'You know why,' she whispered. 'We mustn't ever talk about it, not when … there are bugs everywhere. Spies. They're keeping tabs on us. Can you hear that?'

Lolly had listened but all she could hear was the soft anxious sound of her mother's breathing. 'What?'

A knowing, tight-lipped smile was the only response.

Lolly was still turning this over in her head as she walked to the bed and placed a palm on the grubby sheet. There was no warmth, no indication that anyone had been lying there recently. That wasn't good. She could have been gone for hours. Once, a year or so ago, she'd disappeared for two days and had eventually been found curled up, foetus-like, in the dark space at the bottom of the stairwell.

Lolly went through to the living room, opened the doors that led out to a narrow balcony and leaned over the rail. She scanned the estate, searching for the slim, slight figure of her mother, for the pale blue jacket and the familiar stream of long black hair. No sign. There was hardly anyone about.

She listened carefully but heard only the distant sound of traffic from the high street. An uneasy feeling was starting to stir inside her.

It didn't help that she was starving hungry. She'd gone to bed on an empty stomach and now she was desperate for something to eat. After closing the balcony doors she went to the kitchen and looked in the fridge. It had no light and, despite being empty, a bad smell wafted into her nostrils. She slammed shut the door and went to check the cupboards. She wasn't sure why she was bothering – there'd been nothing in them last night – but she lived in hope of miracles.

On this occasion, like most of the others, her hopes were immediately dashed. Her face fell as she crouched down and gazed at the empty shelves. Not even a few stray cornflakes or a tin of beans. If she wanted breakfast, she'd have to go out and hunt for it.

Lolly put on her thin cotton jacket with the deep pockets (she never knew what she might find), made sure she had the front door key, and left the flat. In the shared hallway she pressed all the lift buttons and waited . . . and waited. There was no indication that anything was happening. They were probably jammed again, or some kids were messing about on the ground floor, keeping all the doors open.

'Come on,' she said impatiently, jabbing at the buttons. 'Come on, come on.'

The estate had only been built about fifteen years ago but already it was starting to fall apart. The once-white concrete walls had turned grey and there were long ominous cracks running up the outside, some of them big enough to slide a finger into. The metal railings were rusting. Damp crept through the building and into the flats, black mould gathering on ceilings like a horrible disease. The whole estate had an air of despondency about it as if the residents, many of them stranded up in the sky, thought of the place more as a high-rise prison than a home.

Lolly couldn't clearly remember living anywhere else, although she knew she had. They'd moved here years ago but she wasn't sure where from. Her mum was always vague when asked, saying things like 'Oh, here and there,' or, if she was in one of her more suspicious moods, 'Who have you been talking to? Has someone been asking questions? You mustn't tell anyone *anything*, Lolly.' As if she had anything to tell. Her memories were vague and dreamlike, odd wisps that floated through her mind.

After a few minutes, Lolly gave up on the lift and decided to take the stairs instead. Fourteen floors was a long way to walk but it wasn't so bad when you were going down. It was the going up that made your legs feel like lead and pulled the air out of your lungs. She sang to herself as she made the descent: 'Knock Three Times' by Dawn.

By now the estate was starting to wake up. She could hear the muffled sound of radios, of voices, of toilets being flushed. The day was going to be a hot one and most people had the upper part of their windows open, the part that was too small for any thieving bastards to climb through. Crime was rife on the Mansfield and anything not nailed down disappeared in five minutes flat. The cops were always around, knocking on doors.

On reaching the ground the first thing Lolly did was to check the base of the stairwell to make sure her mother wasn't there. She approached it with caution, afraid of what she might find. In the event there was nothing scarier than a pile of litter, a load of fag ends and some empty bottles. She stared into it for a moment and then quickly withdrew. It was dark and nasty and stank of pee.

Lolly wasn't alone as she crossed the estate and headed for the main exit. There were people emerging from all three blocks; men and women on their way to work. Most had the same miserable expression on their faces as if the day, even though it had only just begun, was already a disappointment to them.

She set off for the high street. Her favourite spot for discarded food – apart from the market – was round the back of the Spar. Now was a good time to go before the staff came in to open up. As she walked she kept her eyes peeled for her mum. Lolly was always worried about her. Was she sleeping? Was she eating? Was she getting sick again? It was as though their roles had been reversed and she was the parent. There had been a time – she was certain of it – when things had been different, but now she just accepted the situation as normal. Other mothers didn't do the things hers did, but that didn't matter. Her mum was the only one she wanted.

Lolly's gaze made a wide sweep as she left Mansfield Road and turned left into the high street. She looked up and down the length of it – no sign of her mother – before she started checking the pavement and the gutters. Sometimes there were pennies to be found, loose change that had slipped from someone's pocket. Once she had even found a shilling. That kind of luck didn't come too often but it paid to be vigilant. It was surprising how careless people could be.

Halfway down the high street she passed the pawnshop, still with its steel shutters down. It did a brisk trade during opening hours with customers exchanging their valuables – and everything else they could lay their hands on – for ready cash. It was run by Brenda Cecil, a woman who was built like a house and who had clearly never missed a meal in her life. No one messed with Brenda; there were rumours she kept a baseball bat under the counter and wasn't afraid to use it.

Lolly didn't like Brenda, or perhaps it was just that she didn't trust her. Was that the same thing? She was the kind of woman who placed a value on everything from what you were wearing to the furniture in your home. She knew this because Brenda popped round to the flat for a brew from time to time. The woman's eyes would move slyly round the living room as if she were making mental calculations as to what each item was worth.

Lolly's mother didn't have many friends, at least not the sort who stuck by her when she was ill, but Brenda's friendship never seemed quite real; she was always asking questions, always digging in a roundabout sort of way. There was something false about her. Lolly couldn't exactly put her finger on it. She couldn't put it into words. It was just a feeling.

She carried on walking until she came to the narrow alley that led round to the back of the Spar. Here hunger got the better of her and she jogged the last twenty feet until she reached the yard with the old metal bins. One quick glance around to make sure no one was watching and then she dived in. Almost instantly she saw that the pickings were slim. Her mouth twisted with frustration and disappointment. One of the bins was empty and the other only had a few bits of cardboard, a couple of bruised apples and a badly dented tin of corned beef. She grabbed the tin and put it in her pocket. She took the apples too – if she cut the bad bits off, there'd still be some left.

Lolly's next port of call was the chippie. She went back up the alley, along the high street and checked the bin outside the shop. Reaching down she squeezed the scrunched up wrappings until she found a likely prospect. Pulling it out, she opened up the sheets of newspaper to reveal a handful of chips. Last night's leftovers, cold and congealed, but she wasn't fussy. She stuffed them into her mouth, too hungry to care about germs or someone else's spit.

When she'd finished, she crossed over to the green. It wasn't really big enough to be called a park. It was about the size of a football pitch, a grassy oblong with trees and bushes and a few seats. Sometimes her mother came here to sit and gaze into space, but today the benches were all empty. She skirted round the mounds of dog poo and headed back to the high street.

At the café, Lolly pressed her nose against the glass and peered in through the window. Through the fug of fag smoke, she could see there were no women inside, only a load of blokes drinking mugs of tea and reading their papers. The smell of frying bacon and eggs floated in the air making her mouth water. The abandoned chips had taken the edge off but she was still hungry. She'd have killed for a hot breakfast.

With nothing else to do, Lolly wandered back to the Mansfield. She wasn't sure of the exact time now but the traffic was starting to build, the red double-deckers and the cars lining up along the street. She checked the main paths and walkways of the estate, strolling round each of the towers in turn. Once she'd established that her mother was in none of the more obvious places she decided to go home and wait there for a while. There was probably nothing to be concerned about – it wasn't as if her absence was anything new – but she wouldn't stop worrying until she saw her again.

It was a relief to find the lifts were working and she took one up to the fourteenth floor, trying not to breathe too deeply. They always stank. Why did blokes pee in lifts? She didn't get it. Still, it was worth the stench if it meant she didn't have to climb all those stairs.

'Mum?' she called out as she went through the door.

Silence.

Lolly could sense the flat was empty. It had that peculiar stillness, that lonely hollow feeling. Her heart sank. Where was she? With a sigh, she gazed around the living room as if by sheer force of will she could make her appear. It was hard not to imagine the worst, but she tried to push those fears aside. Instead she sat down on the battered sofa, took the tin of corned beef out of her pocket, pulled off the tiny metal key and set about the tricky business of getting it open without slicing off her fingers.

2

Lolly only had one friend on the estate, one other person she could trust. By midday, when her mother still hadn't shown up, she walked down to the twelfth floor and knocked on the door. It was a while before he answered. She jumped from one foot to the other while she waited, playing invisible hopscotch on the floor. Finally, he opened up and looked down at her. Jude Rule was tall and gangly with a lock of dark brown hair that fell over his forehead. He was older than her, sixteen, but he didn't treat her like a little kid.

'Hey, Lolly. What's up?'

'Have you seen my mum?'

'She gone AWOL again?'

'Kind of.'

His eyebrows shifted up a notch before he stood aside to let her enter. 'She'll be okay. You want to come in for a while?'

Lolly followed him through to the living room. It was as

dark as always with the curtains pulled across. A tight white sheet took up a quarter of the wall, and black and white images flickered across the makeshift screen. She stopped and stared. 'Which one is this?'

'*Dead Reckoning*. Bogart and Lizabeth Scott.'

'Why do you always watch old films?'

'Because I like them. You want a sandwich?'

'Yeah, if you're making. Ta.'

'Sit down, then. It'll have to be peanut butter. We've got nothing else.'

Lolly sat down on the green corduroy sofa and stared at the screen. She'd seen this film before although she hadn't remembered its name. It was about Rip and Coral. Rip – Humphrey Bogart – was the good guy, and Coral was trouble. The women in most of the films Jude liked were trouble. They were wild and independent and beautiful, but they didn't behave in the way women were supposed to. And for that they always got their just deserts. Coral was going to end up dead just like she had last time.

Lolly shifted her gaze to the open door of the kitchen. Jude was wearing grey shorts and a dark blue T-shirt. She watched as he buttered the bread, watched the sweep of the knife and his long slender fingers. She knew he was odd but that didn't bother her. She was used to odd. Jude was a film freak and spent all his free time either going to the cinema or watching at home. He didn't seem to like the daylight much.

Lolly knew she could always get food at Jude's, but only if his father wasn't around. His dad, a tall taciturn man, didn't like other people being in the flat. She wasn't allowed in if he was at home. A projectionist at a West End cinema, he worked shifts and was usually out in the afternoons and early evenings.

She shifted her gaze again to the shelves to the right of the screen, all filled with film reels in boxes. In the flickering light, she could see some of the titles scrawled on the sides: *Sunset Boulevard*, *Double Indemnity*, *The Lady from Shanghai*. There must have been hundreds of them. She started to count but lost interest at twenty-four when Jude came in with the food.

'Here you go.'

Lolly made an effort not to snatch the plate from him. Although she'd eaten half the corned beef, that was ages ago and she was hungry again. Jude's sandwiches were like doorsteps, big and bulky, the bread bought from the bakers on the high street. She knew that was where Mr Rule got it because she'd seen him in there. He never bought the sliced stuff from the Spar.

'Where have you looked?' Jude asked, sitting down at the other end of the sofa. 'For your mum, I mean.'

'All over.' Lolly talked with her mouth full, deciding this wasn't rude if the room was dark and no one could see her doing it. 'All round here and on the high street. I went to the green too.'

'She acting funny again?'

Lolly shrugged. 'She thought she was being followed yesterday. I don't know if she slept at the flat. She wasn't there when I got up this morning.'

Jude made a tutting sound with his tongue. 'She shouldn't leave you on your own. It's not right, Lol.'

'She can't help it if she's scared.' Lolly knew that Jude had strong opinions about mothers who didn't look after their kids. His own mum had done a bunk years ago. He said he didn't care but she knew he did. Whenever he talked about her his face got all fierce and red and he'd chew down on his lower lip as if to stop it from doing things he didn't want it to do.

'What's she scared of?'

'All sorts.'

'Did you check the caff?'

'Yeah.'

Jude stretched out his long pale legs and gazed at the screen for a while. Rip and Coral were exchanging meaningful looks. Then, without turning, he asked, 'Why did she call you that?'

'What?'

'Your name. Why did she pick that name?'

'Lolly?'

'No, your real one. Lolita.' Then he split it up, drew it out and said again, 'Lol-it-a.'

She felt instantly defensive as though he might be laughing at her. 'What's wrong with it?'

Jude pushed some sandwich into his mouth and chewed. 'Humbert Humbert.'

'Huh?'

'You ever heard of a fella called Nabokov?'

Lolly shook her head. 'Who's that?'

19

'He's Russian, a writer. He wrote a book called *Lolita*. It's about a middle-aged bloke called Humbert Humbert who falls madly in love with his landlady's daughter. She's actually called Dolores, but his secret name for her is Lolita. And she's only twelve.'

'He's weird, then.'

'Yeah, he's really weird. He even marries the landlady so he can hang about with her. Creepy, yeah? They made a film out of it too. James Mason played the bloke. But they changed the girl's age so she was fourteen instead.'

'What kind of a name is Humbert Humbert?'

'One you remember,' he said, grinning. 'Like Lolita.'

Lolly put the empty plate on the coffee table and wiped the crumbs from her mouth. She slipped her feet out of her shoes, pulled up her knees and wrapped her arms around her legs. She liked making herself small, sinking down into the darkness. 'My mum doesn't have many books.' She didn't tell him there was only one in the flat, a well-thumbed collection of British fairy tales. Once upon a time her mother had read to her, stories called 'Mr and Mrs Vinegar', 'The Secret Room', or 'The Changeling', but now she was too old for make-believe.

'Humbert reckoned Lolita was a nymphet.'

Lolly stared hard at Bogart while she wondered what a nymphet was. There were sprites and nymphs in the fairy stories but she had the feeling this wasn't what he meant and she didn't want him to think she was stupid. She rolled the word over her tongue – *nymphet, nymphet* – while she tried to figure it out.

He saw the expression on her face and laughed. 'Nymphets are birds like Amy Wiltshire.'

Lolly knew who Amy was, one of the popular, pretty girls who all the boys fancied but pretended not to. Although she was the same age as Jude and in the same class at school, she looked older. She had big breasts, a slim waist and green eyes like a cat's. Her hair was long and blonde and she was always swishing it back off her face. 'Do you like her?'

'Boys don't like girls like Amy. They just want them.'

Lolly heard the longing in his voice and felt her stomach shift. She didn't like the idea of him lusting after Amy Wiltshire – or lusting after anyone come to that. Her crush on him, although always carefully hidden, was a constant source of awkwardness and pain. She squinted at him through the gloom. 'What's the difference?'

'Like when you want something that you know is really bad for you. It looks all nice on the outside but ...' He paused, his eyes narrowing a little. 'Inside, it's no good. It's rotten. Except you don't always find that out until it's too late.'

'Is Amy rotten?'

Jude's mouth twisted. 'To the core.'

'Like Coral.'

'Yeah, just like Coral.'

Lolly squeezed her legs more tightly and settled her chin on top of her knees. 'But what makes them bad? I mean, are they born that way or has something awful happened to them? Are they—'

'What does it matter?' Jude roughly interrupted. 'You

can't make excuses for the bitches. They've got bad souls and that's the beginning and end of it.'

Lolly shrank back into the corner of the sofa. She didn't like it when he spoke like this, when his expression became hard and angry. And who was he actually talking about? Was it Amy or Coral? Maybe even his mother. She pondered on what it felt like to have a bad soul. Like a stomach ache, perhaps, or a nagging toothache that throbbed and throbbed and kept you awake at night. Or maybe it didn't hurt at all. Maybe you didn't even know you'd got it.

Jude threw her a glance. 'What's wrong? What's the matter?'

'Nothing.'

'So what's with the face? I'm only saying it like it is. Don't start going all moody on me.'

'I'm not.'

'Yes you are.'

Lolly sighed into her knees. 'I was just wondering.'

'Wondering what?'

She took a moment to gather her thoughts. 'About being bad,' she said. 'What if . . . what if I'm bad too? I could be. I could be a bitch.'

Jude threw back his head and laughed. 'You?' he said. 'Don't be ridiculous! You're nothing like that. You're not that type at all. Jesus, you've no worries on that score.'

By which he undoubtedly meant she wasn't beautiful enough to stir up feelings – be they good or bad – in the pure white souls of boys like Jude Rule. Lolly felt her cheeks burn red and was glad of the cover of darkness. 'You can't *know* that,' she insisted, sounding more petulant than she intended.

'Believe me, I do. What are you thinking?'

Lolly shrugged. 'I don't see how you can tell how people are going to turn out. You can't be sure of anything.'

'Crap,' he said. 'There are plenty of things you can be sure of.'

Lolly leaned forward slightly, letting her long, straight brown hair fall across her face like a curtain. She didn't want him to be able to see her properly. There were tears in her eyes but she didn't dare brush them away in case he noticed. She knew Jude would never love her the way she loved him. She was small and skinny and plain. Her chest was as flat as a pancake. She didn't even know how to smoke. Amy Wiltshire could smoke; she smoked with style like Lauren Bacall.

There was a few minutes' silence between them while the final scenes of *Dead Reckoning* played out on the screen. Lolly watched without really watching, her mind full of Jude. She flinched a little when he spoke again.

'What do you fancy next, then? *The Big Sleep*, *Sunset Boulevard*?'

Normally Lolly would have leapt at the opportunity to spend a couple more hours with him, but not today. She felt all twisted up inside, winded, as though she'd been punched in the stomach. Quickly she jumped to her feet.

'I can't. I've got to go.'

Jude didn't try and persuade her to stay. He didn't even ask where she was going. He wasn't bothered whether she was there or not. 'Okay. See you, then.'

'See you.' While the credits slid down the screen, Lolly made her way to the door and let herself out. As she stepped into the outer hallway she could still hear his voice echoing in her mind: *Lol-it-a, Lol-it-a.* She rubbed at her face with both her palms; her hands felt warm and sticky.

Lolly hit the button for the lift and then, while she waited, walked over to lean on the rail and look down over the estate. It was after one now and the sun was high in the sky. It beat down on the concrete tower, spreading warmth through the stone and the rusting metal of the rail. She breathed in the hot air, feeling its dusty thickness catch in the back of her throat.

As she glanced over to the right her attention was drawn to a crowd gathered outside Carlton House on the patchy square of grass. Something was happening. She leaned out over the rail and shielded her eyes, trying to get a better view. It was probably a bust-up between some of the local lads; they were always knocking seven bells out of each other.

A short ting told her the lift had arrived and she moved back, intending to return to the landing. But just as she was about to look away, the crowd shifted and she was able to catch a fleeting glimpse of what they were all gawping at. Immediately she froze, her blood running cold. Her eyes widened with shock and horror. The hairs stood up on the back of her neck. It couldn't be ... it couldn't. But there was no mistaking that flash of pale blue, that stream of long dark hair.

The crowd moved again like a door closing, and her view was obscured. But she knew what she'd seen. For a moment

Lolly's legs wouldn't move. Her feet were stuck to the ground as though they were glued. She felt sick, dizzy, overwhelmed. And then, just as she thought she might faint, the adrenalin kicked in.

Lolly lurched away from the railing and sprinted back inside. She hammered on the door with her fists. 'Jude! Jude! Jude!'

3

Lolly launched herself down the stone steps as though the devil was on her heels. She ran with abandon, with desperation. No, it couldn't be her. It couldn't. Panic swept through her mind, drowning out every other thought. A sharp screaming pain was cutting through her head. As she descended the stairwell, the floor numbers flashed before her eyes: eleven, ten, nine, eight . . . Her chest was heaving, her heart wildly thumping.

Behind her she could hear Jude's pounding footsteps and the sound of his heavy gasping breath.

'Lolly!' he kept calling out.

She didn't stop. She couldn't.

By the time she was approaching the bottom, Lolly's fear had grown to monstrous proportions. Like a fire-spitting dragon, it threatened to engulf her completely, to incinerate the very foundation of her life. One single word was burnt into her consciousness. *No.* She said it over and over, a mantra to keep the badness at bay. Not far to go now. She jumped the last few steps and hit the ground running. As she was pushing through the crowd, Jude finally caught up with her. He grabbed hold of her elbow and brought her to a standstill.

'You can't,' he insisted. 'You mustn't.'

But she had to see. She had to know. She had to be sure.

'Don't do it, Lolly.'

He was taller then her, taller than most of the other people. He could see over their heads to what was lying on the ground. She could see the look on his face, an expression halfway between horror and disgust.

Lolly struggled free of his grasp and pressed on forward. Nothing was going to stop her. No one. 'Let me through,' she demanded, lashing out with her arms. In the distance there was the sound of a siren, the high whining noise piercing the air. She was suddenly aware of all kinds of odd things, strange disjointed thoughts and memories, as though her life was flashing before her.

She didn't have time to brace herself, to even begin to prepare for the dreadful vision that awaited her. One second she was pushing through the crowd, the next . . . Her heart seemed to stop as she saw her mother's twisted body lying on the grass. The breath flew out of her lungs. A low moan escaped from her throat. *No.*

Lolly sank to her knees and clutched at the sleeve of the pale blue jacket. Her mother's grey eyes were half open and glassy, but she was seeing nothing now. A halo of dark red blood ringed her head, seeping into the long dark hair fanned out across the grass. She was lying awkwardly with one arm thrown out and the other trapped beneath her. Her lips, slightly parted, seemed poised to utter some final words, but there was only silence.

Lolly stared. It was her mother and yet it wasn't. It was what was *left* of her mother: a broken shell, a shattered life. It didn't make sense. What had happened to her? Why was she lying here? She couldn't bear to look at her, couldn't stop looking. She held on to the jacket sleeve, to the flimsy cotton, as if some comfort could be found in it. She prayed to God that it was all a bad dream. She prayed to wake up.

The sun beat down but Lolly didn't feel the heat. Shock had wrapped itself around her like an icy blanket. She shivered and her teeth began to chatter. Sounds came from behind, a gasp or two, shuffling noises, muted voices. She could feel the crowd gawping, curious spectators at a gruesome accident. And then one voice rose high enough for her to hear.

'The poor cow must have thought she could fly.'

It was only at that moment that Lolly realised how her mother had died. Stricken, she raised her face to stare up at the tall tower, at the endless rows of windows, at the walkways that ran along each floor. Which one had it been? She had a sudden image of her mother falling, falling, like an angel from the sky.

Lolly gazed up for a while and then spun round, her eyes blazing. 'Go away! Stop looking! Leave her alone!'

The people shuffled back a little but didn't leave. A drama was playing out and they wanted to be part of it.

Jude crouched down beside her, briefly laid his hand on her shoulder and then removed it again. 'Sorry,' he said. 'Shit, I'm sorry.'

Lolly knew there were no right words. His were as good as any others. It didn't matter what anyone said. Nothing mattered any more. She gazed in silence at her mother's body. How could someone be there one day and then gone the next? It didn't make any sense. She couldn't bear it. She wished she was dead too.

'The ambulance is here,' Jude said. 'They'll take care of her, Lol.' He reached out and gently prised her fingers off the sleeve of the jacket. 'You have to let go now.'

All of a sudden there was a rush of activity, of uniforms, of strangers. Within minutes the police had arrived too, taking charge and forcing the crowd back. But not far enough that Lolly couldn't still hear what was being said.

'Her name's Angela something. She lives in Haslow House.'

'She's a jumper.'

'No, I didn't see it myself, but it was from up there.'

'Yeah, that's her kid.'

The comments flowed over her like cold waves. A jumper? What did they mean? Her mum hadn't jumped. It had been an accident. It must have been. She had leaned too far over the edge and . . . Or maybe she'd been scared, running away from someone. Or . . . She didn't have time to finish the thought. Brenda Cecil appeared from nowhere, a bustling, practical presence. The woman grabbed hold of Lolly's arms and, before she knew what was happening, pulled her to her feet.

'Come on, love. You can't stay here.'

'I have to. I have to be with her. I can't leave her on her own.'

'She's not on her own. She'll be taken care of. I promise.'

But still Lolly resisted. She couldn't stand to be parted from her mother. It wasn't right. It wasn't bearable. She tried to break free but Brenda hung on tightly.

'You don't want her lying out here, do you? You've got to let them take her away.'

'I'll go with her.' Lolly turned towards Jude, pleading with him to come to her rescue. 'Tell her. Tell her I have to.'

Jude, who'd stood up too, was white-faced. He wrapped his arms round his chest and visibly shuddered. 'It's for the best, Lol. They'll ... Look, they'll be careful, yeah? I'll make sure. You go with Brenda. It's what your mum would have wanted.'

Lolly vehemently shook her head. 'No, she wouldn't. She wouldn't want me to leave her. I don't *want* to leave her.'

Brenda's grip tightened, her thick fingers digging into Lolly's skinny arms. 'Come on, love. This is no good. It's time to go. You've got to be brave now; you've got to be a big girl.'

'Jude,' she begged again. 'Please. I can't ...'

'I'll take care of her,' he said. 'I swear.'

Lolly, too weak to fight back, was already being hauled across the grass. The crowd parted to let them through. She turned her head desperate for a final look. There was a tight suffocating feeling in her chest, a taste of bile in her mouth. She heard a terrible sound, a high-pitched keening like an animal in pain. She had no idea it was coming from herself.

4

Five days later Lolly was still at Brenda's. She remained in a state of shock, trying to come to terms with something it was impossible to come to terms with. The loss was too huge, too painful, to face head on. She would creep around it, trying to approach from different angles, casting quick frightened glances towards a truth that made her heart ache. It was the finality that scared her most, the thought that her mum was gone for ever.

Since that afternoon Lolly had barely spoken and she hadn't slept much either. She didn't like it at the pawnbroker's – she wanted to go home – but it seemed she didn't have much choice in the matter. Decisions were being made for her and what she desired was neither here nor there.

People came and went, asking questions, looking her up and down. Police officers and social workers provided sympathetic smiles and spoke in soft wheedling voices. They asked about her father, what his name was, if she ever saw him. The only thing Lolly knew for sure was that he was 'a waste of space'. (That was as much as her mum would say.) When it came to grandparents, aunts, uncles and cousins, she was equally at a loss. It had only ever been her and her mum – and now it was only her.

There were other questions of course. How had her mother been the night before? What had she said? Had she been sad or upset? Confused, perhaps? Lolly kept her answers short. She didn't tell the truth. She didn't tell them about the pacing, the anxiety, the fear her mum had felt about being followed and spied on.

'She was okay.'

'She wasn't worried about anything in particular?'

'No.'

'Are you quite sure?'

'Yes.'

Lolly knew what they thought, that her mum had taken the lift up to the top of Carlton House, climbed over the railing and jumped. She knew this because of what she'd heard five days ago, and because she'd listened in to Freddy and Brenda Cecil talking.

'Christ, she's always been nuts but I never saw that coming. Topping herself like that. You'd think she'd spare a thought for the kid.'

Brenda heaved out a sigh. 'Well, she was never right in the head and that's a fact. I doubt she was thinking straight. And she was always forgetting to take those pills of hers. Still, every cloud has a silver lining.'

'You're not still on about that, are you? It's a load of bollocks.'

'You won't be saying that if it's true.'

'The woman was mad, an out and out screwball. You can't believe anything that came out of her mouth.'

'We'll see. And in the meantime, make sure you're on your best behaviour. You tell them Lolly's welcome here, right? Don't go putting any doubts in their heads.'

That was as much as Lolly had heard. She hadn't been deliberately eavesdropping, just sitting at the top of the stairs, dwelling on stuff. The door to the downstairs living room was open and the voices had floated up to her. She wasn't sure what it all meant, other than the part about her mum being nuts. That bit was easy to understand.

This afternoon, just before another visit from the social worker, Brenda had sat her down and given her 'the talk'. The woman's large frame and plump smiling face created an impression of big-hearted jolliness, but Lolly wasn't taken in. She had always been suspicious of her. Something cunning lurked behind the mask, something false.

'Now, I know things ain't been easy for you, love, what with your poor mum and all, but it'll get better. Everything gets better if you just give it time. And you know you're welcome to stay here, don't you? We're happy to take you in as part of the family.' Brenda paused for a moment, staring hard at Lolly as if she expected her to say something.

Lolly said nothing.

Brenda's smile faded and her voice took on a harder edge. 'Although if you *want* them to take you away to a kid's home, that's entirely up to you. You only have to say the word. No one's going to make you do anything you don't want to. Those places aren't nice, though, not nice at all. I've heard all sorts goes on. And God alone knows where you'd end up. It could be the other side of the country.'

'Why can't I go home?'

'Because you can't live there on your own, sweetheart. You're too young. You need someone to take care of you.'

Lolly reckoned she'd done a pretty good job of taking care of herself over the past few years, but apparently this wasn't good enough. She was left with two options, neither of which held any appeal for her. 'Stuck between a rock and a hard place,' was what her mum used to say. She didn't relish the prospect of making her stay a permanent arrangement but the alternative was even worse. Brenda had spelled it out for her: she would be taken away and could end up anywhere. That would mean being away from Kellston – and from Jude.

'I'd like to stay here, please.'

'Good girl!' Brenda's smile returned to full beam and she patted Lolly on the arm. 'You're better off with us and that's a fact. Now all you have to do is tell Mrs Raynes when she gets here. You can do that, can't you?'

Lolly nodded.

'That's settled, then. You behave yourself and we'll get along just fine.'

Lolly lay in bed, gazing into space. It was FJ's room and it smelled of boy. Every time she breathed in, a musty sweaty odour filled her nose. To keep the worst of the darkness at bay, she had left the curtains open and a thin light slid in from the street lamps on the high street. There were posters on the wall: the Rolling Stones, Goldie Hawn and the West Ham football team.

FJ, Freddy Junior, was Brenda's younger son and as mean as they came. He had the sly, nasty face of a goblin and acted like one too. He hadn't taken kindly to being kicked out of his bedroom and forced into doubling up with his brother.

'Aw, Mum, I'm too old to be sharing. I'm sixteen, for fuck's sake.'

'So start acting your age. Where do you expect me to put her, in the bathroom? And mind your bloody language. It's me you're talking to, not one of your filthy-mouthed mates.'

'I don't see why you have to put her anywhere. She's nothin' to do with us. She ain't related or nothin'.'

'Don't be so selfish. The kid's just lost her mother.'

'So how long is she going to be here for?'

'For as long as it takes. Just get used to the idea and stop whining about it.'

Lolly shifted in bed, pulled up her knees and put them down again. She gazed at the ceiling, wondering what this meant. *For as long as it takes.* She could see the years stretching ahead and couldn't figure out how she'd get through them. It was hard enough getting through each day.

Every time Lolly closed her eyes she saw her mum sprawled out on the grass. She tried to blink away the image, to conjure up a different picture, but it just didn't work. That tightness came back into her chest again, the feeling she couldn't breathe properly. She should have searched until she'd found her. Instead she had gone to Jude's, scoffed a peanut butter sandwich and sat on the sofa watching someone else's life fall apart.

Lolly was haunted by what ifs: what if she'd woken up earlier? What if she'd been able to track her down? What if she'd left Jude's ten minutes before she did? Had she done that she might have seen her mother crossing the estate, heading for Carlton House. She could have leaned over the railing and shouted out.

'Mum! Mum!'

Her mum would have stopped, looked up and waved. She would have waited for Lolly to run down the steps. And then everything would have been different. She wouldn't have gone to that place, wouldn't have taken the lift, wouldn't have ... Guilt slithered its way into her soul. She had let her mother down, failed her. She pulled the blankets over her head, trying to hide from the truth in the hot stuffy darkness.

Lolly wished she were in her own bed, in her own home. She had a sudden urgent need to be in familiar surroundings, to touch the things her mother had touched, to suck in whatever remained of her. The desire was so great she couldn't fight against it. She threw back the covers, got out of bed, got dressed and quietly left the room.

As she crept along the landing, she could hear heavy snores coming from behind Freddy and Brenda's bedroom door. Despite the noise, she tiptoed down the stairs, stopping every time a floorboard creaked. Once she reached the ground floor she paused again, alert to any sound from above that might suggest she'd been rumbled.

When she was sure no one was coming after her, Lolly set off again. She knew there was no way out through the front – the pawnshop was protected by heavy steel shutters pulled down every evening when the business closed – and so she headed instead towards the back from where she hoped to be able to get out into the yard and then into the alley that ran parallel to the high street. The dining room provided her first challenge. The curtains were closed and it was pitch black. She didn't dare put on the light and so frequently stumbled, banging into objects she didn't remember were there: the leg of the table, an armchair, the base of a lamp. She swore softly, rubbing at her shins.

'Shit.'

Eventually, after all these obstacles had been negotiated, she limped into the kitchen where she was faced with the fresh challenge of the back door. She could see more in here – a greyish light, the beginning of dawn was coming through the window – but what she saw only filled her with dismay.

There were two bolts pulled across the door, one at the top and one at the bottom. With the help of a chair, she could probably have solved the problem of the upper one but there was no point even trying. The old iron key that was always in the lock during the day was missing. Lolly hissed out a breath of frustration. Where was it? She began to search the kitchen, peering through the gloom. Not on the table. Not by the sink or on the window ledge. She carefully opened the drawers but there were only trays of cutlery, washcloths and tea towels. She checked the cupboards but couldn't find it there either.

After ten minutes of searching she knew it was useless. She was never going to find the damn thing. She eyed the window, trying to weigh up if she could squeeze through the oblong at the top, the only part that opened. The answer to that was a big fat no. Skinny as she was the space was just too small. She had a mental picture of getting stuck halfway through, wriggling like a fish on a hook with her backside exposed for everyone to see.

Defeated, Lolly sat down on the floor. The key, she suspected, was upstairs, on the bedside table beside Brenda and Freddy. And that was one place she wasn't going to venture into. She had no choice now but to wait until morning. She was locked in, a prisoner. There was no escape.

5

FJ glared at Lolly over the breakfast table, his resentful eyes following every morsel she lifted from the plate to her mouth. But nothing deterred Lolly from eating. She knew what it meant to go hungry and never refused anything that was put in front of her. No matter how tired or sad or sick she felt, her instincts took over when it came to food.

'You'll get fat,' FJ said, 'if you keep stuffing your face like that.'

'Leave it out,' Brenda said, shooting him a warning glance. 'There's not a scrap on her. She needs feeding up a bit.' She smiled at Lolly. 'You dig in, love. Don't mind him; he's always a grouch in the mornings.'

There were only the three of them at the table. Tony, Brenda's other son, had already gone to work, and Freddy was still in bed. From what Lolly had observed over the past five days, Freddy spent a great deal of time in bed and the rest of it doing little that was useful. It was Brenda who ran the pawnshop while he went down the pub or sat in the armchair reading the *Sun* as he smoked his way through a pack of Woodbines.

However, Lolly had more important things on her mind than Freddy's idle ways. She was still set on going to the flat. As she couldn't risk revealing her intentions – what if Brenda refused to let her go or insisted on coming with her after the shop was closed? – she had to find a good excuse to explain her absence.

'I thought I might . . . er . . . go and see a friend today. Is that okay?'

FJ gave a snort. 'What friend? You ain't got no mates.'

'Have so!'

'No you ain't.'

'Do!'

'Don't!'

'Course she's got friends,' Brenda said, standing up to clear away the plates. 'What's her name, love? Does she live near here?'

'Sandra,' Lolly said, glaring at FJ. 'She's only down the road, near the station.'

FJ kicked her under the table, a blow that landed on her bruised right shin. Lolly jumped, gasping at the pain. 'Aagh!'

'What is it?' Brenda asked. 'What's wrong? Are you all right?'

Lolly pulled up her leg and rubbed it. 'Yeah,' she said with her eyes fixed on FJ. 'I just . . . I've got . . . it's just cramp.' She knew better than to dob him in. Nobody grassed where she came from. If you lived on the Mansfield estate you knew how to keep your mouth shut. But that didn't mean she'd forget about it. One way or another she'd get her revenge.

FJ's upper lip curled into a sneer as he pushed back his chair. 'Have a nice time with your *friend*,' he said. 'See you later.'

Lolly watched as he left through the back door. He had the same arrogant, swaggering walk as his older brother. She didn't ask herself why he hated her so much. It was perfectly normal for her to be taunted, to be disliked by other kids. In fact, she would have been more surprised if he'd been nice to her.

Brenda put the dishes in the sink and ran the hot water. She glanced over her shoulder. 'It'll do you good, some fresh air, put a bit of colour in those cheeks. Don't be back late, will you? Tea's at half five.'

Lolly nodded. 'I won't.' She was desperate to get going, but not stupid enough to leave while FJ might still be hanging around outside. Instead she went up to her room, hid behind the curtain and peeked out through the window. He was standing a little way down the high street with a group of lads she recognised from the Mansfield. She prayed that they weren't going to head for the estate.

It was a further five minutes before they moved off in the direction of Connolly's. She gave a sigh of relief. The café was a popular hang-out for the local teenagers, a place where the boys eyed up the girls and vice versa. She had never been inside but had looked through the window often enough. Amy Wiltshire was usually in there after school, flicking her hair while she drank iced Coke through a straw.

Lolly gave them time to get in and settled before putting on her jacket and going back downstairs. She scooted through the living room and into the kitchen.

'Bye, then,' she said to Brenda.

'Half past five. Don't forget'

'I won't.'

Lolly went through the yard, littered with old bikes and bits of rusting metal, out of the gate and along the narrow back alley. It was in an L-shape leading back on to the high street. She had a quick glance up and down the street to make sure the coast was clear before venturing out. Once she was certain she was safe, she half walked, half ran until she reached the main entrance to the Mansfield.

Here Lolly paused, staring down the long path. Her stomach lurched remembering the last time she was here. Her desire to go home, however, was greater than any lingering fears of the place. As she made her way towards Haslow, she kept her gaze averted from Carlton House. She kept her head down, avoiding eye contact with anyone she passed. The last thing she wanted was for someone to stop her and ask how she was.

Lolly rode up in the lift to the fourteenth floor. She took the key from her pocket as she walked round the corner to the flat and quickly opened the door and went inside. The sun was streaming through the windows of the living room, broad stripes of light full of dancing motes. It was all very still, very quiet. She cleared her throat, the noise sounding unnaturally loud in the silence.

The first thing she noticed was that someone had been

there. There wasn't any mess, no major disturbance, but nothing was quite as she'd left it. Everything on the table – the blue bowl, the pile of bills, the jar with its pens and pencils – was in a slightly different position. The chairs were not in their usual place and the cushions on the sofa had been moved.

Not a break-in, that was for sure. The thieving toerags would have torn the place apart. So who? She didn't like to think of strangers in the flat, people touching things, looking at things. It wasn't right.

In her mother's bedroom she noticed that the drawers of the dressing table had been opened but not closed again properly, and the wardrobe door was ajar. Seeing the clothes her mother would never wear again brought tears to Lolly's eyes. Images jumped into her head: the day her mum had been wearing *that* cream sweater or *that* black dress. She reached out, touching the garments with her fingertips. The clothes rocked gently on the hangers; they had an air of despondency, as if they knew they would never be worn by their owner again.

Lolly sat on the bed for a while. She had yearned to come home but now she was here she didn't know what to do with herself. She slid open the drawer of the bedside cabinet, but there was nothing in it other than a small mother-of-pearl button and some dust. Picking up the button she studied it for a moment before slipping it into the pocket of her jeans.

After a while she rose and went to her own room. Stuff had been disturbed here too. She put her school bag on the bed and started filling it with the few clothes she owned. Brenda had bought her new jeans and T-shirts, knickers, socks and a pair of sandals from the market, but she still wanted the old familiar things. Brenda had also made her take a bath and wash her hair.

'We can't have you looking like something the cat dragged in.'

Lolly didn't know when, if ever, she would be back here again. The council might come and change the locks. They might do it tomorrow or the next day. They would want to give the flat to someone else. What would happen to everything? Would they clear it out, throw it all away? She picked up the book of British fairy tales and put that in the bag too.

Worried that she might not get a second chance, Lolly returned to her mother's bedroom and stared into the wardrobe again. What to take? She didn't have much room left in her bag. In the end she decided on the pale pink cardigan, which had always looked nice against her mother's dark hair. Briefly, she raised it to her face and breathed in the scent. Then she wished that she hadn't. It made her feel too sad.

Lolly moved on to the kitchen. What remained of the corned beef was still on a plate on the counter. The two apples were still there too, almost completely brown, rotten to the core. She wrinkled her nose at the sight of them. She would have put them in the bin but couldn't bear the thought of touching the soft pulpy flesh. Instead she turned her back and wandered into the living room.

Despite the sun flooding in, Lolly felt cold. Were there

such things as ghosts? She hugged her skinny chest with her arms. She kept thinking she had caught something out of the corner of her eye but when she turned her head to look nothing was there. A panicky feeling began to stir inside her. There was a prickling on the back of her neck and the hairs rose up on her bare arms.

The feeling that she wasn't alone refused to go away. Eyes were on her; she was being watched. And yet the flat was empty. She knew it was. She had been in every room. If it was her mother's ghost, she reasoned, she had nothing to be afraid of. And yet the sensation she had was one of danger. It was a noise that finally tipped her over the edge, a sudden creak like a footstep on a loose floorboard.

Lolly stood for a moment, rooted to the spot – and then she bolted from the flat as fast as her legs could carry her.

6

Lolly sprinted down the two flights of steps with the bag banging against her thigh. She ran along the walkway and only paused to catch her breath before rapping on the door. Jude answered almost straight away. He looked surprised to see her.

'Hey, Lol. You okay?'

'Yeah, yeah,' she said.

'Why's your face all red?'

'Is it?' She raised a hand to touch her cheek. 'I've just been running, that's all. I was upstairs. I was at the flat.' She wasn't going to admit to having been scared witless; he might think of her as cowardly or weak.

'Who is it?' a male voice shouted from inside.

'Just a mate,' Jude replied, glancing over his shoulder. He looked back at Lolly. 'Dad's here,' he said, lowering his voice. 'You can't come in. Sorry.'

'Oh, okay.' She'd forgotten it was still early and that Mr Rule wouldn't have gone to work yet. 'It doesn't matter.

I'll ... er ... I'll ...' Her voice trailed off. She didn't know what else to say.

Jude must have seen her disappointment, and perhaps something else too, because he hesitated and then said, 'Look, give me five minutes and I'll meet you downstairs.'

Lolly took the lift the rest of the way down. She went into the sunshine, walked a few yards to her right and sat with her back against the wall. Now she was outside with other people around her, the experience in the flat seemed distant and strange. The fear had retreated and she wondered if the feelings, the creak, the sense of being watched had all been a product of her imagination.

It was closer to ten minutes – she was counting off the seconds in her head – before Jude finally showed up. He was carrying two small bottles of Fanta and he passed one over as he sat down beside her.

'Ta,' she said.

'You still at Brenda's?'

'Yeah. She says I can stay if I want to.'

'Do you?'

Lolly shrugged. She took a swig from the bottle, swallowed and resisted the urge to burp. 'They'll put me in a home, otherwise. It could be anywhere, miles away.'

'Right.'

She wanted Jude to say he wanted her to stay, but he didn't. 'I guess it's better than that. Even if I do have to live with FJ.'

'He's a right little shit.'

'Yeah.'

'Don't let him push you around.'

Lolly wasn't quite sure how she was supposed to stop him, but she nodded anyway.

'What about your dad?' Jude asked. 'Do you know where he is? Perhaps you could go and live with him.'

'I don't even know his name.'

'It might be on your birth certificate. Your mum must have had a copy. It'll be in the flat somewhere. Or you can get a copy from Somerset House. That's where they keep all the records: births, deaths and marriages.'

Lolly was always impressed by how much Jude knew; he was the smartest person she'd ever met. 'Oh,' she said. 'Okay.' Up until now she hadn't thought much about her dad. There were lots of kids on the estate who didn't have fathers, lots of single mums. She wondered why she hadn't been more curious, why she hadn't asked more questions. And now it was too late.

'Or maybe Brenda knows who he is. Why don't you ask her?'

'She'd have said something, wouldn't she?'

'Maybe they're trying to find him.'

Lolly recalled what she'd heard: *For as long as it takes.* Perhaps that's what Brenda had meant – for as long as it took to find her father.

'Anyway, it's not all bad,' he said. 'Think of it this way, in another five years you can move out of Brenda's and get a place of your own.'

Lolly couldn't imagine that length of time; it felt like for ever. She drank some more Fanta and put the bottle down on the ground. She had something else on her mind and needed to share it. 'Someone's been in the flat. I was in there and I could tell.'

'It was the police.'

'What?'

'Yeah, a few hours after . . . I don't know, maybe they were looking for a note or something.'

'What kind of note?'

Jude's eyes briefly met hers before he glanced away again. 'From your mum. People leave them sometimes when . . . I suppose they thought she might have.'

'Why would there be a note? She didn't jump,' Lolly said hotly. 'Did anyone see her jump? She didn't do it on purpose. It wasn't suicide. She must have fallen or been pushed.' She gazed up towards the top of Carlton House and shuddered. 'Yeah, someone could have pushed her.'

Jude remained silent.

'She *wouldn't*,' Lolly insisted. 'I know she did some crazy things sometimes but she wouldn't have done that. She wouldn't have just gone off and left me.'

'No, course she wouldn't.'

Lolly stared at him. She knew he was only saying it, that he didn't really believe it. And it was probably what everyone else thought too. A flicker of doubt crossed her mind but she quickly dismissed it. She'd seen her mum in much worse states than she'd been the night before she died. Worried and restless was good compared to the black moods, to the days when she would barely speak and wouldn't even get out of bed.

'Did the police talk to you?' he asked.

'Yeah, they asked me some stuff. How she was and all that. They didn't tell me anything, though. I don't know what they're going to do. I don't know what happens next.'

'I suppose there'll be an inquest, a coroner's report.'

'What's that?'

'It's where they look at all the evidence and come to a decision as to how she died.'

'And then what?'

Jude gave a shrug. 'The funeral, I guess.'

Lolly stared over at Carlton House again, her gaze rising to the upper floors. What if her mum had been right about being followed? Everyone ignored what she said because they thought she was crazy. It was like the story where the boy cried wolf. After a while no one believed a word that came out of his mouth. She glanced back at Jude.

'Don't you ever think about looking for your mum?'

'Why should I?' Jude said. 'It's not up to me. She knows where I am. If she wanted to see me, she could.'

'Maybe something's happened to her, an accident or—'

'Something worse? Maybe it has. Maybe she's dead. I hope so. She deserves to be.'

Lolly stared at him, wide-eyed. 'You don't mean that.'

Jude pushed back the lock of hair from his forehead. He suddenly looked awkward, embarrassed, as though he wished he could take the words back. 'Sorry, I shouldn't have said that. I wasn't thinking.'

'It's all right.'

Jude finished his Fanta, screwed the lid back on the bottle

and left the bottle by the wall. He rose to his feet. 'I'd better head off. I'm going up West with Dad.'

'Oh, okay.'

'See you, then,' Jude said.

'See you.'

Lolly was beginning to feel weepy again. It kept coming over her, out of the blue. One moment she was fine, the next her bottom lip got all wobbly and she couldn't trust herself to speak. She watched Jude stride back towards the lobby. When he reached the door, he didn't turn to wave. He was already thinking about something else, someone else. She picked up his empty bottle of Fanta, unscrewed the cap, glanced around to make sure no one was watching and slipped the cap into her jacket pocket.

Lolly stood up, wondering what to do next. She began to walk in an aimless fashion across the estate. The bag was heavy and she shifted it from one shoulder to the other. It was the first time in days she'd been away from Brenda's and she wasn't in any hurry to get back. She had a free pass until five-thirty and was going to make the most of it.

Without making a conscious decision as to where she was going, she drifted towards Carlton House. She skirted round the square of grass, deliberately not looking over. She was afraid the blood might still be there, an indelible stain, and couldn't bear to see it. At the entrance to the tower, she hesitated before passing into the cool gloom of the lobby. One of the lifts was open and she stepped inside, pressing the button for the top floor. Lolly didn't know exactly where her mum had fallen from. Did anyone? If they did, they weren't telling her. It could have been from lower down, but with no definite information she'd decided to head for the highest point. No one else stopped the lift and she ascended smoothly and alone.

From the eighteenth floor, the view was spectacular; she could see right across Kellston and beyond, for miles and miles. In the distance she could even spot the gleaming dome of St Paul's. She leaned against the rail and lowered her gaze to the estate. The people looked like tiny stick figures, their features soft and blurred.

While she stared down she wondered what her mother had been doing here in the first place. If she had decided to take her own life – and Lolly still didn't believe this was true – then why traipse all the way over to Carlton House? Why not just open the balcony doors of their own flat, step outside and . . .

Lolly glanced to her left and right, searching for evidence that her mum had been here, but there was none. Not even a feeling. She was on the wrong floor, perhaps. She leaned further over, trying to check out the one beneath. It was then, as her gaze flicked to the ground far below, that she felt a weird, pulling sensation, a frightening impulse to lean further and further until there was no going back, until the weight of her body tipped the balance and sent her hurtling towards the square of green beneath.

Quickly she pulled back, tightly gripping the rail as she stood up straight again. Her heart was beating too fast. She retreated from the edge and leaned against the wall for a few seconds before dashing towards the lift. All she wanted was to be on solid ground again, to feel the earth beneath her feet. All she wanted was to be away from here.

7

By September Lolly was back at school. She had returned expecting the usual jeers and taunts but surprisingly they were not forthcoming. She could not say, hand on heart, that anyone was nice to her, but at least they left her alone. In her world this was progress and she was grateful for it. She was smart enough to realise that the break in hostilities was not down to any remorse or sympathy regarding her mother's death, but rather to the fact that she was now living at the pawnbroker's. No one messed with the Cecils, and if Lolly wasn't exactly family she was close enough for the bullies to think twice about singling her out.

Brenda fed her, clothed her, made sure she washed and always sent her to school looking presentable. There was no love there, though, not even a mild affection. Brisk efficiency was the order of the day. Lolly knew she was being tolerated, that she was in some way a means to an end, although she hadn't yet figured out exactly what that end was.

The coroner had made the decision that her mother's death was down to suicide while the balance of her mind was disturbed – and no one cared what Lolly thought. The funeral, a dismal affair, had only been attended by herself, Brenda and Freddy. Even now she could feel the cool chill of the crematorium and hear the priest's voice droning on in the almost empty building. The ashes, collected later, had been interred in Kellston cemetery and marked with a small wooden cross.

'We'll see about a headstone,' Brenda said. 'When we get things sorted out.'

What those things were, Lolly had no way of knowing. Something to do with money, she presumed. What she did know was that there had been a problem with her mother's birth certificate, or rather the lack of one. A search of the flat had revealed nothing. And nothing could be found at the records office either. Angela Bruce – if that was the name she'd been born with – appeared to be untraceable.

There had been much conjecture by Brenda and Mrs Raynes, the social worker, as to why this might be. Had she been using a pseudonym, hiding from someone, in trouble with the law? Lolly had been interrogated at length, but couldn't tell them anything useful. She had no memory of having a surname other than Bruce. Had her mother ever been married? Lolly didn't think so. Well, not during the last six or seven years at least, and her memories of the time before this were too slippery to grasp. What about boyfriends? But Lolly couldn't recall any of those either.

Lolly's own birth certificate was also missing. Without

these two vital documents there was little chance of tracking down other members of the family, if indeed such relatives even existed. She had expected Brenda to be frustrated by this – surely she would want to eject the cuckoo in her nest as soon as possible? – but instead she was oddly pleased.

'Not to worry, love. I'm sure we'll find out where you come from eventually.'

Lolly thought about all this as she took the lift up to the twelfth floor of Haslow House. She wondered what had brought that smug smile to Brenda's lips. There was something unnerving about it. Maybe she would ask Jude. He was older and smarter. Perhaps he could explain it to her.

Now she was living with the Cecils she didn't see Jude as often as she'd like. Brenda kept her on a tight leash, always wanting to know where she was or where she was going. The days of roaming free had gone. And Lolly didn't like to break the rules too often; the threat of Mrs Raynes was always hanging over her. Brenda used this form of blackmail to keep her in line.

'I need you on your best behaviour, Lolly. No trouble, right? You do as you're told or that old bat will have you in care before you can blink, never mind put your bleedin' shoes on.'

Lolly's one escape route was through her imaginary friend, Sandra, but she couldn't afford to overuse it. Already Brenda was asking why Sandra never came round; she was getting suspicious and that wasn't good. Soon Lolly would have to find another excuse, or another 'friend', if she was to continue spending time with Jude. She knew Brenda wouldn't approve of her seeing a boy who was three years older, even if it was completely innocent.

Lolly smiled as she made her way along the corridor. The only time she was truly happy these days was when she was sitting on the green corduroy sofa in the dark, the images flickering on the screen and Jude close enough to touch. He made her feel safe, secure, as if no one could hurt her. Just for a while she could forget about everything else.

As she knocked on the door Lolly wondered which film they'd be watching this afternoon. She waited, swinging her school bag from her arm. Normally Jude was prompt in answering, but not today. Could he be out? Maybe he'd gone up West to see his dad. Her smile faded as disappointment crept over her. She knocked again.

'Jude? Jude, it's me, Lolly. Are you there?'

This time she heard a faint sound from inside, but he still didn't come to the door. Lolly was puzzled. If for some reason his dad was home, Jude would just come and tell her. Could he be sick? Have had a fall? All kinds of terrible scenarios flashed through her mind. The worst could happen – she knew that for certain. What if . . . ?

Panic was starting to overtake her. Lolly rapped much harder and put her ear to the door. 'Jude? Are you okay?'

This time what she heard was instantly recognisable, the sound of whispering followed by a girl's stifled laughter. Lolly jumped back as the truth hit her like a blow. Her stomach lurched. She understood now. She'd got the message loud and clear. Jude had company and she wasn't welcome.

Quickly she walked back to the lift, her cheeks burning

red. She felt embarrassed and humiliated. Why couldn't he have told her he was busy instead of pretending to be out? She wouldn't have minded – well, she would, but she'd have dealt with it. But *this*, this was like being kicked when she was down. They'd been laughing at her. She'd heard them. It was mean and cruel, and she'd never have thought it of Jude Rule.

Lolly didn't go straight back to the Cecils'. She wandered aimlessly round the estate for a while, trying to keep her emotions in check. She walked through the long gloomy passageways, oblivious to the guys who lurked there, young men with pockets full of ludes and speed and marijuana. She rode up and down in the lifts. She went back to the old flat and stood outside the door but couldn't bring herself to put the key in the lock.

At five o'clock, Lolly left the estate and set off for the pawnbroker's. As she traipsed along the high street her spirits were as slumped as her shoulders. What would she do now? She could see the weeks, the months, looming ahead with nothing to look forward to. Without Jude as her anchor, she felt cut adrift, all at sea. But she wasn't going to cry. She was adamant. So he had turned out to be like all the others. So what? She wasn't going to break her heart over it. People let you down. Sometimes they meant to and sometimes they didn't, but the end result was always the same.

Lolly turned off the high street, walked along the alley, through the cluttered yard and into the kitchen. Chips were frying on the stove. FJ was already there, sitting at the table with a football magazine in front of him. He glanced up and gave her one of his looks.

'Someone's had a bad day at school,' Brenda said.

Lolly hung her bag over the back of a chair, but said nothing.

'Or have you fallen out with that friend of yours, that Sandra?'

'No.'

'Well, something's happened. You've got a face like a smacked bum. Like you've dropped a pound and found a penny as my old mum used to say.'

FJ chose this moment to stick his oar in. 'It's probably that lad she's been seeing.'

Brenda frowned. 'What lad?'

'Lolly's got a boyfriend.'

'No I haven't!' Lolly snapped, mortified.

'I should hope not,' Brenda said. 'You're far too young for that kind of thing.'

'He's called Jude Rule,' FJ said. 'He's in my class and he's a right weirdo. Lolly goes round to his flat.'

'He's not a weirdo,' Lolly said, although she had no idea why she was jumping to his defence. It was just some kind of knee-jerk reaction. She glared at FJ, wondering how he knew about Jude and her visits. 'And I hardly ever see him.'

Brenda put her hands on her ample hips and shook her head. 'Weirdo or not, he's too old for you, young lady.'

'He's just a friend. He lives downstairs. I mean, in Haslow, at the Mansfield.'

'You should stick to friends your own age.'

'Yeah,' FJ said. 'What kind of bloke likes hanging out with little girls? Must be a right twisted beggar. Bet they get up to all sorts. You should put a stop to it, Mum. It ain't right. People are going to talk.'

Lolly protested, her cheeks turning red again. 'There's nothing to talk about. Why should there be?'

'You tell me,' he said smugly. 'I'm not the one cuddling up to some weirdo.'

'I'm not cuddling up to him. It's not like that. We're not—'

'I don't know what you're doing,' Brenda interrupted sharply, 'but it stops right now, you hear? I'm not having you mixing with the likes of him. If Mrs Raynes gets wind of it, it's me she'll blame for letting you go round there in the first place. So you stay away, right? From now on, you come straight home from school.'

Lolly shrugged. Yesterday she'd have railed against such a ban, but today it didn't matter. Jude had already dismissed her, pushed her aside. Nothing Brenda said could make the slightest bit of difference.

FJ smirked triumphantly at her from across the table. 'I've done you a favour, Lol. That Jude's a creep.'

'Takes one to know one.'

'Oh, yeah?'

'Yeah.'

'Cut it out, you two!' Brenda said. 'I get enough aggro standing behind that counter all day. I don't need it here as well.'

Lolly sat and ate her meal in silence. There was no sign of Freddy, and Tony hadn't come home either. Brenda treated them to a steady stream of complaints as they chomped their way through fish fingers, chips and peas: rude customers, ungrateful husbands, sons who didn't bother to call when they wouldn't be home for tea. Lolly didn't hear half of it; she switched off, her mind preoccupied by what had happened with Jude.

After the dishes had been done, Lolly said she had homework and went upstairs to her room – although calling it *her* room was something of a misnomer. FJ's posters remained pinned to the wall, his things scattered around, some of his clothes still hanging in the wardrobe. The room was clearly on loan and not a permanent arrangement. She slept in the bed, brushed her hair in the mirror, but the place reflected nothing of her own personality.

Lolly stayed upstairs. She could hear the TV going in the living room but preferred to be alone than with the Cecils. Freddy came home at about eight o'clock, pissed as a newt and crashing into the furniture. Brenda shouted at him for a good ten minutes but then it all went quiet. He'd either fallen asleep or Brenda had killed him.

At nine, Lolly went to the bathroom and brushed her teeth. Back in the bedroom, she got undressed, put on her pyjamas, climbed into bed and lay listening to the sounds of the TV and the cars going by on the high street. Every now and again, she'd hear the creak of the stairs as someone came up to use the loo, followed by a loud flush and the sound of water running through the pipes.

She must have dozed off because the next noise she heard was of a car drawing up outside. It was dark by now, a midnight kind of dark. She didn't even have to think about who it was. She already knew from the soft purr of the engine; it idled for about thirty seconds before being switched off.

Lolly got out of bed and padded over to the window. She pulled aside the curtain and gazed down into the street. The black Jaguar was parked outside the pawnbroker's, directly beneath her. She watched as the passenger door opened and Joe Quinn got out. It wasn't the first time he'd been here and he always came at night.

Joe Quinn owned the Fox pub and, in various ways, most of Kellston too. He was an ageing, ugly, stocky man with a face like a bulldog. Great folds of skin drooped under a flabby chin, and what remained of his hair was combed over his scalp in long oily strands. Even before she had come to live with the Cecils, she'd been aware of him; his name was well known on the Mansfield estate. This was his manor and he ran it with an iron fist, and that included all the pushers and the prozzies too.

Lolly could see why people were scared. He had one of those scowling demeanours as though he was always on the verge of losing his rag. He was rude and charmless, a tyrant who got what he wanted through brute force. Nobody messed with Joe Quinn, no one with any sense that was. He laid down the rules and others obeyed them.

The driver's door opened and a younger, good-looking man got out. This was Terry Street. He was wearing a smart suit and tie, like he'd been somewhere fancy. The two men couldn't have been more different. Terry was only about nineteen or twenty, lean and handsome with dark hair and sharp cheekbones. But it wasn't just his appearance that set him apart from his boss: Terry had a way about him, always ready with a smile or a joke. He was what her mum would have called a Jack-the-lad, but nice with it. All the girls had the hots for him.

The two men walked along the road and turned into the alley. Lolly moved away from the window, crossed over to the door and carefully opened it. She didn't have to wait long before she heard the knock at the back door. The TV went off and the next thing she heard was Brenda's voice.

'Evening, Mr Quinn. Come on in. Hello, Terry. How are you doing?'

And then Freddy saying something she couldn't quite catch. There was the sound of the kettle being filled with water. A welcome brew while they did a bit of business. This was pretty regular, once a fortnight or so. She had eavesdropped several times on these meetings – it was the only way to find out anything – and it didn't take a genius to work out that the goods Quinn came with were nicked.

The pawnbroker's did plenty of honest business, but it didn't bring in big bucks. Lolly knew this because Brenda was always moaning about it. It didn't help, of course, that Freddy drank half of what they earned every week. Brenda was always in a better mood after Joe Quinn had been round. Fencing stolen goods was risky but it was also lucrative.

Lolly stepped tentatively on to the landing, checking to make sure FJ's door was closed before she went to the banisters and leaned over. She could hear the metallic clinks as Brenda sorted through whatever Quinn had brought her – rings and chains, bracelets and brooches.

'I'll have to shift some of this on, get it melted down,' she said.

'That's quality,' Terry said. 'Twenty-four carat.'

'I'm not saying it ain't, love, but it can't go in the window. It's them emeralds; they're what you'd call distinctive. I don't need Old Bill knockin' on the door.'

Brenda always haggled over the price, getting the best possible deal she could. In a few days, after she'd managed to shift the gear, she'd have a big smile on her face and she'd be off down the market to buy a new pair of shoes or a handbag. There would be pork chops for tea instead of fish fingers, and a fresh bottle of gin on the sideboard.

Joe Quinn and Terry didn't stay for long. Ten minutes after they arrived they were off again. The back door had closed and Lolly was about to retreat to her bedroom when she heard something interesting.

'So what's happening with the kid?' Freddy said.

Lolly's ears instantly pricked up. Freddy never referred to her by name, only as 'the kid'. He rarely spoke to her either, acting as if she wasn't even there. She may as well have been invisible for all the notice he took of her. Sometimes, if they passed on the stairs or met at the kitchen table, his forehead would crease into a puzzled frown as though he was trying to remember what she was doing in his home.

'Don't you ever listen to a word I say?' Brenda gave a long sigh, audible even to Lolly at the top of the stairs. 'I took her down Doc Latham's yesterday. He'll have the blood results before long.'

'And then you'll wish you hadn't bothered.'

'I'm telling you, I heard Angela say his name, Mal Fury, clear as day, and not just the once either. She knew that man, I'm sure of it.'

'Read about him more like. Come on, it was all over the papers, headline news.'

'That was years ago.'

'So what? It just got stuck in her head somewhere.'

But Brenda wasn't having it. 'She was scared of him, always looking over her shoulder. She reckoned he was searching for her. Told me she'd lived all over before she came here. Why do you think that was?'

'Why did the crazy bitch do anything? She had a screw loose and you know it.'

'She was on the run, hiding from him. That's what I think. A secret like that, it's enough to drive anyone round the bend.'

'Have it your own way,' he grumbled. 'But if you're wrong, we'll be the ones feeding and clothing the kid for God knows how many years. Have you thought about that? A bleedin' fortune down the drain.'

Brenda snorted. 'What, as opposed to the bleedin' fortune you throw at the bookies every day? I'll take my chances, thank you very much.'

Lolly waited but Freddy didn't reply. From below she could hear the sound of Brenda locking up for the night. Quickly she slipped back into the bedroom and softly closed the door. When she was in bed, her fingers reached for the rough pink plaster that had been stuck over the skin in the crook of her left arm. It had hurt when the needle went in, but not any more.

'Just a quick test,' Brenda had said as they'd walked along. 'Nothing to worry about. We'll be in and out in five minutes.'

'A test for what?'

'To see if we can track down any of your family. That'd be nice, wouldn't it? If we could find some folks of your own?'

Lolly shrugged. What if her own 'folks' were even worse than the Cecils? There was no way of knowing. And she couldn't see how going to the doctor's could help find anyone. It was all a mystery to her. They had turned on to Albert Road where the prozzies hung out, the women who sold sex for money, although there'd been none of them around yesterday. Maybe they didn't work in the mornings. The surgery was at the station end, not far from the corner, in a big old redbrick house. There wasn't even a sign on the front door and inside the place had been none too clean. Lolly thought that was odd.

She hadn't liked Doctor Latham, a middle-aged scruffy man who had a strange chemical smell about him. He didn't speak to her – in fact he barely looked at her – as he jabbed the needle into her arm.

'How long are we talking?' Brenda asked.

'Couple of weeks.'

Lolly had watched the dark red blood leave her arm and travel up into the syringe. And then the needle was pulled out and the plaster stuck on her arm.

'Leave it there,' he said to Brenda. 'Don't let her take it off for twenty-four hours.'

And then Brenda gave him some money and they left. On the way home, they stopped by Woolworths where Lolly had her picture taken in the photo booth. Before she went in, Brenda combed her hair and adjusted the collar of her blouse.

'When the light comes on, don't forget to smile. And try and look nice.'

Lolly, who had never posed for a picture before, wasn't exactly sure how to achieve this feat, but she gave it her best shot. She sat on the stool, put the coins in the slot and smiled at the window. The flash when it came was dazzling. It caught her off guard, made her squint, but she was ready the next time.

Afterwards they'd had to stand by the booth while the photos were developed. The pictures shot out suddenly, a row of four, and Brenda snatched them out of the machine. She stared at them for a moment or two, looked at Lolly and then back at the pictures. 'Well,' she sighed, 'I suppose they'll have to do.'

Lolly had been allowed to keep one of the photos and Brenda had taken the other three. When Lolly had asked what she wanted them for, Brenda had been vague.

'Oh, just a bit of paperwork. Nothing for you to be bothered about.'

Lolly didn't think she looked like herself in the pictures, not the way she was in the mirror. She had a wide-eyed, surprised expression and a lopsided smile.

After tea in the evening, when his mother was out of earshot, FJ had asked her about the plaster on her arm.

'What's that?'

'The doctor put it there. He took some blood.'

'Are you sick?'

'No.'

'Maybe you've got a horrible disease,' he said. 'Maybe you're dying.' He grinned nastily. 'I hope so.'

'Yeah, maybe I am.' She quickly leaned across the sofa and breathed on his face. 'And now you've got it too. You've got all my germs. If I die, so will you.'

FJ had jumped up, wiping his mouth as though she'd spat at him. 'Get off, you filthy bitch! What are you doing? I'll get you for that, I'll bloody well get you.'

'You can't get me if you're dead.'

Brenda had come in at this point. 'Can't you two get on for five minutes? Just give it a rest. If you don't stop right now you'll both be straight off to bed. You understand? All I'm asking for is a bit of peace and quiet.'

Lolly's victories over FJ were few and far between and as she lay in the dark she savoured this one. Doubtless, he would find a way to get his revenge, but for now she had the satisfaction of knowing that, for once, she'd had the last word. His expression had been priceless. She'd remember that look for a long time to come.

Lolly reached down under the bed and picked up the carrier bag she'd put there. Inside was her mum's pink cardigan. She took it out and held it to her nose, breathing in the scent. As she closed her eyes, Lolly's last thoughts were of her mother, of blood and photographs and the mystery of her unknown family. Now that she'd been deserted by Jude she needed someone or something to cling on to, and hope was the only thing she had.

8

Mal Fury shifted his gaze to the left and looked through the window towards the fine view of the lake. This morning there was a ripple on the water, an autumnal breeze catching the surface. The sky was a clear pale blue. It was thirteen years now since Kay had been taken. Where had all the time gone? Sometimes it seemed like only yesterday that Esther had walked into the library, nervously glancing at her watch, asking why Cathy was taking so long.

Yes, he should spare a thought for Cathy Kershaw too, drowned in the calm cold water. An accident was what they'd thought when they first came across the scene; the empty pram lying tilted in the bulrushes, the dead girl floating face down. He had pulled her on to the bank but it was too late by then. Scrabbling like a madman, going under the water again and again, he had searched until he was exhausted, but there had been no baby, no blanket, no sign of little Kay. He could still hear Esther's screams in his head, a wild despairing sound that echoed in his dreams.

They'd expected the worst when the police drained the lake, waited for the dreadful news, but her body hadn't been found. That was when despair had turned to hope. There was still a chance Kay was alive, that she wasn't gone for ever. He had never entirely given up hope but time had dulled the edges of his expectation.

Mal shifted his gaze back to the private detective. He released his breath, unaware he'd even been holding it.

'So, we have another one,' he said wearily. 'It's been a while.'

Stanley Parrish gave a nod. 'Indeed.'

When Mal had originally announced the reward, twenty thousand pounds, for information about his missing daughter, it had opened the floodgates to every shyster and hustler out to make a fast buck. Not to mention the cranks. There had been hundreds of alleged sightings, of babies being seen with people who were not their parents, with women who had not been pregnant, with men who were acting suspiciously. Back then every new lead had filled them with hope, but as each one came to a dead end the agony was almost too much to bear.

The police had been all over the case at first, but as the weeks passed into months and then into years, it had ceased to be a priority. So Mal had employed Parrish to investigate instead. For the last eleven years he had acted as a useful buffer, shielding them from the timewasters and the crooks.

'Go on then,' Mal said. 'What have you got?'

Parrish leaned forward and put his elbows on the desk. He was one of those sad-looking men with a long thin face and bags under his eyes like a basset hound. 'I wouldn't have bothered you with it normally but there are some unusual circumstances. The girl was orphaned recently – her mother was a suicide – and there are question marks over her true identity. No record of a birth certificate, for example, at least not one for the date she claims is her birthday.'

'Which is?'

'June tenth. She's thirteen, of course, born in 1958.'

Mal nodded. Kay's birthday was the first of June. 'And?'

'Well, the other odd thing is that no one's been able to track down a birth certificate for the mother either. She was called Angela Bruce. I don't suppose that name means anything to you?'

Mal turned it over in his mind for a moment, but came up with nothing. 'No.'

'Although that might not have been her real name. So you can see how there's a problem. No birth or marriage certificates, no driving licence, no passport, no official identity papers of any kind. The woman didn't even have a bank account. No tax records or National Insurance. She was living under the radar, so to speak.'

'There could have been all sorts of reasons for that. What about the girl? What's her name?'

Stanley Parrish hesitated before he said, 'Lolita. They call her Lolly.'

Mal's eyebrows went up. 'An unusual choice.'

'Yes. She's currently living with a married couple, Freddy

and Brenda Cecil. They run a pawnbroking business in east London, in Kellston. It was the wife who came to see me. She's already had the initial blood test done. Type "O".'

'She came prepared then.'

'Exactly. And we both know that result doesn't mean anything – half the population is type 'O' – but it also means we can't completely rule out the girl.'

'Have you seen her?'

'Not yet.' Parrish opened a buff folder and slipped out a strip of three passport-sized photos, the black and white type you had taken in a booth. 'I've got some pictures, though.'

Mal felt a fluttering in his chest as he stretched out his hand. No matter how often he went through the procedure, he couldn't help wondering if this time he might finally see the face of his daughter again. His eyes darted eagerly towards the images, absorbing the features – the eyes, the nose, the mouth – and his disappointment was instant and gut-wrenching. The kid looked nothing like him or Esther. She was a pale, washed-out, nondescript thing with long lank hair and a startled expression.

'Brown hair, blue eyes,' Parrish said. 'I know there's not much of a resemblance but—'

'But what?' Mal snapped, dropping the pictures on the desk. 'This isn't my daughter. You only have to look at her to see that.'

'Children don't always look like their parents. Genes can skip a generation.'

Mal glanced down at the pictures again. Both he and Esther were fair-haired, and Kay had been blonde as a baby too. There was nothing about this girl even faintly reminiscent of either side of the family.

'But you're probably right,' Parrish continued. 'You want me to drop it?'

Mal reckoned the chances were a million to one that this was his daughter, but despite the odds he still didn't want to make any hasty decisions. It was the loose ends that always nagged at you, the fear that a lead could slip through your fingers. 'Do you have a picture of the mother?'

'No, there aren't any. Well, none from when she was alive. That's another odd thing – no mother and baby photos. That's peculiar, isn't it? Most people, most mums, would usually have at least one snap taken with their child. There must be pictures of her from the morgue, but there'll be some red tape to go through before we can get hold of them. And I don't know how useful they'll be; she jumped from a high-rise in Kellston.'

Mal winced, wondering how desperate you would have to be to do such a thing. 'What else do you know about her?'

'Not much. Brenda Cecil says she had psychiatric problems, although she didn't quite put it that way. It sounds like the woman suffered from some kind of paranoia. She also claims that Angela mentioned you on several occasions, but whether this is true or not ...' Parrish lifted and dropped his shoulders in a sceptical shrug. 'People say a lot of things when there's a twenty thousand pound reward up for grabs.'

'Mentioned me in what respect?'

'In a rambling kind of respect. Apparently Angela wasn't exactly lucid when she was ill. She'd claim people were looking for her, following her, spying on her. Your name came up on more than one occasion – or so Mrs Cecil says.'

'You don't believe her?'

'I think she's on the make. And I reckon that's the only reason she took the kid in. But, like I said earlier, there are unusual circumstances. For some reason or another Angela Bruce wanted to keep a low profile, cover her tracks, which begs the question why.'

Mal pulled a face. 'Not necessarily. Not if she had psychological problems. If she believed she was in danger – even if she wasn't – she'd behave in exactly that way. There might not have been anything sinister about it.'

'The chicken or the egg.'

Mal stared at him. 'Huh?'

'Did she become ill because she was afraid of something or someone, or did the illness make her believe she had something to be afraid of?'

'You think it's worth doing some digging?'

Parrish pursed his lips, lifted a hand and scratched his scalp. 'That's up to you. If you're sure she's not your daughter then—'

'I can't be sure of anything, can I?' Mal leaned back and gazed up at the ceiling for a while before slowly lowering his gaze again. 'But I don't feel it. Do you understand? When I look at the pictures, there's nothing there. If I was her father, wouldn't I . . . I don't know, but surely I'd recognise something about her.'

Parrish nodded. 'You have to trust your own instincts.'

A silence fell over the room.

Mal drummed his fingers on the desk, concerned perhaps that his instincts *couldn't* be trusted. This girl wasn't how he imagined his daughter to be, but was that just his prejudice talking? He had a preconceived idea of how Kay should look at the age of thirteen – a younger version of Esther, pretty and graceful, clever and charming. Lolita Bruce showed no signs of having any of these attributes. But for all that, he wasn't prepared to dismiss her out of hand.

'Okay, well, there's no harm in making more enquiries. See what else you can find out about the mother. And try to get hold of a picture of her.'

Parrish closed his file, rose to his feet and gestured towards the strip of photographs. 'I've got copies if you want to hold on to those.'

'Write down the address for me. Kellston was it?'

'You're not going to go there are you? I don't think it's a good idea, not before—'

Mal waved away his objections, pushing a sheet of paper across the desk. 'Just write it down, for Christ's sake.'

Parrish did as he was told. 'All I'm saying is—'

'I know what you're saying. You don't need to spell it out for me. I've got no intention of confronting the Cecils, okay? Not right now, at least. You don't need to worry on that score.'

Parrish finished writing and passed the address over to Mal. 'I'll let you know when I've got more news.'

'You do that.'

After he'd seen him out, Mal returned to the library, sat down and stared through the window again. Sometimes he felt a kind of crazy anger towards the lake as if it was deliberately withholding its secrets, refusing to share the truth of what had taken place all those years ago. It was irrational, but the thought never completely left him. Perhaps they should have sold the house, moved away – a fresh start somewhere else – but he hadn't been able to take that step. His ties to the scene of the crime were deep and profound. This was the last place he'd seen Kay and until she was found it was all he had left to hold on to.

The library door opened and Esther came in. She was wearing a blue dress and had a tight, angry expression on her face. She walked over to the desk, folded her arms across her chest and stared down at him.

'What was that man doing here?'

'The usual,' Mal said.

'The usual *shit*, you mean.'

'Would you rather I just turned him away?'

'Yes,' she said. 'I don't want him in the house. I don't want him anywhere near me. He's a creep and a user. Why can't you see that? He's been bleeding you dry for the past ten years.'

'Eleven, actually, and he does what I pay him for.'

Esther gave a derisory snort. 'You pay him for false hope – and that's exactly what he gives you. Why can't you see that? He encourages people to come forward with any damn kid of the right sex and age so he can spend the next six months proving that she isn't Kay. And then he sends you the bill. He preys on you, Mal. He takes you for a bloody fool. It's pathetic.'

Mal listened indifferently to the tirade he had heard a hundred times before. What she really meant, of course, was that *he* was pathetic. Once, back in the dim distant past, her scorn would have cut him to the bone, but now it no longer touched him. Their marriage had fallen apart years ago and all that held them together was the glue of grief and bitterness.

'So what would you like me to do?'

'Nothing,' she said. 'You're chasing after ghosts and you know it. Kay's dead. Face up to it. She's never coming back.'

Sometimes Mal wondered if she was right. Perhaps, as a mother, she knew instinctively that her child was gone, that there would be no second chances. Or was it just her way of coping? Maybe she would rather have no hope than some, especially when that hope only brought recurring pain and disappointment.

'Is this the latest?' she said, leaning over to snatch up the strip of photographs. Esther gazed at the pictures, shaking her head. 'He's really scraping the barrel now. Look at her, for God's sake. Do you really think this could be our daughter?' She flapped the photos in front of his face. 'Well, do you?'

'What do you want me to say?'

'That she isn't Kay. That in your heart you know she isn't. What's the matter with you?'

Mal met her cold stare and shrugged. 'What harm does it do to check it out?'

'You're ridiculous!' she said, throwing the photos on the desk. Esther turned and quickly walked back across the library, her high heels tapping angrily on the wooden boards. She opened the door and glanced back over her shoulder. 'And keep that man away from here. I don't want to see him again. You understand? He makes me sick.'

Mal didn't even flinch as she slammed the door. He was expecting it. He only ever expected bad things these days. Looking down at the photos, he gave a sigh. None of this was the girl's fault; she was a victim too. He felt sorry for her, alone and orphaned, left with the legacy of a mother who had topped herself. 'Well, Lolita, what do we do now?'

9

Stanley Parrish was aware of Esther's eyes on him as he climbed into the old white Cortina. She was standing at the window, her stare as hard and cruel as Medusa's. What was that saying: if looks could kill? He only glanced once in her direction but that was more than enough to grasp the full measure of her anger.

Quickly he chucked the file on the passenger seat, pulled his seatbelt across and turned the key in the ignition. He was relieved when the car started first time – it was getting more unreliable by the day – and he could pull away from the house. He never liked coming here, preferring to see Mal in London, but sometimes it couldn't be avoided. This whole business with Angela Bruce needed sorting before the trail went cold.

As Stanley rounded the bend in the drive he speeded up, lit a cigarette and sucked in the smoke. He knew why Esther hated him and, although it irked him to admit it, she was not entirely mistaken when it came to her suspicions. For the last eleven years, the search for Kay Fury had subsidised his meagre income as a private detective, enabling him to keep his head above water. It had always been in his interest to encourage the con artists and timewasters to come forward, to chance their hand, in order for him to investigate and ultimately dismiss their claims – and then to charge Mal for the time and effort of doing so.

For all that, Stanley was not a completely cynical or dishonest man. Although it was his belief that Kay had probably died on the day she was abducted, he did not know it for certain. As there was no body, there was no proof of her death, and so he gave every new lead his close attention. There was a chance, albeit a small one, that she was still out there somewhere. It was this slim possibility that enabled him to justify his actions.

Stanley liked Mal Fury and had enormous sympathy for him. Over the years he had watched the grief eat into his employer, its effects as corrosive as acid. Once the Furys had been a golden couple, the talk of the society pages – Mal the handsome jeweller, Esther the beautiful actress – and their romance had been played out in a glare of publicity. But the bright lights had gone out long ago. Now their names had faded and they were rarely seen in public.

When it came to Esther, Stanley had fewer fond feelings. He wound down the window and flicked out the ash from his cigarette. He found her cold and superior, the kind of woman who was used to always getting what she wanted. There were rumours of affairs but he didn't know if they were true or not. Anyway, it was hard to like someone who despised you so openly. If the decision had been hers she'd have dispensed with his services almost as soon as he'd started providing them.

'Let the police deal with it,' he'd overheard her say to Mal. 'What can that creep do that they can't?'

But Mal Fury hadn't given in. By then, of course, he had worked his way through half the private investigators in London, always hoping that the next one would turn up something new. Stanley suspected he had been a last resort, perhaps the only detective left who was prepared to keep digging on a case that had long since gone cold. And why not? He needed the money and for most of the time he had nothing better to do.

Someone, somewhere, knew the truth about what had happened to Kay, and secrets rarely stayed buried. Eventually something would rise to the surface, a clue, a link, and then the past would begin to unravel. That something was unlikely to be anything to do with Angela Bruce but he'd still give it his full attention. He was always thorough in his work, checking every detail, turning over every stone. It was a salve to his conscience, a way to help him sleep at night.

Stanley's journey back to London was uneventful. It was only midday and the Friday traffic hadn't started to build up yet. As he passed through the gloomy interior of the Blackwall Tunnel, he pondered on an article he had come across recently, a piece in a magazine about developments in paternity testing. At the moment simple blood tests could only exclude the possibility of a man being the father of a child, but there would come a time, and perhaps it wasn't that far off, when science would be able to offer a more positive outcome.

He sighed. This wasn't good news for him. For now every child with an 'O' blood type was a possible match for the Furys, but if these new tests proved reliable much of the work he carried out would be redundant. There would be no need for him to follow up on those kids who fell into the 'possible' bracket, no need to go chasing after ghosts.

Still, he had to look on the bright side. Those days weren't here yet. Although there wasn't much chance of Lolita Bruce being the missing child, he had permission to carry on investigating. He had a contact at the coroner's, a technician who (for a price) would be able to provide a photo of Angela and a copy of the post-mortem. He could have gone through the legal channels but that would take weeks and a pile of paperwork. This way he could have all the information he needed by Monday.

Stanley made his way to Kellston, parked at the Fox and went inside. The pub was doing a brisk Friday lunchtime trade and he pushed through the crowd, going from room to room. He was hoping to find Pym there but was out of luck. Should he stay for a drink? Better not. One would turn into two or three and before he knew it the place would be closing. Instead he retraced his steps, crossed the road and walked down to the Hope and Anchor.

This was a much less congenial establishment, a spit-and-sawdust pub mainly frequented by local villains and other assorted riff-raff. The furnishings were old and worn and the inside had a chill that wasn't just down to the lack of heating. By choice, Stanley would never have set foot in the place, but needs must.

The man he wanted to see was seated at the bar nursing half a pint of mild. Pym was the eyes and ears of the East End, a sly furtive man who made his living by selling information. He worked mainly for Joe Quinn but was happy to take money from anyone who'd pay him. Stanley walked over and nodded.

Pym looked up and smiled, showing a mouth full of rotten teeth. 'Ah, Mr Parrish. Haven't seen you in a while.'

'Can I get you a drink?'

'Scotch. May as well make it a double.'

Stanley ordered the drinks, two singles, and paid for them. They moved to a corner table, away from the other customers, and sat on the hard wooden seats. He didn't bother with any small talk but got straight down to business. 'Angela Bruce. What can you tell me about her?'

'Who?'

'Angela Bruce,' Stanley repeated.

Pym frowned and shook his head. 'Don't sound familiar.'

'She lived on the Mansfield. A suicide, back in August.'

'Ah,' Pym said. 'The jumper. I remember now. Let me think.' While he was doing this he took a black pouch out of his pocket, unzipped it, removed a pinch of tobacco and slowly rolled himself a tight skinny fag. He licked the edge of the cigarette paper, sealed it and stuck it in the corner of his mouth. 'The crazy lady, yeah? I used to see her around.'

'And?'

Pym gave a careless shrug. 'What's to say? I guess I won't be seeing her around no more.'

Stanley stared at him. 'That's it? That's all you've got?'

Pym lit the cigarette and puffed out a small cloud of smoke. 'What's with the interest?'

'Just trying to track down some family, if there is any. There's a kid, a daughter. She's staying with Brenda Cecil at the moment. No one seems to know where Angela came from; she turned up in Kellston about eight years ago. I'm wondering why she chose here, if she had a connection to the area. '

'You reckon she was looking for someone?'

'Could have been.'

'Can't say I heard nothin'.'

'You ever see her with a boyfriend, girlfriend, anyone she might have been close to? Apart from Brenda, I mean.'

'Not so you'd notice. I mean not recent like. Maybe back when she first arrived, when she was working for Joe.'

Stanley frowned. This was news to him. 'She was working for Joe Quinn?'

'Yeah, in the Fox. Well, it would have been Joe's son, Tommy, who hired her. She didn't last long.' Pym lifted his glass, knocked back the whisky in one and smacked his lips. 'Started scaring the customers away with all that crazy talk of hers. But there may have been a girl she was friendly with.' Pym stared at the empty glass and then glanced at Stanley. 'I'm trying to think of her name but it just won't come to me.'

Stanley took the hint, went over to the bar and bought

another Scotch. He put the glass on the table and sat down again. 'How about now? Anything?'

Pym gave a grin, leaned in close and lowered his voice. He had a ripe unwashed odour, overlain by the smell of tobacco and a whiff of halitosis. 'Maeve, that was it. Maeve Riley. You won't find her at the Fox, though. She don't work there no more.'

'Any idea where I could find her?'

'You could try Connolly's. She's there most days.'

'Connolly's,' Stanley repeated before emptying his glass. 'Thanks. You've got my number. Call me if you think of anything else.' He rose to his feet, dropped a few quid on to the table and walked out of the pub.

As he headed for the high street, he wondered how interested he should be in the Joe Quinn connection – the man was nasty and vicious and not beyond a touch of kidnapping – but realised he was probably clutching at straws. It would be pretty hard to work anywhere in Kellston without Joe having some involvement in the business. The lowlife had his snout in every trough.

The lunchtime rush was over at the café and there were plenty of free tables. Stanley chose one at the back, away from the window and the other customers. There was only one waitress serving, a pretty woman in her late thirties with short brown hair and a tired expression. When she came over to take his order he asked for a coffee and inquired if she was Maeve Riley.

'That's me,' she said.

'My name's Stanley Parrish. I'm a private investigator

trying to track down some family for Angela Bruce's daughter. Would it be possible to have a word? I understand you worked with her for a while.'

Maeve's face fell at the mention of Angela's name. 'Oh, that was just awful, wasn't it? Terrible. I never thought, not for a minute . . .'

'Dreadful,' he said.

'I just can't believe what happened.'

'I've got a few questions, some things you might be able to help me with. I could come back later if you like, after you've finished work.'

Maeve shook her head. 'No, no, that's fine. I'm due a break in ten minutes. We can talk then.'

Stanley drank his coffee while he waited and thought about stuff. Mostly what he thought about was how he was wasting his time. The chances of Kay Fury and Lolita Bruce being one and the same person were about as likely as him winning the football pools. Still, he was getting paid to investigate and that's exactly what he was going to do.

It was almost a quarter of an hour before Maeve finally returned carrying two mugs. 'On the house,' she said, putting one in front of him. 'Sorry I took so long.'

'It's no problem. Thanks.'

Maeve sat opposite, sighed and leaned down to rub her feet. 'So how can I help?'

'Well, anything you could tell me about Angela could be useful. Like I said, we're trying to trace some family for Lolly.'

'Poor girl. She must be heartbroken.' Maeve sat up straight

again, lifted the mug to her mouth and took a sip of tea. 'I don't think Angela ever mentioned family, though. I got the impression it was just her and Lolly.'

'What about Lolly's dad?'

Maeve shook her head. 'She never said. She was pretty secretive about her past.' There was a small hesitation before she continued. 'Perhaps secretive is the wrong word. Maybe she just didn't want to talk about it.'

'But you were friends, yes?'

'Well, I suppose. For a while. But that was when she first came to Kellston.'

'When she got a job at the Fox?'

'That's right. I was working there too.'

'Did she say where she'd been living before?'

'She was kind of vague about it, said she'd lived all over the place. I think she was familiar with London, though. She seemed to know her way around.'

Stanley thought about what Pym had told him. 'Was it Tommy Quinn who took her on at the pub?'

'Yeah, although Joe wasn't too pleased about it. Did his nut, in fact. He wanted Tommy to get rid of her but he wouldn't.'

Stanley's ears pricked up at this piece of information. 'Why? What did Joe have against her?'

'Beats me. I mean, this was all before she got ill and started ... well, you know what I mean. Back then she was fine. Or she seemed to be. She was a good worker, pleasant to the customers.'

'Did Joe often interfere in the hiring and firing?'

'Never,' she said. 'He always left that up to Tommy. Joe's not really interested in the pub – apart from the profits.'

'So did Angela know him? Had the two of them met before?'

Maeve sipped on her tea and thought about it. 'I don't think so.'

'So Joe just took against her because . . . ?'

'I've no idea. Well, he doesn't need a reason. You only have to look at him the wrong way and he's got it in for you.' As if she might have said too much, she put her elbow on the table and briefly covered her mouth with her hand. Her brown eyes widened with alarm. 'You won't tell him I said that, will you? If he hears I've been badmouthing him, I'll be in trouble.'

'This is all confidential,' Stanley said in his most reassuring tone. 'I promise. Completely confidential. You've got nothing to worry about.'

But Maeve didn't seem entirely convinced. 'So who exactly are you working for?'

'I'm afraid I'm not at liberty to say. Just someone who's interested in Lolly's future.'

'I heard Brenda Cecil had taken her in.'

Stanley nodded. 'For now. I'm not sure if she views it as a permanent arrangement.'

Maeve lifted her eyebrows. 'I was surprised she took her in at all.'

'Why's that?'

But Maeve was still wary, not prepared to say too much. 'I don't know.'

Stanley could guess the reason. Brenda Cecil was hardly the most warm-hearted of people; she had a reputation around Kellston and it wasn't for bringing comfort and joy. 'So what else can you tell me about Angela? What kind of a person was she?'

'Nice,' Maeve said. 'Ordinary. But ... ' She paused as if grasping for the right words. 'Not shy exactly, but reserved, I suppose. Not the sort to go shouting her business from the rooftops. We were friendly for a while, but not close. Just pals, really. I mean, we were more or less the same age. We'd go for a drink or to the cinema if she could get a babysitter. But then she hooked up with that lowlife, Billy Martin, and everything changed.'

Stanley made a mental note of the name. 'What do you mean? In what way?'

'That's when she began to act strangely. He started putting all sorts of crazy ideas into her head, saying that people were talking about her behind her back, calling her a slut and plotting to take Lolly away. I told her he was wrong but she wouldn't listen. I couldn't understand it – the bloke was twisted, but it was like he had some sort of hold over her.'

'You think she was scared of him?'

Maeve gave a light shrug. 'Maybe, a bit, but she also trusted him. God knows why. He was one of those control freaks always checking up on her, where she'd gone, what she'd done, who she'd talked to and what she'd said. I told her it wasn't normal but I may as well have been speaking to a brick wall. As you'll have guessed by now, I couldn't stand him; he gave me the creeps. He had this way of looking at you.' She pulled a face. 'Kind of leery and threatening at the same time. Like he was daring you to cross him.'

'Was he local?'

'South London. He put it about that he'd worked for the Richardsons but I reckon it was bullshit. He was just one of those guys who liked to act the big man, to pretend he was something he wasn't. All mouth and no trousers as they say.'

'Was Angela still seeing him when she ... at the time of her death?'

'Christ, no. He did a bunk years ago. He was only around for a few months and then he suddenly took off. She was convinced something bad had happened. I mean something *seriously* bad. She even went to the law to report him as missing.'

'And did he ever turn up again?'

Maeve shook her head. 'No, that was the last we saw of him. I reckon he was in trouble with someone, that's why he scarpered, but Angela wasn't having any of it. She just couldn't accept that he'd up and gone like that. And that's when all the other stuff started.'

Stanley waited but she didn't explain. He drank some coffee and put the mug down on the table. 'Stuff?' he prompted.

Maeve's shoulders shifted up and down again. 'Well, the accusations. She started saying that Joe Quinn had ... you know? Got rid of him. And that the rest of us were covering up. I mean, it was crazy. I'm not saying that Joe's not capable, but he didn't give a damn about Billy Martin. He barely knew the bloke. Anyway, it got so bad that Tommy eventually had to let her go. After that, I hardly saw her.' She sighed. 'I feel bad about it now. She was ill wasn't she? She didn't know what she was saying. I keep thinking I should have done more to help.'

'It's not always easy. You can't blame yourself.'

'I should have . . . I don't know. I should have done something. She must have been in a right state to . . . and now poor Lolly's left without a mum. It's all too sad. I hope you find some family for her.'

'I hope so too.' Stanley took one of his business cards out of his wallet and laid it on the table. 'Thanks for your time. If you think of anything else, give me a call.'

'I will.'

Stanley left the café, not entirely sure if he had learned anything useful. Still, the Billy Martin angle could be worth pursuing. If he could be found, the fellow might be able to provide some information about Angela. To this end, he walked back to the Hope and Anchor, looking for Pym.

There was no sign of him – the stool by the counter was empty – and so he crossed the road to the Fox. Pym wasn't there either. Stanley bought a pint and settled down to wait. He took out his notebook and wrote the name Billy Martin at the top of an empty page. It seemed doubtful that this bloke was the cause of all Angela's problems but he had been, perhaps, the straw that broke the camel's back.

When, after an hour, Pym still hadn't shown up, Stanley gave up and set off for the high street. It was time for another word with Brenda Cecil.

10

At five o'clock, as soon as the shop closed, Brenda thrust an envelope into Lolly's hand and said, 'Take this down to the Fox and give it to Joe Quinn or Terry. No one else, right? And don't open it. I'll know if you do.'

Lolly was glad of the errand. She was glad of anything that got her out of the house, away from the Cecils and especially FJ. He made it his life's work to inflict pain on her; he bit, pinched and kicked and tried to get her into trouble at every opportunity. 'Lolly did it,' was his favourite mantra. And of course Brenda usually believed him.

She had been quick to learn that Brenda Cecil wasn't the type of woman who did anything out of the goodness of her heart. In exchange for her keep, Lolly was kept busy with chores, with washing-up, dusting, even polishing the silver from the pawnbroker's.

It was a warm Friday, one of those late reminders of summer, and as she walked towards the pub she could feel the last of the sun on her shoulders. When she got to Connolly's she glanced through the window. Inside there were lots of older kids from school, drinking Coke and fooling around. By chance her gaze alighted on a pair sitting at the back and she gave a start. It was Jude with a girl called Tracy Kitts.

Tracy was one of Amy Wiltshire's friends, although she wasn't as pretty or as popular. Her red-gold hair was cut into a swinging bob which swayed as she moved her head. Lolly could tell from the way they were leaning in towards each other, smiling and laughing, that they were a couple. His hand touched Tracy's for a moment as he whispered in her ear. Lolly felt a stirring in her chest. Although she couldn't pin down the exact feeling – it was a swirling combination of envy and resentment – she was aware of tears pricking her eyes.

It was only as she kept on watching that she became aware of something else. Jude's attention wasn't completely held by his new girlfriend; he kept glancing over to the next table where Amy was holding court. They were quick, fleeting glances but she could read the expression on his face; it was the same adoring look as when he was watching Lauren Bacall on screen.

Perhaps Jude sensed he was being scrutinised because he suddenly turned towards the window. Lolly froze, a red flush covering her cheeks. She waited for him to wave, to acknowledge her, but he did nothing. A few seconds passed. He'd seen her – she knew he had – but couldn't even spare a nod. Instead he abruptly turned back and continued talking to Tracy.

Lolly hurried on, feeling her knees beginning to shake. She wished now that she'd never looked into the café in the first place. Seeing Jude again reminded her of how much she missed him – but what was the point of missing someone who didn't want to know you? He had made his feelings crystal clear. She was someone to be ignored, thrust aside, now that he was moving in the cool kids' circle.

By the time she reached the Fox the car park was already half full and people were streaming into the pub. Friday was pay day, the end of the working week, a time to relax and splash the cash. Lolly wasn't old enough to go inside and so she went around the side and knocked on the door by the place where the beer crates were stacked.

A blonde woman answered the door and looked down at her. 'Yeah?'

'Is Terry Street here, please?'

'He's busy. What do you want?'

Lolly held up Brenda's envelope. 'I've got a message for him.'

'Give it here,' she said, reaching out. 'I'll pass it on.'

Lolly took a step back, knowing that Brenda would do her nut if she gave the note to someone else. 'I can't. I've got to give it to Terry.'

'Suit yourself,' the blonde said huffily. 'You'll just have to wait, then, won't you?'

The door closed and Lolly wandered over to the low wall where she sat down. She could have asked to see Joe Quinn instead but he scared her too much. Anyway, if Terry was busy, Joe would be too. She waited impatiently, tapping her feet on the concrete as she watched the cars go by on Station Road.

Lolly tried her best not to think about Jude, but of course he was all she could think about. Now he had a girlfriend, she was surplus to requirements. No, it was worse than that: he was embarrassed by her. All those afternoons they'd spent together counted for nothing. What she'd valued was his kindness, the fact that he was different to other boys, but it turned out he was just the same.

The minutes passed by slowly: five, ten, fifteen. She didn't have a watch but she could see the clock on the side of the station tower. What if the woman didn't tell Terry she was waiting? She could be here for hours. And Brenda would get the hump if she was late back, thinking she'd done it deliberately.

Lolly felt in her pocket to make sure the envelope was still there. Her fingers touched on something small and metal. Drawing it out, she saw the cap she'd saved from the Fanta bottle Jude had drunk from. She put it in her palm and stared at it for a while. What was she keeping it for? In a fit of pique she hurled it across the car park and watched as it arced through the air, landed and rolled under the back wheels of an old blue van.

Lolly looked up at the clock again. It had been almost twenty minutes now. She was on the point of going to the main entrance of the Fox and trying to get Terry's attention from there when the side door opened and he finally came out. She jumped to her feet as he strolled over to her, hands in his pockets. As usual he was dressed in a smart dark suit and a shirt so white it almost gleamed.

'Hey,' he said. 'Sorry about that.'

Lolly shrugged as though twenty minutes was neither here nor there. 'It's okay.'

'A bit of business. It dragged on longer than I thought it would.'

Lolly, who didn't know what to say to that, simply held out the envelope. 'It's from Brenda.'

'Ta,' he said. He tore the envelope open, pulled out the note and read it. He glanced over at her. 'Tell her Tuesday. Probably.'

'Probably Tuesday,' she repeated dutifully.

He held up the note. 'You could have given it to Yvonne. Save you waiting. She'd have passed on the message.'

Lolly shook her head. 'Brenda said it had to be you or Joe.'

Terry gave her a long scrutinising look as if he had something on his mind. 'Lolly, isn't it?'

'Yeah.'

'I thought so. How are you doing?' he asked. 'I was sorry to hear about your mum.'

'I'm okay.'

'You like it at Brenda's? Is it all right there?'

'It's okay.'

'When I was a kid, she used to scare the shit out of me.'

Lolly's eyes widened with surprise. She couldn't imagine Terry being scared of a woman, even one as big as Brenda.

Terry grinned. 'But don't tell her I said that.'

'I won't. I swear.'

'I believe you. You strike me as the kind of girl who can be trusted.' He reached into his pocket, took out a handful of change and gave her half a crown. 'Here's something for your trouble.'

For Lolly this was an unexpected bonus. She was used to running errands for Brenda but had never been tipped before. 'Thanks.'

'Actually, I could do with someone reliable. You know your way round Kellston, don't you? How do you fancy earning a bit of extra cash?'

'What would I have to do?'

'Deliver a few messages to people. Nothing complicated. What do you reckon? You could start tomorrow if you like.'

Lolly did like. She couldn't think of anything better than earning money of her own. She could get flowers for her mother's grave and, if she saved up, she might even be able to buy a headstone eventually. 'Yeah, sure, I can do that.'

'Right, good, let's say about twelve o'clock, then. Meet me round the back of the Hope. Oh, and one more thing. It might be better if we keep this between the two of us. Our little secret, yeah? Can you keep a secret?'

Lolly nodded. 'I won't tell anyone.'

'See you tomorrow, then.'

Lolly watched as Terry went back into the pub, pleased by this unexpected turn of events. Now all she had to do was to find a way of escaping from Brenda's clutches tomorrow. The thought of Brenda reminded her of the time and the trouble she was likely to be in. She walked quickly across the car park. As she passed the blue van she glanced down at the discarded Fanta cap lying beside the back wheel. Just leave it there, she told herself. It doesn't matter. You don't want it. But somehow it looked sad lying there on its own so she stopped, bent down and picked it up. Some things, she decided, were just too hard to throw away.

Lolly waited for a gap in the traffic before sprinting across the road, up the high street, down the alley and through the yard. Breathless, she rushed into the kitchen.

'Sorry I'm late. I had to wait. Terry was—'

Lolly stopped dead in her tracks, surprised to find a stranger sitting at the table. The man was middle-aged with a long hangdog sort of face and pouches under his eyes.

'About time too,' Brenda said. 'This is Mr Parrish. He's come to have a word with you.'

11

Even though Stanley had seen the photograph, he was still disappointed by meeting Lolita Bruce in the flesh. She was a small skinny kid, pale and awkward. There was nothing, not the slightest hint of Mal or Esther about her. Of course he had expected this, prepared himself for it, but in the back of his mind there had always been the hope of a miracle.

'Hello,' he said. 'It's nice to meet you at last.'

The kid stared silently back at him, her mouth still open from when she'd stopped mid-sentence. It gave her a stupid, gawping kind of look and he wondered if there was something wrong with her. Maybe, like her mother, she wasn't quite right in the head.

'Well, say hello, then,' Brenda ordered. 'Don't just stand there.'

'Hello,' Lolly said obediently.

Stanley smiled, hoping to put her at ease. He spoke slowly and clearly in case she had difficulty in understanding 'I think Mrs Cecil – Brenda – has explained, that I'm trying to track down some family for you. Maybe you can help. Would you mind if I asked you a few questions?'

'You're wasting your time,' Brenda said before Lolly had a chance to answer. 'She don't know nothin'. I've already asked.'

Stanley extended his smile to include Brenda Cecil. 'Yes, I understand, but the memory's a strange thing. Sometimes there can be information buried deep down, things that need a bit of a nudge to bring them to the surface again.'

Brenda rolled her eyes as if to suggest he was talking ten types of nonsense. 'Well, you go right ahead, do as you like, but don't say I didn't warn you. She talks about as much sense as that mother of hers.'

'Perhaps if I could have a few minutes alone with Lolly?'

'No, I don't think that's a good idea. She's just a kid. I reckon someone should be here with her.'

Stanley suspected that the girl wouldn't speak openly in front of her guardian. He also didn't want Brenda interrupting every thirty seconds – she was the sort of woman who liked the sound of her own voice and wasn't likely to keep her mouth shut for long. 'I'm afraid Mr Fury insists that I talk to her in private. But if you don't think it's appropriate . . . well, maybe it's better if we leave things for now.'

'Leave things?' Brenda snapped. 'Things have been left long enough, ain't they?'

Stanley gave a mild shrug of his shoulders. 'If it was down to me, Mrs Cecil, I'd be more than happy for us all to sit down together, but I can't go against Mr Fury's wishes. I'm sorry, but that's just the way it is.'

'So you want to throw me out of my own kitchen,' Brenda said indignantly. 'How am I supposed to get the tea made? I've a family to feed, you know.'

'No one's throwing you out of anywhere. Perhaps we could go through to the living room if it wouldn't inconvenience you too much?'

'Or the yard,' Lolly said suddenly. 'We could go out there.'

Stanley, pleased with this suggestion, quickly rose to his feet. 'Yes, indeed, the yard would be fine.'

Brenda glanced from one to the other, her mouth in a tight straight line. For a moment she looked as though she was going to object again but instead she flapped a hand. 'Oh, do as you like. It don't make no difference to me.'

Stanley followed Lolly outside. She went to the far end, out of earshot of Brenda, and sat down on one of two metal barrels that had been left by the gate. He perched on the other one, wondering if his first impression of the girl had been wrong. She was, perhaps, smarter than she looked.

'You must be tired of answering questions,' he said. 'I'll try not to keep you too long.'

'Are you from the Social?'

'No.'

'So who's Mr Fury?'

Stanley didn't want to say too much. 'He's the man who employed me to try and find your family.'

'Why would he do that?' she asked.

'It doesn't really matter. What's important is—'

'Is he my dad?'

Stanley hesitated, not wanting to lie but not willing to tell the whole truth either. 'It's unlikely. Did you ever hear your mother mention his name?'

'No, only Brenda. She told Freddy that Mum was scared of him, but I never heard her say it. Why would she be scared of him?'

'I've no idea,' Stanley said. 'He's a kind, decent man. There's nothing about him to be scared of.' And then, before she could ask anything else, he quickly said, 'So your mother never mentioned any relatives, nothing about her own mum and dad, or any brothers and sisters?'

Lolly shook her head. 'She always said it was just the two of us, just me and her.'

'What about a bloke called Billy, Billy Martin?'

'I dunno. She used to talk about a lot of people, mainly the ones who were out to get her. When she was sick, she thought she was being followed.'

'Who did she think was following her?'

Lolly screwed up her face while she thought about it. 'Ted Heath,' she said eventually.

Stanley laughed. 'Ted Heath? The prime minister?'

Lolly kicked her heels against the metal of the drum and glared at him. 'It's not funny. It's not her fault she was ill. People were always mean to her.'

'You're right,' he said. 'I apologise. It can't have been easy for either of you.'

'And now they're saying that she killed herself. But she wouldn't have done that. She *wouldn't*. She'd never have left me on my own.'

Stanley sighed, wondering how you could even begin to

explain to a thirteen-year-old why adults ended up doing what they did. 'No, of course not. So what do you think happened?'

Lolly's face grew pinched and tight. 'I don't know. Maybe it was an accident. She could have leaned too far over the edge and ... '

'Yes, it's a possibility.' Stanley left a short respectful silence before he continued. 'I had a chat with Maeve earlier. She was friends with your mum, wasn't she?'

'She works in the caff,' Lolly said.

'That's right.'

'They used to be friends, but then ... Mum said she and Joe Quinn were in it together.'

'In what?'

Lolly shrugged.

'Was she scared of Joe Quinn?' Stanley asked.

'Everyone's scared of Joe Quinn.'

Stanley couldn't argue with that. And he certainly didn't want to go poking around in the gangster's business if he could avoid it. He went on to ask a few more questions, trying to unearth some childhood memories, but nothing useful came to light. 'What about paperwork?' he eventually asked. 'Where did your mum keep important stuff – the rent book, bills, things like that?'

'In the kitchen drawer,' Lolly said.

'And did you ever see anything else there?'

'Like what?'

'Address book, driving licence, maybe something to do with where you used to live?'

'No.'

'What about personal effects: jewellery, keepsakes, mementoes, anything like that?'

'She had beads,' Lolly said. 'She kept them in a box in the bedside table. It's a tin box with flowers on the front. There's a brooch and some pink ribbon in there too, and buttons, and cinema tickets and hair grips.'

'Do you have the box?'

Lolly shook her head. 'It's still at the flat.' She looked over towards the kitchen window where Mrs Cecil was busying herself in the kitchen, one eye on the sink, the other on the yard. 'Brenda's got the hump. She doesn't like it when she can't hear what's going on.'

'Is that why you wanted to come out here?'

Lolly didn't answer. She transferred her gaze from the window to the wall and began kicking her heels against the drum again.

'Well, thanks for your help,' Stanley said. 'I think that's all for now unless—' He was about to say, 'Unless there's anything else you can think of,' but Lolly was already on her feet and walking towards the door.

The two of them went back inside where Brenda, acting as if she hadn't been watching them, was now setting the table. 'All finished? Good. Go upstairs, Lolly, and wash your hands – and don't take all day about it. Tea's going to be ready in ten minutes.' She waited until the girl had gone before turning to Stanley. 'So?'

'Lolly mentioned a box that belonged to her mother. A tin box with flowers on? She said it was still at the flat, in her bedside table.'

'There's nothing in the flat. I cleared it out weeks ago. Council wanted it back, didn't they.'

Stanley felt a stab of disappointment. 'So what happened to it? To the box, I mean?'

'What box? There wasn't any box. If truth be told, there wasn't much of anything: a few scraps of furniture, some kitchen stuff, an old TV, and that was about it. I brought Lolly's clothes back here and gave Angela's to the charity shop.'

'And you definitely checked the bedside table?'

'It was empty. There was nothing in there but a couple of old magazines.' Brenda eyed him suspiciously. 'What's so important about this box, then?'

'Probably nothing, but it's a shame it's gone missing.'

Brenda's expression changed from suspicious to indignant. 'Before you start throwing accusations around, I can assure you there was no box in the flat, no box at all.'

'No one's accusing you of anything, Mrs Cecil. All I was saying was—'

'Oh, I know what you were saying. You think I was born yesterday?' Brenda wiped her hands on her apron and glared at him. 'What do you take me for? You think I'd rob a dead woman?'

Had Stanley been forced to give an answer to that question, it would have been 'Yes', but there was a time and a place for honesty and this wasn't it. 'No one was suggesting that. No, no, not at all. I don't believe there was anything of value in the box, at least not in a monetary sense, but there may have been some clues to her past. For obvious reasons Mr Fury is keen to get some background, to trace the family history.'

'I ain't seen it, okay? And if I tell you it weren't there, it weren't there.'

'Could it have been removed by someone else?'

'Like who, for instance? There's no one had a key apart from the girl and me.'

Stanley gave a nod, all the time wondering if Brenda had taken the box because there was something inside that provided a clue as to who Angela really was. 'Well, if it turns up at any point, I'd be grateful if you'd let me know.'

Brenda continued to glare at him. 'So what's going on with Mr Fury? We've done the blood test and you've got the results. They must have been okay or you wouldn't be here now asking all your questions.'

'All that the blood tests prove is that Lolita can't be completely ruled out. Unfortunately, as I'm sure you understand, more definitive proof is needed before my client can proceed.'

'What I understand is that it's costing me a bleedin' fortune. I've got enough mouths to feed as it is. Perhaps you could mention *that* to Mr Fury. I'm the one who's paying out and I don't see how that's right, not if she turns out to be his.'

Stanley, who was pretty sure she was receiving money from Social Services for the care of Lolly, took care to keep the disgust from his face. 'I'll be sure to pass on your concerns.'

'You do that,' she said.

Stanley picked up his coat, put it over his arm, said goodbye and left by the back door. As he walked along the alley he pondered on why it was that some people drew the short straw in life. Poor Lolly Bruce, orphaned at the age of thirteen, was both unloved and unwanted. The chances of her being Mal's daughter were negligible, and from what he'd just heard there appeared to be little hope of the Cecils offering any kind of permanent home. Once Lolly ceased to be the goose that laid the golden egg, her usefulness would be over. And what then? She'd be out on her ear, thrown into the system. He sighed into the still evening air. The future for the kid looked bleak and there was nothing he could do about it.

12

Lolly soon settled into her new job with Terry Street. On school days she would scoot round to the Hope and Anchor after the afternoon bell and wait in the yard until he came out. At first he had only given her short handwritten notes to take to this place or that, but now he knew she could be trusted, it was often three or four packages too. She would put the items into her school bag and set off, like the postman, to make her deliveries.

Lolly had quickly learned how to do her job with speed and discretion. She would drop off the packages only when no one else was around and usually in one of the long shadowy passageways that linked the various parts of the Mansfield estate. It hadn't taken long to get to know the regulars: Skinny Mick, Perks and a tall Jamaican called Joseph. They'd been suspicious of her at the beginning but now they were friendly enough, sometimes giving her a few pennies or a stick of gum for her trouble.

Lolly enjoyed the intrigue of it all. Sometimes she'd pretend she was a spy or Emma Peel from *The Avengers*. But what she liked best was feeling a part of something, of feeling needed. And even without the money, she'd have done it just for Terry's praise.

'You're my best worker,' he'd say. 'You're a star, Lolly Bruce.'

For Lolly, who had never heard flattery before, the experience was a novel one.

Her favourite drop was in Albert Road, at the old three-storey redbrick house where the women were always pleased to see her. Here there was usually a glass of Coke on offer and a plate of chocolate biscuits. She'd sit in the kitchen at the back while the women chatted and smoked, the smell of weed permeating the air. Stella was the one she liked best. She wasn't the prettiest but she was the kindest. Stella always took an interest, asked how she was and interrupted the others, trying to protect her when the talk got too close to the knuckle.

'Not in front of the kid,' she'd say. 'She don't need to hear shit like that.'

And then one of them, usually Jackie, would give a snort. 'Best she finds out now rather than later. Life ain't no fairy tale with handsome princes coming to the rescue. If she's old enough to do Terry's dirty business, she's old enough to hear the truth.'

Stella would shake her head. 'There's time enough for that.'

Lolly didn't always understand what they were talking

about, but she got the gist: one way or another, men were trouble. And that was clear enough from the black eyes and bruises that the women frequently sported. But when she asked what had happened they just shrugged it off.

'It comes with the job, love. No point whining about it.'

Lolly pondered on this as she made her way home. Her job, she decided, was a better deal than theirs. She glanced up at the dark sky. It was November, Bonfire Night, and already the smell of sulphur hung in the air. Later, she'd be going to the green to see the fireworks with the Cecil boys. Looking over at the station clock, she saw that it was almost half past five and broke into a run, not wanting to be late. As an excuse for her frequent absences after school, she told Brenda she was doing homework at her friend Sandra's. As it happened, Brenda didn't seem to care much one way or another these days; so long as Lolly was back for her tea she rarely asked any questions.

Lolly was still angry with Brenda after finding out about the clear-out of the flat. Listening on the stairs, she had overheard the revelation to Stanley Parrish. Why hadn't she been told? It made her stomach turn over to think of Brenda going through her mother's things, touching, feeling and discarding them. As she sprinted down the alley she hissed out breaths of anger and frustration. If only she'd thought to take the box when she had the opportunity; now it was gone for good.

When she stepped inside she discovered the kitchen was empty, but could hear voices coming from the living room. On going through she found Brenda, FJ and Tony there along with a girl with long fair hair who she instantly recognised as Amy Wiltshire. Everyone fell silent for a moment, one of those awkward lulls, and Lolly was certain they'd been talking about her.

'So you're home,' Brenda said eventually. 'Go and get your hands washed. Tea's almost ready.'

As Lolly scooted through the room into the hall and up the stairs, she heard Amy say, 'So that's her, then. She's kind of funny looking. Bit small for thirteen, isn't she?'

'Stunted growth,' Tony said.

FJ sniggered. 'She ain't right in the head, either. She's nuts, a basket case. She ought to be locked up someplace, not living here. It ain't safe; we could all be murdered in our beds.'

No one contradicted him or came to Lolly's defence, and she carried on upstairs with a red flush burning her cheeks. By the time she descended ten minutes later, everyone was sitting round the kitchen table. The only person missing was Freddy and he was probably down the pub.

She sat down between Brenda and Tony and opposite Amy. While they ate she tried not to stare at the girl, although it wasn't easy. Amy was so pretty it was hard not to look at her; she had smooth perfect skin, blue eyes and lips that were painted a pearly pink. She could see what Tony saw in Amy, but couldn't figure out what the attraction was for her. He was an eighteen-year-old skinhead with the manners of a pig, and hated everyone and anything that was different to him.

During the meal, roast beef with all the trimmings – the

stops had been pulled out for Amy's visit – the conversation turned to Jude Rule. Lolly's body stiffened as soon as his name was mentioned. She still hadn't got over losing his friendship and thought about him more often than she should.

'I reckon Tracy's going to dump him,' Amy said. 'I mean, he's a weirdo, isn't he? Everyone knows.'

And FJ, of course, had plenty to say on the subject. 'Yeah, he's that all right. What sort of fella hangs out with little girls? Lolly knows all about that.'

Lolly's face burned red again as the whole table turned to stare at her. 'No, I don't.'

'Come on,' FJ urged, 'bet he used to do all sorts to you.'

'He'd better not have,' Brenda said, glaring at her.

Lolly shook her head quickly from side to side. 'He didn't. He didn't do anything.'

'I've told Tracy,' Amy said. 'I've told her he's not right. What's with all those old films? It ain't normal watching that stuff all the time.'

Lolly didn't respond. She got Jude's need for escapism, for a way of retreating from the real world. He had lost his mother just as she had lost hers and the pain was often too much to bear. But she wasn't going to try and explain. How could she? None of them would understand.

'He ain't normal, full stop,' Tony said. 'He needs his fuckin' head kicking in.'

'Language,' Brenda said. 'We don't need that kind of talk at the table.'

'Just saying.'

'He's good looking, though,' Amy said provocatively. 'Don't you think?'

Tony curled his lip and stared at her. 'If you like bleedin' weirdos. And why is he always sniffing around you when he's got a girlfriend of his own?'

Amy smiled smugly. 'What's the matter? You jealous?'

'Of that freak? You're having a laugh. Anyhow, you're way too old for him. He likes his girlfriends young, don't he, Lolly?'

'He's not weird,' Lolly said. 'He's not like that.'

'You don't know what weird is,' FJ sneered. 'You think what that creep does is normal.'

'He doesn't do anything.'

'Yeah, right. Like we all believe that.'

Lolly bowed her head and carried on eating. Jude was nothing to do with her any more. Sometimes she saw him around, but they never spoke to each other. If she could avoid him, she did, dodging into shop doorways or veering down side roads. She didn't want to come face to face with him, to see that look of embarrassment in his eyes.

'Don't be back late tonight,' Brenda said, changing the subject. 'I want you home by ten at the latest. There's school in the morning.'

'I don't have school,' Tony said.

'No, you've got work and I'll be the one having to drag you out of your pit.'

Tony worked for his uncle, Freddy's brother, selling second-hand cars. Well, he claimed he sold them, but Lolly had walked past the place one day and seen him standing on the forecourt washing down a rusty Vauxhall Viva. More dogsbody than salesman, she reckoned, but knew better than to voice this opinion.

'And don't go messing around with any fireworks. Just watch the display and come straight home.'

Lolly had the normal excitement of any kid on Bonfire Night. She was looking forward to it, but not to spending time with the Cecil boys. It was her intention, once they got to the green, to make herself scarce and hide in the crowd. She knew they wouldn't bother searching for her and she could enjoy the rest of the evening in peace.

'And keep an eye on Lolly. I don't need her wandering off and getting lost.'

Lolly frowned, wondering how on earth she could get lost in a place she knew like the back of her hand. 'I'm not going to—'

'Don't worry, Mrs C.,' Amy interrupted with an ingratiating smile. 'We'll take care of her.'

Lolly was aware of FJ grinning and a quick exchange of looks between Tony and Amy. Something was going on and, if past experience was anything to go by, it was probably something bad. Suddenly the prospect of the fireworks didn't seem so appealing. She shifted in her chair, made a swift decision and looked at Brenda.

'I'm not feeling well. I don't think I'll go.'

'Well enough to eat your tea,' FJ said, clearly annoyed by this turn of events.

And Brenda wasn't having any of it either. 'You'll be fine once you get out in the fresh air. I've got the books to sort. I can't be doing with you under my feet all night.'

Which meant, in Brenda speak, that she wanted everyone out of the house. Perhaps Joe Quinn was coming round to do a bit of business.

Amy chipped in again. 'I'll make sure she's okay. I promise. Hey, Lolly, you've got to come. You must. I don't want to be the only girl.'

Lolly shrugged, knowing that she had no choice. She hadn't lied about feeling ill; she had a sick feeling in her guts, an instinctive knowledge that she was being set up.

'Good,' Amy said. 'That's settled, then.'

It was just before six when they all left the house and began walking along the high street. The temperature had dropped and Lolly shivered, although maybe that wasn't just from the cold. Amy linked an arm through hers as though they were best friends, chatting away while the two boys trailed behind.

'So how long have you known Jude?' Amy asked.

'A while,' Lolly replied cautiously. 'A few years. We used to live in the same block.'

'I don't really think he's a wrong 'un. I only said it because Tony doesn't like him. He's jealous, you see. He doesn't like it when other boys fancy me.'

'Oh,' Lolly murmured.

'I'm sure he's very nice. Was he nice to you?'

'I guess.'

Amy left a short pause before asking, 'In what way was he nice?'

Sensing a trap, Lolly answered carefully. 'Just kind, you know, like when my mum was sick.'

'That's sweet. Did he ever kiss you?'

'What?'

'Kiss you. Even if he didn't, I bet he wanted to. You're a pretty girl. I bet boys want to kiss you all the time.'

'No,' Lolly said, astonished by the suggestion. 'I don't like boys.'

Amy laughed. 'Oh, there must be some. What about the Beatles? You must like them. What about Paul McCartney?'

'He's all right.'

'Or the Rolling Stones?' Amy leaned in close and whispered in her ear. 'I really fancy Mick Jagger.'

'He's all right,' Lolly said again.

'So what kind of things did you and Jude talk about?'

'I don't know. Films and stuff.'

Amy gave an impatient little sigh. 'Is that all? You must have talked about something else. Did he ever mention me?'

Lolly hesitated for a fraction too long.

'He did, didn't he? Tell me what he said.'

'Just that you were ... er ... yeah, kind of pretty.' Lolly wasn't going to tell her the whole truth. She could hear Jude's voice in her head: *Boys don't like girls like Amy. They just want them.* 'That's all. There wasn't anything else.'

'Sure there was,' Amy insisted. 'Come on, spill. I won't tell anyone, I swear.'

Lolly stuck to her guns. 'No, really. Just that, just that you were pretty.'

By now they had reached the green, which was full of people. The bonfire had already been lit and smoke was drifting in the air. There was the smell of frying onions and the fizz of sparklers. Lolly's plan was still to slip away, but Amy was hanging on tightly to her arm.

'Let's go and see the fire,' FJ said.

The local kids had been collecting wood all week, everything from old chairs to broken tree branches, and piling it up on the green. Tony and FJ forged a path through the crowd while Amy dragged Lolly along in their wake. A few rockets screamed into the sky, exploding into falling stars of gold and red and green.

FJ glanced over his shoulder. 'You should see the guy. You're going to love it. It's ace.'

Lolly didn't pay much attention. She was too busy drinking in the atmosphere: the people, the noise, the sights and smells. The night air was cold and breath escaped from her mouth in white steamy clouds. As they drew closer she began to feel the heat from the fire and hear the pop and crackle of the flames.

Amy had stopped asking questions. FJ kept turning around to look at Lolly. His nasty little face was red and shiny, his eyes bright with an odd kind of excitement. 'Come on, come on!'

Lolly should have stopped to think, but she didn't. Caught up in the moment, her first impression of the guy was of a bundle of rags: a pair of old boots, blue trousers, a fat stomach stuffed with straw and . . . it took a few seconds for her to register the pale pink garment that was wrapped around his shoulders. When she did, bile rose into her throat. Her whole body began to shake. It couldn't be! Oh, God! *Her mum's cardigan!*

Instinctively she dived towards the fire, but the heat was too fierce for her to get close. 'No!' she screamed. 'No, no, stop it!' But she knew it was too late. Already the flames were at the guy's waist, licking at his chest, burning up the wool before her very eyes. She reached out her arms, her heart beating so wildly she thought it would burst out of her body.

Beside her she could hear the dreadful sound of laughter. Tony had his head thrown back. Amy was grinning like a Cheshire cat. FJ was jumping up and down and pointing.

'Look at it! Ha ha! The guy's wearing Lolly's cardi!'

Lolly felt as though she was watching the last of her mother go up in smoke. Apart from the mother-of-pearl button, it was the only thing she had left, something so precious it could never be replaced. 'What have you done?' she screamed. 'I hate you!' The tears rose to her eyes but she didn't let them fall. She wasn't going to cry in front of her tormentors. She wasn't going to give them the satisfaction.

Instead Lolly turned on her heel and ran. Their laughter echoed in her ears as she pushed through the crowd, clearing a path with her sharp little elbows. How could they? Their cruelty was like a knife slicing though her, and all she could think about was getting away. Why had they done it? But she knew the answer. They were mean to the bone, heartless through and through. She would never forgive them, not ever, not in a million years.

Once Lolly had cleared the green, she swerved left and ran and ran until she reached the Mansfield estate. Her lungs were bursting by the time she passed through the gates. Slowing to a walk, she tried to catch her breath. The gulping didn't help, the great racking sobs that were shaking her body. She couldn't think straight, couldn't think beyond the licking flames and the grotesque laughing mouths.

As she stumbled across the scrubby patch of grass she could hear the sound of bangers going off like gunfire, each one making her jump. She stopped to look up at the tall tower of Haslow House, counting off the floors until she came to the old flat. There was a light on in the window, but she knew she couldn't go there. It wasn't her home any more. Nowhere was home.

Lolly wrapped her arms around her chest, trying to contain her grief and anger. Hate coursed through her veins. She would never forgive them, *never*, and one day she would make them pay. She would get revenge no matter what it took.

13

Stanley Parrish had rented the same space in Whitechapel for years. He stared at the building as he approached. The block was old and decrepit, the six floors divided and subdivided into numerous offices. All were as small and shabby as each other, a testament – if one was needed – to the failure of the people who occupied them. The very walls seemed ingrained with a thousand disappointments, scarred with lost dreams and empty hopes. A sour smell always hung in the air.

Stanley's dreams had faded long ago. He scraped a living and was grateful for it. Once upon a time he'd had a career, first in the army and then the police. The former had been distinguished, the latter not so much. An ill-fated affair with a senior officer had seen him disgraced and booted out. Homosexuality had been illegal then, of course, a perversion that would not be tolerated within the ranks of Her Majesty's Constabulary.

These days Stanley didn't often think of Richard Price, although occasionally he saw his picture in the paper. The 'incident', as the powers that be liked to refer to it, had been hushed up and Richard – claiming a temporary aberration, stress and depression – had managed to salvage his loveless marriage and escape with his career intact. Stanley, on the other hand, had been thrown to the dogs. Cast in the role of the younger, single, predatory male, the blame for the year-long affair had been laid entirely at his feet.

Since then he had shied away from relationships. The fear of getting hurt again was too much to chance. The betrayal had cut deep, but that was love for you. When push came to shove, Richard had chosen public respectability above his own nature and, perhaps, his own happiness.

Stanley walked through the front door of the block and went to the reception area to see if there was any mail or phone messages.

Liz shook her head. 'Sorry, Stan,' she said. 'Nothing today.'

Stanley, unsurprised, gave a nod and thanked her. He climbed the stairs to the third floor, unlocked the door and went into the tiny waiting area of his office. There were three chairs and a coffee table with some old magazines stacked on top. Everything was covered in a fine layer of dust. He made a mental note to run a cloth over the place, but knew he would never get round to it.

He went through to the main part of the office and put on the electric fire. There was a chill in the air and a forecast for snow. He rubbed his hands together, sat behind his desk and thought of the bottle of cheap brandy in the bottom drawer. A small one, perhaps, just to take the edge off. He reached down but stopped himself. Better to wait until after Mal Fury had been to see him. It was hard to disguise the smell of booze in a room this small.

Stanley leaned back, checked his watch and saw that he still had twenty minutes to wait. He stood up, retrieved the Fury file from the half empty metal cabinet and sat down again. Flicking open the folder, he began to read. He knew the contents inside out – eleven years of false leads and dead ends – and yet remained convinced that he was missing something.

Near the front was a list of all the Furys' employees at the time of Kay's abduction, as well as a list of staff Esther had fired over the previous few years: cooks, housekeepers, gardeners and handymen. Any one of them might have held a grudge. Had it been an inside job? Somebody had known the nanny's routine, known that she always took the baby for a walk in the morning.

There was yet another list, this one running into pages, of everyone who had visited the house over the previous twelve months. There had to be over two hundred names here, including party guests and weekend visitors. The Furys had been a sociable couple and the guest list read like a roll call of the rich and famous.

Stanley read through them all again but nothing jumped out. The police had made their own enquiries, checking for form, but nothing untoward had been found. That, however, didn't prove much. Not all of the ex-employees had been tracked down and anyone on the list could have been feeding information to someone else.

He thought about Angela Bruce. There hadn't been a great deal of progress in that direction either. He had tracked down Pym again, but the man had been curiously tight-lipped when it came to Billy Martin.

'To tell the truth, I hardly knew the geezer, Mr Parrish. He weren't around for long.'

'But he and Angela were seeing each other?'

'Might have been. I couldn't really say one way or the other.'

'Billy can't have been too happy when she got fired from the Fox.'

Pym had given him a long hard stare. 'Ain't for me to speak for him. You'd have to ask him that yourself.'

'Bit hard when he's gone missing.'

'Just 'cause he ain't around no more, don't mean he's missing. He's just some place else.'

'And you wouldn't have any idea where that place might be?'

'Like I said, I hardly knew him. People come and go. It were years ago, weren't it? He could be anywhere.'

Despite further probing, Stanley hadn't managed to prise anything useful out of Pym. But he was sure the man knew more than he was letting on. There was something in his manner, a wariness that set alarm bells ringing in Stanley's head. Why had Billy Martin up and left so suddenly? Maybe he hadn't had a choice in the matter. Or maybe the only place he'd gone was to meet his maker.

Stanley sighed and checked his watch again. It was at this very moment he heard the main door open, followed by footsteps on the threadbare carpet through the adjoining room. He closed the file and looked up, expecting to see Mal Fury. But when his own door, which he'd left ajar, swung open it wasn't Mal standing there at all. Instead Stanley found himself staring up into the face of the infamous Joe Quinn.

'Mr Parrish, yeah?'

Stanley was tempted to deny it, but lying to Joe Quinn wasn't a smart idea. 'That's right,' he said, trying to keep his voice steady. He didn't scare easily, but only a fool would be at ease in the presence of the East End gangster. 'How may I help you?'

Quinn walked across the room and stood in front of the desk. 'I reckon it's more the other way round.'

'I'm sorry?'

Another man appeared in the doorway, a great bear of a guy, well over six foot and with the build of a heavyweight boxer. Quinn glanced over his shoulder and then back at Stanley. 'Oh, don't worry about Vinnie. He's harmless so long as you don't make any sudden movements.'

Stanley stayed very still.

Quinn pulled out a chair, sat down, leaned forward and laid his palms on his heavy thighs. He fixed Stanley with his cruel, piercing eyes. It was a stare so menacing the Devil himself would have flinched. 'You got something you'd like to tell me, Stan? Only I've heard you've been poking your nose into my business.'

'I don't think so.'

An unpleasant sound came from Quinn's throat, half laugh, half growl. 'And here was me thinking we were going to get along.'

'Perhaps I should rephrase that. I wasn't *aware* that I was poking my nose into your business. It certainly wasn't deliberate.'

'Did you hear that, Vinnie? Stan here says it weren't deliberate.'

'Yes, guv.'

'Guess he must be the careless type, huh?'

'Looks that way, guv.'

Quinn continued to glare across the desk. 'Be a shame for us to fall out so soon. Here we are, we've only just met and already you're pissing me off. Now I'm a busy man, a *very* busy man, and I can't afford to waste time on some cheap private dick who doesn't know his arse from his elbow. So let's make this easy. Just tell me who you're working for and we can both get on with our day.'

Stanley shook his head. 'I'm afraid I can't do that.'

'Sure you can. It's easy. Just open your mouth and tell me his fuckin' name. Now I'm the reasonable sort, always happy to talk things over, but Vinnie ... well, Vinnie's not so understanding. He has a short fuse if you know what I mean.'

It was a long time since anyone had tried to intimidate Stanley and he felt, perversely, rather flattered. Which wasn't to say he didn't take the threat seriously. He looked over at the goon who, he imagined, rarely had to raise a finger;

his size was enough to make the toughest man compliant. Transferring his gaze back to Quinn, he gave a nod. 'What I can tell you is that the case I'm working on has nothing to do with you. If I've inadvertently crossed a line, then I apologise.'

Quinn seemed less than satisfied with the answer. His eyes flashed with irritation. 'There are three things I can't stand, Stan: pigs, queers and bleedin' liars. They turn my stomach. I can hardly bear to be in the same room as them. You understand?'

What Stanley understood, loud and clear, was that Quinn had been doing his homework. And that meant he was worried. But why? It was either down to Angela Bruce's death or to Billy Martin's abrupt disappearance. Probably the latter. Pym must have tipped him the wink about Stanley's interest in the matter. 'Yes.'

'So?'

'So I'm not a liar,' Stanley said. 'The case in question concerns a child's paternity. Who's the daddy, if you like. I was simply making the necessary enquiries. There was nothing more to it than that.'

Joe Quinn curled his lip. 'You don't seem to be listening to me, Stan. I need a name.' He glanced down at his watch. 'You've got thirty seconds before my patience runs out.'

Vinnie shifted his weight, inching forward as if in preparation.

Stanley's palms were starting to sweat. He was not prepared to reveal Mal's identity, but was aware he had to offer up something credible. He also had to figure out what

Quinn already knew. 'Okay, I don't want any trouble. All I'm trying to do is to track down some family for Angela Bruce's daughter. I believe Angela used to work for you. Brenda Cecil is taking care of Lolly at the moment, but it would obviously make more sense if we could trace the kid's father. Even if he's not prepared to take her on, there could be other relatives we don't know about.'

'Well, it ain't me if that's what you're thinking. I never touched the mad cow.'

'I wasn't.'

Quinn smirked and looked over his shoulder. 'What about you, Vinnie? You ever find your way into Angela's panties?'

'No, guv.'

'So there you go,' Quinn said to Stanley. 'End of story. Time for you to start looking some place else.'

'I'll do that,' Stanley said.

Stanley's heart was in his mouth as Quinn lumbered to his feet. By implying that Brenda was his client he was, at least temporarily, off the hook. But what if the old bastard went to see her or called her up? Well, it was a risk he had to take. And he had the suspicion that Brenda would be less than open. If she came clean about Mal Fury, about the distant chance he could be Lolly's father, then Quinn might try to muscle in on the reward.

Joe Quinn was the type who never liked to leave without one last dramatic flourish. He stared hard at Stanley, raised his hand and pointed a finger at him. 'Don't make me come back,' he said. 'I won't be fuckin' happy.'

Stanley nodded, thinking it wise to keep his mouth shut.

He watched the two men leave the room. When the outer door closed he released his breath in a long sigh of relief. 'Shit,' he muttered. Then he quickly got up, went into the waiting area and pressed his ear against the door. He could hear his visitors retreating along the corridor, the heavy tread of their boots clearly audible on the lino.

Stanley went back to his desk, removed the bottle from the bottom drawer and poured a stiff shot into a mug. He knocked it back in one and immediately poured out another before putting the bottle away again. Christ, he was getting too old for this kind of aggro. As a young man he'd have taken it in his stride but now, at fifty-three, he didn't have the energy or the inclination to go up against the likes of Joe Quinn.

The Fury file was still open in front of him. On reflection, he didn't think there was any connection between Quinn and the abduction of Kay. No, the visit had been all about Billy Martin – even if his name hadn't been mentioned. Stanley had only tried to trace the guy in the hope he might know who Lolly's father was, but in the process he'd opened a whole can of worms. From now on he'd steer clear of anything to do with him. It was none of his business and he preferred to keep it that way.

Another ten minutes passed before Mal Fury arrived at the office. He strode in, took one look at Stanley and asked, 'What's up? What's the matter?'

Stanley felt a small shift inside his head, a discomposure that always occurred when the two of them came face to face. Mal Fury was handsome and charming, but it wasn't just that. Over the years something more than a basic working relationship had developed, a mutual trust, even a kind of friendship. Stanley was, he supposed, a little in love with the younger man, although he'd rather walk over red hot coals than openly admit to it.

'I just had a visit from Joe Quinn and his pet gorilla. He's an East End villain based in Kellston. He—'

'Yes, I know who he is.' Mal interrupted. 'I've heard of him. What did he want?'

'The name of the person I was working for.'

Mal pulled out the chair and sat down. He crossed his long elegant legs and gazed across the desk at Stanley. 'And did you tell him?'

'Of course not. You don't need the likes of Quinn on your back. Anyway, it's none of his business. He doesn't care for the fact I've been in Kellston asking questions. Something's rattled him. I think it's to do with Billy Martin. He didn't come straight out and say but that's the impression I got.'

'Angela's boyfriend?'

Stanley nodded. 'The guy who disappeared.'

'What if Quinn knows something about Kay?'

'I don't think he does. Not unless he's smarter than he acts.' Stanley paused and gave a faint smile. 'What are the odds?'

Mal shrugged.

'No,' Stanley continued. 'I reckon someone's told him I'm looking for Billy and he's got all jumpy about it. If this was to do with Kay then he wouldn't need to ask who my client was. Even a moron like Quinn could take an educated guess at that one.'

'You've got a point. I take it you're not going to pursue the Billy Martin angle, then?'

Stanley hesitated. He didn't want to come across as a man who could be easily intimidated, but didn't want to lie either. 'I don't think there's much mileage in it, but I'll keep my ear to the ground.'

Mal opened his mouth as if about to speak but then closed it again and reached into the pocket of his overcoat. He took out a loosely folded A4 envelope, put it on the desk, smoothed it out and pushed it towards Stanley. 'You'd better keep these. I don't want them in the house. Esther might find them and . . .'

Stanley knew what was inside: photos of Angela Bruce from the morgue, and the autopsy report. 'Of course. Nothing useful, I take it?'

Mal shook his head. 'I don't recognise her. I've never seen her before.'

Stanley hadn't expected anything else. Even if Angela had mentioned the Furys in one of her less lucid moments – and he still suspected the story was pure concoction, invented by Brenda Cecil – it wasn't proof of anything. Thirteen years ago the news of Kay's abduction and her nanny's murder had made the headlines, splashed across the front page of every paper. In her delusional state, Angela could easily have got confused, tangling up the memories of her own life with something she had read.

Mal sighed. 'It's just another dead end, isn't it?'

'It would help if we knew Angela's real identity. Where she came from, where she was living before she turned up in

Kellston. At the moment all we have are questions. Someone has to know who she really is.'

'Does it make a difference?'

On balance Stanley thought the answer was probably no. The chance of Lolly being Mal's lost daughter was less than slim. 'Do you want me to drop it?'

Mal gazed beyond Stanley, staring at the buildings of Whitechapel through the smeared panes of glass. Or maybe he wasn't seeing the outside at all. His blue eyes had a glazed, distant look as if his mind was somewhere else. A few seconds passed before he spoke again.

'Whatever you think best.'

Stanley understood that he wasn't capable of closing the door on any line of enquiry until there was definite proof one way or another. Although in his heart Mal didn't believe Lolly was his, he could not entirely dismiss the possibility. 'I'll give it another week or two, see if anything comes to light.'

Mal glanced down at the envelope. 'A suicide, then? Why do you think she did it?'

Stanley didn't know the answer to that. 'Why does anyone?'

'Because they've had enough. Because they've run out of hope.'

'There's always hope,' Stanley said quickly, alarmed by the despair in the other man's voice. 'You never know what's round the corner.'

Mal's face tightened. 'Sometimes you know exactly what's round the corner.' He rose to his feet, gave Stanley a nod and said, 'Call me if anything changes.'

Stanley didn't like to see him leave in this frame of mind. What if he did something stupid? He racked his brains for words of encouragement but could find nothing but platitudes. 'You know where I am if . . . I'll stay in touch.'

As soon as the door closed Stanley lifted the mug to his lips and drained the last inch of brandy. He was worried. There had been something different about Mal today. Or was he just imagining it? Maybe *he* was the one who wasn't thinking straight. The visit from Joe Quinn had rattled him.

Stanley opened the envelope and spread the photos out on the desk. They didn't make for pleasant viewing. He had looked at them before – there was another set in his files – but had that familiar feeling he was missing something. What had gone through Angela's mind as she'd stood staring down at the Mansfield estate in the final seconds of her life? In the photos her face was waxy and expressionless. Part of her skull had caved in and the damage was ugly. He tried not to stare at it, and to concentrate on her features instead.

'Who are you?' Stanley murmured.

He flicked through the file, removed the strip of photos of Lolly and laid them beside the pictures of Angela. So far as he could see there were no similarities, nothing to indicate they were mother and daughter. Even the colour of their eyes was different. But that didn't mean anything. Lots of kids didn't look like their mums. They might take after their dad or their grandparents. Genetics was a strange thing.

There was nothing helpful in the autopsy report either. Stanley skimmed through it again. No evidence of an injury previous to the fall (although this could have been destroyed by the force of impact). No drugs in her system, and no alcohol either. Her stomach had been empty. Angela had gone to her death stone cold sober, influenced only by the demons in her mind.

Stanley shuddered as if someone had just walked over his grave. He understood despair and loneliness, had himself swayed on the brink on more than one occasion, but had never had the courage to make that final fateful leap into the unknown.

He gathered up the pictures and put them back in the envelope. What now? The woman deserved more, he thought, than to be filed away in a drawer and forgotten about. And Lolly deserved more too. He couldn't give the kid a fairy-tale ending, couldn't wave a magic wand and make everything all right, but perhaps he could try and make a difference. There must be family out there, people who would care for her. All he had to do was find them.

Stanley tilted back his head and gazed up at the old cracked ceiling. There was another advantage to uncovering Lolly's background in that he'd be one step closer to helping Mal draw a line under the faint possibility that she was his flesh and blood. But was that a good or a bad thing? So long as an element of doubt remained, no matter how small, there was still hope and he didn't want to be the person to take that hope away. With these contradictions jostling in his mind, he decided there was only one thing to do – he put the file away, stood up and headed for the nearest pub.

14

It was over a week since Bonfire Night and Lolly still hadn't mentioned the business of the guy to Brenda. There were two reasons for this: the first was that it wouldn't make any difference – the cardigan was gone for ever – and the second was that she'd only make her own life worse by grassing up FJ and Tony to their mother. Not that Brenda would give a damn anyway. She would only raise her eyes to the ceiling and say something like, 'For God's sake, I've got more important things to worry about than some old cardi.'

For Lolly it was a lesson learned. From now on she would take extra care of what little she had. She was saving up the money she got from Terry and already there were five one-pound notes hidden in her room. The idea for the hiding place had come from something she'd seen in a film: a tiny slit cut into the mattress near the seam, just big enough for her to slide the notes in. She was determined that the boys wouldn't get their hands on her hard-earned cash.

She loathed FJ and Tony, hated who they were and what they'd done. There was no place in her heart for forgiveness. And they weren't even sorry. For them it was all one big joke. They smirked at her over the dinner table, their faces glowing with joyful spite.

'You'll be sorry,' she muttered. 'One day you'll be sorry.'

A cold wind was gusting along the high street and she pushed her hands deep into the pockets of her coat. She had just come from Albert Road but there hadn't been much of a welcome today. Stella had grabbed the package and shooed her away.

'You'd better scoot, hon. Terry just called and Joe's on his way over from the Fox. He won't like it if he finds you inside.'

Lolly had been looking forward to getting into the warm for a while and being fussed over – it was the only bit of comfort she got these days – but she made sure it didn't show on her face. 'Okay. See you next week, then.'

She turned and walked down the steps. Perhaps she hadn't hidden her feelings quite as well as she thought because Stella called after her. 'Lol? You all right, love?'

'Yeah, yeah,' Lolly said, painting on a smile and giving a breezy wave. 'See you soon.'

Stella frowned, gave her a searching look but then shrugged and retreated back inside.

Lolly had only walked a few yards when she saw the black Jag approaching. Terry wasn't driving. It was the big bloke, the one called Vinnie. She didn't stare in case she drew attention to herself. Joe didn't know about the errands she ran. In fact she had the feeling Joe didn't know about a lot of things Terry did.

Terry was smarter than his boss, but was careful not to show it. Men like Quinn didn't like being overshadowed – they always had to think they were the best at everything. And Quinn wouldn't have trusted her in the way Terry did. It would never have dawned on him how useful she was and how she could move around Kellston without arousing suspicion. Nobody took any notice of a kid, and especially not the law.

Lolly was heading towards the Mansfield for her last delivery of the day. Joseph would probably be in the east tunnel. It was called a tunnel by all the residents but it wasn't actually underground: the long straight throughway was at ground level and linked the front and back of Carlton House. The ceiling was low with the plaster peeling off and the walls were covered in graffiti. There were six of these passages on the estate. It was where the dealers hung out, the druggies, the gang boys and even the occasional brass if it was chilly outside.

It was dusk by the time Lolly arrived. She peered along the length of the tunnel. As usual a few of the lights were out and the place, full of shadows, had an eerie feel to it. Halfway down there were a couple of lads, a bit older than her, leaning against the wall and sharing a fag, but no sign of Joseph. From past experience, however, she knew he could be at the far end, off to the left where she couldn't see him, hanging out near the base of the stairwell.

Lolly was wary of the lads and scuttled past with her head

down. In the event she needn't have worried. She could feel their eyes on her as she passed by, but neither of them said anything. They were bored but not bored enough to bother with her. She was too young to be of any interest.

Lolly was almost at the end of the tunnel when she heard the raised voices, a boy and a girl in the middle of an argument.

'Why couldn't you keep out of it, you interfering bitch?'

'Jesus, it's not my fault. What are you blaming me for?'

It took a moment for the penny to drop and by then it was too late; she had already turned the corner and was face to face with Jude Rule and Amy Wiltshire. The two of them were standing by the foot of the stairs. Jude was wearing jeans and a black raincoat with the hood pulled up. She could tell how angry he was by the bright red flush on his cheeks. Amy looked defiant; her mouth was a tight straight line and her arms were folded across her chest. As soon as they realised who it was, they stopped arguing and stared at her.

Lolly glanced from one to the other. It was the first time she'd seen Amy since Bonfire Night when, she was sure, the girl had conspired with FJ and Tony in the big 'joke' with the guy. She felt the anger gathering inside, her guts turning over at the memory of it. She hated both of them: Amy for what she'd allowed the brothers to do, and Jude for his betrayal. If she'd been braver she might have confronted them, asked why, but all she wanted to do was get away. The very sight of them made her sick.

Before anyone could say anything, Lolly quickly pushed past, strode across the rear lobby and went through the door.

Outside, the cold air stung her face. She hunched her shoulders and buried her chin in the collar of her coat. She had a lump in her throat but she fought against the urge to cry.

As she headed towards the west tunnel on the other side of the tower, Lolly wondered what they'd been rowing about. Not that she cared. Why should she? If she never saw either of them again it would be too soon. People couldn't be trusted and that was the beginning and end of it. Now that her mum was gone, there was no one special in her life. She was on her own and she'd better get used to the idea.

Lolly had only walked a short distance when she began to feel unsteady on her legs – a delayed reaction, perhaps, to bumping into Jude again. There was a low wall by the scrubby patch of green and she sat down. It was dark now and the windows of the towers were lit up. They made curious patterns, long lines and zigzags. She wondered about the people who lived behind the bright panes of glass, what they were like, what they were doing.

For some reason, Stanley Parrish came into her head. She hadn't seen him since he'd turned up at the pawnbroker's and that could only mean one thing: he hadn't been able to find any family. Not that she'd expected him to. He'd probably given up by now or forgotten all about it. The whole idea was crazy anyway; if there had been any relatives, she'd have known about them.

Lolly was so wrapped up in her thoughts she wasn't sure how long she sat there for. It was the cold that finally pulled her to her feet again. She jogged along the front of the building and ducked into the west tunnel, glad to be out of the wind. She saw Joseph almost immediately and gave a sigh of relief. Time was getting on and she had to be back by five-thirty if she was to avoid a clip round the ear from Brenda. Her bag bounced against her hip as she made her way towards him. He was fifty yards in, leaning against the wall with that faraway look on his face.

There were a few other people coming in the opposite direction and Lolly slowed down to give them time to pass. She wouldn't stop unless the coast was clear. She'd walk straight on without even saying hi. She saw a man sidle up, glancing furtively along the tunnel, before slipping some money into Joseph's hand. The deal was done in the blink of an eye. The man continued on his way as if nothing had happened. Joseph leaned back against the wall, staring into space again.

There was no one else around when Lolly drew level with him. 'Hey,' she said.

Joseph gave a broad smile. 'Hey, Lollipop. How you doin' today?'

'Yeah, I'm good.' She slipped the small package out of her satchel, gave it to him and watched it instantly disappear into the pocket of his jacket.

'You tried telling your face that?'

'Huh?'

'You don't look happy, babe. You look kind of pissed off if you don't mind me saying.'

Lolly tried to force a smile but her lips wouldn't cooperate. 'I'm okay.'

Joseph shook his head. 'I know what okay looks like and

it sure as hell ain't that. What's on your mind? Come on, you can tell me. I won't go blabbing to no one. Anything you tell me is straight up secret, right?'

Lolly was quiet for a moment and then she said, 'I'm just missing my mum. I don't like it without her. I mean, I know she wasn't always . . . but we had each other. Now there's no one.'

'No, well, it ain't easy losing someone close. Takes a good while to come to terms. Nothing you can rush. Just got to take it slow, a day at a time.'

'You got family?'

'Sure,' he said. 'Some. But it ain't always what it's cracked up to be.'

'What do you mean?'

Joseph pulled a face. 'Family's just chance, the luck of the draw. Just 'cause they're your folks don't mean you're going to get along. They say blood's thicker than water but it ain't always true. Sometimes you've got to start from scratch, make your own family.'

Lolly stared down at the ground for a while, thinking about it. Eventually she glanced up again. 'How are you supposed to do that?'

'With people you trust. Mates. I got brothers I'd trust with my life, but we ain't related. That don't matter, though. We got a bond, see. We've got each other's backs.'

Lolly couldn't think of anyone who'd got her back. 'What happens if your mates let you down?'

'Then you have to let 'em go.' Joseph gave her a long steady look. 'Someone screw you over, Lollipop?'

Lolly couldn't bring herself to tell him about Jude – she was too afraid she might start crying – but found herself blurting out the story of her mum's cardigan and the guy, and what FJ, Tony and Amy had done.

'Little bastards,' he said. 'Who'd do a shitty thing like that? Those fuckin' Cecils have got a lot to answer for.'

'I don't like living with them.'

'Can't say I blame you, babe. Wouldn't fancy it much myself.'

Talking about the Cecils reminded Lolly that she was due back soon. 'Do you have the time?'

Joseph stretched out his arm to reveal a flashy gold Rolex. Well, it looked like a Rolex but it probably wasn't real. There was a ton of fakes for sale on the Mansfield estate, everything from watches to handbags.

'Twenty past five,' he said.

Lolly drew in a breath. 'God, I'm going to be late. I've got to go.'

'You take care, Lollipop. See you when I see you.'

'Bye then.'

Lolly hurried through the tunnel, only glancing back when she reached the end. Joseph was in his familiar pose, lounging against the wall. She would have waved but she knew he wouldn't wave back. He wasn't watching her. He'd returned to his own thoughts, to whatever occupied his mind while he waited for the next customer.

Lolly was almost at the main gate when she saw the cop cars arriving, three of them with flashing lights and sirens. There was an ambulance too. She had a sudden recollection of the day her mum had died. It was the sirens, she thought, a sound she now found so ominous that her heart always missed a beat. She watched the vehicles sweep past and pull up outside Carlton House.

She was curious enough to stop and stare but knew she couldn't hang about. Anyway, bad stuff was always happening on the Mansfield. The law spent more time here than anywhere else in Kellston. It would only be a gang fight or some bust-up between a bloke and his missus. Perhaps the latter, as she hadn't heard any commotion as she left the tunnel.

Lolly passed through the gate, crossed the road and was back on the high street when she heard the sound of someone running behind her, their feet pounding on the pavement. She half-turned, instinctively veering to the left to let them pass, but instead they drew up beside her.

'Lolly! Stop! Hold on.'

Lolly jumped with surprise. It was Jude. 'What is it? What do you want?'

He took a moment to catch his breath and in those few seconds, as his chest rose and fell, she saw the terror on his face. A wave of fear rolled over her, a sense of dread. His mouth was partly open, strange and twisted, and there was a weird look in his eyes. Snot was running from his nose as if he'd been crying.

'What is it?' she asked again.

Jude stared wildly around and then grabbed her arm and dragged her away from the street lamps and into the shadows of a narrow alley that ran between the bakery and the newsagent. 'Something . . . something's happened.'

Even through the sleeve of her coat Lolly could feel his fingers digging into her flesh. She flinched and pulled her arm away. 'You're hurting me.'

'I'm sorry, I'm sorry,' he said. 'Christ, I don't know what to do.' Jude raked his fingers through his hair. He couldn't stay still; every nerve end in his body seemed to be twitching. There was a thin film of sweat on his forehead. He covered his face, dropped his hands and then raised them again. He rubbed hard at his temples as if trying to scour some awful image from his mind. 'It's . . . it's Amy. I found her. I left her but then I went back. And that's when . . . she was just lying there, in the stairwell. Shit, shit. They're going to think it was me, Lolly. They're going to think I did it.'

'Did what?' Lolly whispered, although she didn't need to ask. Already she was putting together the pieces, the cop cars and the ambulance and Jude's terrified expression. Her fingers clenched into two tight fists. 'Is she . . . ?'

'I didn't do it. I swear. Please, Lolly, you've got to believe me. I never touched her.'

She stared at him, remembering the raised voices, the argument, the two bright spots of red on his cheeks. He'd been angry with Amy, called her an interfering bitch. And now, less than half an hour later, she was gone. 'Are you sure she's . . . you know? Are you sure?'

Jude's head bobbed up and down. He clawed at her arm, his eyes full of pleading. 'You've got to help me. Please. They'll say I did it. They will.'

Lolly didn't know how to respond. None of it felt quite real. It was like one of those strange scary dreams you couldn't wake up from. At first she didn't understand what he wanted from her – she frowned, confused – but the light gradually dawned. 'I won't tell anyone I saw you. I promise.'

'I've had it,' he said as though she hadn't spoken. He turned away from her and paced a short way up the alley and back again. 'They're going to come for me. They'll take me away, Lolly. They'll lock me up.'

'Not if you didn't do it,' she said.

Jude made a weird strangulated kind of sound, half snort, half sob. His voice rose up an octave. 'That won't matter. I was with her, wasn't I? We had a fight and . . . they'll pin it on me. I know they will.'

'Maybe no one else saw you.'

He shook his head. 'Tracy knew. She knew I went looking for Amy. She'll grass me up. She'll go running to the cops as soon as she finds out.'

'So just tell them what happened.'

'I can't,' he whined. 'Don't you see? You know what they're like. They won't listen. They'll twist everything round. They'll make it look as though . . .' Jude gave a shudder, his face contorting again. 'I've had it. Jesus, what am I going to do?'

Lolly didn't have an answer. She stared at him, wide-eyed. Despite everything that had gone on between them, she still had feelings. She remembered the times he had been there for her rather than the times he hadn't: afternoons on the sofa, peanut butter sandwiches, an old black and white film playing out its tragedies on the screen. She should hate him but she couldn't. Old loyalties died hard.

'I know, I know,' he said. 'I've been horrible to you. I'm sorry, I'm really sorry. You've got no reason to help me. Why should you?'

Lolly waved the apology aside. 'Why were you arguing with Amy?'

Jude glanced away. He stared at the wall for a moment before looking back. 'She told Tracy I'd been coming on to her. But I hadn't. She was just stirring, the bitch was always stirring.' He must have heard the venom in his own voice because he quickly added, 'I mean, she was always causing trouble, mixing it up, but that doesn't mean . . . I wouldn't have . . . I didn't kill her, Lolly. I didn't lay a finger on her.'

'I believe you,' she said.

Jude looked relieved, but then his face darkened again. 'You might but they won't.'

Another cop car sped down the high street with its sirens blaring. Lolly felt her stomach turn over. 'You could run away.'

'What with?'

'I've got some money,' she said. 'Five pounds. You can have it if you want.'

'Where did you get that from?'

'Just odd jobs,' she said vaguely. 'I've been saving up.'

Jude gave a weak smile. 'Thanks for the offer, but I won't get far on a fiver. And anyway, if I run they'll be sure it was me. It's like saying you're guilty, isn't it? It's like admitting to it.'

'I suppose.'

'What I need is an alibi,' he said. 'I need someone to say

they were with me for the last hour, that I was never out of their sight. Could you do that for me, Lolly? Could you tell the cops that we were together?'

Lolly thought about it. She wasn't bothered about lying – if you did it for the right reasons then it wasn't really wrong – but about the practicalities. 'What if someone else saw you at the stairs?'

'They didn't. I'm sure. You're the only one who went past.' Jude's eyes brightened. 'If I can prove I was never with Amy, they can't blame me. We could say we were at the flat, that you came over after school. Why not? That would work.'

'But what if someone saw *me*?' Lolly asked. 'Saw me on my own, I mean.'

Jude, who had started pacing again, instantly stopped. 'Did they?'

Lolly thought back over everything she'd done since four o'clock. She'd met Terry and gone to see Stella, but hadn't stayed long with either of them. And neither of them mattered as they were both en route from school to the Mansfield when she would have been alone anyway. Which only left Joseph. 'Yes, there's someone, but I don't reckon he'll say anything. He'll keep schtum. He doesn't like the law.'

'Are you sure?'

Lolly nodded. 'Yeah, I'm sure. Only . . .'

'Only what?'

'There were other people around on the estate, people coming back from work and the rest. Someone else might have noticed me. I don't know.'

145

Jude raised a hand to his mouth and chewed on his knuckles. The panic had come back into his eyes.

'But they probably didn't,' she said quickly. 'It was dark by then.'

Jude started nodding again. 'Yeah, yeah, it was dark. It should be okay. But if I say we were together, the cops are going to want to speak to you, Lolly. They'll ask all kinds of stuff, how long you were at mine, what we did, what we talked about. We'll have to get our stories straight. They'll try and trip us up. They'll double check everything and if we get it wrong . . . '

'So what do you want me to say?'

'Er . . . what about . . . we could . . . no, not that . . . '

Lolly waited, but she could see he was in no frame of mind to follow through. His head was too frazzled to think straight. If their stories were going to tally, she was the one who'd have to sort it. She didn't stop to consider what she was getting herself into. It was enough that Jude needed her. 'Look, we have to keep it easy so we can both remember. I've got some ideas. Come on, I'll tell you while we walk.'

'What? Where are we going?'

'I have to get back. I'm late enough as it is.'

Jude stared at her as though she was crazy. 'I can't. What if someone sees me?'

'What if they do? There's no reason you shouldn't be here. You've got to start acting normal. You've got nothing to hide, remember?'

Jude gazed over at the high street and swallowed hard.

She could see his Adam's apple bobbing in his throat. He took a few tentative steps, stopped and shook his head. 'I can't. I can't do it.'

Lolly linked her arm through his. 'You can,' she insisted. 'You have to.'

15

As she hurried through the back yard Lolly braced herself for a tongue-lashing, but that was the least of her worries. She was scared Jude would lose his nerve and crumble when the police finally caught up with him. It was all very well agreeing to lie, quite another to be caught out in the process. She wasn't sure if she could trust him to stick to the story. He might crack under the pressure and then they'd both be up to their necks in it.

The light was on in the kitchen and she could see the Cecils seated round the table. How late was she? It was well past half five by now. It must be. She took a deep breath, opened the back door and walked in.

Brenda glared at her. 'Oh, so you've decided to grace us with your presence, have you?'

'Sorry,' Lolly said. 'I didn't realise what the time was.'

'Too busy getting up to no good, I imagine. Where have you been? I don't make your tea for the fun of it, you know.

If you can't be bothered to come home, I don't see why I should be bothered to cook it.'

Lolly tried to look suitably contrite. 'Sorry,' she said again. 'I was only doing homework at Sandra's. I thought it was earlier. I ran all the way back.'

'You don't look like you've been running,' FJ said, sticking his oar in. 'Why aren't you out of breath? And why isn't your face all red?'

Lolly ignored him.

Tony looked up from his half-eaten dessert, something soft and mushy covered in custard, and glanced from her to FJ. 'It's 'cause she ain't got any blood. She's not really alive, you see, she's just one of those zombie things. Like in that film. You'd better watch out or she'll come and get you in the middle of the night.'

FJ gave a snort. 'Hey, Lolly, are you a zombie? Is that true? I bet it is.'

'No, but you might be one. I've heard they haven't got any brains.'

FJ glared at her, his eyes narrowing. 'Zombies are liars. They never tell the truth. They don't know how.'

Brenda lumbered to her feet and went over to the oven. 'It'll be burnt to a crisp by now,' she grumbled. 'Don't blame me if it's not fit for a cat to eat.'

Lolly hung her bag over the back of an empty chair and began to take off her coat.

'And don't go leaving those there,' Brenda snapped. 'Put them where they belong. Go on. I'm not having the place looking like a bleedin' cloakroom.'

Lolly grabbed her bag and went though to the small stretch of hallway that separated the main part of the house from the pawnbroker's. She could hear FJ and Tony laughing, something to do with her, no doubt. It was clear they hadn't heard about Amy yet, but it was only a matter of time. In a place like Kellston, news travelled fast.

She hung up her coat and bag and went back to the kitchen. *Act normal*, she instructed herself, trying to take the advice she'd doled out to Jude. Except it was easier said than done. She sat down, picked up her knife and fork and attempted to eat the dried-up cottage pie. Her throat felt tight and she found it hard to swallow. She pushed the food around the plate, taking tiny mouthfuls while her stomach churned.

The others left the table and went through into the living room. As soon as Brenda's back was turned, Lolly got up, scraped the food into the bin and put the plate in the sink. It was the first time she hadn't finished a meal since coming here. She ran hot water into the bowl and began the washing-up. It was nothing to do with placating Brenda, just something to keep her mind occupied while she waited.

Lolly grew more and more nervous with every minute that passed. How long before the telephone rang or the knock came on the door? She had a sense of foreboding like a weight pressing down on her. She knew what was coming and that it couldn't be avoided. A storm was about to blow through the Cecil household and there was nothing she could do to stop it. Amy Wiltshire was dead, murdered, and the news would reach here soon.

When all the dishes were washed, dried and stacked in the cupboard, she stood in the middle of the kitchen until she couldn't put it off any longer. She had to go through and join the others. It might start to look odd otherwise, like she was deliberately avoiding them.

Lolly sat down in the only space available – between Tony and FJ on the sofa. She stared at the TV without seeing anything, without hearing a word. All she was thinking about was Jude. She wondered if he'd got it wrong. What if Amy had simply slipped and banged her head? It could have been an accident. He might be panicking over nothing. In her heart, however, she knew this was only wishful thinking.

A quarter of an hour passed before Lolly heard the back door open and close. Freddy poked his head into the living room and gestured to Brenda.

'I need a word, love.'

'If it's your tea you're after, you're too late. I'm not going to start cooking again at this time of night.'

'In the kitchen,' he said, abruptly withdrawing.

For a moment Brenda stared at the space where her husband had been, but then she hauled herself to her feet and padded across the room. The kitchen door closed firmly behind her.

Lolly didn't need to hear the conversation to know what it was about. She had seen the look on Freddy's face. Her body stiffened, her pulse starting to race. She had a sick feeling in the pit of her stomach and was glad she hadn't eaten much. Beside her, the boys kept their eyes fixed on the TV; if they were curious about what was happening they didn't show it.

It was a while before Brenda opened the door again. 'Tony,' she said. 'Come here a minute.'

'What is it?'

'Just come here.'

Tony sighed and rose to his feet. 'I ain't done nothing,' he said plaintively as though he thought he was in for a bollocking.

'What's going on?' FJ asked.

Brenda shook her head. 'Not now.'

Once Tony was in the kitchen, the door closed again. FJ, annoyed that he was missing out on something interesting, slouched in the corner. His gaze flicked between the TV and the door.

'No one ever tells me nothin',' he grumbled.

Lolly, pretending to be engrossed in the programme, didn't say a word.

When Brenda, Freddy and Tony came back into the living room, their faces were grim. Tony didn't speak. His eyes were dull, almost glazed. He looked stunned, as though he hadn't quite taken it in yet. He went straight through to the hall, got his leather jacket and came back.

'Let's get it over with, then.'

'Maybe I should come too,' Brenda said.

Freddy shook his head. 'No, you stay here with the kids. It don't take three of us. Call Jim and let him know what's going on.'

'What *is* going on?' FJ asked.

152

There was a long ominous silence before Brenda finally answered. 'It's bad news, I'm afraid. It's Amy. There's ... er ... there's been an accident.'

Lolly felt a fountain of relief bubble up inside her. So Jude had been wrong after all. Amy hadn't been—'

'An accident?' Tony hissed, suddenly finding his voice. 'This wasn't any bloody accident. Why are you saying that? Someone killed her, for fuck's sake! Someone knifed her!'

There was a clear intake of breath from FJ. 'What? No way!'

Lolly gasped too, her relief disappearing like air from a deflating tyre.

'Let's get going,' Freddy said. He took hold of his son's arm and led him away. 'The sooner it's done, the sooner it's over.'

'Where are they going?' FJ asked his mother.

'Down the nick,' Brenda said, 'before they come here.'

'Why would they do that?'

Brenda's mouth tightened into a thin straight line. 'You know what the law are like. Tony's her boyfriend. When it comes to suspects, he'll be top of the list, won't he?'

'But they can't ... they can't think he had anything to do with it.'

'That's what your dad's sorting out now. He'll take care of things.'

'When was it? Where?'

'I don't know all the ins and outs, not yet. On the Mansfield, I think.'

'Only Tony's been at work all day and then he was here for his tea so how could he have—'

'Yeah,' Brenda said. 'Exactly. It won't come to nothing. It'll be fine. You don't have to worry.' Except worry was etched all over her face. 'I've just got to call your Uncle Jim. I won't be long.'

FJ jumped up as his mother left the room. Then, as if he didn't know what to do with himself, sat straight back down again. 'Jesus Christ,' he muttered. 'Amy's dead.'

16

Lolly stared at the floor. The enormity of it all was finally sinking in. She hadn't really thought about Amy until now, not properly. She'd been too wrapped up with trying to help Jude. She hadn't liked the girl – how could she after what had happened on Bonfire Night? – but she'd never have wished this on her.

'She was the same age as me,' FJ said.

'How could anyone do that?'

'Some bastard. They won't get away with it.'

Brenda came back, but she couldn't stay still. She started pacing round the living room, glancing impatiently at the clock, even though it was only minutes since Freddy and Tony had left.

'What did Uncle Jim say?' FJ asked.

Brenda, lost in thought, went from the fireplace to the window, played with the edge of the curtain and stared into space.

'Mum?'

Brenda looked over at him and frowned. 'Huh?'

'Uncle Jim,' he prompted.

'Yes, they locked up at five. Tony was there all day. He didn't leave the car lot, not even at lunchtime, so—'

'So he's in the clear.'

The phone rang and Brenda hurried back into the hall. It was the first of many calls that evening. As the grapevine buzzed, more and more information began to come in. Some of it might have been accurate, but most was just rumour and gossip. What was established, however, was that Amy had still been alive at four o'clock when she'd left school with her friends and headed home to the Mansfield. What had happened after that was simply a matter of conjecture.

Lolly sat and listened, trying to piece together what she was hearing with what Jude had told her. As yet his name hadn't come up and that had to be a good thing. She was on tenterhooks wondering if anyone had noticed her on the estate and, if they had, whether they were going to share this fact with Brenda.

An image came into her head of Amy sitting in the café, flicking back her long blonde hair. That was the day Jude had been there with Tracy Kitts, holding her hand while stealing quick furtive glances at Amy. But that didn't mean anything. All the boys looked at her; she was ... *had been*, the prettiest girl around.

Lolly fought against the flicker of doubt that entered her mind. Jude couldn't have done it. He wasn't the type to carry a knife, not like some of the lads on the Mansfield. And he never got into fights. Occasionally he got angry, but didn't everyone? She tried to figure out how long it had been between when she'd seen the two of them together and when Jude had come running after her. She'd sat on the wall for a while and then chatted to Joseph. Twenty minutes, maybe. Enough time for Jude to have left Amy and for someone else to have attacked and murdered her. That's how it must have been. There wasn't any other explanation.

She thought about that dark space at the base of the stairwell where she had once found her mother, cowering and afraid. It was an ugly place to die. Amy must have been lying in the dirt and the litter like some unwanted piece of rubbish. And Jude must have discovered her there when he'd gone back to look for her. Another question instantly jumped into Lolly's head. Why had he gone back? And he wasn't the one who had called 999 so what had he been doing in the time between his initial discovery and someone else stumbling on the body? Panicking, most likely.

Lolly understood why he'd run. She'd probably have done the same in his position. The police would have him right in the frame. They wouldn't even bother looking for the real killer. Jude would be judged and found guilty and that would be that.

A couple of hours went by and there was still no sign of Freddy and Tony. In between phone calls, Brenda made and drank copious mugs of tea. Sometimes she went out to the yard, walked to the gate and stared along the alley.

'Why aren't they back yet?' FJ asked. 'Why's it taking so long?'

'If I knew that,' Brenda snapped, 'I wouldn't be tearing my hair out, would I? Typical of your dad. He could have called – they've got phones down there – but no, not a bleedin' word.'

'Maybe you should get a solicitor,' FJ said.

'What does he need a solicitor for? Your brother ain't done nothin'. He was at work all day so how could he have …' Brenda shook her head, put her hands on her hips and scowled. 'I always knew that girl was trouble. He should have left well alone.'

'They've only been going out two weeks,' FJ said.

'Yeah, well, it's two weeks too long. I'm going to call the nick, see what's going on.'

Lolly watched Brenda go through to the hall and lift the phone to her ear. Then, as if she had suddenly thought of something, she put the receiver back in the cradle, got out her keys and unlocked the door to the pawnbroker's. She disappeared from sight for a couple of minutes and then came back into the living room holding the oblong metal tin she usually used for petty cash.

'Here,' she said, thrusting it into FJ's hand. 'Make yourself useful and take this down to number eighteen. Tell Marge I'll pick it up tomorrow.'

Lolly heard a rattling as the box was transferred. She could guess what was inside: some of Joe Quinn's dodgy gear, rings and necklaces and the like, stuff she wouldn't want the law to find if they decided to pay a visit.

After FJ had gone, Brenda turned to Lolly. 'And you get yourself up to bed. I can't be doing with you under my feet all night.'

Lolly didn't argue. It wasn't even eight o'clock but she preferred to be out of the way. She went upstairs, had a pee, a quick wash, brushed her teeth, got into her pyjamas and climbed into bed. She switched off the lamp and lay in the dark. It had been a weird, disturbing day and her mind was still racing.

The sound of the TV floated up the stairs, the music from the closing credits of *Coronation Street*. Usually Brenda was glued to it, passing judgement on Elsie Tanner's morals – or lack of them – and revelling in the bad luck that seemed to beset most of the soap's characters. Tonight, however, she had barely given it a glance; she had enough misfortune of her own without watching it on the box.

Lolly closed her eyes and tried to go to sleep. She turned on to her left side and then the right but still couldn't get comfortable. That feeling of dread was growing inside her again, spreading like a poisonous weed. Once Tony had been eliminated as a suspect, the law would start to look elsewhere. Maybe Tracy Kitts was already down the nick, telling her story about dumping Jude, and pointing the finger straight at him.

Lolly lay staring at the green luminous dial of the alarm clock. At some point she must have dozed off because when she woke again the hands read twenty past ten. From downstairs she could hear the murmur of voices. She got out of bed, went out on to the landing and leaned over the banisters.

'For God's sake,' Freddy was saying, 'it was only a pint. Three hours we've been down that bleedin' nick and you're having a go about ten minutes in the boozer.'

'You could have picked up the bloody phone and let me know. I've been sitting here, worried sick.'

'Well, we're back now, ain't we? What's the point of going on about it?'

'The point is that—'

'Jesus,' Tony said. 'Cut it out, can't you? I've had enough crap for one night. I don't need you two laying into each other as well.'

'Sorry, love,' Brenda said. 'How was it?'

'How do you think? Got a grilling, didn't I? The bastards had me well and truly in the frame.'

'You've got a rock-solid alibi. How can they accuse you?'

'Yeah, well, we had to wait for Uncle Jim to come down, and even then they weren't satisfied. Kept going over it again and again. *Exactly* what time did I leave the car lot, *exactly* what time did I get home – as if I'm supposed to know to the very minute. I mean, shit, I don't spend the whole day staring at my watch.'

'You were home by half five,' Brenda said, 'a bit earlier. You must have been 'cause I hadn't put the tea out.'

Freddy spoke again. 'That's what I told them, but it didn't make a blind bit of difference. Not going to take our word for it, are they?'

'Well they're certainly not going to take yours,' Brenda sniped, 'seeing as you weren't even here.'

'I need to call Tracy,' Tony said. 'Find out what she knows.'

'Not at this time of night,' Brenda said. 'The girl's probably in bed by now, and her parents aren't going to thank you for disturbing them. No, leave it for tonight. Do it in the morning.'

Lolly waited but couldn't hear any more. They must have moved into the kitchen. She went back to bed wondering what Tracy Kitts had told the police. They would have talked to her by now – she was Amy's friend – and she would have told them about Jude. Perhaps he was already down the nick being questioned just like Tony had been. If that was the case, it was only a matter of time before she was asked to confirm his alibi.

Lolly pulled the covers round her, tight as a cocoon. Would they come tonight and drag her out of bed? Or would they wait until tomorrow? She went over the story in her head again, making sure she knew it off by heart. She was still reciting the lies when she finally fell asleep.

17

Lolly spent the whole of the next day in a state of heightened anxiety. It didn't help that everyone at school was talking about the murder. She had slept fitfully and she couldn't concentrate. The words on the blackboard danced in front of her, and at break times all she heard was Amy, Amy, Amy. What she saw in the other kids' eyes was a weird combination of fear and fascination. By the time the afternoon bell went she was desperate to get away. She was far from eager, however, to return to the Cecils.

The school gates were crowded with mothers who would usually let their children walk home alone. Today they weren't taking any chances. There was a killer on the loose and they were going to make sure their loved one didn't become his next victim. There was no sign of Brenda, of course, but that hardly came as a surprise.

Lolly walked slowly, taking her time. Usually she would have called in at the Hope to see if Terry had any deliveries, but she knew it was better to avoid him today. If she lied about where she'd been and that lie was then exposed, no one would believe her story about Jude.

By the time she reached the Cecils' back yard, Lolly's heart was thumping in her chest. And the minute she stepped over the threshold she knew she was right to be afraid. There were two uniformed police officers sitting at the kitchen table, one a middle-aged man, the other a younger woman with short red hair.

'Ah, here she is,' Brenda said. 'Lolly, these officers want to have a word with you, some nonsense about—'

'If you don't mind, Mrs Cecil,' the young woman said, shooting a warning glance in her direction. 'We can take it from here.' She turned her attention back to Lolly, and smiled. 'Hello, I'm WPC Sally Windsor, and this is Sergeant Grand. Now there's nothing to be worried about. You're not in any kind of trouble. We're just here to ask you a few questions and it won't take long.'

Lolly pulled out a chair. 'Is this about Amy?'

'In a way,' Sally said. 'Now, as I said you're not in any trouble, not at all, but there's been a bit of confusion and perhaps you can help us out. Would you mind doing that?'

Lolly shrugged as she sat down. 'Okay.'

'So, could tell me exactly what you did after school yesterday. Before you came home, I mean.'

Lolly immediately lowered her eyes, placed her hands in her lap and put on a show of looking nervous. Well, she was nervous so she didn't really need to pretend but it was for a different reason than the one she wanted to convey. She chewed on her bottom lip and refused to meet Sally's gaze.

'Lolly?' Sally prompted.

Brenda jumped in again. 'I've already told you this. She was just round a friend's, doing her homework. Weren't you, love? Go on. Tell them.'

It was the man, the sergeant, who said sternly, 'Mrs Cecil, can you please let her answer for herself.'

Sally produced another of her smiles. 'Lolly, do you know the difference between right and wrong?'

'Yeah,' Lolly mumbled.

'And you know that it's wrong to tell a lie?'

Lolly nodded. 'Yeah.'

'Okay, good girl. So tell me, in your own words, what you were doing after school yesterday.'

Lolly finally looked up, glancing quickly at Brenda – as if she was afraid of how she'd react – before meeting Sally's gaze. 'I went round to the Mansfield to see Jude Rule.' And then she added hurriedly, 'I haven't been there for ages, not since I was told not to, but he borrowed me ... leant me ... this book ages ago and I still hadn't given it back so ... '

Brenda bristled. 'What have I said about going round to that lad's flat? You know you're not allowed.'

'*Please*, Mrs Cecil,' Sally said. 'This really isn't helping.'

Lolly looked suitably shamefaced. 'But I had to give the book back, didn't I? It wasn't fair to keep it. It's not mine.'

'I understand,' Sally said. 'Don't worry about that; it's not a problem. So what time did you get to Jude's?'

Lolly pretended to think about it. 'I'm not sure. About

twenty past four? I went to Woolworths first, you see. Just to look around. I didn't buy anything. So by the time … yes, it was probably about then.'

'And Jude was at the flat?'

'Yeah. I was just going to give him the book and go but he asked if I wanted to come in and …' Lolly shot another seemingly nervous glance at Brenda. 'I only meant to stay for five minutes but then I started watching the film and kind of forgot about the time.'

'The film?' Sally asked.

Lolly nodded. 'It was *Sunset Boulevard*. That's one of his favourites. I like it too. He's got loads of films, a whole shelf full, and a proper screen and everything. His dad works up West in a cinema.'

'And what did you and Jude talk about?'

'Nothing much. He asked how things were going, you know, but mainly we were just watching the film.'

'Did he seem upset?'

Lolly frowned. 'Why would he be upset?'

'He didn't mention that he and his girlfriend had broken up?'

'No.' Lolly gave a light shrug. 'He never talked to me about that sort of stuff.'

'Do you know Tracy Kitts?'

'I've seen her around. She's one of Amy's friends, isn't she?'

'That's right.' Sally Windsor left a short silence and then asked, 'Have you known Jude for long?'

'For ages. From when I lived on the Mansfield with my mum. We were in the same block, Haslow House, except he was two floors down. We were fourteen, he's twelve. Yeah, I've known him for years.'

'And you used to spend a lot of time with him?'

Lolly hesitated. 'Not really. Not a lot. Just sometimes.'

'It didn't bother you that he was older? Most boys prefer to hang out with mates their own age.'

The sergeant was letting Sally ask the questions while he took notes. It put Lolly even more on edge watching him scribble down her answers. She had to be careful what she said, to not make any blunders that could come back to haunt her. *Think before you open your mouth*, she told herself.

'He knew about my mum, how she got sick sometimes, so he'd look out for me, you know? He was just being kind. He'd make me sandwiches and give me a drink, let me hang out in the flat for a while if our place was too cold.'

Sally nodded. 'So, yesterday, you were at Jude's for how long, do you think?'

'Over an hour, I reckon.'

'And Jude didn't go out while you were there?'

'No, I told you. We were watching the film. Then I suddenly saw what time it was – there's a clock on the mantelpiece – and realised I was going to be late for tea. Jude walked me back here, as far as the gate.'

'That was very gallant,' Sally said. And then, as if Lolly might not understand the word, she added, 'Very nice of him.'

'I don't like the dark,' Lolly said. 'When we got to the gates we saw the police cars and an ambulance, but we didn't . . . we didn't know it was to do with Amy.'

'Weren't you curious?'

'Not really. The law . . . the police are always there. You get used to it after a while. I mean, I don't live there any more but I remember what it was like.'

Suddenly the back door opened and FJ walked in. He stopped and stared at the gathering round the table. 'What's going on?'

'The police are just having a word with Lolly,' Brenda said.

'What for?'

Brenda flapped a hand in the direction of the living room. 'Make yourself scarce for five minutes. I'll tell you later.'

'Is this to do with Tony?'

'FJ! I won't tell you again. Just do as you're told.'

FJ pulled a face, walked through the kitchen, went into the living room and closed the door behind him. Lolly was sure he'd have his ear pressed against it, trying to listen in to what was being said.

It was Sergeant Grand who was the first to speak after the interruption. He looked down at his notes and then up at Lolly. 'You mentioned a book earlier. Can you tell me what that was?'

'It's called *Hollywood Greats*. It's all about the movie stars.' Lolly was confident that should they choose to check for fingerprints, hers would be all over it. The book usually sat on the coffee table and she'd picked it up lots of times to flick through and look at the photos. 'I borrowed it in the summer before . . . ' Lolly stared down at the table for a moment. 'I've had it for ages. That's why I had to give it back.'

Sally went on to ask a few more questions, most of them pretty similar to the ones she'd asked earlier only phrased in a slightly different way. Lolly knew what the WPC was doing, trying to catch her out, to see if she'd make a mistake, trip up or change her story, but she was careful to stick to the script she'd agreed with Jude: short and simple with no unnecessary detail. She'd learned the importance of this from the numerous old movies she'd watched, films about murder and betrayal and revenge. People tried to be too clever and that's where it all went wrong.

Finally the ordeal was over and the two police officers rose to their feet. 'We may need to talk to you again,' Sally said, 'but thank you for your help.'

Lolly was relieved that neither of the officers tried to shake her hand. Her palms were clammy and damp. 'That's okay.'

Brenda saw them out, returned to the table and stood over Lolly with her arms folded across her chest. 'So, young lady, you've got some explaining to do.'

'I'm sorry,' Lolly said. 'I know I'm not supposed to go round to Jude's. And I didn't mean to stay. I was only going to give him the book back but I started watching the film and . . . I won't do it again. I swear.'

'Too right you won't.'

FJ came back into the kitchen. 'Have they gone, then?' he asked, all innocence, as if he hadn't been listening to everything.

'For now,' Brenda said.

FJ glared at Lolly before turning to his mother. 'You do know she's lying through her teeth, don't you? Everyone knows Jude Rule killed Amy. He had a big row with Tracy and stormed off to find her. They're all talking about it at school.'

'He couldn't have, could he?' Lolly said. 'Not if he was with me.'

'Yeah, well we've only got your word for that. She's lying, Mum, I'm telling you. She's just trying to protect that murdering scumbag. I mean, all that stuff about the book. I've never seen no Hollywood book in the house, have you?'

Before Brenda could answer, Lolly jumped in. 'That's because I never kept it here. It was at school, in my locker.'

'I bet.'

'You can bet all you like, but it's true.'

'Liar!'

'Not!'

Brenda gave her a hard look. 'If you are lying, Lolly Bruce, you're going to be in big trouble. They'll take you away and lock you up. Do you understand?'

'I'm not. I'm telling the truth. I went to see Jude yesterday. I did!'

FJ strode across the kitchen, leaned down and pushed his face into hers. 'Then you must have been in on it too. What did you do – hold the knife for him?'

'Jude didn't kill Amy!'

Brenda pulled her son away. 'Leave it out,' she said. 'If that Jude Rule is responsible, the law will find out soon enough. He won't be able to hide a thing like that. There are tests and all sorts they can do. Let's wait and see, huh?'

FJ curled his lip. 'I'm telling you, it was that bloody creep.

He did for Amy. And Tony spent half the night down the nick because of it.'

'No one's accusing your brother. He was with your Uncle Jim all day, wasn't he? He's got a rock-solid alibi.'

'Good thing and all.' FJ stood by his mother, throwing evil glances at Lolly. 'When your boyfriend gets sent down, you'll be going with him. That's what happens to lying little brats. I'd get your stuff packed if I was you.'

18

Over the next three days, Lolly listened in to every conversation, to every bit of rumour and gossip about the murder of Amy Wiltshire. She learned that Jude had been interviewed and released by the police, but that didn't stop people from believing he was guilty. And Tracy Kitts was the loudest of his accusers. She was putting it around that Jude must have done it, that he wasn't right in the head, that he blamed Amy for the break-up and had gone looking for her on the Tuesday afternoon she was killed.

Lolly desperately wanted to see Jude, but knew better than to try and contact him. It was better they stayed apart so no one, and especially the police, could claim they were conspiring. She stayed away from Terry too, hoping that he understood her reasons. Usually, on a Friday, there were lots of deliveries to be made but it was too risky at the moment. FJ was watching her like a hawk – and perhaps the law were too. She had no way of knowing.

It was the end of the school week, a time she usually looked forward to, but not on this occasion. The weekend loomed ahead, two whole days of being trapped in the house with the Cecils. Usually she could get out and about, but that seemed unlikely with the current situation. Brenda would be keeping tabs, making sure she knew exactly where Lolly was.

Lolly's thoughts flipped back to Jude. If the police had let him go, then they couldn't be convinced of his guilt. Or were they just waiting for forensics to get back? She'd seen stuff on telly about that and although she didn't understand all the ins and outs, she knew they could test for blood on people's clothes. Had Jude touched Amy when he'd found her? It would be natural, surely, to crouch down and make sure that she was dead.

Lolly wished she'd asked him, but it all been so fast, so panicked, that the details had gone out of the window. She could only cross her fingers and hope. Maybe he hadn't checked. Maybe it had been so obvious that he hadn't needed to. There was no point in going over and over it in her head, but she couldn't help herself.

Lolly was so distracted she didn't notice the panda car parked outside the pawnbroker's until she was about to turn down the alley that led round the back. Her heart dropped like a stone. The police must have come for her. She pulled in a sharp breath, her first instinct being to run. But where could she go? And how? The little money she had was hidden in the mattress upstairs in the house.

She stood for thirty seconds staring at the empty car

before her gaze slid over to the shop. The sign on the door had been flipped to CLOSED, even though it was only four-thirty. Brenda must be in the kitchen, sitting with the cops, waiting for her. She tried to think of somewhere she could hide but knew she couldn't hide for ever. They'd catch up with her eventually. And it was cold outside. A bitter wind snapped at her face.

Eventually, with no other options, Lolly set off down the alley. She trudged along the narrow passage with her shoulders hunched and her head down. She was about to be exposed as a barefaced liar and there was nothing she could do about it. Except to try and explain. Would they give her the chance to do that? But they wouldn't believe anything she said now. She had failed to tell the truth and would have to accept the consequences.

When Lolly walked through the kitchen door what she expected were uniforms and accusations, but all she found was an empty room. She could hear raised voices, however, coming from the shop at the front. The most powerful of these was Brenda's, its boom travelling back along the hall and through the living room.

'I've had enough of this. It's harassment, bleedin' harassment! My boy's already told you everything he knows. Why do you need to speak to him again? It's not on. I'm not having it.'

'We're just doing our job, Mrs Cecil.'

'I didn't do nothin',' Tony said. 'Why haven't you arrested that bastard, Jude Rule? He's the one you're looking for. He's the one who did her in.'

'If you could step this way. Let's not make this any harder than it has to be.'

'It's a bloody liberty,' Brenda said. 'You'll be hearing from our solicitor.'

'If your son has nothing to hide, he's got nothing to be worried about.'

'Bollocks!' Freddy retorted. 'We all know what you lot are like. It's a fuckin' stitch-up, that's what it is.'

Lolly crept closer, trying not to make a sound. She had entered the house convinced she was for the high jump, but it seemed the police weren't here for her at all. It was Tony they were after. She hovered in the hall and wrapped her arms around her chest, relieved and grateful for the last-minute reprieve. Maybe Tony *was* the guilty one. He was capable of murder, she was sure of it. He had a nasty streak and a temper too.

There were a few more protests before she finally heard the door to the pawnbroker's open and close. Lolly shot back to the kitchen, went into the yard and pretended to be just arriving. By the time she made her second entrance, Brenda and Freddy were in the living room going at it hammer and tongs.

'None of this is my fault. What the hell are you blaming me for?' Freddy said.

'Jim's your bleedin' brother!'

'So what? I'm not his keeper, am I? I don't know what he gets up to.'

'Oh, don't give me that! I wasn't born yesterday.'

Lolly made some noise, closing the back door with a bang

to make her presence felt. The voices immediately stopped. Brenda came into the kitchen, gave a brusque nod, went over to the sink and started filling a pan with water.

Lolly hung up her coat and bag in the hall. She could hear Freddy striding up the stairs, escaping to the only place in the house where his wife couldn't get to him – the lavatory. When she got back there was a bag of potatoes on the table.

'Make yourself useful and peel some spuds,' Brenda said.

Lolly sat down, picked up a knife and started work. She wanted to ask about Tony, about why he'd been taken in again, but didn't dare. Brenda had a face on her like a slapped arse; she stood over the pan, muttering to herself.

It was only a few minutes before FJ came in from school. He dumped his bag on the floor, put his head round the living-room door and then withdrew it again.

'Where's Tony? He said he'd be back early. We're supposed to be going to the football this evening.'

'You're brother ain't going nowhere,' Brenda said. 'He's down the nick again.'

'What?'

'Old Bill called round, didn't they? Not five minutes since.'

'Jesus! Why? What for?'

Brenda wiped her hands on her apron and turned to look at him. ''Cause they just found out your Uncle's Jim's a filthy, lying, scumbag cheat, that's why! Seems he wasn't at the car lot when he said he was. He cleared off about two o'clock to see his fancy piece and left Tony to lock up.'

FJ took a moment to digest this piece of news. His mean

little face twisted as he struggled with the implications. 'So what are they saying, the law?'

'What do you think?' Brenda answered. 'Tony told them he stayed until five, but they've found some would-be customer who claims he called by around four o'clock and there was no one there. All locked up and no sign of anyone.'

Lolly listened while she peeled the spuds. If Tony had cleared off early, then he might have gone to meet Amy. She thought back to the evening in question, remembering that Tony had been here when she got back. But that didn't mean he hadn't done it. There would have been time between the point when Jude left Amy and when he found her again for Tony to have killed her and to have run back to the house. She had no idea how long he'd been home when she arrived. It might only have been a few minutes.

'Where was he then?' FJ asked.

'God knows,' Brenda said. 'But not on the Mansfield, that's for sure. He didn't go near that girl. And he only lied about being at the lot to cover for your Uncle Jim. Tony couldn't say Jim wasn't there, could he? Not without landing him right in it with your Auntie Rose. And now look where it's got him. This is all Jim's bleedin' fault; that cheating bastard has never been able to keep it his pants.'

'It's going to look bad for him, though, ain't it – our Tony, I mean – saying he was there when he weren't. The law are going to think—'

'I know what the law are going to think!' Brenda snapped. 'What they always think about the likes of us.' She stomped across the kitchen, through the living room and into the hall. 'Freddy? What the hell are you doing up there? Your son's down the bloody nick in case you'd forgotten.'

'What do think I'm doing? If I need a slash, I need a slash.'

'It doesn't take half an hour to empty your bladder. Have you called Bob Reynolds yet? Tony needs a brief, for God's sake. Someone better than the duty solicitor.'

'So why don't you do it? You're standing by the bloody phone!'

'Jesus,' Brenda muttered.

Lolly listened as Brenda flicked through the pages of the address book, picked up the receiver and made the call about her son. Just as she was finishing, Freddy came downstairs again.

'Are you going over to the nick or what?' Brenda asked.

'Reynolds is on his way.'

'What's the rush? *On his way* means half an hour at least. There's no point me sitting down there doing nothin'. I won't be able to see Tony. He'll be banged up until Reynolds shows his face.'

'Might as well be there doing nothin' as here.'

The two of them came into the kitchen. Freddy lit up a fag, went over to the sink and gazed out of the window at the yard. He pulled furiously on the cigarette, puffing out the smoke in thick grey clouds. 'Bloody idiots! Stupid fuckers! It's just typical.'

Brenda gave a snort and slammed a pan down on the hob. 'What's typical is your bloody brother getting his end away when he's supposed to be at work.'

'I'm not saying it's right, but this ain't all his fault. Maybe you should be looking a little closer to home.'

'And what's that supposed to mean?'

Freddy twisted round and pointed his fag at Lolly. '*That's* your bleedin' problem,' he said angrily, 'not Jim. She's the one providing an alibi for the murdering bastard who did Amy in. If it wasn't for her, Tony wouldn't be banged up right now.'

Lolly's jaw dropped and her eyes widened with shock. She hadn't expected the attack, hadn't seen it coming.

FJ, following his father's lead, turned on her too. 'Yeah, she's the one who's lying. It ain't right. Someone should get the bloody truth out of her. Someone should make the little bitch come clean.'

Lolly looked to Brenda, hoping for some support, but she should have known better. One glance at the woman's face told her everything. The whole family was against her. She shrank into her chair, afraid of what might happen next. In a few minutes she had gone from feeling relieved to feeling terrified. She had never been liked but now she was the enemy.

19

Stanley Parrish could feel the tension in the air when he walked into Connolly's. A young girl had been murdered and the entire community was in shock. Although acts of violence were not uncommon in the East End, this was something different, and with the killer still on the loose there was an edgy nervousness, a fear that he might strike again. There was none of the usual noisy chatter. Instead people talked in hushed tones, their body language tight, their faces drawn and etched with worry.

Stanley took a seat at the back, sat down and opened his paper. The killing was still headline news in the Saturday edition and although the police had taken several people in for questioning no one had, as yet, been charged. He scanned through the article but didn't learn anything new. There was a picture of Amy Wiltshire in her school uniform, her blue eyes staring directly into the camera, her mouth in a wide smile. A girl who knew she was pretty. A girl who had the world at her feet.

He was still staring at the photograph when the waitress came over to take his order.

'Hello again,' she said. 'How are you?'

He looked up to see Maeve Riley standing there with her notepad. 'Ah, hello. Very well, thank you. And you?'

'I'm good, ta.' She nodded towards the paper. 'Dreadful business, isn't it? She used to come in here, you know. I still can't believe she's dead. It's just not right. She was only a kid. There are some terrible people, aren't there? I mean, who could do something like that?'

Stanley shook his head. 'I'm sure they'll catch him.'

'I hope so. I really do. It's enough to give you nightmares.' She paused and then said, 'So what brings you back to Kellston? Any joy with finding Angela's relatives?'

'I'm afraid not. That's why I'm here. I thought I might have another word with Brenda Cecil, see if anything has surfaced since my last visit.'

'Oh,' Maeve said, the corners of her mouth twisting down a little. 'Do you think that's a good idea?'

Stanley raised his eyebrows. 'You don't think so?'

Maeve gave a shrug. 'It's just with . . . You do know her son was going out with Amy Wiltshire?'

'No, heavens, I had no idea.'

'Well, it's up to you, but you might not get the best of welcomes at the moment.'

'Of course. I understand. Thank you for letting me know.'

'Especially with Tony being . . . ' She glanced away, looked back and lowered her voice. 'I probably shouldn't say but the police have had him down the nick a couple of times. I suppose that's normal, him being the boyfriend and all, but I shouldn't think Brenda's too happy about it.'

'No,' he agreed. 'I'm sure you're right. Maybe I'll give it a miss for today.'

Maeve nodded. 'It might be wise. So what can I get you?'

Stanley ordered a full English and a mug of tea, deciding he needed some fuel before planning his next move. He wouldn't normally spend the money – finances were always tight – but yesterday he'd received a small cheque for an insurance job he'd done a few months ago. Anyway, he needed cheering up. He had that sense of despondency that comes from getting nowhere on a case. To date, all his attempts to track down Angela's family had ended in failure. It didn't help that he wasn't even sure of her real name.

While he waited for breakfast, Stanley returned his attention to the paper. It hadn't occurred to him that the Cecils could be involved. Tony was the older boy. How old was he? Eighteen or nineteen, he thought. As the boyfriend, he'd be up there, high on the list of suspects. He wondered what this would mean for Lolita Bruce. Social Services might not be too keen on her staying in a house with a boy suspected of murder.

Stanley felt sorry for the girl. It was only a matter of time. Once Brenda realised she wasn't the pot of gold at the end of the rainbow, Lolly would be out on her ear. And then what? Pulled from pillar to post, probably. Foster care or a home. She might get lucky along the way, catch a break, but the chances were that her future was bleak. Like most of the kids who grew up on the Mansfield, the odds were already stacked against her.

The estate had seen its fair share of tragedy recently: first Lolly's mother, and now Amy Wiltshire. It struck him as a dark, dangerous place, seething with anger and frustration. The three tall towers were home to the disadvantaged and the disenfranchised, people who were mostly without prospects or hope. It was hardly surprising that bad things happened there.

Maeve brought his tea and he thanked her. As he lifted the mug to his lips, he became aware that someone's gaze was on him. A man on the table to his left kept looking over, but whenever Stanley caught his eye he looked away again. The bloke, probably in his late twenties, had a thin, hollowed-out face, as if the skin had been stretched too tightly over his cheekbones. He had the trademark dark shadows under his eyes and all the jumpy mannerisms of a junkie.

It was another couple of minutes before the stranger plucked up the courage to join Stanley at his table. He took the chair opposite, leaned forward and said in a soft rapid tone, 'You want to know about Angela? I can help. I can tell you stuff.'

'What kind of stuff?'

The man glanced nervously around. 'You're not the law, right?'

'No, I'm not the law.' Stanley took out his wallet, opened it and showed his ID. 'Stanley Parrish, private investigator. And you are?'

'That doesn't matter. Do you pay, you know, for information?'

'Depends how good the information is.'

'What are you after?'

Stanley knew better than to trust the man. Junkies would say anything, do anything, to get their next fix. 'What have you got?'

'I knew her, you see. I knew Angela. I used to live along the landing from her.'

'On the Mansfield?'

'Yeah. Carlton House.'

Stanley rolled his eyes. The guy couldn't even get the right tower. He was just a chancer, an opportunist trying to make an easy buck. 'She lived in Haslow House, not Carlton.'

The guy shook his head. 'Not the first time she was here.'

Stanley frowned. 'What do you mean, the *first* time?'

'Just what I'm saying. She used to live right up there on the top floor, you know, where she jumped from. Shit, that freaked me out, man. I mean, why'd she go and do a crazy thing like that? And before you ask, I didn't see nothin'. I wasn't even there when it happened.'

'Hang on,' Stanley said, 'can we just rewind a bit? When are we talking about, here? When exactly was Angela living in Carlton?'

'It was way back: fourteen, fifteen years? She wasn't there for long. About nine months, I reckon. Only I remember her, see, with us being neighbours. And she was pretty, the kind of girl you notice. A looker, yeah? But nice with it. Not up herself like some of them are.'

183

'Okay,' Stanley said casually, rapidly absorbing this new piece of information whilst simultaneously trying not to sound too interested. 'So what else can you tell me about her?'

The guy gave a shrug. 'Like what?'

'Like, do you recall what her surname was back then? Was she using the name Bruce?'

'I dunno. I'm not sure I ever knew it. I was only a kid; you don't take much notice of that kind of thing.'

'Did she have a boyfriend, a husband?'

'Yeah, there was a bloke, a black geezer, not her husband though. Well, he didn't live there with her.' The guy screwed up his face in concentration as if forging a path through the distant parts of his addled brain. 'Calvin or Kelvin, I think. He didn't come from the estate.'

'Did she work? What about a job?'

'Yeah, up West. She worked in a clothes shop, one of those boutiques.'

'Do you know which one?'

'Nah, sorry.'

I don't suppose you know where she'd moved from, where she used to live before she arrived on the Mansfield?'

The guy shook his head. 'People come and go, don't they? No one hangs around the estate if they don't have to. They fuck off soon as they get the chance.'

Stanley wasn't sure how useful any of this was. It was interesting, though, that she'd lived for a brief period in Carlton House. It could explain her reasons for going there on the day of her suicide. Perhaps it had held some memories for her, good or bad. 'And all this was before she had Lolly? She didn't have a child back then?'

The guy frowned. His hands danced on the table for a few seconds as though he was playing an imaginary piano. 'Yeah, that was a bit weird. I'd forgotten until now but . . . ' His voice trailed off.

'But?' Stanley prompted.

'One day she just ups and leaves, right? And then, like a month later, I'm over at Dagenham, visiting my nan, and I see her – Angela, I mean – standing at a bus stop with a kid, a baby, in a pram. So I go over to say hi. She seems a bit off, you know, like she's surprised to see me and doesn't really want to talk. And that wasn't like her; she was always friendly. Odd thing is she hadn't even looked pregnant when she left.'

Stanley's heart skipped a beat. 'Are you sure the baby was hers? Maybe it was a friend's or a relative's.'

'She said it was, said her name was Lolita. I remembered that 'cause it's kind of different, ain't it?' The guy didn't wait for a reply before continuing. 'Anyway, she rushes off down the street, saying she's just remembered something and that was the last I saw of her until she turned up on the Mansfield again.'

Stanley considered the fact that Angela would have had to have been about eight months pregnant when she left the estate if the information was correct. But was it? They were talking years ago and the memory can play tricks, especially on the drug-fuelled mind of an addict. Perhaps, if Angela had been wearing loose clothes, her pregnancy might not have been immediately apparent, or maybe it was a lot more than a month before the guy bumped into her again.

'So?' the guy asked.

'So?' Stanley repeated.

The guy looked agitated. 'What's it worth? You wanted to know about her and I've told you.'

Another thought occurred to Stanley. Perhaps he was in cahoots with Brenda Cecil. This could all be a ploy so he'd believe her story. 'How can I be sure you're telling the truth?'

'Shit, man, why would I lie to you? And look, old Ma Fenner can back me up. She used to live up at the top of Carlton, next door to Angela. She can tell you. She'll put you straight.'

'Used to? Where is she now?'

'They moved her, didn't they? Down to the ground floor. She's getting too old for going up and down in those lifts. It's number eight, the one with the blue door.'

Stanley took a fiver from his wallet and slid it towards his informant.

'Is that it?'

'Well, if you don't want it . . . ' Stanley made to take the note back, but the guy quickly grabbed the money.

Maeve showed up with his full English and put it down on the table. As if spooked by this unexpected interruption, the guy rose to his feet and hurried out of the café without so much as a goodbye.

'Was he bothering you?' she asked, staring after him.

Stanley shook his head. 'No, it's fine. I don't suppose you happen to know his name, do you?'

186

'Darren,' she said. 'Darren Wakefield. Although he usually goes by the name of Daz. And whatever he's been saying, I'd take it with a pinch of salt.'

'Not the reliable sort, then?'

'About as reliable as snow in summer.'

'Yeah, I kind of got that impression. There was something I meant to ask you, though. Were you aware that Angela used to live in Carlton House around fourteen years ago? It was only for nine months or so, before she had Lolly.'

Maeve frowned. 'Really? No, I didn't know that. She never mentioned it. Are you sure?'

'No,' Stanley said. 'I'm not sure of anything.'

'Well, enjoy your breakfast.'

'Thanks. I will.'

Stanley picked up his knife and fork. He tried to curtail the growing sense of excitement, the feeling that he might finally be on to something. No, it was too early for that. Darren could have been feeding him a load of nonsense. He would have to track down old Ma Fenner and see what she had to say. But what if she was part of Brenda's conspiracy too?

He sighed as he ate his bacon and eggs. All he could do was follow the leads and see where they took him. But his thoughts continued to race. If Darren was telling the truth, then Angela had acquired a baby at around the same time as Kay Fury had disappeared. And that, taken in conjunction with the blood tests, the missing birth certificate and Angela's alleged fear of Mal Fury, added up to something more than a coincidence.

20

There was bad feeling in the house and all of it was targeted towards Lolly. She felt the weight of the Cecils' anger and disapproval pushing down on her. Earlier in the morning she'd been interviewed again by the police, this time down Cowan Road station. Brenda had not sat in with her – there was a conflict of interest, perhaps, with Tony being under suspicion – and instead she'd been joined by the social worker, Mrs Raynes. Lolly had been glad of it. It was hard enough lying to the law without having to do it under Brenda's fierce scrutiny.

She thought, looking back, that she had done a decent enough job, sticking to the original story and not wavering even when they'd pressed her. They had tried to catch her out but she hadn't fallen for their tricks. Now all she could do was wait and hope that Jude's name would be cleared.

She put her elbows on the kitchen table, glad that she was finally alone. Freddy had gone to the bookie's, FJ was out with his mates and Tony was upstairs. Brenda was working in the shop and from time to time she heard the ding of the bell as the front door opened. In front of her was a heap of tarnished silver she was supposed to be cleaning, items that would be flogged once they'd got a shine on them again – tankards and trinket boxes, knives and forks and spoons.

Lolly was back to thinking about Jude, wondering how he was doing, what he was feeling, when the knock came. Too soft to be the law so she didn't have to worry about that. She stood up, crossed the room and opened the back door to find Terry Street standing there. His dark hair was wet and slicked down against his head.

'Hey, Lol,' he said. 'Long time, no see.'

Her first thought was that he had turned up to find out why she'd gone AWOL. It had only been a few days but she'd never let him down before. 'Sorry,' she said quickly, glancing over her shoulder to make sure no one was within earshot. 'I've not been able to come. It's been—'

'I know. Don't worry about it. I'm here to see Brenda. Do us a favour and give her a shout. And do you mind if I step inside? It's chucking it down out here.'

'Oh, okay, yeah, sorry.' She stood aside and Terry walked into the kitchen. She caught a whiff of his aftershave as he passed, along with the smell of damp and tobacco. 'I'll just go and get her.'

'Ta,' he said, brushing the rain off the shoulders of his overcoat. He peered around her into the living room, checked that it was empty and quietly added, 'Oh, and Lolly, about our little arrangement: let's just keep it between the two of us, right?'

'I haven't told anyone.'

'Good girl. Brenda mentioned that the law had been to see you. We don't want things getting any more complicated than they already are.'

Lolly's heart skipped a beat. As her eyes met his she realised that he knew the alibi she'd provided for Jude – or at least part of it – was false. While she'd been making the deliveries to Albert Road and to Joseph, she couldn't have been watching *Sunset Boulevard*.

'Cheer up,' he said, looking at her face. 'No need to stress. It'll all get sorted. We're mates, aren't we? I'll watch your back and you watch mine.'

Lolly nodded. She understood what he meant. If she didn't mention running errands for him, he wouldn't mention where she'd actually been on Tuesday afternoon. She recognised, suddenly, that he had something to lose too if the truth came out. The law wouldn't take kindly to him using a kid to do his deliveries – and probably Joe Quinn, for different reasons, wouldn't be too happy about it either. She didn't understand all the ins and outs but she'd already guessed that Terry was doing business behind his boss's back.

'Go on, then,' he said. 'Go and get Brenda for me.'

Lolly went through to the shop where Brenda was standing at the counter in the process of examining a gold wedding band for a thin, scrawny-looking woman with a grizzling baby in her arms. While Brenda studied the hallmark through her magnifying glass, the woman tried to stop the child crying.

'So how much can you give me?' the mother asked.

Even though Lolly could only see her back, she knew Brenda would be wrinkling her nose in that way she always did when she was figuring out the cheapest price she could get away with. If the ring was never redeemed, she would want to be able to sell it with the highest possible profit margin. 'Well, I can't go any higher than—'

Lolly cleared her throat to alert Brenda to her presence.

Brenda turned and looked at her. 'What is it? What do you want?'

'There's someone here to see you.'

'Who?'

Lolly shrugged, not wanting to say Terry's name in front of the customer. She was in enough trouble as it was without providing Brenda with more ammunition. 'He's waiting in the kitchen.'

Brenda glared at her for a moment and then, perhaps recalling that she was expecting someone, gave a nod. 'I'll be two minutes.'

Lolly went back to relay this information to Terry. He was sitting at the table, his legs stretched out, his head tilted back a little as he dragged on a cigarette and blew perfectly formed smoke rings into the air. 'She's with a customer. She won't be long.'

'Ta. You're a diamond.'

Lolly wasn't sure what to do next. She was usually comfortable with him, able to speak openly, but now she felt awkward and self-conscious. This was partly down to the knowledge that Brenda was close by and partly because he knew she was a liar. Although he wouldn't grass her up, she still wanted to explain, to tell him why she was so sure that Jude Rule was innocent.

Confused, she drifted over to the window and stared out at the yard. Behind her she could hear Terry's soft exhalations as he smoked. Should she go or should she stay? It seemed wrong, rude even, to leave him alone, but she couldn't think of anything to say. Fortunately, she was saved from having to make a decision by the sound of footsteps coming through the living room.

Brenda hurried into the kitchen, stopped and frowned at Terry. 'Oh, it's you. Where's Joe?'

'He's busy.'

'It's Joe I want to talk to.'

'And like I said, he's busy. Do you want our help or not?'

Brenda pursed her lips, clearly annoyed by this turn of events. Although she had nothing against Terry, she preferred to deal with the man at the top. She was canny enough to realise, however, that on this occasion she couldn't call the shots. 'Yes,' she said through gritted teeth.

'Good. Right, let's get on with it, then.'

Brenda went through to the hall and shouted up the stairs. 'Tony! Get your arse down here! We've got company.' She returned to the kitchen and, unwilling to offend Terry, vented her frustration on Lolly instead. 'What are you standing there for? Clear off. Go to your room. This is private business, nothing to do with you.'

Lolly didn't need telling twice and gladly made her escape. As she headed for the door, Terry winked at her. She bowed her head and scurried past. She was going up the stairs as Tony was coming down. When she glanced at him, she could see he was furious: his eyes were blazing, his cheeks burning with anger. As the two of them drew level, he suddenly grabbed hold of her arms and pushed her back against the wall.

'This is all your fault, you fuckin' cow!'

She struggled to get free but his grasp was too tight. 'I didn't—'

'If it wasn't for you, I wouldn't have the law on my back,' he hissed into her face. 'You and that bloody Jude Rule!'

Lolly opened her mouth but nothing came out. The speed and shock of his attack had rendered her speechless. And anyway, she knew that anything she said would only provoke him. He was on the verge of losing control. He wanted to hit her, to lash out and maybe would have done if they'd been alone in the house.

'I know your bloody game,' he said. 'You won't get away with it.'

Lolly felt his fingers digging into the flesh of her arms. She stopped struggling, aware that it was pointless, and stared up at him. His angry eyes bored into hers. What now? Her heart was thumping and her mouth had gone dry. She wondered if what she was seeing now was the last thing Amy had seen before she died. But then, as quickly as he'd grabbed her, he suddenly let go and went on down the stairs as if nothing had happened.

Lolly rushed up to her room and closed the door. She leaned against it, her breaths coming in short fast pants. She rubbed at the tender places on her arms, feeling the bruises already beginning to form. When she had agreed to provide an alibi for Jude, she'd had no idea of the repercussions. How could she have known that Tony would bunk off work early and then lie about it? How was that in any way her fault? But he didn't see it that way. So far as he was concerned, she'd landed him right in it.

Lolly waited a few minutes before venturing out of the room again. She glanced along the landing making sure it was empty. Something important was going on and she wanted to know what it was. Terry hadn't come to shift some dodgy gear. 'Help' was what he was offering and that help had to be connected to Tony.

She leaned over the banisters but wasn't close enough to hear clearly. Only muffled words floated up to her. Slowly she crept back down the stairs, being careful to avoid the floorboards that creaked. As she drew near to the bottom, she could feel her heart start to race again. If she was caught in the act of spying, she'd be in big trouble, but for Jude's sake, as well as her own, she had to find out what Brenda was up to.

Lolly crouched down when she reached a point a few feet up from the hallway. The living-room door was open and so was the door to the kitchen. Now she could hear the voices properly, could hear exactly what was going on.

'Her name's Jackie,' Terry was saying. 'Here's a picture. Take a good look at it, Tony. You'll need to describe her to the filth.'

'I don't like this,' Brenda said. 'Isn't there any other way?'

'Not if you want to keep him out of the slammer. You can see that, can't you? No boy is going to want his mother to know he slept with a tom from the Albert Road. It'll explain why he lied to the law about what he was doing on Tuesday afternoon.'

Brenda gave one of her long sighs. 'The whole bleedin' world's going to find out about it.'

'Not necessarily. And even if they do, it's better than people thinking he killed Amy Wiltshire.'

'I'll do it,' Tony said. 'I don't mind.'

'We'll have to go through the times, make sure you're properly covered. And you'll have to be able to describe the inside of the house and the room you used. I don't want to take you down there – it's too risky right now – but I've got some photos for you to look at. There's no reason why you'd remember every detail, just a few things that can prove you've actually been there.'

'And what if the law don't believe it?' Brenda asked. 'What then?'

'It's up to Tony to make sure they do.'

Lolly's fingers curled around the banisters. She felt disappointed at Terry, let down. Why was he doing this? By providing an alibi, he was letting Tony off the hook. She was becoming more and more convinced that Tony Cecil was guilty. He was nasty enough, vicious enough, and she'd seen little evidence of genuine grief at Amy's death.

There was a rattle at the front door – Brenda must have closed up the shop – and Lolly gave a start. What if someone came through from the kitchen to let the customer in? Worried that she might be caught in the act of eavesdropping, she fled back up the stairs and into her bedroom. Here she paced back and forth, angry and confused. If the law believed Tony's story, suspicion would be thrown back on Jude. But even worse than that, a murderer might be about to go free and there was nothing she could do about it.

21

Old Ma Fenner was one of those typical East End matri-
archs, strong and feisty and opinionated. She was the type
who didn't suffer fools gladly and wasn't afraid to show
it. Stanley wasn't sure how old the woman was, but he'd
hazard a guess that she was knocking on ninety. Although
still sprightly, her face was deeply lined, her pale blue eyes
almost hidden by the heavy folds of flesh.

'So you want to know about Angela,' she said.

Stanley sat back in the armchair. 'Anything you can tell
me could be useful. To be honest, she's a bit of a mystery. As
I mentioned, I'm trying to trace some family for Lolly. There
must be relatives out there, aunts, uncles, cousins, but I'm
not making much progress in finding them.'

'And what makes you think I can help?'

'You used to be neighbours, didn't you? I was hoping she
might have mentioned her family, where she came from,
anything about her past.'

Ma studied him closely for a while as if attempting to read

his face while she weighed up the veracity of his words. Trying to decide, perhaps, whether he was the sort of man who could be trusted. Eventually, she came to a decision and gave a small nod. 'Angela was never much of a talker, not that that's a bad thing. Most folk just prattle on for the sake of it, even if they've got nothing worth saying. I can tell you she came from south London, over Lambeth way, but she never mentioned family. I got the feeling – and it was only a feeling, mind – that they may have fallen out. I've no idea if there were brothers or sisters.'

'And what about her name?' Stanley asked. 'Was she calling herself Angela Bruce back then?'

Ma shook her head. 'No, not Bruce. Martin, it was, Angela Martin.'

Stanley leaned forward, surprised by this piece of information. 'Are you sure?'

'I might be old, Mr Parrish, but I ain't senile.'

'Sorry, yes, I just ... Only later, when she came back to the Mansfield, she started dating a guy called Billy Martin. I don't suppose you knew him?'

Ma thought about it for a few seconds but then shook her head. 'Can't say it rings any bells.'

'You see, I had the impression she only met him for the first time then, but maybe that wasn't the case. If she was calling herself Martin fourteen years ago then there could have been more of a connection than I thought.'

'It's a common enough name.'

This was true, but for Stanley it was still too much of a coincidence. 'Was it possible she was married to him when she first came here? Did she ever—'

'No, she never mentioned nothin' about being married. And she lived in that flat on her own. Could have been separated, I suppose, or just using his name.'

Stanley nodded. 'Maybe Bruce was her maiden name, something she went back to. Or, if they were separated, she could have got married again.'

'Ain't there ways you detectives can check that kind of thing?'

'There are,' he agreed, 'if you have some solid information to start with. As things stand, I've got no birth certificate, marriage certificate, nothing to prove she was who she says she was. I could spend days down Somerset House, searching through the records, but if none of these names were actually hers then I'll just be wasting my time.' Stanley rubbed at his face in frustration. The Lambeth lead might be useful – he could check out any Bruces in the area – but what were the odds of finding one related to Angela? 'I feel bad for Lolly. She's been left with no one. As things stand, she's stuck in limbo, not knowing where she came from or who her real family is.'

Ma pulled a disapproving face. 'What she's stuck with is that Brenda Cecil.'

'You don't like her?'

'What's to like? The woman ponces off the poor, takes advantage. Show me someone who got a good deal from Brenda Cecil and I'll show you a bleedin' unicorn. And God knows why she's taken in the child; she ain't got a charitable bone in her body.'

Stanley could have enlightened her on this point but

chose to keep quiet about it. 'At least it's a roof over her head.'

'And that's about all it is. I'd have offered to look after her myself if I was ten years younger.'

Stanley glanced around the room. The decor was dated, the furniture old and brown, but everything was neat as a pin. Lined up on the mantelpiece were numerous photographs of what he took to be kids and grandkids and probably even great grandkids. 'Did you know that Angela was pregnant when she moved out of Carlton House? Did she mention it to you?'

Ma shook her head. 'Pregnant? No, she … No, not a word. She said she'd got a job up in Manchester, something with better prospects. A secretary, I think. She seemed happy about it. She was excited.'

Stanley wondered how that tallied with Angela turning up in Dagenham a month later with a baby in tow. 'You'd have noticed if she was expecting, wouldn't you? I mean, she was a slim girl. It's not the kind of thing she could hide.'

'She'd have told me,' Ma said. 'She wouldn't have kept something like that a secret.'

'Even if she was going to be a single mum? There are plenty of people even today who don't approve of un-married mothers.'

'I don't judge, Mr Parrish. Angela knew that. And anyway, she can't have been pregnant, she—' Ma stopped suddenly as if she was about to reveal something but then had second thoughts. 'No, I'm sure she wasn't.'

Stanley stared at her, his interest piqued. 'Is there something you're not telling me?'

'She asked me not to say.' Ma shifted in her chair, avoiding his gaze. 'I don't like to break a confidence.'

'I understand, but Angela's dead and Lolly has no family. Perhaps the time for secrets is over.'

There was a long silence while Ma studied the floor. Eventually, she looked up again. She sighed as her eyes met his.

'For Lolly's sake,' he urged.

Ma sighed again, a thin whispery sound. 'What if Lolly ain't Angela's daughter at all?'

Stanley felt a tingling run the length of his spine. Darren had already sown some seeds of doubt, but now those seeds were beginning to take root. 'Why do you think that?'

'All I know . . . all she told me, was that she couldn't have kids. It broke her heart. That's what she wanted, really, a family of her own. She was seeing this bloke, Calvin, and it was serious for a while, an engagement ring, marriage plans, but when she told him about how she couldn't . . . Well, some men can't see a future without children. He dumped her, didn't he? That's when she decided to leave and head up to Manchester.'

'I don't suppose you know where he lives?'

Ma shook her head. 'Haven't seen him in years, although I don't get out so much now. Mind, I'm not sure I'd recognise him even if I did see him.'

'Any idea of his surname?'

Ma scratched her temples and frowned. There was a short silence while she thought about it. 'No, I don't recall. It might come back to me.'

Stanley laid his disappointment aside and continued to probe. 'So Angela had some kind of medical problem?'

'That's what she said. When she turned up with Lolly, I thought maybe the doctors had made a mistake, or that she'd adopted the girl.'

'And what did she tell you?'

'She didn't tell me nothin', Mr Parrish, and that's the truth of it. Fact is, she went out of her way to avoid me.' A cloud passed across her face as if the memory upset her. 'I didn't understand it, but there you go. I suppose there were questions she didn't want to answer.'

This made Stanley wonder why Angela had come back to the estate. If she had something to hide as regards Lolly, surely she wouldn't have taken the chance? But then again, with her mental problems she might not have been thinking straight. Or perhaps there was a reason she had to come back, something important that outweighed the risk she was taking.

'So you didn't have much contact after she moved into Haslow?'

'No,' Ma said sadly, 'although it weren't for the lack of trying. By me, I mean. But once she'd made it clear ... well, there's no point in forcing the issue, is there? She didn't want to talk, didn't want anything to do with me, and that was the beginning and end of it.'

'Was there anyone she did talk to?'

'I wouldn't know. She got a job at the Fox but it didn't last long. I heard she was fired. I did see her around with a bloke for a while – maybe it was that Billy you mentioned – but she never looked too happy. And then all that strange business started when she took to wandering about the estate. It was obvious she wasn't well but she wouldn't let anyone help.'

Stanley nodded. 'Was there any sign of her illness when you first knew her?'

'Not at all. She was a nice girl, friendly, normal. That's what made it all so strange when she came back and virtually ignored me. It wasn't like her. She wasn't the nasty sort. She used to pop in all the time when we were neighbours, make sure I was okay and do a bit of shopping and the like if I didn't feel up to it.' Ma's hands trembled a little in her lap. 'Do you know what I sometimes think, Mr Parrish?'

Stanley waited.

Ma took a few seconds to get the words out. 'I sometimes wonder if she came to see me on the day she died, if she thought I was still living up top. She might not have realised I'd moved. Maybe, if she'd found me . . .'

'I guess we'll never know,' Stanley said softly.

'And there's no point dwelling on it,' she said briskly, although the expression in her eyes belied the tone of her voice. 'What's done is done. We can't turn back time. We just have to get on with it. Sorry, I haven't been much help, have I? You're still no closer to finding any family for Lolly.'

Stanley rose to his feet. 'You've been a lot of help,' he said. 'Sometimes it takes a while to build up a picture, for things to start slotting into place. Thank you for telling me about Angela.'

'I often think of her.'

He shook her hand, feeling the thin, papery texture of her skin. 'I'll let you know if anything comes to light.'

'You do that. Ta. I'd be grateful.'

Outside, the sky was low and grey and threatening. Stanley walked halfway along the path leading to the main gate before he turned around and gazed up towards the top of Carlton House. For a second he thought he saw someone standing there, a woman with long dark hair. He blinked twice and the image was gone – just a trick of the light, perhaps, or a figment of his imagination. He took a long, deep breath. What he'd learned today was intriguing but he wasn't going to get ahead of himself. Lolly might not be Angela's daughter but that didn't mean she was Mal Fury's – although, of course, it didn't mean she wasn't, either.

22

It was late on Saturday night when Lolly woke up, wanting a pee. She would have preferred to stay in bed – she could feel the chill in the room – but was too afraid of having an accident to ignore the demands of her bladder. Reluctantly, she slipped out from under the covers and went along the landing to the bathroom. The sound of the TV, a chat show, travelled up from the living room. She heard Brenda say something but couldn't catch the words.

Lolly put on the light, closed the door and slid the bolt across. It was freezing in the bathroom. Someone had opened the top window and she wasn't tall enough to close it again. She lowered the loo seat – it always seemed to be up – and sat down, shivering. While she peed, she thought back over the day.

It was one she was glad to see the back of. First she'd had to endure a grilling from the law, and then Tony had gone for her on the stairs. The attack had left bruises on her arms, dark stains that had turned a yellowy brown. She rolled up her sleeves and studied the damage. He'd been in a better mood in the afternoon after getting back from Cowan Road – his new alibi must have done the trick – but had still stared daggers at her across the kitchen table while they were having tea. She wasn't safe. She knew she wasn't. But what could she do about it other than keep her head down and hope the storm would eventually pass?

While Lolly was sitting on the loo she heard footsteps and voices coming along the alley. A group of people, five or six, stumbled into the back yard. Their voices were drunkenly loud and aggressive, and she could make out Tony's in the middle of it all.

'You should have seen their fuckin' faces,' he said. 'They thought they had me bang to rights and then I pulled this one out of the bag.'

There was some laughter and shuffling of feet, and then a clink like the sound of a bottle being put on the ground.

'Good one, Tone.'

'Yeah, good one, mate.'

And then a girl's voice. 'You ain't going to be properly off the hook until they find out who done it.'

'I know who bloody done it! That Jude Rule. If it weren't for the stupid bitch giving him an alibi—'

'Maybe it wasn't him.'

'You've changed your bloody tune. Since when did you start defending the murdering bastard?'

'I've just had time to think, that's all. I mean, I don't *know* he went after Amy. And even if he did, it don't mean he found her. Anyone could have killed her.'

'That's not what you were saying last week.'

'Yeah, well, it were a shock, weren't it? You know how crazy it was. I couldn't think straight back then.'

Tony gave a snort. 'And now you can?'

'I'm just saying. I heard Old Bill pulled that Joseph in too, you know the one who hangs out in the tunnel.'

'What? The coon?'

'Yeah, I heard they had him down the nick for hours.'

'She's right, Tone,' another bloke chipped in. 'I heard that too.'

Lolly sat very still, not wanting to alert them to her presence. If they looked up, they might see the light, but she had the feeling they were all too pissed to take any notice. It was news to her about Joseph. She was sure he couldn't have murdered Amy – she'd been talking to him in the tunnel around the time it must have happened – and hoped he was okay. But the law was well known for stitching up people, especially the blacks.

'How come I'm only just hearing about this?'

'We should head over to the Mansfield and have a word with him, see what he's got to say for himself.'

'Who's up for it?' Tony asked.

A chorus of voices, cruel and eager, rose up through the air. 'Yeah, man'; 'Too right'; 'Let's do it.'

'Best get tooled up then.'

Lolly's hands clenched as she listened to the gang moving about the yard. She could hear the clanging of metal as they sifted through the junk searching for weapons. A shudder ran through her. She didn't understand how suspicion had suddenly shifted from Jude to Joseph. She wanted to jump up and yell that Joseph was innocent. He *couldn't* have done it. But if she did that, she'd be blowing her alibi for Jude. It wasn't possible for her to have been in two places at the same time.

Within a few minutes the gang had departed. Even Tracy had gone with them. They were all hyped up and looking for trouble. She had to find a way to stop them before something terrible happened. Lolly stood up, flushed the loo and went out on to the landing. She stood there, the panic rising inside her. What could she do? Go and tell Brenda and Freddy what she'd heard? But it was probably too late to catch up with Tony and his mates by now. The Cecils could only call the law and they wouldn't grass up their own son. It crossed her mind to slip downstairs and dial 999 herself – if she spoke quietly she might not be heard over the sound of the TV – but was too scared of Tony to go through with the plan, too terrified of what he might do if he found out.

Lolly went back to her bedroom, pushed aside the curtain and looked through the window. There was no sign of the gang. She felt small and helpless and cowardly. Joseph had been kind to her and God knows what was about to happen. It was cruel and crazy. Her only hope was that they wouldn't find him – or that if they did he'd be able to outrun them.

Eventually, with the cold seeping into her bones, she crawled back into bed. She curled up into a ball and wrapped her arms around her knees. Closing her eyes, she prayed hard for Joseph's safety. 'Please God,' she whispered, 'take care of Joseph. Don't let them get him. Don't let them hurt him. *Please.*'

23

Lolly woke on Sunday morning to the distant sound of church bells. A grey light slid through the gap in the curtains, and rain was lashing against the window. For a moment she didn't remember, but then it all came back to her in a rush. She lay trembling under the covers. Had Joseph escaped? Had Tony come back? She hadn't heard him if he had, but she could have been asleep.

For a long while she remained staring up at the ceiling. Her heart was heavy, the kind of weight that comes from doing something bad – or, in this case, not doing anything at all. But maybe she was worrying over nothing. Joseph might not even have been there. The best course of action, she decided, was to get up, get dressed and go over to the Mansfield. She had to warn him if it wasn't already too late. She had to tell him that Tony was after his blood.

Lolly leapt out of bed, pulled on her clothes and hurried

downstairs. Brenda was in the kitchen, cooking bacon and eggs for Freddy and FJ. Usually the smell of food made her mouth water, but this morning it only made her feel ill.

'If you want something cooked, you'll have to wait,' Brenda said.

'It's okay,' Lolly said. 'I'll just have cereal.'

FJ stared at her. 'What's wrong with you?'

'Nothing.'

'She must be sick,' FJ said with a snigger. 'Are you sick, Lolly?'

'No.'

'So why aren't you stuffing your face like you normally do?'

Lolly ignored him, concentrating instead on Brenda and Freddy. They didn't seem unduly concerned about anything, their major worries swept away now that Tony had acquired a watertight alibi for the time Amy Wiltshire was killed. But where was he this morning? She wanted to ask but didn't want to draw attention to herself. Instead she poured out a small bowl of cornflakes, threw some milk over them and started to eat.

FJ continued to bait her. 'Maybe you're sick with worry,' he said. 'I would be too if I was lying through my teeth. Tony could have been banged up because of you.'

'No one's getting banged up,' Brenda said.

'That Jude Rule is,' FJ said. 'And so will Lolly when they find out what she's done.'

Freddy turned over the pages of the *News of the World*, lifted his mug to his lips and took a noisy slurp of tea while he waited for his breakfast. 'How long does it take to fry a few rashers? I'm bloody starving here, woman.'

'Make it yourself if you want it any quicker,' Brenda retorted. 'You should be grateful I'm feeding you at all after what your Jim did.'

'And what's that got to do with me? It's not my fault he's being getting his end away with some little slapper.'

'Nothing's ever your fault.'

'Jesus,' Freddy said, rolling his eyes.

'You can Jesus away as much as you like. If he hadn't cleared off and left Tony on his own, I wouldn't have had to go cap in hand to—' She stopped suddenly, remembering they weren't alone in the room. 'I don't like being beholden to no one. You know that.'

'Who are you talking about?' FJ asked.

'None of your business,' Brenda said.

'It is my business if it's to do with Tony.'

'And how do you figure that one out?'

'He's my brother, ain't he? I've a right to know what's going on.'

Brenda pushed the frying pan around the ring, making the fat pop and splutter. 'The only rights you have in this house are the ones I say you have.'

FJ looked at his father.

'Don't drag me into this,' Freddy grumbled. 'I'm in enough trouble already, thank you very much.'

Brenda served up the breakfast and sat down. As the three of them tucked in, Lolly took her chance to make a bid for freedom.

'Is it all right if I go over to Sandra's?' she asked. 'We're doing a project. It has to be in for tomorrow.'

'Project liar,' FJ muttered under his breath.

'It's pouring down,' Brenda said. 'What do you want to go out in this for?'

Lolly stood up and took her empty bowl over to the sink. 'I have to.' Before any further objections could be raised, she scooted through to the hall, grabbed her coat and returned to the kitchen. 'I won't be long.'

'Stay as long as you like,' FJ said. 'We're not going to miss you.'

Brenda gave an exasperated shake of her head. 'Don't blame me if you catch your death of cold.'

Lolly opened the back door, went out into the yard and pulled up her hood against the rain. As she closed the door behind her, she caught one last comment from Brenda.

'There's something wrong with that girl.'

As Lolly made her way along the alley, she wondered if there *was* something wrong with her. She knew she was different, that she didn't fit in. But what could she do about it? A while back it hadn't mattered – she'd still had her mum – but now the world felt like a lonely place. She had no one to ask for advice, no one to turn to.

On the high street, she sloshed carelessly through the puddles, not bothered that the water was seeping through her shoes and soaking her socks. As she drew closer to the estate, her breath quickened. If she could just find Joseph, discover he was okay, she wouldn't feel so bad. Maybe then the sick feeling in her guts would go away.

Lolly reached the main gate of the Mansfield and began to jog towards the east tunnel. She would try there first as it was the nearest of the two tunnels where Joseph could usually be found. But she hadn't covered more than twenty yards when she saw that the entrance to the passageway had been sealed off by long lengths of police tape. Her heart skipped a beat. All her worst fears came bubbling to the surface. She was too late. She hadn't acted when she'd had the chance and now . . .

She stopped dead and stared, her eyes widening with alarm. There was no sign of the law – they must have been and gone – which meant that whatever had happened had taken place a while ago. Like last night, for example. She cursed herself for doing nothing. What if Joseph was dead? What if Tony and his gang had killed him? Her teeth began to chatter.

Eventually, she got up the courage to approach Carlton House and the opening to the tunnel. Her legs felt unsteady as if they might suddenly buckle. She took slow, careful steps, the rain squelching in her shoes. When she reached the entrance she stopped again and peered into the gloom. So far as she could make out there was nothing to see apart from the usual litter, some broken glass and more police tape down the other end.

Lolly kept on staring. There might be little to see, but the tape told its own story. Something seriously bad had happened here. She swallowed hard, her mouth turning dry. Eventually, she retreated back on to the path, hoping that someone would come by and she could try and get some answers. But as the minutes passed she quickly realised there was little chance of that. The estate was deserted, the heavy rain keeping everyone inside.

She glanced towards Haslow House and then back at Carlton. That was when she noticed old Ma Fenner looking out of a window on the ground floor. The net curtain was pulled aside, gripped by an old gnarled hand, and the witch was staring directly at her. Lolly thought of her as a witch because that was what her mum had told her.

'You stay away from that woman, do you hear? She eats little girls like you for breakfast.'

That had been years ago but Lolly hadn't forgotten. Whenever she saw Ma Fenner, she still thought of Hansel and Gretel, and the house in the woods made of gingerbread and cake. Suddenly the old woman waved at her. She quickly averted her face, pretending she hadn't seen, and strode off along the path. As she walked she could feel Ma's eyes on her, a hungry gaze boring into her back.

Lolly had no clear idea of where she was going or of what to do next. All she knew was that she couldn't go home until she'd found out about Joseph. Having seen the tape, she was imagining the worst. What else could it mean? Her nerves were on fire, her stomach queasy with fear. She had no idea where he lived on the estate – the only time she ever saw him was when he was lounging against the wall of the tunnel waiting for his next customer.

As she drew adjacent to Haslow House, the front door opened and Jude's father walked out. She watched as he crossed to the parking area and got into a battered blue

Vauxhall. It was then she thought of going up to see Jude. Surely he'd know what had happened. But could she take the risk? While the investigation was going on, she wasn't supposed to talk to him – in fact, she wasn't supposed to talk to him, full stop – but desperate times called for desperate measures.

Lolly waited until Jude's dad had left before strolling casually towards the door. Would she know if she was being tailed? She wasn't sure. Glancing over her shoulder, the coast appeared to be clear. Anyway, she didn't think the law would bother; they had better things to do than follow a kid around.

Inside the lobby, she went into one of the lifts and studied the buttons. Rather than pressing number twelve, she pressed number nine instead. That way, if someone was on her tail, they wouldn't know for certain where she was going. The lift lumbered up making an ominous scraping noise. It stank of pee and fags and dope, but at least it was empty. She got out on the ninth floor and took the stairs for the remaining three.

At each landing she stopped for a moment and gazed down on the estate. She couldn't see anything suspicious, no one loitering or paying any particular attention to the building. It was not quite as deserted as when she'd first arrived – a few people hurried along, their heads bowed against the rain – but there was no one in the vicinity who looked like a cop.

Lolly was extra cautious when she came to the twelfth floor. She paused, looking up and down the corridor, before advancing to Jude's flat. Her footsteps sounded unnaturally loud as she covered the distance from the landing to the door. She knocked softly, not wanting to alert the neighbours, and waited.

When Jude answered, it was not exactly the welcome she'd been hoping for. His face fell when he saw her. 'What are you doing here?'

'Let me in. I've got to talk to you.'

He shook his head. 'You can't. My dad's inside.'

'No he isn't,' she said, shocked by the lie. 'I just saw him.'

Jude flushed. 'We're not supposed to talk to each other.'

'It isn't about that. Come on. Let me in before someone sees.'

Reluctantly, Jude stood aside. 'It had better be quick.'

Lolly went through to the living room and immediately felt a stirring of emotion. The green corduroy sofa and the shelves full of films reminded her of old times, of peanut butter sandwiches, of easy chats and hours spent watching the ill-fated lives of others play out on the makeshift screen. It felt like for ever since she'd last been here. So much had changed over the past few months, and not for the better.

Jude didn't even try to hide his agitation. 'What is it? What do you want?'

'I need to know what happened to Joseph.'

'Who?'

'Why were the cops here last night?'

'They weren't. Why would they be? I had nothing to do with Amy's death. I've told them that. I didn't—'

'No, I don't mean *here*,' she interrupted, 'I mean on the

estate. There's tape across the tunnel. Something happened. Did Joseph get hurt?'

'I don't even know who Joseph is.'

'Yes you do. The black bloke who hangs out in the tunnel. You must have seen him around. He's always there.'

'Oh, right, *him*.'

'I think Tony and his crew might have come after him last night. I heard them talking in the yard. Tracy said Joseph had been picked up over Amy. She said he'd been down the nick for hours. She said—'

'What was Tracy doing there?'

'I don't know,' Lolly said, frustrated by the lack of answers. 'They all took off and came here looking for Joseph.'

'There was an ambulance. Someone got taken away. Yeah, it could have been him. I think it was.'

Lolly's heart sank. 'Was it bad? Could you see?'

Jude shrugged. 'I dunno. Does it matter? And if he killed Amy—'

'But he didn't. He couldn't have. I saw him in the tunnel just before . . . it was like maybe a quarter of an hour before you caught up with me. And I was chatting to him for ten minutes, maybe longer. So he couldn't have done it, could he? It's impossible.'

'You can't tell the law that. You can't say you were with him.'

Lolly saw the panic in his eyes and knew that the only person he was thinking about was himself. He was scared she'd go back on her alibi. 'I know. I'm not going to. But what if he dies?'

'So what if he does? It's one less lousy dealer on the estate.'

Lolly was stunned by the words. She stared at him, open-mouthed.

Jude hissed out a breath. 'Jesus, what are you looking at me like that for? It's true, isn't it? Anyway, why were you even talking to him?'

She didn't want to tell him about her job with Terry and so she said instead, 'He was just ... just asking how I was doing. He said he was sorry to hear about my mum and all.'

'Yeah, as if he gives a damn. Why were you even on the estate? What were you doing here?'

'It's a free country, isn't it?' Lolly retorted. 'I can go where I like.'

Jude paced over to the window, looked out, turned around and came back. 'Sorry, I didn't mean ... It's just if you tell the police all this, we're both going to be in big trouble.'

'I won't. You know I won't. I just don't want Joseph to get blamed for something he didn't do. It isn't fair.'

'Well, what can you do about it? Anyway, if the guy's innocent, he's got nothing to worry about.'

Lolly could have said the same for him, but of course she didn't. Despite his attitude, she still wanted him to like her. When she looked at his face, at his eyes and mouth, her stomach flipped over. 'Not if Tony spreads it around that he's guilty. I mean, that's what he wants, isn't it? For the law and everyone else to think that Joseph did it. That way he's off the hook. First it was you and now—'

'Did Tracy really say that she thought I was innocent?'

'Not exactly. She said something like she wasn't sure.'

'But that's still good. That's better than ... Has she told the police that?'

Lolly shrugged. 'I don't know.'

'When did they last talk to you?'

'Yesterday. In the morning.'

'What did they say?'

Lolly shrugged again. 'The same old stuff. What time I got here, what time I left, what film we were watching.'

Jude put his hands in his pockets and nodded. Suddenly his voice grew silky soft. 'Thanks, you know, for what you're doing. I appreciate it. I mean, it was just bad luck that I found her like that.'

'Who do *you* think killed her?'

Jude seemed surprised by the question. 'How should I know? She was always winding people up. You know what she was like.'

'Maybe it was Tony. He was her boyfriend and he's always looking for someone else to blame.' She was tempted to speak out about the fake alibi, but wasn't sure if she could trust him. What if he told the law? Tony would find out and then he'd kill *her*. No, she'd better keep quiet about it. Instead she asked, 'Did you see him after you'd talked to Amy?'

Jude shook his head. 'No, I don't think so. I can't remember. I was kind of distracted after ... I mean, I wasn't really looking. Just walking around, trying to work things out.'

'So he could have been here.'

'Anyone *could* have been here,' he replied sharply. 'Unless we can prove it, it's not much use, is it?'

Lolly turned her face away, not wanting him to see the tears in her eyes. She felt he should be nicer after everything she'd done. It wasn't easy lying to the law – or having Tony Cecil on her back twenty-four hours a day. She concentrated on picking at a loose thread on the back of the sofa, trying to stop her lower lip from wobbling.

'Sorry,' he said. 'I didn't mean ... I can't think straight at the moment.'

Lolly instantly forgave him. 'It's okay.'

'I just want it to be over, to get on with things. You should see the way people stare at me, like I'm a kind of monster.'

'They'll find out who did it. I'm sure they will.'

Jude didn't seem convinced. 'And if they don't? I'll be the person who might have killed Amy for the rest of my life.'

'You won't,' she insisted. 'You've got an alibi.'

'As if that's going to stop them talking.' He glanced impatiently at his watch. 'Look, you'd better go. There's going to be trouble if someone finds you here.'

Lolly wondered how anyone was going to find her there seeing as his dad had gone to work, but could see he wanted to get rid of her. It hurt her feelings, made her ache inside, but she still made excuses for him. He was in a state, scared and anxious; the murder of Amy had turned his life upside down.

'Okay,' she said.

Jude looked relieved. 'You'd better not come back until ... you know, until all this is over.'

'Okay,' she said again.

He went over to the door, opened it and peered left and right along the corridor. 'Right, quick, it's all clear.'

Lolly was bundled out with barely enough time to say goodbye. It was only when she was standing by the lifts that she realised Jude hadn't asked how she was or how she was doing. He'd been too wrapped up in his own problems to even think about hers. As she slowly travelled down the twelve floors, she tried not to dwell on this. After providing him with an alibi she'd been hoping, perhaps, to rekindle the easy friendship they'd once had.

Outside, the rain was still coming down. She put up her hood and looked towards Carlton House and Ma Fenner's ground-floor window. It was empty now, with the white net curtain back in place. If she'd had more courage she might have knocked on the door and asked about Joseph – Ma was the type of woman who knew everything that went on around the estate – but she still had that vision in her head of a red-hot oven, stoked up and ready to receive the next unsuspecting child.

Lolly shuddered, turned and headed for the pawnbroker's. She felt sad about Joseph and Jude and just about everything else in her life. She felt afraid too. The atmosphere in the Cecil house was taut and strained and growing darker by the day. It was only a matter of time, she thought, before things reached breaking point and then ... She raised her face to the heavens and hoped her mum was looking down on her. At the moment she needed all the help she could get.

24

Lolly walked through the kitchen, shaking the rain from her like a drenched dog. She was cold and wet and miserable. Loud laughter came from the living room. Tony and FJ. The sound put her on edge and if she could have avoided the brothers she would have, but there was only one way to get upstairs. She had just reached the door when Tony came out with something that made her stop dead in her tracks.

'He was squealing like a pig. Shit, you should have heard him. It was hysterical. So I stamped on his fuckin' head, didn't I? I swear to God his eyeball went straight into his brain.'

'No way,' FJ said.

'It was bloody classic, I'm telling you.'

'And then what?'

'What do you think? We fuckin' scarpered before the law showed up.'

At that very moment, alerted perhaps by the intake of her

breath, they both glanced across the room and saw Lolly. Tony's face grew dark, a scowl settling over his features. He leapt to his feet, strode over and grabbed her arms.

'What are you doing?' he snarled.

'N-nothing,' she stammered. 'I'm not—'

'Yes you are! You're a dirty little snoop!'

'How long has she been there?' FJ asked.

'Too long,' Tony said, tightening his grip. 'The little bitch has been spying on us.'

Lolly winced in pain as his fingers pressed into the bruises inflicted the day before. 'I haven't, I swear. I've only just—'

Tony pushed his face into hers. 'Shut it! We all know what a filthy liar you are. You say one word about this to anyone and I'll close your stinking mouth for ever. Do you get it? Do you understand?'

'I didn't hear anything. I didn't.'

'Don't give me that. I know you, Lolly Bruce, always sneaking around, always poking your nose into other people's business. We take you in and this is all the thanks we get. You should be grateful but instead all you do is cause trouble.'

FJ stood up too and came to stand by his brother's shoulder, egging him on. 'Yeah, that's all she's done since she's got here. She's sick in the head like her weirdo mum.'

'Yeah, she's that all right.' Tony laughed, expelling a blast of stale, beery breath. 'She needs teaching a fuckin' lesson.' He bared his teeth as he glared at her. 'You know what happens to sneaky little brats like you? They end up with their throats cut in the middle of the night.'

Lolly stiffened at the threat. She could feel her lungs pumping, her pulse starting to race. She turned her head away but didn't try to get free. The more she struggled, the more he would hurt her. 'Leave me alone. I've not done anything.'

'You hear that, FJ? Says she ain't done nothin'.'

FJ sniggered. 'Funny idea of nothin'.'

'She's a bloody curse. They should have drowned her at birth. That's what they usually do with the runts. The sooner we get rid her of her the better.'

Lolly yelped as his fingers squeezed her arms even tighter. 'Let go! Let go of me!'

'You should finish her off,' FJ said. 'Put her out of her misery.'

Lolly let out another cry. 'You're hurting!'

Suddenly, Brenda's voice came from the front of the house. 'What's with the racket? What's going on back there?'

'Just messing about,' FJ called back.

'Well, do it more quietly. I'm trying to do a stocktake here. I can't hear myself think.'

Tony released his grasp but didn't immediately get out of Lolly's way. Instead he leaned down and whispered in her ear, 'See you later, darlin'. See you when it gets dark.'

Lolly pushed through the two boys, ran through the living room, into the hall and up the stairs. She dashed into the bedroom, closing the door behind her. She was terrified, sure now that Tony meant what he said. After what he'd done to Joseph, she knew what he was capable of. And maybe he'd killed Amy too. Why else would he have needed that fake alibi?

She began to pace around the room, trying to work out what to do. She couldn't stay here. It wasn't safe. She had to get away, somewhere, anywhere. Perhaps Stella would take her in. Or Terry? But no, she didn't entirely trust Terry now. He might bring her straight back to Brenda and then she'd be in even more trouble.

Lolly put her school bag on the bed and began to gather up her belongings. It didn't take long. She would have to leave most of her clothes behind; there wasn't room for them. The precious book of fairy tales was the last item she packed, wrapping it in a T-shirt so it wouldn't get damaged. There was only one thing left to do. First, she went back out on to the landing to make sure neither of the brothers was hanging about. She hung over the banisters until she was sure she could hear them talking in the living room.

Quickly she returned to the bedroom, knelt down by the bed and eased out the five one-pound notes from the slit in the mattress. Where to put them? Not in the bag. It might get nicked when she was out there on her own. In the end, she decided that the safest place was on her own body. She carefully rolled them into a cylinder and slid them down the side of her sock.

Lolly went over to the window and stared out at the lashing rain. All she had to figure out now was how and when she was going to leave. This afternoon, after dinner, seemed the best option. She didn't dare wait until night. What if Tony came for her before she had a chance to get away? And anyhow, the back door was always locked before Brenda went to bed and she still had no idea where the key was kept.

Glancing up and down the street, she wasn't that scared at the prospect of being out there on her own – at least not as scared as she was of staying put. While her mum was sick, she had learned how to scavenge and how to take care of herself. The only problem was where she would sleep. It was cold out, and wet. She would need a warm jumper if she wasn't going to freeze to death.

Now that she'd made up her mind, Lolly felt calmer, as if a weight had been lifted from her shoulders. Her only problem would be getting Brenda to let her go out again. She'd have to come up with a good excuse, like she'd left something at Sandra's and had to go and pick it up. How long would it be before they realised she was missing? Not before teatime, she reckoned, which gave her a good few hours.

Lolly left the window and sat down on the bed. With the cash she had, she could catch a train or a bus and go to . . . but here her imagination failed her. For the past five years, she had rarely been outside of Kellston. Her mum had taken her up West occasionally to look at the shops or to see a film – she remembered the bright lights and the bustling crowds, the wide hoardings with their bright advertisements – but the thought of going there alone was daunting.

Maybe she could find somewhere to hide in Kellston. She'd be okay if she stayed out of sight, slept during the day and only ventured out at night. Under cover of darkness, she could search the bins for food. Although she planned to buy provisions, bread and the like, she didn't want to spend too much of the money she'd been saving for her mum's headstone.

All she had to figure out now was where to go. There were the railway arches and the cemetery, even tucked-away places on the Mansfield. As she thought about the estate, she was reminded of Joseph. She hoped he was still alive. She hoped his eye wasn't buried in his brain. Lolly flinched as the gruesome image jumped into her head. She didn't want to think about it, couldn't stop thinking about it. How could Tony have done such a thing? He was crazy, deranged. She remembered his threat and a tremor ran through her. There was no going back. If she didn't get out of here soon, she would end up as his next victim.

25

Brenda always cooked a roast on Sundays. Today it was chicken with all the trimmings: potatoes, carrots, cabbage, and sage and onion stuffing from a Paxo packet. Lolly sat down opposite Tony, the only space left at the table. She could feel his eyes on her and deliberately avoided his gaze. She was scared of what she'd see there, what she might read on his face.

Aware that this was the last hot meal she might have for a while, she tried to fill her belly. The food was the only thing she'd miss when she left. Well, that and TV, and the fact the house was always warm. But those things didn't matter. All she wanted was to feel safe again and there was no chance of that while she was living here.

The conversation flowed around her, the usual chit-chat, the two-and-fro between Brenda and her sons. Freddy rarely said much. And Lolly wasn't expected to contribute; no one wanted to hear what she had to say. At least it gave her a chance to think. She still had to come up with a good excuse for why she had to leave the house again. What if Brenda refused to let her? Maybe she shouldn't even ask. Maybe it was smarter to just sneak out when no one was watching.

'You know what, Mum?' Tony said. 'You really should get some sharper knives. These ones are rubbish. They wouldn't cut through butter.'

Lolly flinched and looked up from her dinner.

FJ sniggered, in on the joke.

Brenda shook her head. 'What are you going on about now? There's nothin' wrong with them knives. They're top quality, silver-plated.'

Tony made a show of trying to saw through his chicken. 'See, they're almost blunt. What do you reckon, FJ?'

'Yeah, you're right. I mean, if you want to cut through things . . .'

'Exactly.'

'Well, if you want them sharpening,' Brenda grumbled, 'you can do it yourself. I've got enough on my plate without making even more work for myself.'

Tony grinned, staring at Lolly. 'Maybe I will. I've got nothin' else on this afternoon. I can get them all nice and sharp.'

'You should,' FJ said. 'You should get them *really* sharp.'

Lolly inwardly shivered. She could imagine the sound of the creaking floorboards as Tony came to grab her in the middle of the night. Maybe he wasn't planning on doing it in the house. Maybe he'd drag her out of bed, take her somewhere dark and lonely, slit her throat and leave her body in the dirt.

'Lolly could help me,' Tony said. 'Make herself useful for a change. How about it, darlin'? You and me, sharpening up the knives together?'

'I can't,' she said, dreading the thought of being alone with him. 'I've . . . I've got homework.'

'Thought you did that this morning.'

'It's not finished yet.'

'I can wait,' Tony said slyly. 'We can do it later.'

After the meal was over and the dishes washed, Lolly flew upstairs and took refuge in the bedroom. She had to get away, and fast. She didn't dare ask Brenda if she could go out again – if she said no, she'd be trapped. Instead, she opened the window and gazed out on to the wet street. It was a long way down, too far to jump. She'd probably break her neck if she tried.

Lolly went out on to the landing, leaned over the banisters and listened. The TV was on, a football match from the sound of it. She waited until she heard Brenda go back into the pawnbroker's before returning to the bedroom and picking up her bag. It was suspiciously full, bulging in fact. She hung it over her left shoulder, hoping its size would go unnoticed as she tried to make her escape.

She went quietly down the stairs and grabbed her damp coat from the hallway. All she had to do now was negotiate the living room. She took a few deep breaths, telling herself not to rush, not to do anything that might alert the boys to her plans. As she walked through the door and across the room, her heart was thumping in her chest. If she got stopped now ...

But no one even looked up. Freddy was still reading the *News of the World*, and the brothers were glued to the TV. She gave a sigh of relief when she reached the far side of the kitchen, opened the back door and stepped out into the yard. She softly closed the door behind her, pulled on her coat and hurried towards the gate. But her sense of relief was short-lived. No sooner had she reached the alley when Tony and FJ came flying out after her.

'Where the hell do you think you're going?' Tony asked.

Lolly stopped, her stomach turning over. 'Nowhere,' she said stupidly.

'Looks like a pretty heavy bag to be going nowhere with. What have you got in it?'

Lolly had a split second to make a decision. The boys were advancing and if she waited any longer they'd be on her. As the adrenalin kicked in, she decided to make a dash for it. She took off, sprinting down the alley, hoping to outrun them. Were they coming after her? She didn't know. All she could hear was the slap of her shoes on the concrete, the breath pumping from her lungs. Fear drove her on – she thought she was getting away – but then disaster struck. As she reached the corner she ran slap bang into a couple of uniformed officers.

'Hey, where's the fire?' one of them said.

'Sorry,' she mumbled.

'Lolly, isn't it?'

She nodded, looking up. 'Yeah.' Then she glanced over her shoulder towards the gate to the yard. Tony had disappeared but FJ was still standing there, watching her.

'We've met before,' he said. 'I'm Sergeant Grand. I came to talk to you about Amy.'

'Yeah,' she said again, wishing he'd get out of the way.

'Where are you off to, then?'

'A friend's,' she said. 'Er ... homework. I've got some homework to do.'

The other cop, a younger one, laughed. 'You must be keen. I never rushed anywhere to do my homework.'

'It's raining,' Lolly said, in case they hadn't noticed. 'I don't want to get wet.' She hopped from one foot to another, impatient to be off. 'Can I go now?'

'I think you'd better come with us,' Grand said.

Lolly's heart sank. 'Is it about Amy again?'

Grand shook his head. 'No, this is something else. Let's go to the house, shall we, before we all get soaked?'

Lolly glanced over at FJ. She could see him glaring at her. 'I c-can't,' she stammered. 'I'm late already.'

Grand put a hand on her shoulder and began to gently propel her back along the alley. 'This won't take long. You can spare us five minutes, can't you?'

Lolly was tempted to try to wriggle free and make a run for it again, but she reckoned the younger cop could catch her in a few strides. And then she'd have some explaining to do. But she didn't want to go back to the house. Once the cops had left, she'd be in big trouble. Brenda would ground her for a month if she found out she'd been intending to run away. And Tony – well, she didn't even want to think about what he'd do.

But the matter, it seemed, was already out of her control. She saw FJ shoot inside, following in his brother's footsteps. Lolly bowed her head as she was forced towards the gate. By the time they got there, Brenda had been alerted and was standing at the back door with her hands on her hips and a face like thunder.

'What's going on? What do you want now?' she growled at the officers.

'Your Tony in, Mrs C.?' Grand asked.

'No,' she lied.

'Mind if we come in and check?' Grand didn't bother waiting for an answer but simply pushed past her into the kitchen.

'Yeah, I do bleedin' well mind,' Brenda protested. 'Why can't you leave us in peace? Don't you know it's Sunday? The boy ain't done nothin'. You're hounding him, that's what you're doing. I'll be putting in a complaint.'

'You do that, love. Whatever makes you happy.' Grand turned to his colleague and said, 'Better check upstairs, Dave, case the lad slipped in when his mother wasn't looking.'

'I've told you, ain't I? He's not here.'

While Brenda was arguing with the cops, Lolly dropped her bag on the floor and nudged it under the table with her toe. With a bit of luck she could smuggle it back upstairs when all the fuss had died down. Brenda, at least for the moment, was too distracted by the visit from the law to ask what Lolly had been doing outside.

'Do you know where your son was last night, Mrs C.?'

Freddy came into the kitchen from the living room. 'He was here with us. We were all watching TV.'

'That's right,' Brenda said. 'He never set foot outside the door.'

Grand lifted his eyebrows. 'Of course he didn't.'

It was less than a minute before the young cop came down the stairs with Tony in tow. 'Look who I found hiding in the bathroom.'

'I wasn't bloody hiding. I was taking a slash.'

Grand stepped forward and said, 'Tony Cecil, I'm arresting you on suspicion of—'

'Hey, hang on there,' Freddy interrupted. 'What the hell are you playing at? My boy had nothin' to do with that girl's death. How many times do you need telling?'

'If you'd just let me finish,' Grant said. 'I'm arresting you on suspicion of the attempted murder of Joseph Clayton. You have ...'

The rest of what Grant said floated over Lolly. All she was thinking was: *attempted* murder. That meant Joseph wasn't dead. At least, not yet. And now the law had come for Tony. Hopefully, they'd lock him up and throw away the key. She stared at the wall trying to appear suitably solemn, but inside she was jumping for joy.

'This is crap!' Tony said. 'It's a stitch-up. I was here. I never stepped foot outside the door.'

'Not according to half a dozen witnesses in the Dog,' Grand said. 'C'mon, you can tell me the rest down the station.'

'I don't even know this Joseph guy.'

Brenda scowled at the sergeant. 'Those bloody witnesses are lying! How could he have . . . I've told you he was here all night. FJ, tell him.'

FJ nodded. 'Yeah, course he was.'

Brenda turned to Lolly. 'Tell him.'

The last thing Lolly wanted to do was to provide an alibi for Tony, but what choice did she have? Reluctantly, she nodded. 'Yeah.'

'You see?' Brenda said.

But Grand wasn't interested. 'Save it for the jury, love.' He got out his cuffs and snapped them on to Tony's wrists.

'There's no need for that. What are you doing?'

'There's every need. Your son's under arrest.'

After Tony had been taken away, Brenda turned to Freddy. 'Get on the blower. He'll need his brief.' Then she looked at FJ. 'And you'd better tell me everything you know, right now.'

'Why would I know anything?'

'Don't give me that. I can read your face like a bleedin' book. Now are you going to tell me or am I going to have to shake it out of you?'

FJ scowled at her. He shuffled about for a while, looking everywhere but at his mother, but eventually gave in. 'Shit, the guy deserved it. He's a scumbag dealer and everyone's saying that he killed Amy, only the law can't prove it. And all Tony did was beat him up a bit; it weren't attempted murder.'

'For Christ's sake,' Brenda said.

'She was his girlfriend. He's got the right to—'

'He ain't got the *right* to do nothin'. We've only just got that other business sorted and now he's back down the nick again.'

'Yeah, well, we all know whose fault that is.' He poked a finger into Lolly's shoulder. '*She's* the one you should be talking to. She's the little bitch who grassed him up.'

'What?' Lolly said, stunned by the accusation. 'I did not.'

'Liar! I saw you with my own eyes. You were listening in on me and Tony, don't say you weren't, and next thing we know you're down the alley chatting to the law.'

'I didn't tell them anything. I didn't! I didn't even know they were going to be there.'

'You've had it in for us ever since you got here.'

'I haven't. I swear. I didn't say a word. I'd never ... I wouldn't.'

Brenda's eyes narrowed as she glared at Lolly. 'What were you doing out in the alley, then?'

'I was going to Sandra's. I forgot something.'

FJ bent down, picked up her bulging bag and put it on the table. 'So what did you need this for?'

'Get your hands off that!' Lolly tried to snatch it away from him, but he held on tight.

'You see?' FJ said to his mother. 'She's hiding something.' He unzipped the bag, opened it up and started pulling everything out. 'Jesus, look at this! She's got all her stuff here. She was going to clear off. She grassed up Tony and then—'

'I didn't!' Lolly protested.

Freddy came in and said, 'What did I tell you? I could see she was trouble from the moment she got here.'

Lolly shook her head. There was no more she could say, at least nothing that would help. She could see from the expressions on their faces that she'd already been tried, judged and found guilty.

'Go up to your room,' Brenda said coldly. 'I don't want to see you again today. I can't stand the bleedin' sight of you.'

Lolly grabbed the bag and her things and scurried out of the kitchen. The last voice she heard as she ran up the stairs was Freddy's.

'I've had enough, woman. Sort it out, yeah? That girl's a bloody curse. The sooner she's out of here the better.'

26

By Monday morning, Stanley still hadn't called Mal Fury. He was waiting until he heard back from his contact at the coroner's. The autopsy report didn't tell him what he needed to know – whether there were any visible signs on Angela's body to show that she had once given birth – and now he had the ominous feeling it was all too late. Unless the pathologist could remember, there wasn't any way to go back and check. Angela had already been cremated.

Despite having no definitive proof, Stanley was starting to feel convinced that Lolly wasn't Angela's daughter. The junkie, Daz Wakefield, was hardly a reliable witness, but what he'd said tallied with the evidence provided by Ma Fenner. And the latter, so far as he could tell, had nothing to gain by lying to him.

Stanley boiled the kettle and made another cup of coffee, his third that morning. He flipped open the file and stared at the photo of Lolly. Where had she come from? Who did she really belong to? Brenda's claim of a connection to the Furys had to be taken with a pinch of salt. It was more likely that the kid had been adopted – although the lack of a paper trail made this impossible to corroborate – or acquired by less legal means. Maybe Angela, desperate for a child, had found a woman willing to give one up.

He made some more notes in his neat sloping hand-writing. The Billy Martin connection still irked him. He didn't like loose ends and this was a big one. Despite Quinn's threats, and his own sense of what was smart to do and what wasn't, he had put out some feelers to his contacts on the force, trying to establish whether the man was a known felon or had any form at all. As yet, he'd heard nothing.

The phone rang at a quarter past nine. Stanley snatched it up, hoping it was a call from the coroner's office. It wasn't. The strident tones of Brenda Cecil came down the line, bat-tering his eardrums. He had barely had the chance to say hello before she launched her attack.

'What's going on with the girl, Mr Parrish? I need to know. My Tony's been arrested again and . . . Well, she can't stay here now. To be honest, I've had enough. I really have. It's not right. A decision needs to be made. Does Mr Fury want her or not?'

'I'm still looking into it, Mrs Cecil.'

'You've had months to look into it. Tell Mr Fury he's got twenty-four hours to make up his mind. Yes or no. After that I'm ringing the Social.'

'There's absolutely no proof that Lolly is the missing child. The blood tests were inconclusive and—'

'I don't care if she is or she ain't. She's not staying here no more and that's final.'

Stanley gave a sigh. 'He's not going to take on a child that isn't his.'

'Fine,' she said. 'She'll have to go into care. There's nothing else for it.'

'I don't understand the rush. Surely you can wait a few more—'

'It ain't working out, Mr Parrish. That's the beginning and end of it. You talk to the Furys and let me know.'

And with that she hung up.

Stanley put the phone down and immediately picked it up again. He tried the number in Kent but got no reply. Eventually he got hold of Mal at the store in Hatton Garden. He filled him in on the latest developments and explained the situation as regards Brenda Cecil.

'Is she serious?' Mal asked. 'Or is she just trying to put the pressure on?'

'Oh, I think she's serious. I don't know exactly what's been going down, but from the sound of it Lolly has certainly outstayed her welcome.'

'So what next?'

'That's up to you. There's increasing evidence that Lolly isn't Angela's child, but that's about as far as it goes.'

There was a long silence at the other end of the line, so long in fact that Stanley wondered if they'd been disconnected.

'Mal? Are you still there?'

'Yes. I was just thinking.'

'I suppose we'll have to let things take their course. If anything changes in the future, you can always—'

'Would you be able to pick her up this afternoon, after school? Bring her over to the house. I'll be home by four.'

Stanley was startled by the suggestion. 'What?'

'Yes, let's do that. I can't see any point in messing about. Maybe you could give that Cecil woman a call and let her know the arrangements.'

'You do realise it's highly unlikely that Lolly is your daughter?'

'I *know* she's not my daughter. But she's got nowhere to go, has she? Surely living with us is preferable to going into care.'

'You haven't even met her.'

'Oh, I'm sure we'll get along.'

'But what about the Social?' Stanley asked. 'I can't just truck up and whisk the girl away. There are formalities to go through: meetings, interviews, paperwork. You haven't even got a connection to Lolly. You just said you're sure she's not yours so—'

Mal interrupted him with a snort. 'Don't worry about all that. I'll make a few calls, clear the way. I don't see how anyone could object to us giving the kid a decent home.'

'What about Esther?'

'What about her?

'Don't you want to discuss it with her first? It's a big decision, one that's going to affect her too.'

'It won't affect her that much,' Mal said. 'She's in

Cornwall until the weekend. They've just started filming. Did I tell you she was working again?'

'No, I didn't realise. But—'

'So she won't even be here. Anyway, she'll see it the same way I do once I've explained the situation.'

Stanley wasn't quite so sure of that. From what he knew about Esther, she wouldn't take kindly to Mal making a unilateral decision over something so important. And he doubted there would be much enthusiasm from her either at the prospect of sharing her home with an unrelated – and slightly odd – kid from the East End. 'Maybe you want to think about it for a while.'

'What's there to think about? Nothing's going to change in a day or a week. The girl's still going to need a home, isn't she?'

Stanley could tell he'd made up his mind and nothing was going to change it. 'All right,' he said. 'If that's what you've decided.'

'It is.' Mal paused and then added, 'I suppose the Cecil woman's going to want some money.'

'You can't pay her the reward. Lolly isn't yours.'

'No, but we don't want her getting difficult. It's better to keep her on side. Let's suggest a contribution towards the girl's bed and board for the time she's spent there, something modest but tempting. I'll leave it up to you to decide. Use your judgement.'

'Look, are you absolutely sure about this? About taking on Lolly, I mean.'

'Yes, I'm sure. You can't live in the past for ever. I want

to move on, do something positive. If you think that's a problem then—'

'No, of course not,' Stanley said quickly. 'I understand. I'll head over there right now and have a word.'

'Any trouble, just give me a ring.'

'I will.' Stanley said goodbye and hung up the phone. He was not entirely comfortable with Mal's decision and still worried about how Esther would react. It didn't feel right putting Lolly into a potential war zone, but then it didn't feel right letting her go into care either. Once she was in the system, she'd probably be stuck there until she was eighteen.

Stanley closed the Fury file and slipped it into a drawer. He wondered if the truth about Kay would ever come out. As the thought entered his mind, he had one of those eerie sensations as if someone had just walked over his grave. He took a quick intake of breath, the cold washing over him. Then he rose to his feet, put on his overcoat and headed for Kellston.

27

When Lolly got home from school it was to find Stanley Parrish sitting in the kitchen with Brenda. She had spent the whole day debating whether to come back at all – the atmosphere in the house was grim – but in the end she'd felt too exhausted (and too afraid of Brenda's wrath) to cope with the consequences of running away. Also, with Tony banged up, she didn't have to worry about any murderous midnight visits.

'Hello, Lolly,' he said. 'How are you? It's nice to see you again.'

'Hi.'

'I have some news.'

Lolly, recalling their last conversation, felt her spirits rise. Maybe something good had finally happened. 'Have you found my family, then?'

'Not exactly.'

Her face dropped. 'Oh.'

'The next best thing, though,' Brenda said with a forced kind of cheeriness. 'Mr Parrish has found a nice new home for you in Kent. You'll like it there. Lots of fresh air and green fields; you can run around to your heart's content.'

Lolly's eyes widened. She felt like an unwanted dog being shipped off to the countryside, but didn't raise any objections. In fact, she'd have been perfectly happy to move into a kennel if it meant living under a different roof to the Cecils.

'Okay,' she said.

Stanley appeared surprised by the easy acceptance of her fate. 'They're called Mal and Esther Fury. I've mentioned Mal before. Perhaps you remember? I'm sure you must have lots of questions. If there's anything you'd like to ask, just go ahead.'

Lolly was still thinking about this when Brenda, who was clearly eager to get rid of her as soon as possible, glanced at the clock and said, 'Yes, well, there'll be plenty of time for that on the way there. I've packed a bag so everything's ready. There's no point in dragging it out, is there? Best to get it over and done with.'

'I need the loo,' Lolly said.

'Well go on then, but be smart about it.'

Lolly hurried off, wanting to make sure that Brenda hadn't forgotten anything. As she passed the pawnbroker's, she could see Freddy serving a customer. He glanced over his shoulder, gave her a hard look and turned his back on her again. Upstairs, she took her money from the mattress – she'd hidden it again after yesterday's nightmare – and quickly checked the drawers, including the bedside table where she usually kept the book of fairy stories. All empty. She didn't need to worry about the mother-of-pearl button; she always kept that in her pocket.

In the bathroom, she slipped the five notes down the side of her sock. Everything was happening so fast, she wasn't sure what to feel or think. She'd heard of Kent – that was where they grew the hops – but wasn't sure how far it was from London. She was nervous at leaving the East End, but glad of it too. The only place she wanted to be at the moment was as far away from Tony Cecil as possible.

Lolly had a pee before she went downstairs again. By now Stanley and Brenda were both on their feet and hovering by the back door. Stanley was holding a battered, brown suitcase she had never seen before. This, apparently, contained all her worldly possessions.

'Ready then?' Brenda asked curtly.

Lolly gave a nod.

There were, unsurprisingly, no tender farewells or goodbye kisses, not even a friendly pat on the arm. Brenda bundled them out of the kitchen as if she couldn't wait to see the back of them both. Her parting words were addressed only to Stanley.

'You'd better make sure the law knows about the change of address, case they want to talk to her about that Amy business again.'

'I will,' he said.

'And you'll be in touch about that other matter we discussed?'

'There'll be a cheque in the post.'

As they were walking along the alley, it occurred to Lolly that Stanley Parrish might not be a private detective at all. What if he was one of those men teachers were always warning them about? The sort you were not supposed to take sweets from. But then he hadn't offered her any sweets so she supposed he must be okay.

'I'm sorry,' he said. 'This must all feel a bit sudden. Try not to worry too much. Mal and Esther will take good care of you.'

The car was parked on the high street, a few yards away from the pawnbroker's. While Lolly got in, Stanley put the suitcase in the boot. As she sat and waited, her gaze travelled over the seats and the dashboard. The interior, although not plush, had a reassuring tidiness about it. The last occasion she'd been in a car was for her mother's funeral. It felt like a long time ago although she knew it wasn't.

Stanley sat down beside her. 'Ready?'

'What if they don't like me?'

'Why wouldn't they?'

But Lolly knew her track record was none too great on that score. She gave a shrug. 'Will I have to come back?'

Stanley shook his head. 'No one's going to make you do anything you don't want to do.'

Lolly hoped he was right, but she didn't have much trust in adults and what they said. She leaned forward a little as the car drew away from the kerb, catching some last-minute impressions of the place she'd called home. It was almost dark now and the street lamps were on. She turned around to catch a final glimpse of the three tall towers. Her only regret was that she hadn't had the chance to say goodbye to Jude.

'How far is it?' she asked.

'About an hour, depending on the traffic. Just over, probably. The house is in a village called West Henby. You'll like it.' He cleared his throat, glanced at her and smiled. 'It might seem a bit quiet after the city, but it's a nice enough place.'

Lolly fidgeted in her seat. She had a lot of questions running through her head and wasn't sure which one to ask next. Eventually she settled on what seemed to be the most obvious. 'Why do they want me to live with them? I mean, I'm not family or anything.'

'Well, they haven't got any kids of their own, so ...' He hesitated as if not quite sure what to say next. 'They heard you'd been having some problems here and thought you might be happier with them.'

Lolly sensed there was more to it, something he wasn't telling her. 'But they don't even know me.'

'They know *about* you,' he said.

Lolly didn't like the sound of that. What had they been told? Brenda could have said all sorts, painting a picture of her that was a thousand miles from the truth. The Furys might have judged her before they'd even met, before she'd had the chance to put her side of things. 'It isn't true about Tony,' she blurted out.

'What isn't?'

'The Cecils think I grassed him up, but I didn't. I had

no idea the cops were going to be in the alley. They're all blaming me for something I didn't do.'

'Brenda mentioned he'd been arrested. Is it to do with the Amy Wiltshire case? He was her boyfriend, wasn't he?'

Lolly could have told a story about that – a tale of false alibis and deceit – but, as yet, she didn't trust him well enough for those sorts of confidences. 'Kind of.'

Stanley gave her a curious look as if he was waiting for her to say more. 'He was kind of her boyfriend?'

'No, I meant it's kind of to do with the Amy case. In a way. Sort of.'

'It sounds complicated.'

Lolly stared out through the windscreen. The wipers went back and forth, back and forth, making a small squeaky sound every time they flipped from left to right. 'It wasn't me, though. I swear. I never said a word.' She felt a sudden surge of anger at what Tony had done. 'He did it, though. He beat up Joseph. I heard him tell FJ.'

Stanley's face swivelled round to look at her again. 'And who's Joseph?'

'He lives on the Mansfield. And he's not a bad person. He didn't kill Amy. I know it for a fact.'

'For a fact, huh?'

Lolly knew she'd said too much and quickly glanced away. She could feel her cheeks starting to burn. 'He wouldn't do a thing like that,' she mumbled.

'You don't have to worry about any of that now. You can leave it for the police to sort out.'

Lolly's face twisted. She didn't have much faith in the

police. And she knew how rumours spread on the Mansfield. Until Amy's killer was found, Tony's accusations about Joseph would stick. No smoke without fire, they'd say. Which meant that someone else might have a go at him as soon as he got out of hospital.

'Are you all right' Stanley asked. 'It sounds like you've had a lot to deal with recently.'

'I'm okay.' She gave him a sideways glance. 'But ... '

'There's always a but,' he said. 'What's on your mind?'

Lolly didn't answer straight away. She thought about it for a while before she asked, 'How do you ever know whether you've done the right thing or not? I mean, what if ... I don't know, what if helping one person means hurting someone else?'

Stanley took his left hand off the wheel and laid it on his stomach. 'You rely on what your gut tells you.'

But Lolly's guts weren't telling her anything other than the fact she hadn't eaten since lunch. She had loyalty to Jude and guilt over Joseph. 'What if it's fifty-fifty?'

'That certainly complicates things. I guess you have to weigh up the good against the bad and take it from there.'

She went back to staring at the wipers, aware that her love for Jude, whether right or wrong, was absolute. He was the only real friend she'd ever had. But she felt sick at how she'd turned her back on Joseph. She could still tell the police she'd seen him, been talking to him, at the time of Amy's murder, but she knew she wouldn't. She had made a choice and she would stick with it.

'Anything I can help with?' Stanley asked.

Lolly shook her head. 'I don't think so.' And then, before he could probe any further she said, 'So what are they like, the Furys? I don't know anything about them.'

Stanley sneaked a few quick glances at Lolly as they drove through the dimness of the Blackwall Tunnel. It was hard to know what she was thinking. She was a curious kid, a child who had seen and experienced too much for her years. Although she had asked about Mal and Esther, he had not sensed any particular interest in the information he'd been providing for the past fifteen minutes. In fact, he'd rather wondered if she was listening at all. Her thoughts appeared to be somewhere else, perhaps back in Kellston with the troubles she'd had there.

For his part, he was still anxious about removing the child and taking her to Kent. What if she was rejected again? Mal wasn't a problem, but he knew what Esther could be like. A prize bitch when she put her mind to it – and even when she didn't. The woman wouldn't take kindly to having a cuckoo in the nest. It would be disastrous, he thought, if Lolly was thrown out of yet another potential home. He considered warning her about Esther – that she could be difficult – but didn't want to colour her opinion before the two of them had even met.

It had surprised him to discover Esther was working again. She had not made a film since Kay's disappearance thirteen years ago. He had no idea whether this resumption of her career would be a good or bad thing for the Fury marriage. From what he'd observed, their relationship was already a volatile one. Add Lolly into the mix and there was no saying what might happen.

Stanley was also worried about his investigation into Angela Bruce. It was starting to look as if she might not be Lolly's mother after all. How would the kid cope with news like that? She seemed the resilient type but maybe that was all show, a way of coping with the endless grief that had been thrown in her direction. It seemed a particular act of cruelty to deprive her of the one certainty she had in her life.

As they came out at the other end of the tunnel, he tapped his fingers against the wheel. 'So you still don't recall your mum ever mentioning Mal or Esther?'

'No,' Lolly replied. 'Did she know them?'

'I don't think so. I'm not sure.' He was about to add that Angela might have read about them in the papers but decided against it. It might lead to questions about what had happened to Kay. And that, he decided, was up to Mal to explain.

By the time they reached the narrow roads that led to West Henby, it was pitch black. The only light came from the two strong beams of the car's headlamps. All that could be seen either side were the hedgerows and the dark silhouettes of trees.

'What do people do here?' Lolly asked.

Stanley grinned. 'Good question. I'm a city boy myself, but I'm sure there are ways of keeping occupied.' Personally, he wasn't too keen on the country, preferring the hustle and bustle of the capital. 'You'll be okay. You'll soon make new friends.'

Lolly said nothing. She bowed her head, her long hair falling across her face.

Stanley realised in that moment that Lolly Bruce was the type of kid who probably didn't have many friends, if any at all. She'd have always been the one who was marked out as being different, the one who had a crazy mother, the one who was never as clean as she ought to be, the one with the hungry eyes. He knew what it was to be different, to not fit in. His reasons were not the same as hers, but he understood the feeling of isolation.

'If you ever want a chat, just pick up the phone,' he said. 'I'll leave you my number. You can call any time.'

Lolly gave him a quick sideways glance, but didn't reply.

'If you need anything or . . . well, you know what I mean.' He thought, on reflection, that she probably had no idea what he meant. He wasn't even sure if *he* knew what he meant. He just didn't want her to feel she was entirely on her own.

It was a few more minutes, minutes spent in silence, before they came to the tall wrought-iron gates set into a high brick wall. 'Here we are,' he said. 'This is it.' Stanley pulled up, stretched his arm out of the window and pressed the buzzer. The gates immediately swung open. He drove through and they set off along the approach to the house, a long curving driveway illuminated by tiny white lights glittering in the darkness. As they drew closer, he could see Lolly's body tense.

'Don't worry,' he said. 'Everything will be fine.'

Stanley tried to sound confident and reassuring. He glanced up at the starless sky, hoping he wasn't wrong, hoping this wasn't all a dreadful mistake.

28

Lolly gazed at the house, awed by the size of it. She blinked in astonishment. It was lit up like a Christmas tree, bright and white and sparkling. They got out of the car and Stanley went to the boot to get her suitcase. As she stood waiting, the front door opened and a tall, fair-haired man bounded down the flight of shallow stone steps to greet them.

'Stanley,' he said. 'Good to see you. And you must be Lolly. Welcome! Welcome! I'm so glad you could come. I'm Mal Fury. Call me Mal. How do you do?'

Lolly took the proffered hand and shook it. His fingers were warm and smooth. 'I'm good,' she said. Then, remembering her manners quickly added, 'Thank you.'

'Excellent. Now let's get in from the cold before we all freeze to death.'

As Lolly walked up the steps, everything felt faintly dreamlike. And if she'd been impressed by the outside of the house, the inside was something else entirely. In the grand hallway there was a marble floor and big paintings hanging on the walls. Rooms ran off to the left and right and straight ahead was a wide staircase leading up to the next floor.

'It will all feel strange at first,' Mal said, 'but you'll get used to it. And to us, of course. At least, I hope so. We're not too bad when you get to know us. I'm afraid Esther's away until the weekend but she can't wait to meet you.'

Lolly might have been mistaken but she thought she saw Stanley throw Mal Fury a querying look. Her attention, however, was diverted by the appearance of a thin-faced, middle-aged woman wearing a dark brown woollen dress and a stern expression.

'Ah, Mrs Gough,' Mal said. 'I'd like to introduce you to Lolly, the latest member of our household. Lolly, this is Mrs Gough, our splendid housekeeper. God knows what we'd do without her. She'll show you up to your room. I'm sure you want to get unpacked and settled in. And then we'll have some supper. You must be starving by now.' He turned to Stanley. 'You'll join us, won't you? Before you set off for home again.'

'Of course. I'd be glad to.'

Mrs Gough gave a nod, took the suitcase from Stanley and set off up the stairs. 'We've put you in the Peacock Room,' she said. 'You should be comfortable. There's an en suite and a view of the garden.'

'Ta,' Lolly said, even though she didn't know what an en suite was. Although the stairs were easily wide enough for four or five people to walk abreast, she stayed behind the housekeeper, unsure of her place in this new world she'd entered.

In the hallway, Stanley asked Mal, 'So you've talked to Esther?'

'Of course.'

'And what did she say?'

There was a short hesitation before Mal replied softly, 'Oh, give her time. She'll get used to the idea.'

Mrs Gough turned left at the top of the stairs and walked briskly along the landing. She stopped at the third door, pushed it open and stood aside for Lolly to enter. 'Here we are.'

Lolly's eyes almost popped out of her head. It was the biggest bedroom she'd ever seen, with a four-poster bed, a rose pink carpet and heavy velvet curtains. The walls were papered with a design of peacocks, their tails fanned out to reveal pretty shades of turquoise and green. There was even a fireplace with a small pile of logs waiting to be lit.

Mrs Gough laid the suitcase on the bed and opened it. She stared at the contents with a tight-lipped look of disapproval. 'Is this it?'

Lolly nodded. 'Yes.'

'You haven't got much.'

Lolly smiled faintly, not sure what to say. She wasn't sure what to do either as Mrs Gough began taking out the items and placing them in the wardrobe and drawers. She felt ill at ease, awkward in her plush surroundings. Her fingers closed around the mother-of-pearl button in her pocket, something safe and reassuring, something from the past, something to hold on to in this strange new place.

'I'll make a list. Theresa can take you to the shops tomorrow.'

It was only when Mrs Gough lifted the volume of fairy tales from the case that Lolly stepped forward. She held out a hand for the book, relieved to see that Brenda had packed it. 'I'll sort that out.'

The housekeeper glanced at the title before passing it over. 'Bit old for fairy tales, aren't you?'

Lolly backed away, holding the book to her chest. 'My mum gave it to me.' Because she wasn't looking where she was going, she banged into the bedside table and almost knocked over the lamp. It rocked back and forth, on the verge of falling, before she quickly reached out to save it.

'Be careful!'

'Sorry.'

Mrs Gough raised her eyebrows, clearly unimpressed by Lolly's clumsiness. 'You'd better take off your coat if you're planning on staying.' She snapped shut the lid of the case and placed it in the bottom of the wardrobe. 'Right, that's done. I'll leave you to get settled in. Supper will be in twenty minutes, six o'clock sharp. The dining room is at the end of the hallway, last door on your right. Don't be late.' She glanced around the room, sighed and looked back at Lolly. 'And try not to break anything.'

After she'd gone, Lolly stayed where she was for a moment, taking it all in. Then she put down the book and began to explore. The first thing she discovered was the bathroom, gleaming white as if it had never been used. She went in and ran her fingers along the cool porcelain of the basin and the shiny metal taps. There were soft white towels, three in all, neatly folded on a wicker laundry basket. A patterned rug lay in front of the bath. She had to stand on tiptoe to see her face in the mirror, and didn't much like what she saw. She pulled her fingers through her tangled hair and rubbed away a mark at the side of her mouth.

Lolly returned to the bedroom and stared at the peacocks. There must have been over a hundred of them, scattered across the walls. It wasn't long, however, before her gaze was drawn back to the bed with its cream and gold bedspread, and gold drapes fastened in the middle to each of the posts. She sat down on the edge of the mattress and bounced a few times. She supposed she should be pleased, but all she felt was a growing sense of bemusement. What was she doing here? Stanley's explanation didn't really cut it. There had to be something more, something she didn't yet understand.

She stood up, crossed the room, pulled back the curtains and pressed her nose against the glass. It was too dark to see anything much. Rain splattered against the window. She opened it and leaned out. The air smelled different to how it was in London: colder, crisper, stranger. She sniffed at it like some small nocturnal animal trying to get its bearings.

After a while she closed the window and looked around again. There was a bamboo chair with a turquoise cushion, and a dressing table with brush and comb and clothes brush. On the mantelpiece were a number of ornaments she didn't dare touch, including a pair of china ballerinas. There was a clock too. She realised with a start that the hands read five to six. She'd better hurry if she wasn't going to be late for supper.

Lolly made her way down to the hallway and along the corridor to the dining room. She could hear voices as she approached the open door.

'You made the calls then?' Stanley asked. 'You didn't have any problems?'

'Everything's fine. We're giving her a home, aren't we?'

'It's not always that straightforward.'

'Well, that depends on who you know.'

There was a pause in the conversation as Lolly stepped into the room. Then Mal said, 'Ah, here she is. Come in, come in. Supper awaits. Mrs Docherty has done us proud with one of her excellent beef stews. I hope you like stew, Lolly?'

Lolly, who had never had the luxury of being fussy about food, nodded as she advanced towards the large dining table. 'Yes, I like everything.'

'Good. That's what I want to hear. A woman after my own heart.' Mal waved a hand towards the empty seat beside him. 'Sit down and make yourself comfortable.'

Lolly did as she was told. She was worried that it was all going to be weird and awkward – she still didn't have a clue what she was doing here – but Mal tried to put her at ease.

'I don't like new places,' he said. 'So I understand if this all feels odd. But I hope you'll be happy in our home. *Your* home if you want it to be. You strike me as the kind of person who's prepared to give it a go and that's all we ask. I know we're not family, but that's not always the most important thing. We're all friends here and that's what really matters.'

Lolly was instantly reminded of Joseph and what he'd said to her in the tunnel. *They say blood's thicker than water but it ain't always true. Sometimes you've got to start from scratch, make your own family.* She didn't know why the words had stuck in her head but they had. Maybe it was a sign, something she should take note of, but no sooner had the thought crossed her mind than a bowl of stew was placed in front of her and all she could think about was eating.

The woman who served the food was small and wide with a large bosom. 'I hope you've got a good appetite, love. There's plenty more where that came from.'

'Ta,' Lolly said.

'And feel free to come down to the kitchen any time. I'm always glad of the company.'

'Mrs Docherty makes the best cakes in the world,' Mal said.

'Oh, get away with you. When was the last time you ate one of my cakes?'

Mal patted his stomach and smiled. 'I've got a middle-age spread to worry about. Lolly doesn't need to be concerned about her waistline.'

Mrs Docherty laughed and left the room. While Lolly dug into the most delicious stew she'd ever tasted, Mal and Stanley kept up a steady flow of conversation. Occasionally, one or other of them would ask her a question, but on the whole she was left to get on with her meal. It was only when Stanley said, 'You'll have to find a school for her. Have you thought of anywhere?' that she stopped eating and looked from one to the other.

'Do you like school, Lolly?' Mal asked.

'Not much,' she replied honestly. 'I'm no good at anything.'

Mal smiled. 'Everyone's good at something. You just haven't found out what it is yet. What do you like doing?'

Lolly frowned as she thought about it. Her only happy memories were of being with her mum – and those days had gone for ever – or sitting with Jude on the green corduroy sofa. 'Films,' she said eventually. 'I like watching old films.'

'Ah, well that's a turn up. Did you know Esther's an actress? In fact, she's filming right now in Cornwall.'

'What's it called?'

'*Jamaica Inn*. It's based on a novel by Daphne du Maurier. Have you read it?'

Lolly shook her head. 'What's it about?'

'Oh, shipwreckers and smugglers and women in peril. We may have a copy somewhere. I'll see if I can dig it out. Esther's only got a small part, but I'm sure it will lead to greater things. It's been a while since she last worked.'

'Why's that?'

There was a short, uneasy silence. Mal seemed on the verge of saying something, but then changed his mind. Another few seconds ticked by. Stanley cleared his throat. Lolly wished she hadn't asked.

'It's a long story,' Mal said. 'I'll save it for another day.'

Stanley rose to his feet with what sounded like a sigh of relief. 'Thank you for supper, but I'd better make a move. I don't want to get back to London too late.'

'You'll call?' Mal asked. 'If you get any news?'

'Of course.'

Lolly wondered what the news might be about, but kept her curiosity to herself. The three of them walked to the front door together where Stanley said goodbye and trotted down the steps towards his car. He was just about to get in when she realised she couldn't let him go without asking something. Quickly she launched herself down the steps after him.

'Mr Parrish! Wait!'

He turned, looking startled, as if she might be about to beg him to take her with him. 'What is it? Are you all right?'

'Yes, but could you ... could you do me a favour?'

'If I can.'

'Could you find out how Joseph is? You know, the guy I told you about? Joseph Clayton. Could you ring the hospital? I just want to know if he's okay.'

Stanley nodded. 'Joseph Clayton. I'll see what I can do.'

'Thanks.'

'You take care,' Stanley said. 'Oh, I almost forgot.' He took out his wallet, removed a small white business card and passed it over to her. 'My number. You can call me any time. Leave a message if I'm not there and I'll ring you back.'

Lolly shoved the card into her pocket and ran back up the steps where she stood with Mal and waved as the car began its journey down the drive. She watched until the tail-lights disappeared from view. She had a curious feeling in the pit of her stomach, as though she was watching her last link to Kellston slip away for ever.

'Will he come back?' she asked.

'Of course. Why wouldn't he?'

Lolly shrugged, knowing that sometimes people went away for good.

'It's cold out here,' Mal said. 'Let's go in.'

But still they stood for a while longer, side by side, gazing silently into the darkness.

29

When Lolly woke the next morning it was to the vision of a hundred peacocks. She had left the curtains partly open and light slid through the gap. While she gazed at the birds, she reviewed her situation, trying to decide how she felt. Relief was at the top of the list – there would be no Cecils to face this morning – but also a sense of trepidation. Everything was new and weird and different. From past experience, she knew how hard it could be to fit in, to be accepted.

She got out of bed and padded over to the window. The view across the garden took her breath away. There were wide lawns and winding paths, trees, shrubs and hedges, and straight ahead the silvery expanse of a lake. No cars or buses, no sounds of traffic at all. Even the spitting rain couldn't detract from the beauty of the scene spread out before her.

Last night, Mal had provided a guided tour of the house, each room – or so it seemed – grander than the last. Her eyes had grown large as her feet had sunk into the deep-pile carpets.

She had never seen such stylish furniture before, or so many statues and paintings. There was even a library full of books. What she had noticed most, however, were the clocks. They were everywhere, all shapes and sizes, from tall plain grandfathers to smaller, fancier ones flanked by golden cherubs.

'My father was a clockmaker,' Mal had explained. 'Or an horologist if you want the technical term.'

'Did he make all these?'

'Only some of them. He was a collector. He liked beautiful things.'

'Do you make clocks too?'

'No, I'm not smart enough for that. And I haven't got the patience. I just sell them. Although it's more watches than clocks these days. Do you have a watch?'

Lolly had shaken her head, glancing at her bare wrist as if one might have suddenly materialised while they were walking round the house.

'We'll have to get you one. I'll take you to the store and you can choose your own.'

Lolly left the window and looked over at the clock in her own bedroom. It was five past eight. Usually, at this time, she'd be getting ready for school but today she didn't have to face that particular horror. No lessons, no maths or French. It was like being on holiday, although she wasn't quite sure what she was going to do with herself.

She went to the bathroom, had a wash and brushed her teeth. She thought about Mal Fury as she got dressed. He was an easy sort of person to be with, not like some adults, but she was still wary of him. People weren't always what they seemed to be. Her instincts told her she could trust him, but she'd reserve judgement until she got to know him better.

Lolly went downstairs and along the hall to the room where they'd eaten supper last night. The table was empty. She pushed her hands into the pockets of her jeans and stared at it, not sure what to do next. A voice behind her made her jump.

'If it's breakfast you're after, you'll have to go to the kitchen.'

Lolly spun round to find Mrs Gough standing by the door. 'Oh, right, okay.'

'Mrs Docherty will fix you up with something. It's downstairs. Do you know where the stairs are?'

'Yes,' Lolly said, remembering the way from the tour Mal had given her.

'And don't forget that Theresa's coming at ten. She'll meet you in the hallway. Make sure you've got your coat on.'

'Okay.'

Mrs Gough gave another of her disapproving looks before quickly turning and heading off towards whatever urgent business needed her attention next. Lolly wasn't upset or even offended by the woman's attitude. A spot of mild disapproval was nothing compared to the outright hostility of some people. She was thinking especially of the Cecil boys, and was glad she was finally free of them both.

Downstairs, the kitchen had a big wooden table and numerous pots and pans hanging from hooks on the wall.

Mrs Docherty greeted her with a smile. 'Hello, love. Did you sleep well?'

'Yes, ta.'

'Now, what can I get you for breakfast? You must be hungry. Do you like eggs?'

Lolly nodded.

'Boiled, poached or scrambled?'

'Scrambled, please.'

'That's fine. And I'll do a few rashers of streaky to go with it. You can manage a bit of bacon, can't you?'

'I think so.'

'Good. You sit yourself down and I'll get it sorted. Won't take me long. I've got to say it's nice to have some young blood in the house. And with Mrs Fury back at work, it's all change for the better. Perhaps we'll see some life around the place again.'

Lolly watched as Mrs Docherty put a pan on the stove and heated up some oil. 'Is she a famous actress?'

'Well, she was when she was young. Not that she's old or anything now – of course she isn't – but I mean when she was in her late teens and early twenties. She won an Oscar, you know. Best Actress. She was Esther Gray back then. It was before she was married and there was all that awful business with ... ' Mrs Docherty paused and gave a sigh. 'Still, perhaps things are looking up for her again. I hope so.'

Lolly wanted to know what the 'awful business' was, but didn't like to ask. Instead she said, 'What was the film called?'

'Oh, it had a strange name – *Dark Places*. Not very cheerful, is it? But everyone said she was wonderful. A real star. Which is something to be proud of, considering she was so young and all at the time.'

Lolly tried to remember if she had ever seen the title on Jude's shelves, but didn't think she had. Thinking of Jude made her sad. She felt a long way away from Kellston and wondered if she'd ever get the chance to see him again. 'What was it about? The film, I mean.'

'I don't recall all the ins and out. It's years since I saw it now.'

The smell of frying bacon made Lolly's mouth water. She heard the spit and crackle as Mrs Docherty flipped the slices over in the pan. For all her sadness, there was something comforting about being down here in the basement; it felt warm and safe. She yawned even though she wasn't tired.

'You need some fresh air. What are your plans for today, then?'

'I'm supposed to meet someone called Theresa at ten. Mrs Gough says she's going to take me shopping.'

Mrs Docherty glanced over her shoulder as she stirred the scrambled eggs. 'You'll like Theresa. She's from the village, a nice girl, although her mouth tends to run away with her at times. I wouldn't believe everything she tells you.'

'What sort of things?'

Mrs Docherty laughed as she served up the food. 'You ask a lot of questions, don't you? Here, get this down you. It'll set you up for the day.'

While Lolly ate, Mrs Docherty poured herself a mug of tea, spooned in three sugars and sat down at the table. 'It makes a change to see someone with an appetite. Half of what I make in this house goes to waste. Mrs Fury hardly eats a thing, and he's more often out than in. Most times, when he gets back from work, he only wants a sandwich.'

'It's very nice,' Lolly said between mouthfuls.

'Maybe things will buck up now you're here. The place has been too quiet for too long.' Mrs Docherty took a sip of tea and gazed at Lolly over the rim of the mug. 'I was sorry to hear about your mum, love. You must miss her.'

Lolly stopped eating for a second, her fork poised mid-air. She couldn't count the number of ways she missed her mother, but didn't know how to put it into words. 'Yes,' she said eventually. 'I do.'

'Course you do. And nothing's quite the same as your own kin, but you've got friends here. Any time you fancy a chat, you just come on down. There's never a need to be lonely.'

'Okay.'

'I mean it. You'd be doing me a favour. I could do with a bit of company myself.'

Lolly still had an hour to spare after breakfast. She thanked Mrs Docherty again, ran upstairs to get her coat and then descended to the ground floor where she went through the rear doors into the garden. With time to kill, she may as well explore the grounds.

Outside, the air was crisp with a cold snappy wind. She jogged down the wide flight of steps. At the bottom were two big terracotta pots, one either side, like guards to the house. They were filled with ivy and winter pansies and some other plants she didn't know the names of.

Lolly pushed her hands into her pockets and set off along the path that led towards the lake. She passed an abandoned tennis court on the way, the net removed, weeds pushing up through the concrete. When she stopped and listened she could hear nothing apart from the wind running through the trees. As she drew closer to the water, the ground became soft and pulpy underfoot. She danced around the puddles, relishing her freedom from school. It wouldn't last for ever so she might as well make the most of it.

Eventually she came to another smaller path that skirted the lake. Did it go all the way round? It was impossible to tell. The weeping willows leaned over, obscuring her view. She knew that was their name because her mum had said so when they'd seen one in a park. It had stuck in her head because it was so sad.

'Why are they called that?'

'Because they come from China and they're missing home.'

Lolly wasn't sure if this was true – her mother hadn't always been the most reliable source of information – but she wanted to believe it. She gazed at the long, trailing branches, their tips skimming the water. She was missing home too. A lump formed in her throat but she swallowed it back down. It wasn't good to think about the past too much.

Crouching on the bank, she dipped her fingers into the cold water and quickly pulled them out again. Freezing. She sucked in a breath and wiped her hand on her jeans, trying to get it dry. The wind caught the surface of the lake, creating choppy waves that rolled and ran and eventually disappeared to nothing. By her feet were large clumps of reed-like things with dark brown velvety heads.

Lolly straightened up and walked a short distance along the path. She didn't want to go too far in case she got back late to the house. Apart from the wind, there was no other sound. It felt odd, kind of wrong, to be in a place without people; she was used to the busy streets of London, to the roar of traffic and the constant hum of life.

After a few metres, she stopped again and gazed out across the water. It was then, as her eyes scanned the horizon, that she got a strange prickling sensation on the back of her neck. She whirled around but there was no one there.

'Hello?'

Nothing.

She peered into the bushes and up the gentle slope. Had she heard a sound too, like the snapping of twigs? It was just an animal perhaps, a fox or a . . . Well, she didn't know what other animals there were in the country apart from cows and sheep and pigs. She stamped her feet on the ground in the hope that whatever it was would go away, but still the feeling persisted, like it had when she'd been in the empty flat at Haslow House.

Lolly scratched her neck, trying to scrape off the sensation. She didn't like the feeling; there was something bad about it, something threatening. A ripple of fear ran through her. She hunched her shoulders and shuddered. Here, in this quiet place, anything could happen and no one would be any the wiser. You could scream and scream and nobody would hear.

It was this thought that finally propelled her into action. She turned tail and fled, running as fast as her legs would carry her . . . and didn't slow down until the house was in sight again.

30

By the time Lolly reached the rear door, she was windswept and breathless, her cheeks red from running and her long brown hair hanging in tangles round her face. As she hurried through the house she caught sight of her reflection in one of the mirrors and grimaced. Waiting in the hall was a teenage girl, maybe seventeen or eighteen, leaning against the banisters and examining her nails. Lolly only had time for a few fleeting impressions – a ponytail, pale skin and freckles – before the visitor looked up and smiled.

'Are you Lolly?'

Lolly nodded. 'Yeah, that's me.'

'Hi, I'm Theresa.'

Although Lolly wasn't late – it was only five to ten – Mrs Gough emerged from one of the reception rooms glancing at her watch in a pointed fashion. 'Ah, you're here. I was wondering where you'd got to.'

'I was in the garden,' Lolly said.

'I can see.' Mrs Gough stared hard at the floor where Lolly had walked in a trail of mud. 'Perhaps you could think about wiping your feet next time.'

Lolly looked down. 'Oh, sorry.'

'Sorry doesn't keep the floors clean and polished. Just be more careful in future.'

Theresa caught Lolly's eye and grinned.

Mrs Gough turned on the girl, frowning. 'And what are you smirking at? It's no laughing matter, I can tell you.'

'I was just being friendly, Mrs Gough. No harm in that, is there? Now, have you got that shopping list only I have to be home by one.'

Lolly was surprised and impressed by the way Theresa talked to the housekeeper. She didn't seem to be intimidated by her at all.

Mrs Gough walked over to the hall table, muttering under her breath, and returned with a white envelope which she handed over to Theresa. 'There's a list in here, and money. I'll need a receipt so make sure you don't lose it.'

'I won't.'

'And use some common sense. We don't want the child looking like a hippy.'

Theresa, who was wearing flared jeans, boots and an Afghan coat, laughed as she put the envelope in her suede bag. 'Leave it to me, Mrs Gough. I'll make sure she gets everything she needs.' She looked over at Lolly. 'Come on, then. Let's get a shuffle on.'

The two girls left the house together and started walking down the drive. Theresa gave her a nudge with her elbow.

273

'You all right, love? You shouldn't let her boss you about. She's no better than anyone else. Just the hired help, that's all – although to listen to her sometimes you'd think she owned the bleedin' house.'

Lolly gave the older girl a sideways glance. 'I only got here yesterday,' she said, hoping this might pass as a reasonable excuse.

'Well, don't let her walk all over you. You've got to stand up to people like that or they'll just push you around.'

Lolly, who viewed being pushed around as a natural state of affairs, raised her eyebrows a fraction. Her usual survival tactic was to try and stay under the radar, to be as invisible as possible. 'I don't think she likes me.'

Theresa gave a snort. 'I wouldn't worry about that. Mrs G. doesn't like anyone apart from Esther Fury.' She gave Lolly a curious look. 'So, are you related or what? To the Furys, I mean.'

'No.'

'So how come you're living here now?'

Lolly wished she had the answer to the question. Despite Stanley's attempts at explaining, she was still pretty much in the dark on that score. 'Just 'cause my mum died,' she said eventually. 'I had nowhere else to go so . . .'

Theresa, who appeared no have no inhibitions whatsoever, asked, 'What happened to her, then?'

'It was an accident.'

'Oh, right.'

Theresa didn't say she was sorry or press for any further information, for which Lolly was grateful. It made her sad to talk about her mum. It produced a dreadful yearning in her chest as though her heart was being crushed.

The drive seemed shorter than it had last night and they soon reached the end of it. Theresa went through a small gate, set to one side of the big double ones. 'It's not far to the village from here. Only a few minutes. We'll go to Moffat's. It's a bit dull but I'm sure we'll find something that suits you. Where are you from? London, is it?'

Lolly nodded. 'Kellston.'

'I go to London sometimes. There's a station in the village. You can get straight through to Victoria. The shops in the West End are brilliant; that's where I got my coat.'

'It's nice.'

Theresa smiled and ran her fingers down the fur at the front, clearly proud of her purchase. 'Yeah, it's cool, isn't it?'

They turned right onto a narrow hedge-lined lane and walked for a few minutes before reaching a wider, busier street that had cars and people and which led eventually to the centre of the village. West Henby was larger than Lolly thought it would be. When people talked about villages, she always imagined a few country cottages and not much else, but this had shops and cafés, a pub and a restaurant. It was a busy, bustling place far removed from the quiet of the house.

Moffat's was opposite the pub, a double-fronted store with a selection of clothes in the windows. They pushed open the door and went inside. Theresa took the list out of the envelope and scanned the contents. 'Right,' she said. 'Shall we start with the coat? What colour would you like?'

Lolly shrugged. She wasn't used to choices, to having to make decisions for herself. 'Blue?' she suggested. 'Red? I don't know. I don't really mind.'

Theresa looked at her as though she was mad. 'You're the one who's got to wear it. You may as well get something you like. Come on, we'll go and see what they've got.'

For the next hour, Lolly was in and out of the changing room, trying on coats, trousers, shirts, skirts and jumpers. It was all new to her but the novelty soon wore off. She was happiest in a pair of comfy jeans and a T-shirt, and quickly grew bored of all the endless changes she had to make. 'Are we done yet?'

'Blimey,' Theresa said. 'Hark at you! I wish someone would buy me a whole new wardrobe. I wouldn't be complaining.'

Lolly, who didn't want to appear ungrateful, quickly replied, 'No, no, it's not that. I'm just—'

'That's okay. I was only kidding. I was the same at your age: I couldn't wait to get out of the shops – it was all so boring – and now I can't wait to get in them.' Theresa laughed. 'I bet in a couple of years you'll be exactly the same.'

Finally, all the shopping was done, including new shoes and underwear. While they waited by the till for the items to be folded and packed and totted up, Lolly's gaze alighted on a small trinket box sitting at the side of the counter. It was made of wood, covered in tiny seashells and varnished. She picked it up and lifted the lid. The inside was lined with red velvet.

'Do you like that?' Theresa asked.

'It's pretty.'

'Do you want it?'

Lolly did, but she hesitated. 'It's not on the list. What about Mrs Gough?'

'Oh, blow Mrs Gough. Everyone needs a box to put their bits 'n' bobs in.' Theresa took it out of her hand and handed it to the sales assistant. 'We'll have this too.'

Of all the purchases that were being made, this was the item Lolly was most excited about. Her mum had owned a box – one that had mysteriously disappeared – and now she had one too. It was the nicest thing she'd ever owned in her life. 'Ta.'

Theresa produced one of her grins. 'No need to thank me, love. I'm not paying for it.'

When the bill had been settled and the receipt handed over, Theresa took the two heaviest bags and gave the other one to Lolly. They left the shop and set off back along the street, retracing their steps from an hour earlier.

'I suppose the lovely Mrs Fury will be home soon.'

Lolly glanced at her, hearing an edge to the girl's voice. 'At the weekend,' she replied. Not that she was looking forward to it. Mal's response to Stanley, a comment she wasn't supposed to hear, didn't exactly inspire her with confidence. *She'll get used to the idea.* It had sounded as if there was trouble ahead – and Lolly was sick of trouble. 'What's she like?'

'Haven't you met her?'

Lolly shook her head. 'Not yet.'

'How strange.'

'She's in Cornwall,' Lolly said.

'But you've never met, not even once?'

'I don't think so.'

Theresa swung the bags by her side and laughed. 'Oh, you'd remember if you had. No one forgets Esther Fury in a hurry.'

Lolly had the feeling this wasn't meant as a compliment. 'So what's she like?' she asked again.

'She's ...' Theresa paused as if searching for the right words. 'She's definitely what you'd call a princess. Blonde and beautiful and disgustingly rich.'

'Like Grace Kelly?'

'Sure, just like Grace Kelly. And Esther always gets exactly what she wants. Apparently she wasn't so bad before ... well, you know ... but now it's different. There used to be big parties at the house, massive, with music and dancing and fireworks. All the stars came, all the great actors and actresses, and they'd stay until the early hours. My dad used to park their cars for them. Alfred Hitchcock came once. Have you heard of him?'

'Of course,' Lolly said.

'And Elizabeth Taylor.'

'Did you go?'

'No, I was too young. Not that I'd have got an invite anyway. This is years ago, after Mal and Esther got married but before ... It all changed then. She stopped making films and they never had another party.'

'What happened?'

Theresa pulled a face. 'Hasn't anyone told you?'

Lolly shook her head. 'Told me what?'

'If I tell, you've got to promise you'll never say it was me. I mean, you're going to hear about it anyway, you're bound to, but—'

'I won't. I swear. Cross my heart and hope to die.'

Theresa gave her a long searching look. 'Okay then.' She lowered her voice even though they'd now reached the quiet lane and there was no one else around. 'It was a terrible thing. Mal and Esther had a baby about thirteen years ago. She was called Kay. But when she was a few months old, she was taken. You know, stolen or kidnapped or whatever. Someone pounced on the nanny when she was taking Kay for her morning walk, snatched the poor baby and she was never seen again.'

Lolly stared at her, horrified. 'What, never?'

'Never. The pram ended up in the water and the police drained the lake, but she wasn't there. They thought she might have fallen out and drowned, you see.' Theresa's eyes grew bright as she elaborated on the story. 'My mum says she was the prettiest baby ever. Like an angel. And the kidnapper never made contact. There wasn't any ransom note, not a word, but that was probably because it had all gone wrong. He couldn't risk asking for money after what he did to the nanny. She must have fought back, tried to stop him, but she couldn't.'

'What happened to her?'

Theresa ran her tongue over her lips, relishing the gory details. 'She drowned, didn't she? And not by accident. The police reckoned she was held underwater. Mr Fury found her floating there, but it was too late to do anything by then.

279

She was called Cathy, Cathy Kershaw, and she wasn't much older than I am now.'

Lolly, recalling what Mrs Docherty had warned her about earlier, gave Theresa a sceptical look. 'Is this all true or are you making it up?'

'Cross my heart and hope to die,' Theresa said, echoing Lolly's earlier pledge. 'It was in the papers and everything. That's when the parties stopped. Well, you wouldn't fancy it, would you? Not after that. And everyone felt sorry for them, naturally, because it was just the worst possible thing in the world. But then Esther fired everyone who worked at the house and there was a lot of bad feeling about it in the village. I mean, some of them had worked there donkey's years, way back from when Mr Fury's father had the place. She couldn't trust them, you see, thought they might have been involved, but no one from round here would ever do a thing like that.'

'I was at the lake this morning,' Lolly said.

'You should be careful.'

'It's all right. I can swim. I learned at school.'

'Cathy Kershaw could probably swim, but it didn't do her much good. Anyway, they say the lake is haunted, that on some days you can hear a baby crying.'

Lolly felt a chill run through her, remembering the strange feeling she'd had when she was down by the water. 'Do you believe in ghosts, Theresa?'

'Not really. But better to be safe than sorry, eh? I wouldn't hang around there on my own if I was you.'

Lolly, who had no one else to hang around with, gave a

shrug. She didn't want to come across as a scaredy cat. 'I'm not bothered.'

'Yeah, well, perhaps you should be. That place is definitely creepy. There's something weird about it. Don't you think?'

'Maybe. I've only been there once.'

'It feels ... I don't know, *bad*. It makes the hairs on the back of my neck stand on end. I only have to see the water and ...' Theresa gave an exaggerated shudder. 'But it might just be me. It gives me the heebies thinking about what went on there.'

They reached the gate and passed through it. Lolly glanced up at the darkening sky, at the great rolling clouds gathering overhead. 'What do you think happened to Kay?'

'Who knows? Some people reckon she's dead and others that she's still out there somewhere. Mr Fury has never stopped searching. He's hired private detectives and everything.' Theresa gave her a sideways look. 'In fact, when we heard there was a girl coming to the house we wondered if it was Kay. You're about the right age. We thought he might have finally found her.'

Lolly shook her head. 'It's not me. I'm not her.'

'Oh, I know that now. I can tell just by looking at you. You haven't got the Fury cheekbones or the fair hair or ... Still, I suppose it'll be nice for them having a kid around. Might cheer the place up a bit.'

Lolly, who didn't have much confidence in her cheering abilities, thought she was likely to be a disappointment on that score. And what would happen then? The carrier bag swung against her leg as she walked. Perhaps they would send her away. She peered through the trees at the grey sheen of the lake, trying not to think about Cathy Kershaw and her watery grave. But suddenly that was all she could think about . . .

31

Stanley Parrish had two messages when he checked with reception on Tuesday morning. He took the slips of paper from Liz, glanced at them and thanked her. One was from Ma Fenner, the other from his contact at the coroner's office. Up in his office, he turned on the electric fire before sitting down at his desk and picking up the phone. He rang the coroner's first and asked to be put through to Mr Miller.

'It's Stanley,' he said. 'What have you got for me?'

'Nothing definitive, Mr Parrish, but I've had a chat with the pathologist and he's checked his notes. There's nothing in them to suggest Angela Bruce ever had a child, but then that wasn't what he was looking for. Truth is, he can't recall much about her – there's a lot of bodies pass through the morgue.'

It struck Stanley as profoundly sad that even the man who had cut her open and removed all her vital organs couldn't clearly remember her. She had been, apparently, as anonymous in death as she had been in life. 'Okay, Charlie,' he said. 'Thanks for that.'

'Sorry I couldn't have been of more help. The trouble with these people is that they never want to say too much in case it comes back and bites them on the bum. But if you want my opinion – for what it's worth – I reckon Mackenzie would have written down everything he'd seen. He's the meticulous type, known for it. So if it isn't there ...'

'It probably didn't exist.'

'Exactly.'

Stanley thanked him again and hung up. He wasn't much further on as regards absolute evidence but he trusted Charlie's judgement. And it tallied with what Ma Fenner had told him about Angela being barren. Ma was his next port of call. He felt a faint flurry of excitement as he dialled the number. She wasn't the sort to get in touch unless she had something useful to say.

Ma picked up after a couple of rings. 'Hello?'

'Mrs Fenner? Hello, it's Stanley Parrish. I'm sorry I missed your call. How are you?'

'Still alive, thank the good Lord. It's always a good sign when you wake up breathing at my age. But that's beside the point. What I called you about was that Calvin. You remember? Angela's boyfriend. Only my daughter was round yesterday and I mentioned your visit and she reckons he's working at that bottling plant in Hoxton. Or at least he was six months back. Her old man had a job there too before ... well, that's another story, but she remembers Calvin. She used to see him around the estate.'

'Is she sure?' Stanley asked. 'Only that's quite a while ago. We're talking fourteen years or so.'

'Yes, she's sure. Calvin Cross, that's his name. She'd meet George at the plant occasionally and that's when she saw him again.'

Stanley jotted it down in his notebook. 'That could be useful. Thank you.'

'If anyone knows about Angela's past, he will.'

'I don't suppose you could give me a description?'

Ma sighed down the line. 'No, it's too far back for me. He's a coloured fella, though. Well, half and half. Tall.' She left a long pause as though she was searching her memory, but nothing else came to her. 'Sorry. I could ring my Jeanie if you like. She'd be able to tell you more.'

'No, it's all right. I can ask at the plant.'

'Do you have any news on Lolly? She was here at the weekend, on Sunday. Just standing there, staring at nothing. Pouring down with rain it was. I'm surprised she didn't catch her death.'

Stanley didn't want to say too much. 'She's gone to stay with a foster family in Kent. Hopefully, it will work out for her.'

'Well, I hope so too. Can't be any worse than living with the Cecils,' Ma said bluntly. 'Brenda's oldest, that Tony, just got arrested again.'

'Is that to do with the Joseph Clayton business?'

'Yes, that's it. Put the bloke's eye out, by all accounts. He's a wrong 'un, that lad, pure evil.'

'He's still alive, though? Clayton, I mean.'

'So far as I know.'

Stanley made another quick note to call the hospital and get an update. He'd made Lolly a promise and felt obliged to keep it. 'Okay, thanks, Mrs Fenner. I'm grateful for your help. It's much appreciated.'

He replaced the receiver and checked his watch. It was almost eleven. Kettlers, the bottling plant, probably broke for lunch about midday. As he had nothing else to do – no new jobs had come in – he decided to head over to Hoxton and see if he could track down Calvin Cross. With luck, the man might have something useful to tell him.

He crouched down and turned off the fire, taking a moment to warm his hands. Winter was setting in and it was cold outside. As he straightened up, he could feel the creak of arthritis in his knees. It bothered him to think he might kick the bucket without ever getting to the bottom of the Fury case. Not that he was old, not really, but he was no spring chicken either. He no longer had the energy he used to have, or the drive. Sometimes it was an effort just to get up in the morning.

Stanley locked his office, went downstairs and walked round the corner to where his car was parked. He had a fog in his head from the brandy he'd drunk the night before. There was a bad taste in his mouth too. He lit a cigarette and blew the smoke through his nose. Maybe he should give up the booze, although he couldn't think of what else he'd do with all the long, empty hours. It was a way of getting through, of lurching from one day to the next.

The traffic was bad, but he still had twenty minutes to kill by the time he got to Hoxton and found a place to park. He went into a newsagent and bought a birthday card for his nephew, Nick. Seventeen already. It saddened Stanley that he rarely saw the kid now that he was no longer welcome in his sister's house. And that wasn't down to her – he and Patsy had always been close – but her small-minded bigot of a husband, Maurice Trent.

Maurice couldn't stomach the fact that his brother-in-law was homosexual. He had the same twisted view on queers as Joe Quinn, believing they should all be hung, drawn and quartered for their 'unnatural desires'. And even that was too good for them. Of course, Stanley had always been discreet, even to the point of playing along with talk of girlfriends and 'settling down'. But then there had been the trouble with Richard. It had been hushed up but somehow Maurice had found out – probably through his Masonic pals – and from that day forth Stanley had been persona non grata when it came to visiting the Trent household.

He didn't blame Patsy – the poor woman had to live with the bastard – but he missed seeing Nick and watching him grow up. And he resented Maurice's insinuations that he was in some way a threat to his nephew, an affront to morality, a contaminating force that had to be eliminated.

Back in the car, Stanley wrote out the card and enclosed a tenner. It was more than he could afford but he didn't begrudge it. Perhaps, once Nick was eighteen, they would be able to re-establish some kind of relationship. Patsy rang occasionally, always when Maurice was out of the house. The marriage wasn't a happy one but, like so many women, she lacked the will or the confidence to end it.

Stanley wrote the address on the envelope and attached a stamp. He got out of the car and walked across the road. 'Happy birthday,' he said as he slipped the card into the post box. 'Have a good one.'

By the time he'd walked round the corner to the bottling plant, the workers were already filing out. Stanley scanned the crowd, looking for a likely candidate, but there were lots of black men in their thirties, any one of which could have been Calvin. In the end, he stopped a young woman and asked for her help. She gazed around for a while and then pointed towards a group coming through the door.

'That's him there, the one with the stripy shirt.'

The first things Stanley noticed were his height – he was over six foot tall – followed by the nut-brown eyes and then the gold wedding band on the third finger of his left hand. He went over and introduced himself, opening his wallet to show his ID. 'I wonder if I could have a word? It's about Angela Martin.'

Calvin smiled, his eyes lighting up. 'Ange? God, how is she? I haven't seen her in years.' But then his smile gradually faded. 'Shit. Something's happened, hasn't it?'

'Let me buy you a coffee,' Stanley said. 'I'll tell you all about it.'

32

Calvin Cross put his elbows on the café table and rubbed his face with his hands. 'Jesus, I still can't believe it. Why'd she go and do a thing like that? Why would she?'

Stanley didn't have a straightforward answer for him. 'I don't know. She had some serious problems, including a kind of psychosis, perhaps. I think it had been going on for a while. But why she finally decided to . . . I've no idea. Did you know she'd gone back to Kellston, that she was living on the Mansfield again?'

Calvin shook his head. 'No, the last time I saw her . . . it was years ago. After we split up, we didn't have any contact.'

'She had a child with her, a girl called Lolita.'

'A kid?'

'I've heard that Angela couldn't have children. Is that true? We think Lolly must have been adopted although we haven't been able to find the paperwork.'

'Yeah, it broke her heart. That's all she wanted: kids and

a family of her own. The doctors reckoned they couldn't do anything for her.' Calvin played with his wedding ring. 'It's why we broke up. She said it wasn't fair on me, that one day I'd resent her for it. I told her it didn't matter, as long as we had each other, but ... it caused endless rows. She didn't believe me, *couldn't* believe me. I don't know, she just couldn't get beyond it. And maybe she was right. Maybe I wouldn't have been able to cope. In the end it all got too much and we split up. Do you have kids, Mr Parrish?'

Stanley shook his head. 'No.'

'I've got two boys. My pride and joy. Now they're here, I can't imagine life without them. Perhaps she knew me better than I knew myself.'

Stanley nodded, lifted the mug to his mouth and took a few sips of the black coffee he'd ordered. 'We're trying to track down some family for Lolly, but it's proving difficult. Angela was using the surname Martin when you met, wasn't she?'

Calvin's face twisted. 'Yeah, she was still married to him. That bastard has a lot to answer for. If anyone screwed her up, it was him.'

Stanley leaned forward, keen to verify what he already suspected. 'Are we talking about *Billy* Martin here?'

'Who else? That lowlife was the biggest mistake of her life. Her family didn't approve, and they were right. But she couldn't see it, of course. She was mad about him, infatuated. When they tried to stop her seeing him, he persuaded her to do a runner. She was little more than a kid then – only sixteen – and he was twenty-five. They got married up in Gretna, and it was all downhill from there.'

'I take it he wasn't perfect husband material?'

'He was a shit, Mr Parrish, if you'll pardon my language. Once he'd got her, he stopped being interested, except as someone to torment. Handy with his fists too, when he was in the mood. She soon realised it had all been a big mistake, but she was too scared to leave him. Anyway, she had nowhere else to go. She was too ashamed, too humiliated, to go crawling back to her parents, so she stuck it out until she had a bit of luck. Billy got nicked for robbery and sent down for a long stretch. While he was away she got herself a job and a flat and began to realise there was more to life than being Billy Martin's punchbag.'

'And that's when you met her?'

'My sister worked in the same shop up West. She was the one who introduced us. I liked her straight off; there was something about her. She was a genuine sort of person.'

'Was there any sign back then that she . . .' Stanley paused, looking for the right way of putting it. 'Would you say she was depressed or anything like that? Did she ever act irrationally?'

Calvin spooned some sugar into his mug and gave the tea a stir. 'No, not at all. I mean, there was the whole business with not being able to have kids – that used to get her down – but she coped with it. And she was afraid of Billy. That was understandable. Of course, she didn't have to worry about him so long as he was banged up. He wasn't happy about her filing for divorce but there wasn't much he could do about it.'

'Until he got out,' Stanley said. 'And tracked her down.'

Calvin's face grew dark. 'Did he do that?'

Stanley nodded. 'He did, unfortunately. For some reason, about eight years ago, she moved back to Kellston. She was calling herself Bruce by then, Angela Bruce, but he still managed to find her. Does that name mean anything to you? I'm thinking it could have been her maiden name or that she might have got married again, and that Lolly was her husband's child.'

'Why would she go back there? The estate would be the first place he'd look. He'd have had the address from the divorce papers.'

'I don't know,' Stanley said. 'It's been bothering me too. There must have been something that drew her back, but I just can't figure out what it was.' He shared the frustration of the younger man, unable to fathom what Angela had been thinking in returning to the Mansfield. 'What about the name? Does it ring any bells?'

Calvin waved a hand in a brief, dismissive gesture. 'No, I've never heard it before. *Parr* was her maiden name. But if you're thinking of contacting her parents about the kid, I wouldn't bother. Her mum died years ago, and her dad wouldn't be interested even if she was Angela's flesh and blood.'

'Is it Lambeth? Is that where she came from?'

'That's what she said.'

'He might not even know she's dead.'

'Oh, she was dead to him years ago, from the moment she ran off with that lowlife.' Calvin stared down at his untouched sandwich for a moment before lifting his head again. 'Have you talked to him, to Billy?'

292

'I can't find him. No one seems to know where he is. He disappeared a few months after he caught up with Angela. And that's another strange thing. You'd have thought she would be pleased, wouldn't you? Glad to see the back of him. But apparently she kicked up a stink, reported him missing to the police and everything.'

'He's a manipulator, a control freak. He'd have found a way to get inside her head. That's what he's like.'

'Rumour has it that he could be six foot under.'

'Let's hope so,' Calvin said. 'It couldn't happen to a nicer guy.'

Stanley heard the venom in his voice and wondered if he knew more than he was saying. 'Have you heard something?'

Calvin hissed out a breath. 'Shit, man, don't start looking in my direction. I don't know zilch about Billy Martin, other than he made Angela's life a misery.'

'I wasn't suggesting that you did.'

'I don't even know what the bastard looks like.'

'No, I understand,' Stanley said. 'I didn't mean anything by it. I wasn't implying . . . I'm just scrabbling around in the dark, trying to get some answers.'

A silence fell over the table. Then Calvin sighed. 'Sorry. It's been a shock. I still can't believe she's gone. What's going to happen to the kid?'

'We've found a place for her with a family in Kent. I guess she'll stay there if we can't trace anyone else.'

'Bruce,' Calvin murmured, his eyebrows coming together in a frown.

'You thought of something?'

'Only that Angela had a dog called Bruce when she was young. I just remembered. She told me about him once; he was a boxer. She could have ... Only if she was hoping to stop Billy from finding her ...'

Stanley nodded. Unable to risk reverting to Parr, she had maybe chosen it as a reminder of happier times. 'It's one way of choosing a new name.'

'For all the good it did her.'

Stanley, sensing that he'd come to the end of the road as regards any further useful information, rose to his feet. 'Thanks for talking to me.'

'I still don't get why she did it. She must have loved that kid. Why would she have taken her own life? Why would she have done that to her?'

'I've no idea. Who knows what goes on in someone else's head?'

'It's a bad business.'

Stanley couldn't argue with that. As he left the café, he glanced back over his shoulder. Calvin Cross was staring at the wall with a dazed expression on his face. There was always a legacy with suicide, feelings of guilt and regret. Calvin was feeling them now and one day Lolly would feel them too. Perhaps not today or tomorrow, but eventually they would come to haunt her. She would wonder what she'd done wrong, what she'd said or hadn't said; why she hadn't been important enough to live for.

33

Everywhere Lolly went in the house she was reminded of time passing. The clocks tick-tocked, chiming on the hour and sometimes more often. The sound echoed through the empty rooms, a lonely kind of noise breaking through the silence and leaving an eerie echo in its wake. It was Friday, four days since she'd arrived, and Esther Fury would be coming home soon. She wasn't looking forward to it.

By now she knew her way around and already had her favourite places. One of these was the den, a small room with a squashy sofa and easy chairs. Here there was a TV, a radio and a record player, along with hundreds of LPs. She had discovered albums by, amongst others, the Rolling Stones, Bob Dylan, David Bowie, Marvin Gaye and Janis Joplin. In a box packed full of singles she had found 'Hey Jude' by The Beatles. She'd already played it over twenty times, the song reminding her of her old friend.

Mal had given her some good news last night after he'd

got back from work. He had been in touch with the police and they wouldn't need to talk to her again. Their enquiries into Jude's connection to the murder of Amy Wiltshire were over.

'So he's in the clear?'

'Looks that way.'

Lolly had been relieved. 'Do they know who killed her?'

'Not yet, but I'm sure they'll find out eventually. Anyway, you don't have to worry about it any more.'

Lolly, thinking back on the conversation, was surprised he had any confidence in the cops at all, bearing in mind his own experience. But maybe he'd only said it for her benefit, to stop her worrying about a murderer being on the loose. He still hadn't mentioned Kay and she wondered if he ever would. The police hadn't been able to find *her*, so what chance they'd find Amy's killer? Of course, it was staring them straight in the face – it had to be Tony Cecil – but they'd been fooled by the false alibi Terry had provided.

As she walked into the library, Lolly's stomach churned at the thought of Tony. She hoped he was still banged up because she knew he blamed her for his arrest. What if he came looking for her? She had no idea if Brenda had her new address or not. And what if he came when Mal wasn't here? There would be no one to protect her.

Lolly sat down in one of the big leather chairs by the window. It had a view of the garden and she briefly gazed out at the lawn before turning her attention back to the room. At first she'd been daunted by it, by the endless shelves of books running from the floor to the ceiling, but as she'd explored further she'd found all sorts of interesting things: books on exotic birds and butterflies, all with big glossy pictures that had a peculiar and yet strangely pleasing smell. There were books on travel too, with photographs of India and Egypt, China and Japan.

When she thought of China, she thought of the weeping willow, and when she thought of that she was reminded of the lake. Despite Theresa's warning, she'd been back several times, trying to prove to herself that she wasn't afraid of ghosts. She'd heard nothing, seen nothing, since that first occasion. If poor Cathy Kershaw did haunt the place, she was keeping a low profile.

Early this morning, just as the sun was rising, she'd heard footsteps outside and got up to look through the window. It had been fear that propelled her from her bed – fear that Tony Cecil had come – but it was only Mal walking down the path towards the water. She couldn't see his face but she reckoned he was sad from the way his shoulders were hunched up.

Lolly liked spending time with him. He was funny and kind and didn't ask too many questions. Last night he had shown her the insides of a clock – the movement, he'd called it – all the tiny metal parts that made it work. She had never thought about it before, what made the hands turn and the clock chime, and some of the names had stuck with her: the mainspring, the ratchet, the pinions. He'd been patient with her, never snappy, even when she couldn't quite grasp what each of the parts was supposed to do.

Lolly heard the distant ringing of a phone – the door

to the library was solid and heavy – and shortly after, Mrs Gough came in and announced there was a call for her.

'It's Mr Parrish. He wants to talk to you.' There was disapproval in her voice as if she objected to Lolly receiving calls at the house – or maybe she just objected to Lolly, full stop. 'You can take it in the hall.'

Lolly went through and picked up the phone. 'Hello?'

'Hi, it's Stanley. How are you?'

'All right, thanks. Do you have any news on Joseph?'

'I do. He had some nasty injuries, but he'll live.'

Lolly, who still felt guilty, gave a sigh of relief. He wasn't dead, at least. 'What about his eye?'

'They weren't able to save it, I'm afraid. But Tony Cecil's been charged so I don't think he'll be around for a while.'

'Is he locked up?'

'Locked up and staying locked up. I've heard his mates are going to give evidence against him so he'll definitely go down.'

But Lolly knew this wouldn't stop him from blaming her. 'What about Amy? Is there any news?'

'None that I know of. Look, I know I've asked you this before, but does the surname Martin mean anything to you in relation to your mum? I mean, did you ever see letters or envelopes addressed to her in that name?'

Lolly frowned. 'Our name's Bruce not Martin.'

'Yes, I know but . . . Maybe on the bills or in that tin box that went missing?'

'I don't think so.'

'Okay, it doesn't matter.'

And then something came back to Lolly. She could remember pulling out the strings of beads, her fingers pushing aside some folded sheets of paper. 'Hang on, I'm not sure but there might have been a few letters. They didn't have envelopes though, nothing with Martin on it.'

'Can you recall who they were from?'

In her mind she could see the writing, big and untidy and sloping to the left. *Dear Angela* . . . But try as she might, she couldn't remember any more. Had she ever read them? If she had, the words had slipped from her memory long ago. 'No, sorry, it was ages back.'

'That's all right. You've got my number if you think of anything.'

'Okay. Could I ask you something?'

'Ask away.'

Lolly, who was on the verge of inquiring as to whether Theresa's story about Kay Fury was true, suddenly became aware of Mrs Gough's presence in the hallway. The housekeeper was carefully running a cloth along the sides of a long gilt mirror, dusting or at least pretending to. What she was really doing was earwigging. As an expert on snooping, Lolly could see exactly what she was up to. 'No, don't worry. It's not important. Thanks for letting me know about . . . Thanks.'

'No problem. You take care of yourself.'

Lolly said goodbye and hung up.

Mrs Gough smiled at her. It was a fake sort of smile that didn't get close to reaching her eyes. 'So what did Mr Parrish want?'

'Nothing.'

The smile slipped a little. 'Well, he must have wanted something or he wouldn't have made the effort to call.'

'Just to see how I am,' Lolly said. 'That's all.' She suspected Mrs Gough of ulterior motives, of trying to do more than merely make conversation. There were things the housekeeper wanted to know, although she wasn't sure why.

Mrs Gough gave a disapproving sniff. 'Well, think on. Mrs Fury doesn't care for him, and she'll be home tomorrow.'

It was said like a threat – as if she was expected to choose sides – but Lolly refused to go along with it. If her betrayal of Joseph had taught her anything, it was that sometimes you didn't get second chances. 'He's always been nice to me.'

'Nice?' Mrs Gough replied mockingly. 'Oh, I'm sure he's been that. After all, you're his meal ticket, you and your like.'

Lolly had no idea what she meant by this. She stared at her blankly. 'What?'

'All I'm saying is that I wouldn't get too comfortable. You might not be here for long.' And with that parting shot, she turned on her heel and click-clacked away along the hall.

Lolly wondered if it was true. Maybe, in a day or two, she'd be off somewhere else. Maybe Stanley would come and pick her up and take her to another house where she would have to start all over again. The very idea made her feel tired. With a sigh, she went upstairs to her bedroom and sat down on the bed.

Beside her, on the bedside table, was the seashell box. She remembered when Mrs Gough had plucked it from the Moffat's carrier bag on Tuesday and held it aloft.

'What on earth is this?'

'For Lolly's bits 'n' bobs,' Theresa had said. 'It wasn't expensive.'

'I can see that. If she'd wanted a box, there are plenty in the house. I could have found her something decent.'

Lolly still couldn't understand Mrs Gough's disdain. She loved the box and hoped she'd be allowed to keep it even if she was sent away. She ran her fingers over the pretty varnished shells and then opened the lid and looked inside. There, nestled in the red velvet, was the mother-of-pearl button, the Fanta cap, the photo she'd had taken in Woolworths and Stanley Parrish's business card.

The latter reminded her of what Mrs Gough had said. What had she meant by a meal ticket? She couldn't figure it out. What she did understand, however, was that her presence wasn't welcomed by everyone in the house. Tomorrow, when Esther Fury returned, she could be packing up her things again. Lolly closed the lid on the box and put it back on the table. She felt a flutter of anxiety. There was a storm brewing, no doubt about it, and she was right in the middle.

34

Mal Fury gazed at his wife. Dressed in a pale green dress and fur coat, she was looking extraordinarily beautiful, but this wasn't why he was smiling. It was her anger that pleased him. These days he was only ever able to provoke two emotions and these were rage or contempt. He preferred the former to the latter, and preferred either to complete indifference.

'Have you gone mad?' she asked. 'Have you gone completely insane?'

'There's nothing mad about it. She needs a home and we can provide one. What's wrong with that?'

Esther flung off her coat and threw it over the back of a chair. She turned back to him, her eyes flashing. 'Listen to yourself! For God's sake, she isn't Kay. How many times do you need telling?'

'Of course she isn't,' he replied calmly. 'That isn't why she's here.'

'So you've just decided to take in some waif and stray,

some random kid you know nothing about? Why would you do that? Why would you even consider it?'

'I know plenty about her. I know she has no one and nowhere to go. Do you think *that's* right?' He sat back and shook his head. 'Come on Esther, have a heart. If Kay was out there in the same situation, wouldn't you want a family to take her in, to take care of her?'

'Kay isn't out there. And you can't just bring a child here without discussing it first.'

Mal shrugged. 'It's done,' he said. 'She can't be returned like some unwanted bit of shopping. It doesn't work like that.'

'This is all down to that Stanley Parrish. He's a bloody pariah! And who's going to look after her? If you think it's me, then you'd better think again.'

'From what I've seen, she's perfectly capable of looking after herself. Anyway, it's not as though you're going to be around much. Didn't you say you had a couple more films in the pipeline? You won't be here so you hardly need to worry about taking care of Lolly.'

'Oh, is that what this is about? You're annoyed that I've gone back to work, and so you're looking for a way to punish me.'

Mal rolled his eyes. 'Jesus, I hate to break this to you, Esther, but not everything is about you. I don't give a damn whether you work or not. I feel sorry for the kid, okay, and all I'm hoping is that her future with us might be marginally better than spending the next God knows how many years in care.'

'And since when did you become so charitable?'

'And since when did you become so heartless?'

Esther gave a snort. 'She's not staying here. I won't allow it.'

'It's too late – unless you want to throw her on to the street. And that wouldn't reflect too well on you. I mean, everyone in the village already knows we've taken her in. What are they going to say if you kick her out again?'

'I don't give a damn what they say.'

'And what about the papers? What if they get to hear of it? They'll be interested now you're back on the scene again. They'll be digging up the past, poking their nose into our business, looking for some juicy gossip.'

Esther leaned over the desk and snarled into his face. 'Don't try and blackmail me.'

'I'm just saying it like it is.'

'I don't want her here. Do you understand?'

'Loud and clear. But I'm sure you'll get used to it. All I'm asking is that you're kind to her. She hasn't had much of a life so let's not make things worse.'

Esther straightened up, her face tight and angry. 'You're the only one who's making things worse. Trying to play daddy to some scruffy East End orphan. What's all that about? What's going on in that twisted head of yours? You can't replace Kay with this Lolly. And *Lolly*, for Christ's sake, what kind of a name is that?'

'Short for Lolita.'

'I know what it's short for. What sort of mother calls her daughter that?'

'One who doesn't read much? I don't know. What does it matter? It's not the girl's fault. She didn't choose it.' Mal tilted his head and stared at his wife. He was certain she'd been speaking to Mrs Gough on the phone, getting the lowdown on Lolly's lack of social graces. 'She's a nice kid. She won't be any bother.'

'Not to *you*, perhaps, seeing as you're out at work all day.'

'She'll be at school once I get it sorted.'

'She should be at school now.'

Mal shrugged. 'It's only a few weeks until they break up for Christmas. She can start in the New Year.'

Esther folded her arms across her chest and went to stand by the window. Anger made her shoulders tight. 'You've got no right to do this,' she said. 'It isn't fair. This is my house too and I should have a say in who lives in it.'

'You'll hardly notice she's here. No one's asking you to be her mother or to play happy families. It isn't like that. I'm simply her guardian, taking care of her until she's old enough to take care of herself.'

Esther looked back over her shoulder. 'There isn't any *simply* about it. What do you even know about this girl? I mean, other than that her mother threw herself off a high-rise block of flats? And what sort of problems do you think that's going to cause long term? The kid's going to be damaged. You might not see it now, but it's going to be there.'

'All the more reason to take her in.' Mal didn't mention the fact that Angela probably wasn't even Lolly's mother. Or that Lolly had recently been involved in a murder investigation. Esther held enough prejudices already without him adding to them. 'She needs some stability in her life.'

Esther barked out a laugh. 'Stability? And you think she's going to get that here?'

'Why not?' he retorted. 'It has to be better than being in care.'

'You won't be saying that when she's sneaking around behind your back, dating boys and getting into trouble.'

'Well, we'll cross that bridge if and when we come to it.'

'Oh, we'll come to it. There isn't any doubt about that.'

Mal pulled a face. 'You haven't even met her and already you've written her off. Why can't you give the girl a chance?'

'She's of no interest to me. I've made my feelings clear. It's up to you what you do about it.'

'I won't be doing anything. The girl's staying, end of story. I'm not offering her a home, a future, and then snatching it away again.'

Esther rounded on him, storming over to the desk. 'You had no damn right to offer it in the first place. This isn't a bloody orphanage. How many more are you planning on bringing in? Three, four? Why not make it a round ten?'

'Just Lolly,' he said. 'I think she deserves a break.'

'And what I think doesn't matter?'

Mal gave her a faint smile. 'Of course it matters, sweetheart. It just isn't going to change anything.'

'Don't you sweetheart me, you patronising bastard.' Esther crossed the room, opened the silver box on the table, took out a cigarette, put it in her mouth and lit it. 'I can't believe you're doing this.' Realising it wasn't a battle she was going to win, she inhaled and expelled the smoke in a long resentful stream. 'I won't forget it.'

'You never forget anything. That list of grudges must be getting pretty long by now.'

'And whose fault is that?'

Mal raised his arms in a mock gesture of surrender. He studied his wife while she glared into the middle distance. She always smoked like she was on set, her right hand bent back at the wrist, elegantly poised as if waiting for the director to say *Action!*

'Don't expect me to take an interest in her. She's your responsibility, no one else's.'

'Yes,' he agreed. 'All I'm asking is for you to be civil to her.'

'Civil?' she echoed, her lips curling into a sardonic smile. 'And how exactly am I supposed to do that?'

'You're an actress, aren't you? I'm sure you'll figure it out.'

35

Stanley Parrish viewed the approach of Christmas with a dull sort of dread. It wasn't even December yet and the shops were already full of baubles and tinsel. As he no longer got an invitation to spend the day with his sister's family, he knew it would be time spent alone. In general, he didn't mind his own company, could cope perfectly well with it, but the festive period was more challenging. For a couple of days everything would close down and the only company he'd have would be during the brief hours the pub was open.

Stanley tried to take his mind off this by concentrating on the Fury case. He had brought the file home, and now had the sheets of paper spread out in front of him on the table. As he'd done so many times before, he was going right back to the beginning to look at the day of the abduction itself. The house had been protected by a good alarm system, along with serious locks on the doors and windows, but there had been no real security as regards the grounds. Although the main gates were locked, a smaller side gate was often left open during the day to enable staff to come and go. This was probably how the intruder had got in.

The abduction had been well planned – someone knew the nanny's routine – and yet it had all gone badly wrong. Cathy Kershaw must have fought to save the baby and in the process had lost her own life. But why had she been killed? It had either been a moment of panic or a deliberate act to prevent her from identifying him. So someone she knew, perhaps, a former member of staff or a visitor to the house.

Stanley could still remember going to see Cathy's parents. It had been about three years after her murder, but time hadn't dulled their grief. Agonised eyes stared out from pale, tight faces. They could have no closure – if such a thing was even possible – as the police had still not caught their daughter's killer. He knew from experience that at the time of Kay's abduction, Cathy's innocence would not have been taken for granted. Questions would have been asked about friends and boyfriends, questions guaranteed to cause additional pain. Personally, Stanley didn't think she'd been involved. She'd been a nice girl who'd been in the wrong place at the wrong time. She was as much the victim in all this as Kay Fury.

And what of Angela Bruce? He'd made some progress since dropping off Lolly in West Henby. After trawling through what felt like thousands of records, he'd finally discovered that Angela had changed her name from Martin to Bruce by deed poll in 1959, a year or so after Lolly was born.

Despite the name change, Billy had still managed to

track her down. He must have known that Lolly wasn't hers, couldn't be, but had he ever found out where she'd come from? Stanley was still mulling over this when the phone call he'd been waiting for finally came through.

DS Donal Stewart worked out of West End Central, and was a colleague from way back. They went through the usual friendly exchange before getting down to business. 'Okay, I've got something for you – if it's the right Billy Martin. I'm presuming it is: right name, right age, a small-time villain from south London, in and out of jail for robbery and GBH. That's the good news. The bad news, for you at least, is that he was still banged up in fifty-eight so he couldn't have had anything to do with the Fury business. Well, not unless he organised it from behind bars.'

Stanley wasn't overly disappointed. It had always been a long shot that Billy could have kidnapped Kay and then given her to Angela to look after. 'I don't suppose you have an address?'

'Nothing recent. And he's been off the radar since … hang on, just let me check. Yes, we're talking January 1963 when they kicked him out of the Scrubs. Not so much as a parking ticket since then. So he's either a reformed character, cleared off abroad or gone to meet his maker. Take your pick. I'm leaning towards the latter.'

'Yeah, you're probably right. I don't suppose you've got any known associates on record, have you? Or any family?'

'He did a couple of jobs with the Grayling brothers, but they're both brown bread now. And there's a sister who used to live in Lambeth. Sheila Barstow. Do you want the address? It's old, she could have moved, but someone might know where she is.'

'Thanks. I owe you one.' Stanley scribbled down the details, said his goodbyes and hung up. He thought it could be worth trying to look up the sister, if only to establish whether or not she'd heard from Billy in the past few years. He suspected not. If Joe Quinn's reaction was anything to go by, the delightful Billy had stopped breathing a long time ago.

And that was something else to think about. If it got back to Quinn that he was asking questions about Billy Martin, he could expect another visit – and this one might not end with all his limbs intact. Was it worth the risk? The problem was he had nowhere else to go. Even though he didn't really believe Lolly was Mal and Esther's daughter, he still felt a compulsion to prove it one way or the other.

Stanley drank some coffee, put the mug down and scratched his head. Someone out there must know what had happened that autumn morning in 1958. He thought it unlikely the kidnapper had been working alone. You couldn't just throw a baby in the back of a car and drive off. You needed someone to take care of it, to stop it from crying, and later on, to feed and change it while the ransom negotiations were going on. A woman, he presumed, if that wasn't being too sexist. A man looking after a baby alone was going to arouse suspicion.

Of course, there was always the possibility that it hadn't been a kidnap at all, but that Cathy Kershaw had always been the intended victim. Was there any evidence for

311

this? No, but it couldn't be completely ruled out. It could have been an attempted rape, during which the pram had rolled into the lake. But if that was the case, why was the baby taken?

No ransom demand had ever been made, but that wasn't surprising. The abduction of Kay Fury had been headline news with the police crawling all over the case. Stanley tried to put himself in the kidnapper's shoes. It would have been too risky, perhaps, to go through with it, especially if Kay was already dead. And if she wasn't? Then surely the logical thing to do was to cut your losses and leave the baby somewhere she'd be found.

Stanley looked again at the long list of staff, work colleagues, friends and guests that the Furys had compiled thirteen years ago. Suddenly, as his eyes scanned down the page, one of the names jumped out at him. He pulled in a breath, reminded of something Lolly Bruce had said. As he picked up a pen and underlined the name, his heart was starting to thump. Quickly he picked up the phone and made a call. He asked the questions and listened carefully to the answers. When he put the receiver down, his pulse was racing. After years of working in the dark, there was finally a glimmer of light. He sat and thought about it for a while. Then he picked the phone up again and dialled the number for Mal Fury.

36

Lolly had never met a woman as beautiful as Esther Fury before. She was tall and willowy and blonde, with the kind of face you usually only saw on the covers of magazines. Her skin was smooth, her grey eyes darkly lashed, her mouth a wide perfect bow. Even her smell was exquisite, a scent that floated in the air like summer roses. She was wearing a pale green dress that clung to every curve of her body.

As she circled Lolly, looking her up and down, Esther wore a disappointed expression. 'Oh, dear,' she murmured. 'This won't do at all.'

Mrs Gough stood with her arms folded across her chest. 'You see what I mean?'

'I do indeed.'

'I can't imagine what Mr Fury was thinking.'

'Mr Fury doesn't think; that's the problem.' Esther gave a weary sigh. She took a step back and narrowed her eyes as though this might improve the view. 'Well, we can only do what we can do. A haircut might help. She can barely see out from under that fringe. And where did all these awful clothes come from?'

'They came with her. I sent Theresa to Moffat's to buy some new ones, but I can't get her to wear them. She's stubborn, Mrs Fury. That's the trouble with these London types – they don't appreciate anything you do.'

Lolly could have piped up and said that the reason she hadn't worn the new clothes was that she didn't want to spoil them, but was too overawed to open her mouth and explain. She stood very still, not enjoying the scrutiny, but weirdly entranced by Esther. She was like one of those fairy-tale princesses, a being from another world. Even her voice was enchanting, soft and sweet and melodious.

'There are worse things than being stubborn, I suppose. She might grow out of it.'

Mrs Gough made an unpleasant noise in the back of her throat. 'And I dare say that Mr Parrish has been filling her head with all sorts of nonsense.'

'Yes, I dare say he has.'

Lolly glanced from one to the other, feeling awkward. It was no surprise she'd been judged and found wanting – she was used to little else – but her cheeks were starting to burn with embarrassment. She lowered her gaze to the deep pile carpet of the library. It was only then that Esther addressed her directly for the first time.

'And what are we going to do about this name of yours?'

Lolly looked up again, not understanding.

'You see, Lolly is all very well when you're small, but

314

you're growing up now. You need something a little more . . . sophisticated. And I don't think we want to call you Lolita.' Esther gave a tiny shudder. 'No, that wouldn't do at all.'

Lolly was saved from having to make a response by the timely appearance of Mal. He strode into the room, came over and shot his wife a warning glance. Although he was smiling, his voice had an edge to it.

'Leave the poor girl alone, darling. There's nothing wrong with her name.'

'Oh, please. There's *everything* wrong with it. How's she going to cope when she gets older? She can't be called Lolly for the rest of her life.'

'Why not?'

Esther tossed her head with impatience. 'For heaven's sake, she's got enough disadvantages without adding to them. No, we need to choose something more acceptable. How about Lita?' She looked at Lolly as if assessing how well the name suited her. 'Yes, I think that would do quite well.'

'Doesn't she get a say in the matter?'

Lolly, sensing the tension between them, didn't want to be the cause of more trouble. 'I don't mind it,' she said quickly. 'I don't mind Lita.'

'There!' Esther said triumphantly. 'It's settled then. Mrs Gough, you can let the staff know. And now all we have to do is sort out a school.'

'She can go to the village school,' Mal said.

Esther frowned at him. 'I thought you wanted the best for her, to give her a chance.'

'It's a perfectly good school.'

'Not good enough for your parents to send you to, though.'

'That was their choice, not mine.'

But Esther wasn't giving in. 'You can't say one thing and do another. Either you want her to get a good education or you don't. Or would you rather she just ended up on the scrapheap like most of the kids round here? I think Daynor Bridge could be perfect. It's not too academic and it has a decent reputation.'

'I'll think about it.'

'You'll have to make a decision soon if she's going to be enrolled for next term.'

'I said I'll think about it,' Mal snapped. 'Can we drop the subject now? We'll discuss it later.'

Esther arched her eyebrows as though his tone was totally unreasonable. 'Perhaps I'll make some enquiries, just so we're prepared. It can't do any harm, can it?'

'Whatever makes you happy.'

Esther left the library with Mrs Gough, both of them looking decidedly smug.

Mal walked over to the window and silently gazed out at the garden. Lolly continued to stand there, not sure what to do next. She'd just started to compose a letter to Jude when Esther had arrived, and the sheet of silky white writing paper was still lying on the side table. She hadn't got further than writing her new address and *Hi Jude, How are you?*

Mal glanced over his shoulder. 'I'm going to take a walk into the village. Would you like to come?'

Lolly nodded. 'Okay.'

'Go and get your coat. I'll wait for you at the front.'

By the time Lolly got back, Mal was standing at the bottom of the steps. She jogged down to join him and they began to walk together along the drive. He took long strides and every now and again she had to break into a trot to keep up. A light drizzle was falling but she didn't bother to put up her hood.

'You shouldn't mind Esther,' he said. 'She can be a little overenthusiastic at times.'

Lolly looked up at his face, tight and drawn. 'I don't mind being called Lita.'

'You shouldn't do it just because she wants you to.'

'I don't mind,' she repeated. And, in truth, she really didn't. People had always made fun of her name or questioned her about it. Perhaps it was time for a change. *Lita Bruce.* No, it wasn't so bad. And there was the added advantage that if Tony Cecil ever got out of jail and came looking for her, it might not be so easy to track her down. No one would know her as Lolly any more.

'It's up to you. You're the one who has to live with it.'

'I'll give it a go.'

'And the school?' he asked. 'What do you think about that?'

So far as Lolly was concerned one school was much the same as another. 'Is it far away?'

'If you went to Daynor Bridge, you'd have to board. It's in Suffolk. You'd come back for the holidays, of course, and I could visit some weekends, take you out for a few hours.'

Lolly hadn't realised it was a boarding school. She knew they were for posh girls and wasn't sure how she'd fit in. Not

317

that she fitted in anywhere, so perhaps it didn't matter. She was savvy enough to know that Esther wanted her out of the house, and that it wouldn't be sensible to cross her. Strangely, she didn't resent Esther for this. She understood she was a poor replacement for a child that had been lost and at very best would only ever be tolerated.

'Have a ponder on it,' Mal said. 'You don't have to make a decision right now.'

They came to the end of the drive, went through the gate and on into the country lane. A few minutes later they were in the village. As they passed through the centre, Mal was acknowledged by most of the people they passed. She could see he was liked, but also that the villagers kept a respectful distance. She wasn't sure if this was because he owned the big house or because of the tragedy of his lost daughter.

They called in at the florist, where Mal bought a bowl of blue hyacinths, before walking on to the church. This was at the far end of the village, a pretty stone building surrounded by an old graveyard. As they tramped across the wet grass, Lolly paused to try and read the inscriptions on the headstones. Some were so weathered they were barely legible. She breathed in the damp air and hurried to catch up with Mal again.

The final resting place of the Furys was an imposing monument, a wide oblong flanked by pillars, engraved with scrolls and doves and topped by a grey stone angel. There were lots of names on it, the oldest going back to 1803, the most recent that of Catherine Jane Fury who had died in 1959. His mother, she presumed.

As Mal bent to place the bowl of hyacinths at the foot of the headstone, Lolly studied the angel. Its wings were spread out, its eyes downcast. It looked sad, full of pain, and she felt a sudden rush of grief at the loss of her own mum. There was only a simple wooden cross to mark *her* final resting place in Kellston. Lolly still had the money she had started saving for a headstone, the five one-pound notes that were now rolled up in a sock at the back of a drawer in the peacock bedroom. As yet it was too early to know who she could trust and who she couldn't.

Mal took a cloth from his pocket and wiped the November dirt from the headstone. He picked out the debris that had blown into the white crystal stones at its base: the leaves and the litter and the little twirly things from the Sycamore trees. Lolly crouched down and helped him. They worked in silence for a while, both lost in their own thoughts. The only sounds were the thin patter of the rain and the light rustling of their fingers.

Mal looked over at her. 'You don't have to worry,' he said. 'I'll take care of everything.'

Lolly wasn't entirely sure what he meant, but she nodded anyway and smiled. Glancing up at the angel again, she asked, 'Do you think all good people go to heaven?'

'Of course. Why wouldn't they?'

Lolly stared at the fancy headstone, wondering if God took such things as nice masonry into account when deciding whether to open the pearly gates or not. If he did, her mother was in big trouble. 'Even poor ones?'

'Especially poor ones,' he said.

Lolly didn't mention her mum's cheap wooden cross, not wanting him to think she was asking him to buy something better. That was up to her. She'd sort it out when she had enough cash.

'Come on,' he said, rising to his feet. 'We'd better get back before it starts tipping down.'

But already it was too late. The heavy clouds began shedding their load even before they'd reached the church gates. The rain ran off Lolly's head, through her hair and into her eyes. Within seconds, they were both drenched, their clothes dripping wet. They laughed as they raced through the village and along the lane, trying to avoid the puddles. Anyone who didn't know better would have taken them for father and daughter. It was an easy enough mistake to make.

Their smiles only faded as they jogged round the curve in the drive and saw the police car parked outside the house. Mal stopped dead and stared at it. Lolly's heart skipped a beat. Had her lies finally caught up with her? Maybe they'd found out about the false alibi she'd given Jude and had come to arrest her.

'Now what do *they* want?' Mal murmured.

They set off again, this time at a walking pace. Lolly was filled with dread, convinced she was about to be dragged off down the station and exposed. And then, perhaps, they would send her to prison. Well, not prison exactly – she was too young for that – but somewhere similar. Her stomach was churning as they climbed the steps and walked through the front door.

Esther was on them immediately. She came out of the big reception room on the right and hissed at Mal. 'Where have you been? The police are waiting. They've been here for twenty minutes.'

'Yes, I saw the car. What's going on?'

'And look at the state of you both. You're dripping. You're like two drowned rats.'

'What's going on?' Mal repeated.

Esther's nose wrinkled. 'It's about that Stanley Parrish.'

'What about him?'

'Apparently he's—' She stopped abruptly and glanced at Lolly. 'Go downstairs and get Mrs Docherty to find you a towel. And have a hot drink while you're at it.'

Lolly glanced towards the reception room, desperate to know what the police were doing there, but it was clear Esther wanted to get rid of her. Reluctantly, she turned and headed off along the hall towards the stairs that led down to the kitchen.

In the basement, Mrs Docherty was in a flap. There were numerous books open on the big wooden table, their pages old and stained. She was busy scribbling down notes. Her face was red and flustered, her eyes bright with what might have been excitement but could equally well have been panic.

'Can you believe it?' the cook asked, looking up. 'Mrs Fury wants a big do just before Christmas – and that's not many weeks away. And a party of twelve for next weekend. They're all coming back to the house after filming has finished. One minute there's no one here and the next . . . Well, I'm not complaining, I like to keep busy, but—'

'Do you know why the police are here?' Lolly interrupted. 'They're upstairs.'

Mrs Docherty shook her head. 'Now how would I know a thing like that? It's Mr Fury's business, not mine.'

But Lolly didn't believe her. Mrs Gough was always loitering, always listening outside doors. If the cops had been here for twenty minutes, she would have found out and been straight down to share the news. And that wasn't because she was friendly with Mrs Docherty – the two women didn't really get on – but because she liked to lord it over her, to show that nothing happened in the house without her knowing everything about it. 'I think it's something to do with Stanley Parrish.'

'Well, maybe it is and maybe it isn't. You should get that wet coat off before you catch your death.'

Lolly took off her coat and put it by the Aga to dry. She wondered if Stanley had told the cops about Tony Cecil, about what she'd overheard . . . But would he do that? She had no idea. The trouble with grown-ups was that you never knew what they were capable of. Seeing that she wasn't going to get anything more out of Mrs Docherty, she gave up trying, poured herself a glass of milk and went back upstairs to wait in the den.

It was a further fifteen minutes before Mal came to find her. He walked in with one of those grim expressions on his face, sat down and said, 'I'm afraid I have some bad news.' He placed his hands on his thighs and stared at the carpet for a moment before lifting his gaze again. 'It's about Stanley.' He paused, as if gathering his thoughts before proceeding. 'Unfortunately, he was in an accident. He was hit by a car and . . . Well, sadly, he didn't make it.'

Lolly, who had been expecting to hear something quite different, flinched at the news. Her eyes widened with shock. 'What? Is he . . . is he dead?'

Mal nodded. 'He didn't suffer. It was very fast. He wouldn't have known anything about it.'

She wondered if this was true or if it was just one of those things people said to make it all seem less awful than it actually was. Although she hadn't known Stanley well, she felt bad for having suspected him of grassing her up. Then she remembered how he'd kept his promise to check out how Joseph was. And that he'd been searching for her relatives. There would be nobody to find them now. Instantly, a wave of guilt flowed over her for thinking about her own problems instead of what had happened to him. 'He was nice,' she said, not knowing what else to say.

Mal nodded again. 'Yes, he was a decent man.'

'When did he . . . ?'

'Last night. In London.' Mal sat back and sighed. He closed his eyes for a few seconds as if it hadn't quite sunk in yet. 'It was raining and . . . I'm not sure . . . he must have been crossing the road but the driver didn't see him.'

Lolly felt as sorry for Mal as she did for Stanley. She could see that he was shaken up, shocked by the unexpected death. Although he was technically Stanley's employer, they must have built up a friendship over the years, and she knew what it was like to lose a friend. Jude might not have died but it had still felt like a bereavement when he'd stopped spending time with her.

The door opened and Esther poked her head into the room. 'Oh, Mal, here you are. I've been looking for you.'

'I was just explaining about Stanley's accident.'

'If it *was* an accident.'

'And what's that supposed to mean?'

Esther leaned against the door frame, put a hand on her hip and shrugged. 'Why else would the police have come here? You're not a relative or anything. They must think there was something suspicious about it.'

'Don't be ridiculous. It was just routine. They thought, quite rightly, that I'd want to know. He worked for me, didn't he?'

'If you can call it that. Anyway, he's hardly a great loss to the world. I'm sure we'll all get by without him.'

'For God's sake, Esther, show a bit of respect. And if you can't do it for him, do it for me.'

'Respect?' she echoed mockingly. 'That's a joke. I haven't seen much respect for *me* over the years. But then what I wanted didn't matter, did it? The two of you just went ahead with your stupid rewards and your ludicrous blood tests. That man never gave *my* feelings a second thought. You know what?' A small triumphant smile appeared on her lips. 'I think he got what he damn well deserved.'

Mal rose to his feet. 'Stop it! Lolly doesn't need to hear all this.'

'Lita,' Esther said. 'I thought we'd decided on Lita.'

'Jesus,' he murmured.

'What? Are you going to give me a lecture on priorities now? Would you prefer me to be a hypocrite, to say how sorry I am about Stanley Parrish? Well, I'm not ... and I won't.' And with that she turned away and flounced off down the hall.

For a moment, Mal stared at the empty space where she'd been standing, and then he looked at Lolly. 'She doesn't mean it. She's just overwrought.'

But Lolly knew venom when she heard it. She guessed it was all connected to Kay, although she didn't understand why Esther had objected to Stanley's search for her. She remembered the odd-smelling doctor on Albert Road and the needle he had put in her arm.

Mal raked his fingers through his damp hair and took a few deep breaths. 'Sometimes we all say things we regret.'

Esther Fury left the house on Sunday afternoon. She didn't say goodbye to Lolly but just got in her Mercedes, waved goodbye to Mrs Gough and disappeared down the drive. Lolly watched from the first-floor window, standing to one side so she wouldn't be seen. She wasn't sorry to see Esther go. Somehow the house seemed a safer place without her in it.

37

It was during the run-up to Christmas that everything changed again. One tall glittering tree went up in the hall, and another outside the front door. Suddenly the house was always full of people. Lolly would run into complete strangers in the corridors, men in smart tailored suits and women who looked like they'd stepped off a movie set. There was music and dancing and the constant sound of laughter. The champagne corks popped until dawn. Cars came and went, a procession of flashy motors that filled up the drive making it look like an upmarket showroom.

Occasionally, if their paths happened to cross, Esther would introduce her to whoever she was with.

'Oh, yes, this is Lita Bruce, Mal's ward. I told you about her, didn't I? She's an orphan, poor thing. Her mother died in quite tragic circumstances.'

And Lolly, who never knew what to say to the strangers, would smile and hop awkwardly from one foot to another until she could make her escape. Usually she sought refuge down in the kitchen where Mrs Docherty would be flapping around like her clothes were on fire. Girls, including Theresa, came in from the village to help serve the food and drinks and wash up the dishes. The chauffeurs gathered here too, smoking cigarettes, drinking endless mugs of tea and chatting to each other.

When Lolly grew tired of the bustle in the kitchen, she'd hide in the den or the library. Occasionally she would run into Mal who would be sitting reading a book or staring into the bottom of a glass. He seemed worn out by all the company. His face looked gaunt and strained and he often had a faraway expression in his eyes, as though his thoughts were a million miles from the guests who were occupying his house.

Esther, on the other hand, was in her element. She was the perfect sparkling hostess, always at the centre of things, always the focus of everyone's attention. Basking in the spotlight, she positively glowed. Mrs Gough was happy too, having gained a much welcome opportunity to exert her authority and boss around the additional members of staff. She was like the cat that got the cream.

On this particular Saturday night there was an even larger party than usual and the house was full to bursting. Theresa spent most of the time, when she should have been working, gawping at the guests before dashing back to the kitchen to give Mrs Docherty a rundown of who was there, what they were wearing and who they were flirting with. Lolly didn't recognise half the names mentioned, but she was sure that Jude would have known every one of them.

Lolly put on her coat and slipped out the back way into the garden. The air was crisp and cold and smelled of wet grass. There was a full moon shedding light on the ground. She took the path towards the lake, glad to escape all the people and be on her own for a while. It gave her space to think. As she tramped down towards the water, she wondered how Jude was getting on. First thing every morning she checked the hall table where the mail was left, but as yet she'd received no reply to her letter. It would come eventually. She was sure of it. She just had to keep on believing.

The further Lolly got from the house, the more the music faded, until she could barely hear it at all. What she could hear as she grew closer to the lake, however, was the sound of voices, a man's and a woman's. She stopped in her tracks and listened. They must be sitting on the iron bench by the water's edge, the place she'd been heading for herself. The smell of cigarette smoke drifted in the air.

It was the woman who was speaking now. 'You don't really believe that ridiculous story, do you? I mean, his *ward*, for heaven's sake. Everyone knows it's just nonsense.'

'Caroline, darling, by everyone I take it you mean yourself?'

'Oh, don't be so naive! It's clear as day. Esther tries her best but she can't disguise what she really feels. And who can blame her? No wife wants her husband's bastard child littering up the place.'

Lolly, who seemed to spend too much of her life eavesdropping on other people's conversations, might have walked away if the subject had been anything other than this. As it was, she stood very still and continued to listen. Her mouth had dropped open in surprise.

'You can't be sure the kid is Mal's.'

'What other reason could there be for him taking her in like that?'

'Altruism? The desire to help someone less well off than himself?'

The woman gave a high-pitched, slightly drunken laugh. 'That might be what he *wants* you to believe, sweetheart, but it's about as far from the truth as you are from being stone-cold sober. No, mark my words, she's his all right. Probably the result of some sordid little affair while Esther was away filming. I feel sorry for the woman, I really do.'

This time it was the man's turn to laugh. 'Like hell you do. You couldn't be more pleased than if *Jamaica Inn* was the biggest flop at the box office this century.'

'Oh, do you think it will be?'

'Is that the green-eyed monster putting in an appearance? No, my dear, I think it's going to do just fine. And even if it doesn't, that won't be down to Esther's contribution. I hear she was positively electrifying.'

'Now you're just trying to depress me.'

'I wouldn't scowl like that, darling. It'll give you frown lines.'

The woman sighed into the night air. 'God, I need another drink. Let's go inside. It's cold out here.'

Lolly quickly slipped in behind some shrubs and crouched down out of sight. She waited until they'd gone past, and then a little while longer, before emerging again. Then she went to sit on the empty bench. She sat and stared out across the moonlit water, thinking about what she'd heard. It was rubbish, of course. There was no way she was Mal's daughter. If she was, he'd have told her. You didn't keep something like that a secret. And anyway, he'd never even known her mum. At least she didn't think so. Although Brenda had told Freddy she'd mentioned Mal Fury on more than one occasion. But then you couldn't believe everything Brenda said.

Lolly swung her legs back and forth, confused by this latest turn of events. Perhaps the woman wasn't the only one who thought she was Mal's flesh and blood. Did Esther suspect it too? It would explain why she didn't want her there. But she still thought Esther's reasons were more to do with the child she had lost.

Out of nowhere, Lolly suddenly recalled her mum sitting on the bed and reading her a tale called *The Changeling*, where the fairies stole a baby and left in its place one who cried and fretted day and night, who was skinny and squinty-eyed, and who never grew however much he was fed. The ending, when the impostor was chased out of the house and the real child returned to his mother, was supposed to be a happy one, but something about it had never sat quite right with Lolly. She had always wondered about the strange little creature that nobody wanted. What had happened to him? Where had he gone? Perhaps he was still roaming the world searching for someone to love him.

Becoming overly conscious of the silence, she stood up and put her hands in her pockets. She often came to the lake even though it had the power to scare her. Perhaps that was why she came. She wanted to overcome her fears, face up to them. And there was nothing here really but water and mud and the bent sweeping branches of the weeping willows. Her anxiety was mostly created by her own imagination. Bad things had happened here, but they happened everywhere – in tall blocks of flats, on wet London streets, in the back rooms of East End houses.

Nowhere was safe.

It was when she was walking back towards the house, towards the light and the music, that she had the familiar sensation of not being alone. She shivered as she hurried forward, icy fingers running down her spine. It seemed, suddenly, that the ghosts of the dead were all around: her mother, Stanley, Cathy Kershaw, even Amy Wiltshire. Voices whispering in her ear, sad and pleading, as if they wanted something from her. But what? She held her breath, afraid of what she couldn't see and didn't understand.

38

1976

When Lita Bruce looked in the mirror she could see little external evidence of the shabby, bewildered girl who had been delivered to the Furys' home five years ago. Her skin was tanned golden brown by the sun, and her hair, although still long, was glossy and perfectly cut. She had grown a few inches, although she was still not as tall as most of her contemporaries. No one would describe her as a beauty but she was, to all intents and purposes, the finished article – a well-turned-out, confident young woman of reasonable intelligence who could move in polite society without embarrassment to herself or others.

That she had somehow managed to pull this off still amazed her. The transformation seemed miraculous. How on earth had she done it? She wasn't fooled, however, by outward appearances. If she gazed long enough at her reflection, at the pair of wry blue eyes staring back at her, she knew that Lolly was still there, buried deep inside along with all the old fears and insecurities.

Lita turned away from the mirror in the Peacock room, opened the trunk she had left on the floor and began to unpack. It would be the last time she'd ever do this. School was over, finished for ever, and she felt a mixture of relief and regret. On balance, it hadn't been as bad as she'd expected. She had coped with the work, proving herself to be neither brilliant nor stupid, and had emerged with a few certificates, a smattering of French and Italian and a working knowledge of how to get out of a sports car without showing her knickers to the world. The other girls hadn't been too dreadful. Anyway, she had quickly learnt to adapt, changing her accent, her appearance, even the way she walked so she would fit in more easily. In addition, her general kudos had been vastly improved by her connection to Esther.

Esther's career had taken off again after the huge success of *Jamaica Inn*. She had gone on to have starring roles in a number of acclaimed films and been nominated for two more Oscars. Of course none of this had done anything to change her feelings towards Lita. At best she was coolly indifferent, at worst downright hostile. As if by unspoken agreement, they kept their distance from each other and when Lita came back for the holidays it was often to find that Esther was away filming.

This time, however, it was different. Esther was home, and Lita wouldn't be going back to school. She was eighteen and at the end of the summer she'd be starting work full time at Fury's. In stark contrast to her rocky relationship with Esther, her connection to Mal had grown and flourished. He had kept his word and frequently come to visit her at

Daynor Bridge, taking her out at weekends for drives in the country and leisurely lunches.

When she was home, she often went with him to the store in Hatton Garden. It was here that she'd begun a different type of education, learning all about clocks and watches, what they were worth, who the best makers were, how to take them apart, fix them and put them back together again. She had learned about precious stones too, about diamonds and rubies and sapphires. In the past year she had even been let loose on the customers, Mal teaching her how to sell without being pushy.

After she'd finished the unpacking, Lita changed into her old blue jeans and a white T-shirt. All around, she could hear the sounds of a house in turmoil. Tonight Esther was having one of her grand parties and every member of staff was rushing about making sure that all was as it should be. The carpets were being vigorously hoovered, every surface of every room cleansed of any trace of summer dust, every coal scuttle and bathroom tap polished until it positively gleamed. Tables were being laid with plates and cutlery and glasses. Outside, the gardeners were mowing the lawn and hanging strings of lights and Chinese lanterns on the trees.

As Lita walked downstairs to the hall she could smell the heady scent of the lilies being arranged in tall Chinese vases by Mrs Gough. The housekeeper looked up but didn't smile. Relations hadn't exactly thawed on that front either. To Mrs Gough she would always be an unwelcome guest, an interloper, someone who had no place in the Fury household.

'Anything I can do to help?' Lita asked.

Mrs Gough paused, a lily held mid-air, while she tried to think of something suitably unpleasant she could throw her way.

Theresa came out of the big reception room with a cloth in one hand and a tin of polish in the other. 'If you're after a job, Mrs Docherty needs some coffee from the village, the good stuff from Braddock's. Tell them to put it on the bill. I was going to go myself but if you don't mind . . . '

'Not at all,' Lita said quickly. In truth, she'd be glad to get away from the chaos. She turned to Mrs Gough. 'That's if you don't need me for anything else.'

'If Mrs Docherty did a proper stocktake, she wouldn't run out of things,' the housekeeper grumbled. 'There's enough to do without her adding to the list.'

Theresa rolled her eyes and grinned at Lita. 'Good, that's settled then.'

As Lita set off for the village, she could feel the heat on her bare arms. It was a sunny day and the sky was a cloudless blue. Mal had told her all about the party on the journey back from school, feigning an enthusiasm he obviously didn't feel.

'It will be fun,' he said. 'Everyone's going to be there.'

She often wondered why he put up with the constant invasion of his house, suspecting it had something to do with the tricky art of compromise. Was it the price he had to pay for Esther allowing her to stay? Lita never asked and, unsurprisingly, he never volunteered the information. She didn't really understand the Furys' relationship or why they stayed together. They treated each other with a simmering contempt, slept in separate bedrooms and only ever displayed any signs of affection when they were in public.

But then what did she know about love or sex or marriage? She'd never even had a proper boyfriend. Most of her information was gleaned from books and the not altogether reliable evidence of other girls at school. Her own personal experience of romance was restricted to a few unsatisfactory kisses and some embarrassing fumbling in a dark corner of a dance hall.

Lita didn't care much for lads her own age. Most of them were dull and immature with only one thing on their mind. And she'd heard how they talked about girls: if they slept with a boy they were a slapper, and if they didn't they were frigid. So much for equality. It was one rule for them, another for the girls. She wanted something different, *someone* different, but her ideal man wasn't yet fully formed in her imagination. She supposed he'd be smart and funny and interesting, but her ideas were still a rough sketch with none of the finer detail drawn in.

The sun had brought everyone out and the village was busy. Lita made her way through the crowd to Braddock's and got the coffee for Mrs Docherty. It would be needed in the morning when the guests who'd stayed over woke with blurred memories and raging hangovers. The boxes of Krug, which had been delivered yesterday, were piled high in the basement. The amount of champagne consumed at Esther's parties was legendary.

Lita was in no hurry to get back to the house and so wandered round the village for a while, looking in the shop windows. She remembered the first time she'd been here when she'd come shopping with Theresa all those years ago. A lot had changed since then. Theresa was now married to one of the gardeners who worked at the house; she had a little boy called Sam and another baby on the way. Her own life had also undergone a major transformation. She had passed from child to adult – well, almost – and was on the brink of a whole new chapter. It was exciting but scary too.

Lita was still thinking about these things as she walked past a café set back from the road with a courtyard full of tables and chairs and pots of geraniums. It was doing brisk business and most of the tables were taken. Out of the blue a voice called out.

'Lolly! Hey, Lolly!'

Lita swung round, automatically responding to a name she hadn't heard in years. At first she couldn't locate the person who'd shouted, but then a young man stood up in the courtyard and waved at her. It took a moment for her to recognise him, not because he had changed that much, but because she hadn't ever expected to see him here. As he hurried towards her, she felt the blood rushing to her cheeks. It was Jude! Her heart leapt into her mouth. With no time to compose herself, she greeted him with a shocked rather tremulous smile.

'God, what on earth are you doing here?'

He laughed. 'What sort of greeting is that for an old friend?'

'Sorry,' she said. 'I just ... I can't ... I can't believe it's you.' And in a second, what remained of her somewhat superficial confidence slipped away and she was back to being that tongue-tied child who had always been in awe of him.

'Have you got time for a catch-up? I've got a table. Come and have a drink.' He flashed his widest smile. 'Please say yes. It's been for ever and I've got so much to tell you.'

Lita glanced at her watch as if she was the sort of person who had places to go and people to see. She was trying to hide how flustered she was, but probably not succeeding. 'Okay. Yes. Why not?'

'That's great. Come on, I'm just in the corner over there.'

As she followed him across the courtyard, her pulse was racing. She had convinced herself she would never see him again and yet here he was. He was taller, but just as lean, and his hair still flopped over his forehead in that way she had always found so endearing.

As they sat down, Jude beckoned over a waitress. 'Hi, could we have another cappuccino, please?' He glanced at Lita. 'Is that all right or would you rather have something else?'

She would have preferred a cold drink, a Coke or a lemonade, but was afraid it might make her look unsophisticated. 'No, that's lovely. That's great. Thank you.'

After the waitress had gone, Jude inclined his head and stared at her across the table. 'You look different.'

'Do I? Is that in a good or a bad way?' And then she blushed bright red again, aghast at the idea he might think she was fishing for compliments. So, before he could answer, she quickly added, 'Well, it's been five years. It would be strange if I hadn't changed a bit.'

'Yeah, you're looking well. What are you up to these days?'

'I'm starting work at the end of the summer. I've finished school and I've got a job with Mal – he's my guardian – in his jewellery store in London. How about you?'

'Oh, this and that. I'm doing some writing now, freelance stuff mainly, but I'm hoping it'll lead to other things.'

'Are you still living in Kellston?'

'Yes.'

'In the same place?'

'Yes.'

Lita wondered if he had a girlfriend, someone special he was seeing. And why wouldn't he? He was smart and good looking. 'Hey, you still haven't told me why you're here.'

Jude rubbed at his forehead and frowned. He placed his elbows on the table, looked at her, looked away and then met her gaze again. 'I wanted to say sorry. I feel bad about ... well, you know, everything really. I should have got in touch ages ago. I kept putting it off and the time just went by. I suppose I thought ...' The sentence trailed off into a shrug. 'I don't know what I thought. I'm just a lousy friend.'

Lita thought of the three letters she'd written, none of which he'd replied to. 'So why now?'

Before he had a chance to reply, the waitress came with her coffee and put the cup down on the table. Lita thanked her and then turned her attention back to Jude. 'Why now?' she asked again.

'I wanted to check you were okay, see for myself. But

then I got here and started wondering if it was a bad idea, if maybe you wouldn't want to see me. I mean, why would you? I suppose I got cold feet. So I stopped off to grab a coffee while I thought about it. To be honest, I was on the verge of going home when I saw you walking past.'

It made Lita's stomach flip to think that he could have turned around and gone away without her even knowing he'd been here. 'Why wouldn't I want to see you?'

'It was bad all that stuff that happened back then, your mum and everything. I should have been there for you and I wasn't. I only ever thought about Jude Rule.'

'Not always,' she said. 'Don't beat yourself up about it. You had your own problems to deal with. Anyway, it was a long time ago. It's in the past.'

'Do you really mean that?'

'Of course. It's forgotten. Water under the bridge. We were just kids back then.'

Jude smiled at her. 'Thanks. You're a star. But at least let me do something to make it up to you. How about dinner tonight? I noticed a nice little restaurant down the road. I could book a table. What do you say?'

Lita's heart skipped a beat. Was he asking her on a date? Well, perhaps not exactly, but sometimes one thing led to another and ... Suddenly, she remembered where she was supposed to be this evening. 'Oh, I can't,' she said, disappointment sweeping through her. 'I'm sorry. There's a party at the house and ... But why don't you come to that? Yes, say you will. Would you like to?'

Jude pulled a face. 'I wouldn't want to gatecrash.'

'You wouldn't be. Lots of people are going to be there. One more isn't going to make a difference. And anyway, I'm inviting you. You can come as my guest.'

Jude hesitated as though this hadn't been exactly what he'd had in mind. 'I'm not sure.'

Lita, who couldn't bear the thought of losing him so soon after he'd walked back into her life, tried a different tack. 'Do you know Mal's wife is an actress? Esther Gray. She won an Oscar once. You've probably heard of her. Are you still into films?'

'Yeah, that's what I write about mainly. And I'm working on a screenplay too.'

'There you go. You'll love it! The party's going to be full of movie people. You can't possibly miss out on an opportunity like this.'

'Are you sure?'

'Of course,' she said. 'It starts at seven. It's early, but some people have to work in the morning so ... Do you know where the house is?'

Jude nodded. 'I looked up the address on the map. Will I be able to park there?'

'Yes, that's fine. I'll leave your name at the gate. You won't have a problem.' Lita glanced at his jeans and T-shirt. 'It's going to be kind of dressy, though,' she said. 'Not black tie but ... Will you be able to find a jacket by this evening? Or I could ask Mal if he could lend you one. You're about the same height. He wouldn't mind.'

'Don't worry. I'm sure I can find something to make me look respectable.'

Lita took a few sips of the coffee, licking the froth off her lips with the tip of her tongue. There were so many more things she wanted to ask, questions tumbling through her head at a hundred miles an hour, but she didn't need to ask all of them now. She had the whole evening to get her answers. Just the thought of it gave her a warm glow. She stared across the table at Jude and smiled. Suddenly that picture of her perfect man was starting to look a little clearer.

39

Lita rummaged through the wardrobe, dismissing one garment after another. She had no idea exactly what she was looking for, but was certain she'd know it when she saw it. She paused when she came to the little black dress, always a safe option when it came to parties, but then moved on. She wasn't after safe. She wanted something more glamorous, more seductive, something to remind Jude Rule she wasn't a child any more.

The thought of him made her hands shake and her heart beat faster. And okay, maybe he had only come here to salve his conscience, but that still meant he'd been thinking about her. This was enough to give her hope. She must have been on his mind, and that made her happy. Of course, she had often thought about him too. Did she believe in fate? Well, today she did.

Lita's fingers made contact with dark red silk. She pulled the dress from the wardrobe, pulled it over her head and looked in the mirror. It had been an impulse buy, something she'd spotted in a sale but never worn since its purchase six months earlier. Although simple, it was sophisticated too. The silk was soft and clingy, the neckline low-cut enough to show off some cleavage without making her look cheap. She gazed at her reflection and gave a nod. Yes, this was the one.

It was almost seven by the time Lita had brushed her hair until it shone and put on her make-up. She sprayed Chanel No. 5 on her neck and wrists. Finally, she took the ruby necklace Mal had bought her for her eighteenth birthday out of the box and fastened it around her neck. Would she do? She cast one last critical eye at her reflection, wondering if the lipstick she'd been put on was the right shade. But it was too late to do anything about it now. As she left the bedroom, she could feel the butterflies fluttering in her stomach.

Theresa was standing at the bottom of the stairs with a tray of drinks in her hand. Her eyebrows went up as she saw Lita. 'Well, someone's looking fabulous.'

'I like to make the effort.'

'So what's his name?'

Lita feigned innocence. 'I've no idea what you mean.'

'Hey, this is me you're talking to. Spill!'

'Jude,' Lita said, liking the sound of his name on her lips. 'Jude Rule. But he's just an old friend, no one special.'

'Yeah, right. Not special at all.'

'Just someone I know from when I lived in London.'

Mrs Gough walked past and glared at them. 'By the door, Theresa. You're supposed to be standing by the door.'

'Yes, Mrs Gough. I'm on my way.' She glanced at Lita and grinned. 'See you later. Good luck.'

It wasn't long before the house started filling up. The guests poured in and the noise level quickly rose: the sound of voices, of laughter, and the chink of champagne glasses. She could hear the rhythmic beat of the swing band playing in the garden. Lita stayed in the main reception room, chatting to anyone, killing time while she waited for Jude to arrive. She tried not to glance at her watch more than once a minute.

By twenty past seven, she was starting to wonder if he'd had second thoughts. By seven-thirty she'd convinced herself he wasn't coming. Perhaps he wasn't a party person. Perhaps he didn't like crowds. She sipped on her champagne, wishing she hadn't refused his invitation to dinner. But then, just as she was beginning to despair, as all hope was ebbing away, she felt a small nudge to her elbow and turned to find Jude standing right behind her.

'Lolly Bruce!' He looked her up and down, smiling widely. 'How amazing do you look?'

Lita gazed back at him, her eyes drinking him in. He was wearing a stylish dark suit and tie, and his hair was slicked back. He seemed utterly familiar and yet a stranger at the same time. As she pulled in a breath, she managed to say, 'You don't look so bad yourself.'

Jude gave a mock casual shrug. 'Oh, this old thing? It's just something I found in the back of the wardrobe.'

Lita laughed, at the same time wondering whether he'd driven back to London or had already had the suit with him when he'd turned up at West Henby this morning. Something he'd intended to impress her with when he took her out to dinner? The idea gave her a warm feeling inside. 'You do know that no one calls me Lolly any more? I'm Lita now.'

'Lita,' he repeated. 'Okay. That's nice.'

'Let's find you a drink. And are you hungry? There's food next door.'

'Starving,' he said. 'Lead the way.'

Lita took Jude through to the room where a hot and cold buffet had been laid out. Jude filled his plate, but she was too excited and nervous to eat much. She found a few dainty sandwiches, something she could force down, and asked, 'Shall we go into the garden?'

The evening air retained the day's heat. The sun was low now and the air smelled of dust and grass and perfume. It was busy outside and all the chairs had been taken. Jude took off his jacket and laid it on the lawn for her.

'Sit on this,' he said. 'You don't want to spoil your dress.'

For the next hour they talked non-stop, an easy exchange without any awkward silences. She learned about his writing and she told him about school and her own hopes for the future. It all felt so natural, the years apart just melting away. While they chatted, Jude's gaze roamed over the garden, his eyes widening as he spotted a famous actor or a director he admired.

'God, you're so lucky living here.'

Lita wasn't sure if he meant the house or the people who were currently occupying it. She suspected the latter. Not wanting to spoil his enjoyment, she kept her personal opinion of the guests to herself. Most, she thought, were shallow and bitchy with icy hearts and brittle egos. When she looked into their eyes, she saw a kind of blankness – or maybe that was just the booze in them.

It was after eight when Esther came into the crowded garden and immediately everyone turned to stare. She looked stunning in a sparkling ivory gown. Her fair hair was piled on top of her head, her skin was the colour of honey, and a diamond necklace adorned her long swan-like neck. In a matter of seconds, she was surrounded and disappeared from view.

'That's her, isn't it?' Jude whispered, his voice filled with awe. 'That's Esther Gray.'

Lita nodded. 'Yes, that's her.'

He peered over, trying to catch another glimpse. 'She's very beautiful. What's she like? As a person, I mean.'

Lita could have told him the truth, but she bit her tongue. She knew that wasn't what Jude wanted to hear. Instead she went down the diplomatic road. 'You know, I hardly get to see her these days. She's very busy. She's always away filming.'

If Jude noticed the evasion, he didn't comment on it. 'She's an incredible actress. Have you seen *Dark Places*?'

Lita shook her head.

'You should,' he said. 'It's a classic. It's up there with the best.'

Lita, who only wanted to please him, asked, 'Would you like me to introduce you?'

Jude's eyes lit up. 'Seriously? Would you do that?'

'Of course.' But then as soon as she'd said it, she wondered if it was a big mistake. What if Esther was vile to him? Or just plain dismissive? It would spoil the whole evening, ruin it completely. And it might even colour the way he felt about *her*. The more she thought about it, the more uncertain she became.

He must have seen her hesitation because he quickly said, 'I'll understand if you'd rather not. I don't mind. You must get sick of people asking. Don't worry about it.'

But she could see his disappointment and couldn't bear to be the cause of it. 'No, it's not that, not at all. I was just thinking we should wait a while, pick a moment when there aren't so many people around. That way you can have a proper chat.'

'I don't want to be annoying.'

'Why should you be?'

Jude pulled a face. 'It's a private party. She won't want to talk to a fan.'

'You're not a fan. Well, not *just* a fan.' Lita was still trying to reassure him when she saw Esther leave the group of people she'd been standing with and start walking towards them. A young man was tagging along beside her. Jude leapt to his feet, and Lita had no choice but to stand up too.

Esther leaned down and, rather surprisingly, kissed her on the cheek. 'Lita, darling, are you having a lovely time? And who's this? I don't think we've been introduced.'

'This is Jude,' Lita said. 'He's a friend from London. He's a writer.'

'How interesting,' Esther said. 'I just adore writers!'

Jude shook her hand. 'A struggling one, I'm afraid, but I have had some of my work published.'

'How wonderful! You must tell me all about it.' Esther turned to Lita, still smiling. 'Could you be a dear and try to find Mal? Mr Trent here wants a word. He was around earlier but he seems to have gone missing. He's probably hiding out in the library or the den. You know what he's like.'

Lita glanced at Jude, not wanting to leave him, but he was completely oblivious. He had eyes only for Esther.

'Don't worry about your friend. I'll take good care of him until you get back.'

Lita, unable to refuse, gave a nod. 'All right.' She gazed at Trent, a rather plain and undistinguished looking man. 'This way,' she said abruptly.

'Thank you.'

Lita glanced over her shoulder as she led him through the crowd in the garden and back towards the house. Esther had slipped her arm through Jude's and the two of them were talking, their heads close together, as they strolled across the lawn. She supposed she should be glad – Jude must be overjoyed at meeting a real-life film star – but she didn't trust Esther. A spasm of alarm passed through her. Esther could be sly and scheming and was more than capable of putting the knife in. What if she said something to turn Jude against her?

'I'm sorry to be a bother,' Trent said.

'You're not,' she lied.

'Mr Fury didn't mention anything about a party.' He made a gesture towards the clothes he was wearing, a pair of jeans and a dark blue shirt with the sleeves rolled up. 'As you can see, I didn't come dressed for the occasion.'

Lita scanned the faces as they walked, hoping to catch sight of Mal. The sooner she found him, the sooner she could get back to Jude. 'It doesn't matter.'

'When I called, he just said to come to the house at eight o'clock.'

'He won't care what you're wearing.' Lita, who had her mind on other things, presumed he was a dealer, something to do with clocks or watches. She wasn't sure why she jumped to that conclusion, but couldn't imagine any other reason for his meeting with Mal. 'He won't mind in the slightest.'

Lita stopped at the top of the steps and gazed out across the garden, partly looking for Mal but mainly trying to spot Jude and Esther. She drew a blank. There were too many guests, a noisy shifting mass of silk and glitter. The band was taking a break, and the sound of chatter and laughter filled the air.

Trent placed his hands on the wooden rail and leaned forward a little. 'All the beautiful people,' he murmured.

Lita glanced at him, catching the sarcasm in his tone. 'You don't approve.'

'Don't take any notice of me. I can be a churlish sod when I put my mind to it.' He gave a wry smile. 'And even when I don't, to be honest.'

She gave a shrug. 'I can't see him. We'd better try inside.'

But Trent kept on leaning on the balcony, kept on staring out. 'It's a far cry from Kellston.'

Lita jumped. 'What?'

Trent turned to look at her. His eyes were slate grey, not cold exactly but sharp and calculating. 'Isn't that where you grew up? You are Lolly, aren't you?'

'And just who are you?'

'Nick Trent.'

Lita shook her head. 'Is that supposed to mean something to me?'

'No, we've never met before. But you knew my uncle. Stanley Parrish?'

She drew in a breath. It had been a long time since she'd even thought about Stanley. 'Oh,' she said. And now that she looked at Trent more closely, she could see the resemblance, the rather long gaunt face and the mouth that curled down at the corners. 'He was a nice man. I'm sorry about ... It was sad, what happened to him.'

'The accident?'

'Yes,' Lita said.

'If it was an accident.'

Lita frowned. She had a sudden memory of Esther saying exactly the same thing all those years ago. 'What do you mean? Do you think—'

'I don't think anything as yet,' Trent said. 'I'm keeping an open mind. But I'm hoping Mr Fury may be able to shed some light on it all. Maybe I could talk to you too. I don't mean right now or tonight, but tomorrow perhaps? If you could spare half an hour, I'd be very grateful.'

'I suppose,' she said reluctantly, 'but I only met him a couple of times. I'm not sure I could tell you anything useful.'

'Well, who knows what's useful and what isn't? We'll wait and see. If I come here tomorrow afternoon about two o'clock, would that suit you?'

'All right then. Two o'clock.' As Lita left the balcony, leading him through the house and into the coolness of the hallway, she experienced a strange shivery sensation. It might just have been the change in temperature after the warmth of the garden, but it felt like something else: ghosts from the past, perhaps, coming back to haunt her.

40

Nick Trent's life was in the toilet. As he waited in the library – Lita had left him there while she went off to search for Mal Fury – he had plenty of time to muse on this truth. He was twenty-two, jobless and living in a crappy London bedsit that was barely big enough to swing the proverbial cat. He had no direction, no future and a rapidly dwindling bank balance. And whose fault was all of that? His own, of course, as his father never tired of telling him.

Nick's career in the police force had been short and not in the slightest bit sweet. He'd only stuck it out as long as he had because of his mum. She'd been so proud of him, following in his uncle's footsteps, and he hadn't wanted to let her down. But the truth was he'd never been cut out to be a cop. He didn't like taking orders and didn't care for the mentality of most of his colleagues.

The death of his mother – it had only been six months ago – still filled him with a raw, cruel pain. Her life, although she'd never complained, hadn't been a happy one. She had married the wrong man but, like so many women of her generation, had made the best of a bad job. Had she ever considered leaving him? It must have crossed her mind, especially after Stanley had been banished from the house. He hoped she hadn't stayed for his sake, in some mistaken belief that a son needed his father.

It was his mother's will, ironically, that had freed him from the shackles of a job he'd come to loathe. She had left him two thousand pounds, money that she must have scrimped and saved from the meagre housekeeping his father had provided. He'd handed in his notice the day the cash had gone into his account and had been living off it ever since.

Nick had found his uncle's work files when he was helping his father to clear out the garage, half a dozen boxes filled with brown folders. 'What should I do with these?'

'Just throw them in the bin. God knows why your mother kept all that rubbish.'

But Nick hadn't thrown them away. Instead he'd stashed them in his car, half in the boot, half on the back seat, and taken them home. In truth, most of it had made for tedious reading: insurance jobs, divorce cases, investigations into missing cats and the like. It was only when he'd come across the Fury file that his interest had been piqued. It was a thick folder covering years of work, a tale of child kidnap, of murder, of interviews, clues and leads and a string of dead ends. All of which had led him here to Mal Fury's house.

He stood up and walked over to the French windows

that overlooked the garden. The party was in full swing, the champagne flowing, but all Nick could think about was a murdered girl and a lost baby. It was clear from his uncle's long and meticulous notes that he believed Kay Fury had drowned on the day of her abduction – but still the search had gone on. Without any definitive answers, all that had been left was hope.

He sighed, turned away from the revellers and began to pace around the library. Why was he getting involved in this? It was partly down to his conscience, he thought, a means of assuaging his guilt: if he couldn't be a cop – even for his mother's sake – he could at least try and find out the truth about how and why her brother had died. And he'd liked Stanley too. They'd been close when he was a kid, before his father had refused to have him in the house.

Nick rolled his eyes at the thought of it. He hadn't known at the time but there had been a scandal involving Stanley and another man. Back then, homosexuality had been a dirty word, or at least it had been in the Trent household. What had his father been so afraid of? That it might be catching, perhaps, or that Stanley could have perverse designs on his nephew? He could still remember opening the card on his seventeenth birthday to find the ten-pound note inside. By then Stanley was already dead and his mother's eyes were red from crying.

It was down to his mum's sentimentality that so much of Stanley's stuff still existed. When she had emptied his flat and his office, she had kept all the paperwork, including the phone bills. It was from the last of these that Nick had been able to see that Stanley had made two calls on the day he died, one to West End Central police station and the other to Mal Fury.

When Nick had called the house this morning, he hadn't even expected to be put through to Mal. The rich and privileged had ways of protecting themselves from unwanted intrusions. But amazingly the man had taken his call, had been polite, even pleasant when he'd told him who he was, and then invited him over this evening.

'About eight o'clock,' Mal said. 'Would that suit?'

He hadn't mentioned a party and, after driving to West Henby and giving his name to the uniformed guy on the gate, Nick had been surprised to find a drive full of expensive cars and a house full of people. And not just any people. These were the rich and the famous, the crème de la crème. He had recognised the faces as he strolled through the grounds; men and women he'd seen at the cinema or who graced his TV screen.

However, he wasn't the type to be starstruck, and was more curious than in awe of them. They were like a different species inhabiting a different world, a place where the superficiality of fame was all that really mattered. He had noticed Esther straight away and not just from the thick sheaf of press cuttings in the Fury file. She was one of those women who stood out in a crowd.

It had been obvious from Stanley's notes that he'd neither liked nor trusted Esther Fury. At best he had held a grudging sympathy for her (who couldn't feel sorry for someone who had lost a child in such tragic circumstances?) but had, maybe, seen her more clearly than those who were blinded by her beauty. Even now, at the age of thirty-eight, she was enough to take your breath away.

Nick could have asked anyone where he could find Mal Fury but had chosen to put the question to Esther. He had wanted to get up close to her, to get a sense for himself of what she was really like.

'Mal?' she had said, looking round. 'Oh heavens, I've really no idea. He's probably in the house somewhere. Why don't you—' But at that very moment, her attention had been caught by a young couple sitting on the grass a few yards away. 'Actually, I've got a better idea. Come with me.'

Nick had seen that the girl was none too impressed at being despatched to find Mal. And he had seen something else too, the way the guy called Jude looked at Esther. Was he Lita's friend or her boyfriend? It was hard to tell, but the guy only had eyes for the actress. And perhaps the actress liked what she saw too. He was one of those handsome, moody looking blokes, the type who probably modelled himself on James Dean.

It had taken him about thirty seconds to make the connection between Lita and Lolly, the girl the Furys had taken in when she was thirteen years old. He wouldn't have known her from the black and white passport photo Stanley had in the file. She'd looked an odd sort of kid, but then those booths weren't exactly flattering. The grown-up Lita certainly wasn't a beauty – not in the Esther league – although she did have an interesting face. And he didn't mean that in a disparaging way. Bland, pretty girls were ten a penny but there was something about Lita that made you want to look twice.

Nick wasn't sure what to make of her yet. It struck him that she didn't quite fit in with these showy, glittering people, and that the Kellston Lolly still lurked in her somewhere, hidden beneath the fancy clothes and the smoothed-out accent. He knew that Stanley had been concerned about bringing her here, about leaving her here, but perhaps the alternative had seemed too bleak a prospect.

Nick had just returned to the window when the door to the library opened and Mal Fury came in. He was suave and elegant, older than the man in the newspaper clippings but still undeniably handsome.

'My apologies,' he said, striding over to Nick and holding out his hand. 'It's good to meet you. I'm sorry to keep you waiting.'

'And I'm sorry to disturb you. I didn't realise you had guests. We could have arranged a different time.'

Mal shook his head. 'No, really, it's quite all right. Do sit down; make yourself comfortable. Let me get you a drink. Scotch? Or would you prefer a brandy?'

'Scotch is fine, thank you.'

Mal poured the drinks and handed a glass to Nick. 'I liked your uncle,' he said. 'He was a decent man. He had integrity. What happened – well, it was a tragedy.'

'Yes,' Nick agreed. 'It was very sad.' He took a sip of the Scotch; the whisky was deep and smooth, slightly smoky, and slid easily down his throat. 'And I really don't want to cause any upset. I appreciate how delicate the situation is, how painful for you and your wife. I didn't come here to—'

'You just want some answers, right? That's fine. I understand.'

'It's the loose ends,' Nick explained.

'If I can help, I will. You have my word on it.'

'Thank you.' Nick drank some more whisky while he collected his thoughts. Where to start? He was playing this pretty much by ear, wanting to keep the man on side while he tried to squeeze as much information as he could from him. Stanley had liked Mal Fury, which made Nick inclined to like him too, but when it came to murder it didn't pay to trust anyone. 'What I've been wondering is what Stanley spoke to you about on the day of the accident.'

'He didn't.'

Nick frowned. 'I'm sorry?'

'I didn't talk to him that day. I'm sure of it.'

Nick reached into his pocket and took out a phone bill. 'According to this, he made two calls, one to West End Central police station, the other one to here. This is your number, isn't it?'

Mal took the bill and stared down at it. 'Yes. Mrs Gough or Esther must have answered the phone.'

'The call lasted for six minutes.'

'I can only presume that they went to look for me.'

Six minutes seemed like a long time to Nick, but then again it was a big house. 'And he didn't leave a message, not even to let you know he'd called?'

'No. Or maybe they forgot – whoever answered, I mean. I can ask, see if anyone remembers, but after all this time . . . '

'Yes, of course.'

'Do you think it might have been important?'

Nick countered with another question. 'Did he often ring you here?'

'Sometimes here, sometimes at work. But no, not that often. I suppose it could have been about Lita. She hadn't been here long. He might have wanted to check how she was.' Mal Fury gazed at him over the rim of his glass. 'What are you thinking?'

'He called someone at West End Central, had a fifteen-minute conversation with them – well, thereabouts, depending on how long he was on hold – and then immediately tried to call here. It might just be a coincidence, but it suggests he found out something he wanted to talk to you about.'

'It could have been anything.'

'And then a few hours later, he was killed in a hit-and-run in Kellston.'

'You don't think it was an accident?'

'It's never crossed your mind?'

Mal tilted back his head, was silent for a while and then released a sigh. 'The police gave the impression it was straightforward, that the driver panicked and drove off. I mean, why would anyone want to deliberately kill him?'

'Maybe he'd found out something. Maybe he was getting a little too close to the truth.'

'That's a lot of maybes.'

Nick glanced towards the window. From where he was sitting he could see the guests in all their finery parading through the garden. The evening light had a fading quality about it. He returned his attention to the matter in hand, dug into his pocket again, took out another sheet of paper and passed it over. 'And then there's this. The name underlined in red: what can you tell me about him?'

Mal stared down at the list. 'Not much.'

Nick thought the man's face had paled a little but couldn't be sure. 'You knew him, though? You must have done.'

'Briefly, and it was a long time ago. He was a friend of Esther's, one of those down-at-heel actor types, waiting for the big break that was never going to happen. He had a problem.' Mal nodded towards his glass. 'A bit too fond of the hard stuff from what I remember. But he was harmless enough.'

'Did the police ever interview him?'

'I don't know. It was about a year since we'd seen him by then, maybe longer. I don't think he was even in the country. There was a rumour he'd gone to Spain, looking for work on the Spaghetti Westerns. Almeria, I think; they shot a lot of those films in the Tabernas Desert. But the movie business is full of rumours. I've no idea if it was true or not. Anyway, he was never a suspect. Most mornings Teddy was barely capable of tying his shoelaces, never mind pulling off a kidnap.'

'Even drunks need money,' Nick said. 'And it wasn't exactly "pulled off", was it? It all went badly wrong. Hardly the work of a professional.'

'No, I can't see it. Teddy wasn't the type.'

'And what is the type?'

Mal played with his glass while he thought about. 'Cruel, brutal, ruthless? He was none of those things.'

'Vengeful?'

'Why would Teddy want revenge? He had no reason to hate us. On the contrary. We were always good to him.'

Nick wondered whether being the recipient of the Furys' largesse would be enough to trigger a simmering resentment. 'So Stanley never mentioned him to you, never asked you about him?'

'No, never.'

'And you've no idea why he might have underlined the name?'

Mal gave a shrug. 'I really can't think of any reason.'

A silence fell over the room. Nick kept his eyes fixed on Mal Fury. He had the feeling he was being lied to. It was a gut instinct, a kind of inner prompting, but those feelings were often the most telling. Something was wrong – he was sure of it – and he wasn't going to give up until he found out what it was.

41

It had taken Lita longer then she'd expected to hunt down Mal. After leaving Nick Trent in the library, she'd checked all the usual places and then had to go from room to room, pushing through the crowds of people, getting more and more frustrated by the minute. All she'd wanted was to get back to Jude, to make the most of the time they had together. It was Theresa who'd eventually pointed her in the direction of the drive where she found Mal standing by a shiny black Ferrari and chatting to one of the chauffeurs.

'Christ,' he said, when she told him about Trent. 'Is it eight o'clock already?'

'A quarter past. Why is he asking about Stanley after all these years?'

'I've no idea. I suppose there's only one way to find out.'

'He wants to speak to me too. Tomorrow, though, not tonight.'

'You don't have to if you don't want to.'

'I've said I would.'

'You can always change your mind.'

Lita might have pursued the subject if Mal hadn't been hurrying towards the library and she hadn't been distracted by two other thoughts that were jostling for dominance in her brain: one was that Esther could be openly mocking her to Jude, the other that he might at this very moment be having his head turned by some glamorous, seductive girl who'd made a play for him.

Her second search proved as long and frustrating as the first. She began in the garden, weaving between the guests as she crossed the lawn, but he wasn't where he had been. She checked out the area near the band – not there either. Quickly she backtracked to the house where she found Esther in the main reception room surrounded by her entourage. No sign of Jude. This was good in one way – at least the woman wasn't whispering in his ear – but it didn't do anything to allay her other fear. What if he was currently scribbling down the phone number of some predatory blonde and making arrangements to meet up with her in London?

Lita silently cursed Nick Trent. This was his damn fault. If she hadn't had to go chasing after Mal, she wouldn't have had to leave Jude's side. Talk about bad timing. She continued to look – in the room where the food was, the room with the piano, and even in the bathrooms. Eventually she went out to the garden again and began another tour of the crowded lawn. It was then, just as she was starting to lose hope, she finally got lucky. There he was! He was sitting on a low wall near the path to the lake, all alone, watching the party go on around him.

She felt relief and a jumble of other emotions too. As she approached, she didn't just see the man but also the boy he had been. She could clearly recall him standing in the kitchen in the Mansfield flat, buttering bread for peanut butter sandwiches. She saw him come back into the living room and slump down on the old corduroy sofa, his eyes already fixed on the screen. A rush of memories made the breath catch in the back of her throat.

'Ah, there you are,' he said. 'I was just about to come looking for you.'

Lita sat down beside him. 'Sorry, I couldn't find Mal. It took me for ever. Are you having a nice time?'

'The best,' he said, smiling widely. 'Thanks. I've never been to such an amazing party. Did you know Denis Peterson was here? I love his films. And I just saw Maggie Donovan walk past.'

Lita smiled back, glad he was enjoying himself. 'Good. That's great.'

'And you won't believe this, but Esther's offered to read my screenplay. It's a sequel to *Dark Places*. Did I tell you about it? No, I don't think I did. It's not finished yet but ... Anyway she's invited me to come and stay next weekend. She's having some people over, movie people, including a couple of directors and a producer.'

'She's done what?' Lita spluttered.

Instantly his face fell. 'Oh God, I'm sorry. I should have asked you first, shouldn't I? Do you mind? Please say you don't. This could be my big break. And it would give us a chance to spend more time together . . . although maybe you don't want to. I'd understand if you didn't.'

Lita's head was in a whirl. What the hell was Esther playing at? Why would she invite him to stay? It was some kind of weird game, she was sure of it. She felt confused and bewildered, at sea as to what to say next. Of course she wanted to spend more time with him – she couldn't think of anything she wanted more – but on *her* terms, not Esther's. However, when she looked at him, she knew she couldn't say no. It would have been like stamping on his dreams.

'I don't mind. Why should I? But . . . '

Jude jumped to his feet, paced a couple of steps away from her, turned and came back. He grimaced. 'God, I always hate it when there's a 'but'. You'd rather I didn't come next week, right? I'm a complete idiot. I've just come barging into your life again and now—'

'That's not it,' Lita said. 'Honestly.' She stood up too as she struggled to find the right words, to try and warn him that Esther wasn't all she appeared to be. But she couldn't think of a way of doing it that wouldn't crush his hopes. 'I just don't want you to be disappointed. Be cautious, okay? Sometimes people say things or make promises they don't keep.'

'I realise that,' he said dismissively. 'But it's a foot in the door. Don't you see? In this business, it's who you know, not what you know.'

Lita nodded, having done the best she could. 'Well, I'm sure the screenplay's brilliant. I'd love to read it too.'

'So you don't mind me coming next week?'

'Of course not.'

Jude grinned like a little kid who'd just been told he could have a puppy for Christmas. 'Thanks. I can't wait. It's going to be amazing.'

Lita smiled too, despite her reservations. His excitement was contagious. Perhaps she was worrying about nothing. Perhaps, just for once, Esther was doing something nice for someone else. But what were the odds? She chose to push aside that warning voice inside her head, the voice that told her none of it was going to end well.

Jude put his arm round her shoulder and gave her a hug. 'You're my lucky charm, Lolly Bruce, do you know that?'

Lita was too distracted by the closeness of his body, by the feel of his hand on her bare skin, to remind him that no one called her Lolly any more.

42

Lita had gone to sleep thinking about Jude Rule and woke up thinking about him too. It felt like a miracle that he had walked back into her life again, something akin to fate or destiny. He had left the party early, about ten o'clock, claiming that he had to get back to London to work on his screenplay. After he'd gone she'd drifted around for a while before deciding that a party wasn't a party without him and clearing off to bed. The music and dancing had continued until the early hours and she'd dozed on and off until it quietened down.

There was no sign of Esther or Mal at breakfast. Out in the garden the great clear-up was in progress, and as she sat at the table and ate her toast she saw Theresa collecting abandoned glasses from the lawn. In her head, she replayed the evening, going over everything Jude had said, and what she'd said back. She winced a little at the recollection, wishing she'd been wittier, cooler and less eager to please.

Playing 'hard to get' was something the girls had talked about at school. But it was different, wasn't it, between her and Jude? You didn't have to play games with someone you already knew.

They had exchanged phone numbers, but she was determined not to call him before next weekend. Or would that look like she wasn't interested? No, if he wanted to speak to her he could ring the house. She didn't want him to think she was the type of girl who did the chasing. They might have history but five years had passed since they'd last seen each other. Things had changed – they were both adults now – and the rules had changed.

After breakfast, Lita went to the den and set to work repairing an old Omega watch. Usually the intricacy of such work calmed her down but this morning she couldn't concentrate. Her fingers felt thick and clumsy, and nothing would fall into place. After half an hour she gave up and, putting the watch aside, picked up her book and headed out for a walk.

It was going to be another hot day. She ran down the steps and then veered off to the left, taking one of the smaller side paths in order to avoid the people on the lawn. Lita didn't do this because she was lazy or didn't want to help, but because Esther had once caught her picking up some post-party litter and been none too happy about it.

'It's not your place,' she'd said sharply. 'That's what we have staff for.'

But Lita struggled with the concept of what exactly her place was. She didn't feel like a member of the family, but nor was she employed. It left her in a kind of limbo, somewhere in between. The idea of 'them' and 'us' didn't sit comfortably with her: she had not forgotten where she came from and never would. She was an East End girl with an education and a fancy wardrobe. And none of that made her better than anyone else.

All in all, it was easier when Esther wasn't around. Mal didn't care how much time she spent with Theresa or Mrs Docherty, or perhaps he simply didn't notice. She always felt like she was stepping on eggshells when Esther was in the house. And now there was the situation with Jude.

Lita found a quiet spot and sat down on the grass. She opened the novel, stared at the first page and put it down again. What if Esther didn't like Jude's screenplay? What if she laughed in his face and sent him away? And then there was that other niggling worry: what if Jude's *only* reason for coming back was to pursue his career? Maybe he hadn't meant what he'd said about spending more time with her.

Several hours later Lita was still mulling these things over when she returned to the house for lunch. As soon as she stepped into the dining room she could sense the atmosphere between Mal and Esther, fraught and tight as a wire. She had caught the name Teddy as she'd come through the door but it didn't mean anything to her.

Esther, who was wearing a pair of Prada sunglasses, asked, 'What does he want to know about him for?'

'It was just something Stanley Parrish had in his notes.'

Esther gave a snort. 'Stanley Parrish! I thought we'd heard

the last of that man. What's his game, this bloke? What's he after?'

Mal glanced towards Lita and gave a nod. 'The truth, I suppose – whatever that might be.'

'Money, more like. He'll be looking for a way to put the screws on. That type are all the same. Why didn't you tell him to push off? He's only here to cause trouble.'

'He's Stanley's nephew.'

'So what?'

Lita sat down, quickly gathering that they were talking about Nick Trent. She hadn't really cared for the guy herself – not that she'd been paying him much attention – but Esther's antipathy made her warm towards him a little.

'So he deserves some answers,' Mal said. 'I can hardly refuse to speak to him.'

'You can do exactly as you like.'

Mal smiled thinly. 'I already have done.'

One of those cold, unpleasant silences fell across the table. Lita helped herself to chicken salad, wanting to get lunch over and done with as fast as possible. From past experience she knew that a disagreement between the two of them could rapidly escalate into a full-blown row. With no desire to get caught in the crossfire she kept her mouth shut and stayed out of it. So far as she knew Mal hadn't mentioned that Nick Trent was coming back this afternoon and she wasn't about to break the bad news to Esther.

For a while the only sound was the scraping of knives and forks against plates. And then Esther, clearly itching for a fight with someone, turned to Lita and said tightly, 'Well, there's no need to thank me.'

Lita looked at her, bewildered. 'I'm sorry?'

'I thought you'd be grateful that I'm giving your boyfriend a helping hand. Do you have any idea how many scripts I'm asked to read?' A sigh escaped from her scarlet lips. 'Sometimes I wonder why I bother.'

Lita felt her cheeks reddening. 'He's not my boyfriend.'

'What's this?' Mal asked.

'Lita's little friend from London. He wants to be a writer, apparently. I said I'd give his script a read-through. It's probably terrible, bound to be, but I like to be supportive when I can. I've got some people coming down at the weekend and—'

'What, again?' Mal said. 'This house is like Piccadilly Circus. Jesus, can't we have some peace and quiet for a change?'

'You might enjoy being a hermit but some of us prefer a bit of life around the place.' She gave Lita the kind of disparaging glance that suggested she fell well short in this department. 'Anyway, I invited him down to meet a couple of directors. Someone might be interested in taking him on.'

'Maybe you should have asked Lita before you did that.'

'Oh dear,' Esther said, without a hint of remorse. 'Have I gone and put my foot in it?'

Lita could see the amusement on her face, and was quick to deliver a rebuttal. 'It's fine. I don't mind what he does. Why should I? If he wants to ... It's not a problem. It's entirely up to him.' All of which came out sounding rather desperate, a far cry from the cool disinterest she'd intended to portray.

'Well then,' Esther said smugly. 'Everyone's happy. Let's say no more about it.'

Lita had to bite her tongue. She often wondered what would happen if she stood up to her, but preferred to avoid confrontation. She knew that Esther, like all bullies, despised her perceived weakness. But what if she did lash out? There would be repercussions, bad ones, and they would probably start with Jude. He would never forgive her if she blew his big chance – and that, for the moment, was more important than anything else.

Lita ate her lunch as quickly as possible and then excused herself from the table. As she left the room, Esther was starting up with Mal again. Her voice was high and peevish, filled with resentment.

'Why is he bringing Teddy into it after all those years? It stinks, all of it stinks. He's out to cause trouble and you know it. And what are you doing? *Encouraging* him, that's what. It's complete madness. The creep doesn't even—'

Lita closed the door behind her, shutting off the ongoing rant. She found herself curious about this Teddy, whoever he was. She could have put her ear to the door and tried to find out more, but she didn't need to. Nick Trent was the man with the answers and he'd be here in less than an hour.

43

Lita stood on the second-floor landing where she had a perfect view of the drive. Just before two o'clock she saw a dark blue Vauxhall approaching the house, and hurried down the stairs and out of the door. Had she been the type of girl who judged a man by his motor, Nick Trent would have been condemned out of hand: it was old and dented and scratched, with one of the headlamps held together by sticky tape.

He got out and grinned. 'I can see you're admiring my car. It's what I like to describe as vintage.'

Lita suspected he had a chip on his shoulder – she recalled that comment he'd made about the 'beautiful people' – and that this was his method of deflecting criticism. Make a joke and pretend you don't care. 'That's one way of describing it. An old banger would be another.'

'Would you like me to park it somewhere else?'

'What for? It would look equally bad wherever you put it.'

Nick laughed. 'Say it like it is, why don't you?'

Lita glanced towards the house, hoping that Esther – if she looked out of the window any time over the next half-hour – would presume the car belonged to one of the people involved in the clear-up. By now everything had been more or less returned to its former glory, but some final tidying was still in progress. 'I thought we could take a walk. It's too nice to be inside.'

'Sounds good to me.'

Worried that Esther might spot them – in her present mood she was more than capable of ordering him off the premises – Lita quickly led him round the house to the back lawn and then chose the path leading down to the lake. She wanted to go somewhere quiet, somewhere she was sure they wouldn't be discovered. In all the time she'd lived here, she had never known Esther go near the water; it was a place with too many bad memories for her.

'Mr Fury didn't warn you off, then?'

Lita looked at him. 'Why would he do that?'

'Some people don't take kindly to the past being raked up.'

'Mal liked your uncle. I'm sure he wants to help if he can.'

'Perhaps.'

Lita threw him another glance, this one more wary than the last. 'And what's that supposed to mean? He agreed to talk to you, didn't he? That's hardly a sign of *not* wanting to help.'

'It depends on how you look at it.'

They came to the wooden bench and Lita sat down. She was starting to wonder if Esther had a point. Maybe Nick

Trent was only here to cause trouble. She waited until he was seated too before asking, 'And how do *you* look at it?'

'With an open mind.'

'It isn't sounding that way.'

'In my experience, such as it is, I've found that people with something to hide want to know what someone else might know – if you get my drift. That's why they agree to talk to you. It doesn't have anything to do with openness or honesty. It's all connected to self-preservation.'

Lita rolled her eyes. 'I think you're being completely ridiculous. No one has anything to hide. Why would they? Mal and Esther are victims too. You don't even know for sure if Stanley was deliberately killed and already you're throwing accusations around.'

'Hey,' he said, raising his hands for a second, 'I'm not accusing anyone. I'm just being straight with you, telling you how it is. Would you rather I lied? Would you rather I was sly and devious, creeping about, saying one thing and doing another? Only that's not my style. I prefer to be upfront, to put my cards on the table. What happened to Stanley ... Well, something isn't right about it.'

'People have accidents,' she said. 'What makes you think this is any different?'

'Did you know he rang here on the day he died?'

Lita shook her head. 'There's nothing unusual about that. He was working for Mal. I'm sure he rang him all the time.'

Nick Trent leaned back and stretched out his legs. 'Except that no one can remember this particular call.'

'It was five years ago. Could you remember a call from that far back?'

'I'd remember if the person died the same day. I mean, that kind of thing tends to stick in your mind, doesn't it?'

Lita didn't like the way the conversation was going. 'I don't know what you're getting at.'

'Nothing,' he said. 'Forget it. I'm just thinking aloud. You ever heard of a bloke called Joe Quinn?'

The sudden change of tack caught her off guard. 'What's this got to do with him?'

'I've no idea. But he paid Stanley a visit at his office. There was a note about it in his files. He was a very meticulous man, my uncle. He recorded everything.'

'Joe Quinn's a gangster,' Lita said.

'*Was* a gangster. He's been dead for years.'

This was news to Lita, but then she hadn't exactly kept up with events in Kellston. And she couldn't really say that his death brought her any grief. The man had been a brute, an animal. Everyone had been afraid of him. 'Really? I didn't know that. But what could he have wanted with Stanley?'

'To warn him off.'

'Off what?'

'I guess that's the million-dollar question. Stanley wasn't sure, but he thought it was to do with Billy Martin. The guy disappeared years back and hasn't been heard of since.'

'Yes, he asked me about him. The name didn't mean anything. I didn't . . . I can't remember my mum ever mentioning him.'

Nick Trent gave her a strange look.

'What?' she asked.

'I thought . . . No one told you?'

'Told me what?'

Nick pulled a face. 'I thought you knew.'

'Knew what?' Lita gave a sigh of exasperation. 'For God's sake, just tell me, whatever it is. I thought you were all for being honest and straightforward.'

He took a quick breath. 'Okay, she was married to him, right? When she was young your mum was married to Billy Martin.'

Lita barked out a laugh. 'No she wasn't. She wasn't ever married. What makes you think that?'

'Because I've got a copy of the marriage certificate. They ran off to Gretna Green when she was sixteen. It didn't last – she left him – and later they got divorced.'

'What?'

'I'm sorry. I didn't realise. I thought you would have known.'

All kinds of thoughts were running through Lita's head. 'No, she never told me. No one told me.' A tiny flower of hope blossomed in her chest. 'So is he my dad, then? Is this Billy Martin my father?'

Nick shook his head. 'No, there's nothing to indicate that. She left him when he was in jail and that was a good few years before you came along. Then he showed up again in Kellston when you were about five, stayed a few months and disappeared again. Stanley tried to trace him, but he didn't have any luck. Word must have got to Joe Quinn about it, and he didn't seem too pleased. He threatened Stanley, told him to keep his nose out of his business.'

Lita swallowed down her disappointment about having perhaps found her father – although the jail bit didn't sound too good – and stood up and walked over to the water's edge. She gazed out across the lake for a while before glancing back at Nick again. 'You think Joe had something to with Billy's disappearance?'

'Maybe.'

'And Stanley's death?'

'It's not impossible.'

'But how is any of that linked to Kay's abduction?'

Nick stood up and came to stand beside her. 'I haven't a clue. Maybe it doesn't have anything to do with it.' He paused and then said, 'Does the name Teddy mean anything to you?'

Lita probably hesitated a little too long – it had to be the same Teddy she'd heard being discussed at lunch – but then shook her head. 'No, I don't think so.'

'Teddy Heath,' he said.

'No,' she said again. But then the name suddenly clicked into place. She remembered her mother rambling on about him in her less lucid moments, but of course everyone – including herself – had thought she was referring to Ted Heath. She frowned. 'You know, maybe my mum did mention him, but I always presumed she meant the prime minister. Well, he was at the time.'

Nick Trent's eyes brightened with interest. 'Really? What did she say?'

'It was a long time ago. That he was following her, spying on her? But she said that about all sorts of people. When she

379

was ill, she got confused about stuff. Does it mean anything? Do you think it could have been the same guy?'

'It's not that uncommon a name, but there might be a connection. Unfortunately, our Mr Heath seems to have disappeared too.'

A light breeze ruffled the surface of the lake. Preoccupied by their own thoughts, a silence fell between them. It was Lita who eventually broke it. 'What do you think happened to Kay?'

'Stanley thought she drowned on the day of the kidnap.'

'And what do you think?'

'Maybe she did, maybe she didn't. But of course, that's where you come into it. Brenda Cecil had you in the frame as the missing child and it was Stanley's job to investigate the claim.'

Lita gave a dry laugh. 'He was barking up the wrong tree there.'

'It would appear so, yes. But he had to follow through, especially after he discovered Angela wasn't your actual birth mother.'

The words came out of the blue and hit Lita like a punch to her guts. 'W-what?' she stammered hoarsely. 'What are you saying? What do you mean she wasn't—'

'Shit,' he said quickly. 'I didn't . . . I presumed . . . ' Nick's face twisted, his mouth widening into a grimace. 'I'm really sorry. I honestly thought you knew.'

'It's a lie!' Lita yelled at him. 'You're talking rubbish! Why are you saying these things? What's wrong with you?' Her hands clenched into two tight fists. It couldn't be true. She wouldn't allow it to be. 'You're just a vile, nasty person, trying to stir up trouble. You're sick, do you know that? You're sick in the head.'

Nick reached out a hand as if to try and console her, but then dropped his arm back to his side. 'I wouldn't have ever wanted you to find out like this. If I'd thought, even for a minute that—'

'You're twisted,' she continued. 'You come here and ... How could you? Do you get some kind of kick out of trying to hurt people? Is that it? Is that your game?'

'If you don't believe me, ask Mal Fury. Stanley told him all about it.'

Lita's whole body went cold. She couldn't move, couldn't think straight. She felt angry and nauseous and utterly bewildered. He was lying. He had to be. Or he'd just got it horribly wrong. Angela Bruce was Lita's roots, her flesh and blood, her *mother*, for God's sake. And now this disgusting man was trying to snatch away the last good thing from her past. Her mouth opened and closed but no more words came out.

'I'm sorry,' he said again.

Lita couldn't even bear to look at him. She turned away and started to sprint back along the path, her pumps pounding against the path, her chest heaving. When she reached the house, she ran up the steps, through the large reception room and along the corridor to the library. She burst through the door and advanced towards Mal who was sitting by the window.

He stood up, frowning. 'What is it?'

'Tell me it isn't true,' she said, still trying to catch her breath. 'Angela was my mother, wasn't she? She was! Just tell me that she was!'

44

Mal gazed silently back at her with a pained expression. And in that moment Lita knew the answer to her question. She covered her face with her hands as the bottom of her world fell out. The one sure thing in her life and now ... It was like losing her mum all over again, the pain as sharp and visceral as the first time.

'Why didn't you tell me?'

'Sit down,' Mal said. 'Please. Let me explain.'

'I don't want to sit down.' Lita paced around the room, trying to come to terms with this devastating truth. Anger bubbled up inside her. 'How could you have kept it a secret? All these years and ... How could you? Didn't you think I had the right to know? Instead you let me hear it from Nick Trent, a total bloody stranger.'

Mal rose to his feet, shaking his head. 'I didn't realise he knew. I swear. He didn't say anything to me last night, nothing to indicate that—'

'And that makes it all right, does it? That makes it okay? You've lied to me for years. How could you?'

'That isn't true.'

Lita wrapped her arms around her chest, her heart beating so hard she thought it would explode. 'And in what way isn't it true?'

'Because we didn't know for sure, not a hundred per cent. Nothing was ever proved one way or the other. Stanley heard things, was told things, but it was all hearsay. I didn't want to burden you with that, not after everything you'd been through. Why would I want to put that doubt in your mind when you had so much else to deal with?'

Lita, seeing a glimmer of hope, stopped pacing and stared at him. 'So Nick Trent could be wrong?'

'Sit down,' Mal said again. 'I'll tell you everything I know.'

For the next ten minutes Lita sat and listened while Mal went through everything Stanley had discovered. But with each new piece of information – what Ma Fenner and Calvin Cross had said, what the junkie Darren had claimed and what the pathologist remembered – her new-found hope began to flicker and fade. She felt a lump forming in her throat and tried to hold back the tears gathering in her eyes.

'It sounds pretty cut and dried to me,' she said, her voice thin and wavering.

'But not *proven*. I should have told you, you're right, and I'm sorry that I didn't – but I wanted to protect you. She was still your mother in all the important ways. She cared for you as best she could. She loved you.'

'Not enough to stay with me.'

'Maybe, if she wasn't your biological mother, she was scared of the truth coming out, of you being taken away from her. She was ill, confused, probably suffering from some kind of paranoia. And Stanley couldn't find any official adoption papers. There was nothing definitive, nothing to say that she absolutely wasn't your mother.'

'Apart from the fact she couldn't have children.'

'Women have been told that before, but still gone on to have them. Doctors aren't infallible. Sometimes they get it wrong.'

Lita's heart battled with her head. She desperately wanted to cling on to the slender chance Angela Bruce was her mother but it was becoming increasingly difficult to do so. It was as if the fragile edifice her life had been built on was gradually crumbling. Who was she? Where had she really come from? A hundred questions lobbied for dominance, jostling in her mind, but the one that eventually found its way to her lips seemed odd and irrelevant, like a stranger plucked at random from a crowd.

'What about this Teddy Heath?'

'What about him?'

She heard something in the retort – fear, defensiveness – and as she glanced up again, she met Mal's eyes for a second before his gaze slid away. 'You were talking about him at lunch. You and Esther.'

'He has nothing to do with this.'

'Nick Trent was asking about him.'

'Forget about it,' Mal said. 'It's not important.'

As the information about her mother began to sink in,

Lita's head started spinning. She couldn't think in a straight line, couldn't concentrate properly. Her lungs felt hot and tight as she gulped in a breath. Quickly she jumped to her feet.

'Lita?'

She shook her head, her mouth too dry to speak. When she looked around she felt like the walls were closing in on her. She had to get out. She was suffocating. Her legs were unsteady as she stumbled across the room. When she opened the door she had the impression Mal was saying something else, but her brain couldn't process it.

Lita wasn't sure how she got upstairs. By the time she reached her bedroom, she was on the point of collapse. Hot tears were streaming down her face. She lay on the bed, wrapped her arms around her knees and curled up into a ball. Great heaving sobs racked her body. She cried for a long time until she was too exhausted to carry on.

For a while she lay and stared blankly at the peacocks on the wall. Her own breathing filled the silence, a weird rasping sound. She felt desolate: alone, betrayed, abandoned. As if her heart had been ripped out, a sense of emptiness lay at the centre of her, a dreadful void that could never be filled.

Eventually she pulled herself up into a sitting position. Her gaze flicked aimlessly around the room until it finally settled on the bedside table. She reached out for the sea-shell box, placed it on her knees and opened the lid. Inside were all the remnants of her childhood. She took out the tiny mother-of-pearl button and held it in her palm. At this moment she no longer knew what it meant or what it signified. Through the years it had offered her solace, a link to the past, but now all of that felt like a sham.

Lita thought about those old World War Two bombs that were sometimes found on beaches or building sites, a dormant threat no one was ever aware of. They lay there, buried secrets in the ground, dark and ominous, just waiting to blow everything apart. All it took was for someone like Nick Trent to come along and . . .

A low groan slid from between her lips. It was hard to believe how happy she'd been when she'd woken up this morning, filled with optimism and thrilled to have Jude back in her life. Now everything was falling apart. She felt a sudden need to hear his voice, to have the comfort of it. He would understand what she was going through and maybe even help her to make sense of it all.

Lita put the box back on the bedside table and placed the button beside it. After checking the coast was clear, she went downstairs and hurried along the hall. There was a phone in the den and she'd be able to talk in private. Once inside she sat down on one of the old leather chairs, flicked over the pages of her address book – she had meticulously copied down Jude's number last night – and snatched up the receiver. She dialled the number with trembling fingers.

'Please be there,' she murmured. 'Please be there.'

But the phone rang and rang and nobody answered.

Long after she knew it was pointless, Lita continued to sit there with the receiver pressed against her ear. She didn't know what else to do.

45

The following week passed in a blur for Lita. She got up, ate her meals, walked in the grounds, watched TV, had a bath and went to bed. Mal made a few tentative approaches – *If you want to talk about anything* – but she shook her head. She wasn't ready yet. She hadn't come to terms. Nick Trent phoned the house a couple of times but she refused to take his calls. She didn't want to speak to anyone but Jude.

Lita hadn't tried to ring him again. She thought, on reflection, that it was probably fortunate he'd been out. Her emotions had been too fierce, the shock too fresh and raw, for any coherent exchange to have taken place. And having some hysterical female blubbing down the line was probably not conducive to the process of creative writing. No, she would wait until she could talk to him face to face. By then she might be able to share the information without bursting into tears.

A strange calm had descended on her. Or was it just

emptiness? She was wrung out, exhausted by the revelations. She walked around in a daze, barely aware of where she was or what she was doing. The secrets and lies bobbed around in her mind like so much flotsam. She wasn't sure if she'd be able to forgive Mal. Maybe, eventually, she could. There was nothing malicious in what he'd done but she still felt betrayed. As for her mum – well, could she even call her that any more? All that she'd thought she'd known had been wiped away by Nick Trent's careless words. Angela had turned from mother to stranger in the space of a few minutes.

As Lita walked through the garden she could smell the scent of summer roses. She breathed in deeply, trying to fill her soul with something more soothing than anger or resentment. Not knowing exactly where she came from had sparked off too many tumultuous feelings. She had raged, wept, accused and blamed, until her emotions had finally closed down and sent her into this strange trance-like state. In some ways nothing had changed – her childhood memories remained the same – but in other ways, everything. When your life is built on shaky foundations, it only takes the smallest tremor to bring everything crashing down around your ears.

From out of nowhere she suddenly recalled standing in the tunnel on the Mansfield estate with Joseph (and what had happened to him?) talking about family. Once upon a time she might have agreed that flesh and blood wasn't the most important thing, but that was before she had ceased to have any. Now it felt like the most important thing in the world.

Lita climbed the back steps to the house, slipped inside

and walked through to the hall. After the heat of the sun, the coolness gave her goose bumps on her arms. She noticed a large oblong parcel lying on the table and went over to look at it. It was addressed to Esther and she guessed what it was: an advance copy of Jude's script. She thought the thin spidery handwriting was his – although all she had to go on was the phone number he had written out for her – and picked it up to take a closer look. It had a London postmark but no return address on the back.

Lita would have liked to read the script – she was curious as to what it was about – but would have to wait. As she put the parcel back down on the table, she noticed a letter for herself. For a second she thought it might be from Jude, but then realised the handwriting was different. She tore it open and pulled out the sheet of white paper. It was a brief apology from Nick Trent, along with a phone number should she wish to 'contact him'. She curled her lip, screwed up the note and shoved it into her back jeans pocket. It would be going in the first bin she came across.

Lita was on her way to the den – perhaps there was something mindless she could watch on TV – when Mrs Gough and Esther emerged from the main reception room.

'There she is!' Mrs Gough exclaimed, as though Lita had been hiding from them all morning. 'I said she'd show up eventually.'

As the two women advanced on her, Lita could tell she was in trouble, although she had no idea why. Mrs Gough was holding something aloft in her right hand. Her face had a look of triumphant malice.

'Perhaps you'd like to explain *this* to Mrs Fury.'

It took Lita a moment to focus on what exactly 'this' was. She peered up at the housekeeper's hand. 'Oh, it's my button,' she said. 'What are you doing with it?'

'You see what I mean?' Mrs Gough sneered, turning her head towards Esther. 'Didn't I tell you? Little Miss Innocent.' She glanced back at Lita. 'More to the point, what are *you* doing with it?'

Lita stared at her, bemused. She had left the button on the bedside table, unwilling to put it back in her seashell box of treasures. Somehow it had seemed out of place there after what she'd learned.

'What's the matter?' Mrs Gough persisted. 'Cat got your tongue?'

Lita shook her head. 'What's the matter? What's going on? It's only a button.'

'Just answer the question. Where did you get it?'

'It was my mother's,' Lita said. 'I've had it for years.'

Mrs Gough gave a snort. She leaned in close to Lita and hissed into her face. 'You're a filthy little liar!'

Lita jumped back, shocked and confused.

And all the time Esther was simply glaring at her, her lips compressed, her eyes flashing with a barely contained anger.

'Tell the truth!' Mrs Gough demanded, advancing again. 'Did you find it? Was it on the ground? Was it down by the lake? Is that when you got the idea?'

'I've already told you,' Lita snapped back. 'It's mine. I didn't find it anywhere. Look, I don't know what's going on but—'

Mrs Gough grabbed hold of her arm, her fingers digging into the flesh. 'Don't come that one with me, young lady. I know exactly what your game is, and so does everyone else. You think we were born yesterday?'

'Get off!' Lita cried out, struggling to free herself. She had a disturbing flashback to Tony Cecil grabbing her as they passed on the stairs at the pawnbroker's. It was as if she had wandered into some weird surreal nightmare where everything had been turned on its head and nothing made sense.

'You won't get away with it,' Mrs Gough said. 'Whatever you're planning, you won't—'

'Let go! Let go of me!'

The door to the library opened and Mal strode out. 'What's with the noise? What the hell is going on out here?'

Esther tossed back her hair and spoke for the first time. 'You should ask your greedy little ward that question. It would appear that food, clothing, a roof over her head and an expensive education isn't enough for her. No, she wants a lot more than that.'

Lita, who had finally managed to shake off the house-keeper, turned her face towards Mal. 'I don't know what she's talking about.'

Mrs Gough held out the button to him. 'I found this in her room. She's claiming it belonged to her mother.'

Mal took the button and held it in the palm of his hand. His gaze took in all three women before settling on Esther. 'Just because it looks similar, doesn't mean—'

'It's not *similar*,' Esther snapped. 'It's exactly the same.'

'Okay, so it's exactly the same. It's still only one of . . . I don't know, thousands of these must have been made, millions even. It's not *that* unusual.'

Esther glared at him. 'Oh, I might have known you'd take her side.'

'This isn't to do with sides.'

'So it's just a coincidence, is it? It's just freak chance that she happens to have a button like that? Well, you believe what you like but I know a devious little gold-digger when I see one.'

The housekeeper piped up again. 'It's obvious what she's up to. She and that Trent are in it together. First he comes along and claims—'

'Mrs Gough!' Mal said sharply. 'You're really not helping.'

'I'm just saying, that's all.'

'Well, I'd rather you didn't. And please, don't let me keep you. I'm sure you have things you want to get on with.'

Mrs Gough looked less than happy at being dismissed. She glanced towards Esther but finding no immediate support there gave a reluctant nod, threw one last dirty look at Lita and retreated down the hallway.

'Perhaps we could continue this conversation somewhere more private,' Mal said.

Esther shook her head. 'You do what you like. I've got guests to prepare for.'

'We need to sort this out.'

'There isn't anything *to* sort out. She's had her card marked and that's the end of it. Whatever she was planning stops right here.'

Lita stared at her, wide-eyed. 'I wasn't planning anything.'

But her protest fell on stony ground. Esther walked away without another word.

Lita quickly turned to Mal. 'I don't understand. What am I being accused of? I don't get it. I don't know what I've done wrong.'

'Come to the library. We'll talk about it there.'

Lita followed him, feeling shaken and bewildered. She hadn't been in the best frame of mind even before this had happened and now she was totally shell-shocked. All this fuss over a button. It was crazy. Except it was more than a fuss.

'Are you all right?' he asked.

Lita shrugged. 'I just don't understand.'

Mal closed the door to the library behind them, walked over to a mahogany bureau in the corner, opened it and took out a framed photograph. He passed it over to her. 'On the cardigan,' he said. 'Do you see?'

Lita gazed down at a picture of Esther and Kay. The pretty fair-haired baby was dressed in a pink lacy frock and a white cardigan – and on the cardigan was a row of small mother-of-pearl buttons. It was only then that the penny dropped. She gasped in surprise. 'What, they think ... but it can't be the same. It was in my mum's drawer in her bedroom. I swear. I've had it for years.'

Mal nodded. 'I believe you. Like I said, there must have been thousands of these buttons made. It doesn't mean anything.'

Lita continued to stare at the picture. The frown between

her eyes grew deeper as the full implication of her attackers' words sank in. 'So they think I'm trying to ... What? Pretend that I'm Kay or something? Is that what they're saying? But it's crazy! Why would I ever do that? It's sick. It's horrible.'

'You wouldn't. It's all right. Don't get upset. None of this is your fault. I'll talk to Esther, to both of them, and clear all this up.'

'She won't believe you.'

'Of course she will, once she's calmed down, once she realises that she hasn't thought it through. It's just the emotion talking, Lita, nothing else. Someone's been whispering in her ear, stirring up trouble and ... '

And Lita knew exactly who that someone was. Mrs Gough had always disliked her, right from the day she'd arrived. Not that Esther had ever been her biggest fan either. She passed the picture back to him. 'I've never even seen this photo before so how could I have known what the buttons looked like?'

'It's in Esther's room – and it was all over the newspapers at the time.'

'I've never been in Esther's room.' She knew that Mal could have added that the picture had also been in the bureau, right here in the library where she often came to read. And even though it had been out of sight – perhaps too painful for him to look at – she could still have come across it. 'This is the first time ... I haven't seen it before. I swear.'

'I know, I know. Don't worry about it.'

But how was she supposed to do that? Lita couldn't get

394

her head round what had happened – and her head wasn't in the best of places to start with. It was just one disaster after another. Mrs Gough must have found the button on her bedside table, concocted this bizarre story and gone running to Esther with it. How long before the whole house knew about it, maybe even the whole village? And then ... then everyone would think ...

'Here,' Mal said, holding out the button to her.

Lita shrank back, shaking her head. 'You keep it,' she said. 'I don't want it.'

46

Nick Trent was still feeling bad about what he'd inadvertently done. He winced as he relived the moment, recalling Lita's face and the devastation on it. Shattering someone else's life hadn't exactly been top of his agenda when he'd decided to carry on where his uncle had left off. He could, he supposed, justify his actions by claiming he'd had no idea she was in the dark about her mother, but it didn't sit well with him. He should have thought before he'd spoken.

'Moron,' he murmured. 'Idiot.'

His attempts to apologise had, unsurprisingly, fallen on stony ground. It was hard to say sorry when someone wouldn't take your calls. She'd have received his letter by now but he wasn't expecting her to ring. Lita wouldn't want to see him again unless it was to shoot the messenger. His clumsy stupidity had done more than injure another person – it had also cost him a couple of the best leads he had. Neither she nor Mal would be likely to welcome him back in a hurry.

As he flicked through the Fury file, he wondered if Stanley had been in the grip of an obsession. And not just about the disappearance of baby Kay. There were three photographs of Mal and only one of Esther. Perhaps he had slipped over that tenuous line between the professional and personal, developing the kind of feelings for his employer that went above and beyond the call of duty.

Nick pondered on whether he was in danger of becoming equally fixated on a mystery that might never be solved. Eighteen years was a long time. If Kay was still alive – and it was doubtful – she could be anywhere. That, however, wasn't the focus or the purpose of his investigation. It was the circumstances of Stanley's death that bothered him. What had really happened that night in Kellston? He was sure it hadn't been an accident but was still without a shred of evidence to prove it.

'There's something in here,' he muttered as he flicked through the Fury file. 'There has to be.'

It was probably a bad sign, talking to himself. Or did everyone do it in the privacy of their own home? As the word 'home' entered his head, he glanced up at the four dingy walls of his bedsit. If he ever wanted to get out of this dump he'd have to get a proper job. There were two application forms on the table, one for a store detective and the other for Securicor. Neither prospect filled his heart with joy but beggars couldn't be choosers; he needed to address the problem of his shrinking bank balance before it disappeared into the red.

Nick returned his attention to the file. He thought about Teddy Heath for a while, more convinced than ever that Stanley had underlined the name for a reason. And hadn't Mal's responses been a little too rehearsed, a little too casual? Maybe, but it was hard to say for sure. His gut instinct at the time had been that he was lying. And perhaps that explained why Mal hadn't thought to warn him about Lita and the doubts relating to her mother; the man had been too preoccupied with covering his own back.

'Teddy Heath,' he said out loud. 'What the hell do you have to do with all this?' Well, Lita had confirmed that Angela had mentioned him. That must mean something. He had tried calling Equity but drawn a blank. If Teddy was still alive, he was either working under a different name or had ceased to tread the boards long ago.

Nick bent his head and quickly read through the notes Stanley had made on his conversations with Brenda Cecil, Maeve Riley, Ma Fenner, Calvin Cross and Lolly (as Lita had been then). The other loose thread, apart from Teddy, was Billy Martin. It was questions about Billy – Angela's ex – that had given rise to an unwelcome visit from Joe Quinn. Still, that was one thing Nick didn't have to worry about. The old gangster was dead and buried, gone for ever. His threats were as meaningless now as the vicious reputation he'd once had.

It was this thought that prompted Nick into action. The

sun was shining and it wasn't the time to be cooped up in a rabbit hutch. Kellston might not be everyone's ideal destination for a hot summer's day, but that was where he was headed. If in doubt, return to the scene of the crime. Perhaps with Joe out of the way, people would be more prepared to talk.

47

Twenty-four hours, including a restless night's sleep, had done nothing to improve Lita's mood or quell her sense of indignation at being wrongly accused. How was she supposed to defend herself against an accusation that was so monstrous, so appalling as to be almost beyond comprehension? The more she protested her innocence, the guiltier she was likely to look. And all because of a stupid button she had plucked from a drawer five years ago. She cursed herself for leaving it on the bedside table in clear view of Mrs Gough's suspicious eyes. It was the equivalent of leaving out a bullet for her enemy, a bullet that had then been loaded into a gun and fired directly back at her.

Lita's thoughts were running riot. She paced up and down the path by the lake. But Mal trusted her, didn't he? She couldn't bear to think of even a flicker of doubt crossing his mind. He had been her saviour, her white knight, her protector. He had taken her on when no one else wanted her and offered her a future. Yet only a week ago she had been wondering if she could trust him. Now the tables had been turned. Would the two events drive a wedge between them, create a barrier they couldn't overcome? She shuddered at the very idea of it.

And today she had something else to stress about. Jude would be here soon and she had no idea how Esther would react. What if she threw his script back at him, laughed in his face? What if she refused to introduce him to the movers and shakers who could change his life? Lita stopped walking, sat down on the bench and immediately stood up again. It didn't bear thinking about – and so of course she couldn't stop thinking about it. There was no reason for Esther to help Jude. Why would she after everything that had happened?

Lita heard the sound of a car coming down the drive and hurried back towards the house. Already six of the weekend guests had arrived, three expensively dressed business types with their glamorous wives in tow. Surely this had to be Jude. She sent up a silent prayer – *Please God* – that Esther wouldn't spoil everything.

By the time she got to the front of the house, Jude was just getting out of his car. Her heart skipped a beat at the sight of him. He was wearing a light summer suit with a white shirt, and with his dark hair and eyes he looked almost Italian. She slowed down, not wanting to give the impression of being over eager. As she sauntered towards him, she was still trying to decide whether or not to warn him about Esther – but where to start?

In the event, the decision was taken out of her hands. They had barely said hello, barely exchanged smiles, before Esther appeared and came down the steps to greet him.

'Ah, Jude. So you've finally arrived!'

Jude glanced down at his watch. 'I'm not late am I?'

'Not so late that we can't forgive you for it,' Esther said. 'We know what you creative types are like – no sense of time whatsoever. But Mr Leighton is an impatient man so we shouldn't keep him waiting.'

'*Claud* Leighton?'

'Who else? And unfortunately he's brought that terrible little wife with him so we'll have to rely on Lita to keep her occupied while we discuss that excellent script of yours. That's if she doesn't mind.' Esther turned to Lita and flashed a bright, false smile. 'Do you mind, darling? It's a huge favour, I know, the woman's a dreadful bore but I'm sure you can think of some way of distracting her for a couple of hours.'

Lita, who had already seen the flush of excitement appear on Jude's cheeks at the word 'excellent', could hardly say no – not without coming across as someone who didn't give a damn about his future. But she wasn't happy about it. She knew she was being sidelined, deliberately manoeuvred into doing exactly what Esther wanted, and although she inwardly railed against this manipulation she couldn't see a way of avoiding it. 'Well, okay, I'll try.'

'You're a dear,' Esther said as she linked her arm through Jude's. 'Anna's in the garden. We'll see you at lunch.'

Lita watched the two of them walk up the steps. She

waited, half expecting Jude to turn around but he didn't. He had forgotten she was even there. As they disappeared inside, she felt two conflicting feelings – relief and resentment. At least Esther wasn't venting her anger on Jude – that was good – but maybe she had a more devious plan.

Lita found Anna Leighton on the lawn, sunbathing on a striped lounger with a glass of something long and cool beside her. She introduced herself and sat down. Anna was a striking brunette with wide brown eyes and a sulky mouth. She was in her thirties and had the confident air of a woman who knew how attractive she was.

Anna fanned herself with her hand. 'God, it's so damn hot. Is there a pool here?'

'No, only the lake, but no one swims there.'

'Well, they wouldn't would they? I hate the country. It's so bloody boring. What do people do with themselves all day?'

Lita shrugged. As soon as the woman had opened her mouth, she had recognised the accent. 'You're from London, aren't you?'

'Chelsea,' Anna said. Then she gave a low husky laugh. 'Not really. I was born in Mile End. Common as muck, me. Still, I haven't done too badly for myself.' She stopped fanning and held out the hand palm down. On her wedding finger were a gold band and an engagement ring with a huge sparkling diamond. 'The price of love,' she murmured with a cynical smile.

Lita, who knew a bit about diamonds, could tell it was a good one – and worth a fortune. 'It's lovely. Stunning. I grew up in Kellston. That's not so far from Mile End.'

Anna nodded. 'We've both done all right then, haven't we?' She paused before adding, 'Depending on how you look at it.'

Lita wasn't sure what to say to that. She wondered how Jude was getting on and wished she was inside with him instead of stuck here trying to make conversation.

Anna leaned back and yawned. 'Jesus, I'm so bored.'

Lita, who couldn't help but take offence at the woman's attitude, decided to match bluntness with bluntness. 'Why are you here if you hate the country so much?'

Anna arched her eyebrows. 'What, and let Claud come on his own? I don't think so. Do you have any idea how many women want to get their claws into him? I know what these weekend parties are like. It all starts off perfectly civilised but after a few drinks . . . And he's not the type of man who likes to say no, if you get my meaning.'

'I think this is more of a business type thing.'

'Oh, they're all *business type* things,' Anna said with a dismissive wave. 'At least that's how they start off. Plans for this film or that, movie talk, location talk, money talk. It's so damn tedious. And before you know it, they're all pissed as newts and looking for a little fun.'

Lita rolled this information around in her head. From across the other side of the lawn, she could hear the sounds of a game of tennis being played, the thwack of the rackets, the gentle pock of the balls, the occasional exclamation. It must have been the other two wives. Were they here looking for a little fun too? 'My friend Jude has written a screenplay. Esther invited him down to meet your husband.'

404

'Jude,' Anna repeated. 'I don't think I've come across him before.'

'He's a writer. Well, obviously. Anyway, Esther said the script was excellent. It's a sequel to *Dark Places*. Didn't Claud direct the original version?'

'Yes, back in the day.'

'I've never seen it. Have you?'

Anna gave a groan. 'God, yes. I've had to sit through that bloody film more times than I care to recall. Past glories, you see. Claud got his only Oscar for it.'

'And Esther.'

'Yes, of course. And Esther. He says she was a nightmare to work with although that didn't stop him screwing her.' She smiled and lit a cigarette. 'Oh, you're not shocked are you? There's a lot of screwing goes on in the movie business. I'm surprised they ever find the time to make any films.'

Lita couldn't imagine Esther with the balding man she'd seen arrive in the Rolls Royce. 'I guess that was before she was married.'

'She might have been single but he certainly wasn't. Wife number two, or was it three? I've lost count of how many he's had. He has to keep on making films just to pay the alimony. Those greedy bitches want every penny he earns.'

Lita heard the resentment in her voice and quickly tried to change the subject. 'So what's it about, *Dark Places*?'

Anna took another long drag on the cigarette. 'It's about beauty and greed and sex. It's about a woman who can't stand the sight of her husband any more and gets her lover to murder him.'

'And does she get away with it?'

'Of course not. It's the men who control the movie business, darling. They don't let women get away with anything.'

Lita found herself thinking about all those films she'd watched with Jude, most of them with similar stories, most of them conveying the message that strong, clever, beautiful women were always destructive. 'Is Claud interested, do you think, in making a sequel?'

'I've no idea.'

'He's not said anything?'

'Oh, he never stops talking. I just don't listen to what he says. To be honest, I wouldn't get your hopes up; you can't trust anyone in this business.'

'Esther says she likes the script.'

Anna gave her an enigmatic smile. 'Are you sure it's just the script she likes?'

'What do you mean?'

'Nothing, nothing at all.' Anna yawned again. 'Do you know, I think I might have a nap before lunch. I feel quite worn out.'

48

There were ten of them in all at lunch and Lita found herself seated next to Mal at the opposite end of the table to Esther and Jude. Although she tried to dismiss it, Anna's insinuation was still firmly stuck in her mind. She watched them surreptitiously while the chatter and gossip flowed around her. It couldn't be true – the woman was just stirring – but even if it was, Jude wouldn't be interested. Esther might still be beautiful but she was so much older than him. He couldn't possibly . . .

But she didn't like the way Esther leaned in to whisper in his ear, or the light flush that rose into Jude's cheeks. And she didn't care for the way he looked at Esther either, a look she had seen once before when he'd been infatuated with Amy Wiltshire. Or was she just being tired and emotional? It had been a rough few days and she wasn't thinking straight.

The wine flowed freely, and only Lita and Mal stuck to

water. She wanted to keep a clear head. Mal made some small talk but for the most part he was quiet; he seemed distracted, solemn, in a world of his own. Had he talked to Esther about the business with the button? Even if he had, she wouldn't believe him. She would choose to think the worst of Lita, just as she always had.

The lunch seemed to go on for ever. It was a quarter to three before everyone finally rose from the table and drifted off in different directions. Lita grabbed the opportunity to have a word with Jude on his own. They went out into the garden and wandered down past the empty tennis court. She could remember the state of it when she'd first come to the house, but since then all the weeds had been destroyed, the court resurfaced and a new net put up.

Eventually they found a shady spot to sit under the canopy of an old oak tree. She could smell the booze on him as he talked, and he talked non-stop, unable to contain his excitement. It was mainly about the script and what Claud had said to him and what he'd said back, a sentence-by-sentence recitation of the morning's events.

It was only when he paused for breath that Lita was able to ask, 'So has he read it already?'

'Well, no, not the whole thing, but he's read the treatment – and he likes the *idea*. That's the main thing. The rest is just detail. It's amazing, isn't it, Lolly? I can't believe it. Claud Leighton actually wants to work with *me*.'

Lita smiled, not wanting to rain on his parade. This wasn't the time to urge caution. He was too caught up in the thrill of it all. 'It's amazing. Well done.'

'And the three of us are meeting up in London next week. Esther says—'

'Esther's going to be there?' she asked sharply.

'Yes, of course. This is going be her biggest part since she started making films again. I mean, she's going to want some input when it comes to the script. It has to be right, exactly right.'

Lita tried to make her next question sound casual. 'What do you think of her, of Esther?'

Jude stared into the distance for a moment. 'She's . . . well, she's one of *those* women, isn't she?'

'*Those* women?'

He gave a soft laugh. 'Oh, you know, beautiful and dangerous, selfish to the very core. The type who always get what they want, whenever they want it.'

Lita was reminded of something Jude had said long ago. 'Like Amy Wiltshire, you mean?'

Jude's head snapped round, his face instantly darkening. 'Jesus, what are you bringing *her* into this for? What's the matter with you?'

Lita shrank back. 'Sorry, I didn't mean to . . . I just . . .'

'Why are you trying to spoil everything?'

She stared at him, wishing she could take it back, wishing she hadn't spoken.

Jude's jaw was set, his faced twisted. His eyes flashed brightly although whether it was with anger or tears she couldn't really tell. He was quiet for a while, staring down at the ground, before slowly lifting his gaze to look at her again. 'Shit, sorry, I shouldn't have . . . It just brought it all back for a second, finding Amy like that and then the police and everything. It was such an awful time. A nightmare. I don't ever want to think about it again.'

Lita, still stung by his response, said nothing.

'Please don't look at me like that. I didn't mean to have a go. I've had too much to drink and . . . You're the one person I'd never want to hurt.' Jude reached out and gave her arm a friendly squeeze. 'You're my lucky charm, Lolly, remember? And all of this, what's going on now, is down to you. If you hadn't invited me to the party, I'd never have met Esther and she'd never have introduced me to Claud. I'm really grateful. You do realise that, don't you?'

An earlier suspicion snaked its way back into Lita's head. What if Jude's appearance in the village last Saturday hadn't been a coincidence? Maybe he'd already known about the party and was angling for an introduction all along. Maybe he'd had more on his mind than an outstanding apology over something that happened years ago. It was an ugly thought and she tried to push it away.

'It's okay,' she said stiffly. 'And people call me Lita now, remember?'

'I can't get used to that.' Inclining his head to one side, he smiled at her. 'Please say you forgive me, Lita. I'm just a drunken idiot. Tell me how I can make it up to you. I'll take you for that dinner, yeah, next week? What do you reckon? Is it a date? Come on, please say yes.'

Lita, still wary of his motives – and not wanting to look like a pushover – gave a shrug. 'I'll think about it.'

'Good. That's all I want. And now tell me what's been

going on. I've been rambling on about myself for ever. I haven't even asked about you.'

Lita hesitated, not sure if she wanted to confide in him right now. 'Not much.'

'You're the worst liar in the world. Something's up. I mean something more than my awful behaviour. You can tell me. You know you can.'

'It doesn't matter.'

'It clearly does. Come on, just tell me, yeah?'

She glanced at him and looked away. 'It's a bit weird.'

'I can do weird.'

She hesitated again. 'Do you ... do you remember that guy who turned up at the party looking for Mal? Esther brought him over. He was called Nick, Nick Trent.'

Jude nodded. 'What about him?'

And Lita couldn't hold it in any longer. The rest quickly spilled out – Angela's marriage to Billy Martin, the stuff about Teddy, Stanley's 'accident' and, finally, the coup de grâce, the fact that her mother might not be her mother at all. She paused for breath, drawing the thick summer air into her lungs. 'So there you go. If she couldn't have kids, I'm either a modern-day miracle or I'm not actually her daughter.'

'Jesus, what was Mal thinking keeping something like that a secret?'

'I suppose he was trying to protect me.'

'From what? The truth?'

'He didn't know what the truth was, not for sure.'

'He had a pretty good idea.'

Lita pulled up her legs and wrapped her arms around her

knees. 'It's not his fault, not really. He just didn't want to see me get hurt.'

'Why are you defending him? He had no right to keep you in the dark.'

'But it's not an easy decision to make. I think, after Stanley died, he decided it would be kinder to let things lie. I'm not saying it's right, just that I kind of understand it.'

Jude didn't seem to share this point of view. He pulled at the short grass with his fingers, dragging it out by the roots. 'People like him reckon they can do whatever they like. Just because they have money and influence, they think they can walk all over the rest of us.'

'Don't be like that.'

'It's true, though. So what are you going to do now?'

'I don't know. I need some time ... I don't know.'

Jude left off tormenting the grass, put his hands behind his head and leaned back against the trunk of the oak tree. He half closed his eyes and gave a sigh. 'I always used to dream that my mother wasn't my real mum. It would explain why she left like that, just buggered off without a word. I mean, she could have got a divorce, for God's sake, if she wasn't happy. She didn't have to ... Anyway, what the hell. I've done all right without her. And you'll be all right too. I know you will.'

Lita nodded. 'I'll survive.'

'Of course you will. And if you look at it a different way, maybe she did you a favour in the end.'

'A favour?' Lita echoed, not understanding what he meant.

'Well, if she hadn't topped herself like that, you'd never have ended up here.'

Lita stared at him. 'That's a horrible thing to say.'

'Is it?' He frowned. 'I didn't mean it to be, but have you forgotten what it was like back then? Half the time you had nothing to eat, no gas, no electricity. What kind of life is that for a kid? You could have starved to death and she wouldn't have noticed. She wasn't fit to look after you.'

'She was sick. It wasn't her fault.'

Jude rolled his eyes in exasperation. 'Why do you always make excuses for everyone?'

'I don't. I just . . . '

'Yes, you do. You need to get some backbone, Lolly, start standing up for yourself. You're not a kid any more, you're a grown woman. Don't let other people run your life.' He jumped to his feet, brushing the grass off his trousers. 'Figure out what you want and go get it. That's sure as hell what I'm going to do.'

'Where are you going?'

'I need a pee,' he said. 'I won't be long.'

Lita watched him walk over to the house, her gaze fixed on his back. Sometimes Jude was hard to like. He was full of contradictions, kind one moment, cruel the next. But perhaps that was what attracted her. He'd always been different to other boys.

After a while Anna sauntered across the lawn, a cigarette in her hand. 'So that's Jude Rule,' she said, despite having seen him at lunch. 'You should watch out. Your boyfriend is too handsome for his own good.'

'He's not my boyfriend.'

'No,' Anna said slyly. 'I don't believe he is.'

49

It probably wouldn't be the smartest move in the world to approach Terry Street in his own pub and ask if he knew anything about the death of Stanley Parrish, but Nick Trent was running out of ideas. He sat in the Fox, sipping on a pint of London Pride while he thought about it. He'd been in Kellston for over an hour and had already faced two major disappointments. The first had come with the discovery that Ma Fenner had passed away three years ago. Would she have had anything to add to what she'd already told his uncle? Well, he'd never know now. The second had been arriving at Connolly's only to find that Maeve Riley had finished her shift and wouldn't be in work again until tomorrow.

A visit to the pawnbroker's hadn't yielded much of interest either. Brenda Cecil had given him short shrift. She'd welcomed him with a generous smile when he first walked in, but that smile quickly faded at the mention of Lolly Bruce.

Glaring at him through small angry eyes, her whole face had tightened, her jaw jutting out like an attack dog ready to pounce.

'You're wasting your time. I ain't got nothin' to say about that ungrateful little cow.'

'And what about Stanley Parrish?'

'What about him?'

Nick had watched her carefully as he told an outright lie. 'The police are reopening the inquiry into his death. It appears it might not have been an accident after all.'

But Brenda hadn't been fazed. Either that or she was damn good at hiding her feelings. 'Yeah? And what's that got to do with us? Or are the filth going to try and pin that on my Tony too?'

Nick took a few more sips of his pint as he went over the exchange in his head. He couldn't really see a motive for the Cecils killing Stanley. Brenda might have been pissed off at the lack of return she'd got on her investment in Lolly, but it was a big leap from that to cold-blooded murder. No, he couldn't see it, not unless he was missing something.

He glanced across the room at Terry who was currently chatting to a slim but well-developed blonde who kept throwing back her head and laughing too much. To the gangster's right was a guy who looked big enough and mean enough to deter any Tom, Dick or Harry from asking his boss awkward questions. It was, he presumed, the infamous Vinnie who'd accompanied Joe Quinn on his visit to see Stanley.

Nick had done his homework on Terry Street. He knew

that he'd slid effortlessly into the gap left by Joe Quinn and was rapidly becoming even more powerful than his former guvnor. Whether he'd created that gap himself was still a matter for conjecture. Quinn's two sons had gone down for their father's murder but it wouldn't be the first time the law had got it wrong. Anyway, it was a rumour that did little to damage Terry's reputation, reminding his enemies – if they needed reminding – that he wasn't a man to be messed with.

Back when Stanley had died, Terry would only have been nineteen or so, just starting out on his criminal career – which begged the question of how much he might actually have known about Quinn's activities. And even if he had been in on the hit-and-run, was he likely to tell? The answer to that was a big fat no, but Nick was still interested to find out what his reaction would be. It was a risky ploy, however, and perhaps one best left to a time when Vinnie wasn't glued to his side.

Nick, having made a sensible decision for once, finished his pint and left the Fox. He got in his car, drove along Station Road to the place where Stanley had been knocked down and pulled over. It was only a stone's throw from Albert Road, where the toms plied their trade, and he wondered if this was where his uncle had been, or was headed, on the evening he died. But why? Certainly not to indulge in the pleasures of the flesh. When it came to sex, Stanley had had about as much interest in women as Nick had in men.

He sat there for a while hoping for some inspiration but

receiving none. So what now? Reluctant to call it a day – he was no further on than when he'd started – he decided on one last-ditch attempt to find out something, anything, that could shed a little light on Stanley's death.

It turned out to be surprisingly easy to find Sheila Barstow. She was still living at the same Lambeth address recorded in the Fury file five years ago. When she answered the door he passed over one of the cheap business cards he'd had printed – *Nick Trent, Private Investigator*, with a fake West End address and his own phone number – and, smiling pleasantly, asked if she was Billy Martin's sister.

Sheila laughed in his face. 'If it's money you're after, you've come to the wrong place. I ain't seen him in years.'

'No, this is about Angela.'

'What about her? If she wants to know where Billy is, I don't have a clue. I told her straight last time she came round here, kicking up a rumpus, going on about how Billy had "disappeared". The only place he'd disappeared to was some other woman's bed, but she wasn't having it. She was in a right old state.'

'You haven't heard, then?'

'Heard what?'

'I'm afraid Angela is dead.'

Sheila instantly stiffened, her face becoming tight and wary. 'And what's this got to with Billy? What are you saying, that he—'

'No, no, nothing like that. It was five years ago. A suicide.'

'Oh, I see.' When she realised she wasn't about to get

417

dragged into a messy murder inquiry, her body visibly relaxed. 'That's a shame. Poor girl. I'm sorry to hear it.'

Nick gave her the spiel about searching for Angela's relatives and finally got invited inside. Now that he was here, he was almost wishing he wasn't. It was bedlam in the Barstow house. He sat at the kitchen table while a horde of kids ran riot, chasing each other round the living room and up and down the stairs. A dog was barking, the TV blaring out. From the floor above, a baby cried intermittently, thin piercing wails that Sheila appeared oblivious to. He had thought the hardest part would be getting over the threshold but was rapidly revising this view. A dull pain was starting to throb in his temples. While Sheila made a brew, he told her about Lita, that she was eighteen now and hoping to track down some family.

'Well, she's not Billy's if that's what you're thinking.'

'No, I'm aware of that. Angela couldn't have kids, could she? And it's all a bit vague as to where Lita came from. Did your brother ever mention anything to you?'

'Half-brother,' she corrected him. 'And no, he told me sod all. He only came round here when he wanted something. Borrowed a score off me, didn't he? Swore he'd have it back by Friday and that was the last I ever saw of the bastard.' She placed a mug of strong tea in front of him. 'We were never what you'd call close. He has a mean streak, Billy. Gets it from his dad.'

'What about you and Angela? Did you see much of each other?'

'Hang on a moment.' Sheila strode to the door and yelled

418

into the living room. 'Will you lot shut the fuck up! I'm trying to have a conversation here.' She came back to the table and sat down opposite him. 'Not after they split up. I didn't hear from her for years, not until Billy was back on the scene again. And God knows what all that was about. I mean, she knew what he was like. What was she thinking? You don't make the same mistake twice.'

'No,' Nick agreed. 'You wouldn't think so.'

'But there you go. Some women never learn.'

'So you've no idea where Billy is now? Or how I could contact him? No old friends, mates he may have stayed in touch with?'

'Not a clue, love. And I can't say I'm sorry. Life's a damn sight more peaceful when he's not around.'

Nick tried a different tack. 'I don't suppose you've ever heard of a guy called Teddy Heath? Not Ted Heath, the old PM, another one.'

She shook her head. 'Sorry.'

'Billy never mentioned him?'

'No.'

Nick guessed that Sheila wasn't the type to volunteer information even if she had any. She came from a world where you shielded your own no matter what. Billy might not be her favourite person but he was still her flesh and blood. She'd keep her mouth shut unless she had a big enough incentive to open it. 'Lita would be very grateful for any help you could give her. *Very* grateful.'

Sheila lit a fag, puffed out some smoke and stared across the table. 'She got money then, this Lita?'

Nick smiled back. 'Private investigators don't come cheap.'

Sheila thought about this for a while. She took a few more drags on her cigarette and drank some tea. 'How much are we talking?'

'It depends on what you know.' With his finances in a less than healthy state, he couldn't afford to fork out too much. 'A score?' he suggested. 'That way you get back the money Billy owes you.'

'Fifty.'

Nick shook his head. 'No way. Come on, the girl just wants to know who her parents are. That's not too much to ask, is it?'

'And what if I know something important?'

'Do you?'

'Well, not where Billy is, that's for sure, but there is something. I didn't take much notice at the time – Angela wasn't making any sense when she came round – but she kept muttering on about a secret she'd been made to keep. It was something to do with the kid.'

Nick raised his brows in a sceptical fashion.

'Straight up,' she said. 'I'm not having you on.'

'What kind of secret?'

'I dunno. It wouldn't have been a secret if she'd told me, would it?'

'And you want paying for that?'

'No, I want paying for the name she mentioned. I reckon this person might be able to help you – and Lita.'

'Mal Fury?' he asked, unwilling to throw his money away on a lead he already had. 'Esther, Teddy, Brenda Cecil, Joe Quinn?'

Sheila didn't blink at any of the names he threw at her. 'Joe Quinn's dead.'

'So tell me.'

'Forty quid,' she said.

'Thirty – and that's my final offer. Take it or leave it.' Nick held his breath while he waited. Perhaps, finally, he was going to get the break he needed.

50

Lita never did get her dinner with Jude. She had been looking forward to it, even planned what she was going to wear,
when he rang to postpone.

'Sorry, but I'm not feeling too good,' he said. 'I think it's
a dose of summer flu. You don't mind leaving it, do you?'

'No, of course not.'

'But we'll get together soon, yeah? I'll give you a call.'

Lita wasn't sure if she believed him, about his flu *or* the
call. She felt disappointed, let down, but that was nothing
new when it came to Jude. What she should have done was
put him completely out of her mind. What she did was to
think about him constantly.

To make matters worse, there was an awful atmosphere in
the house. Ever since the weekend party, Mal and Esther had
been at each other's throats. Sometimes it was just low-level
sniping, other times there were full-blown rows. Voices were
raised and doors were slammed. When they were in the same

room, the tension was palpable, a simmering antagonism that threatened to explode at any moment.

Lita wasn't sure what the arguments were about. She caught only snatches, hurled accusations that were not explicit in their content. Both sides attributed blame – but blame for what? For what had happened to Kay, perhaps. She wasn't sure. All she knew was that things were escalating and that it would all come to a head sooner rather than later.

Most days Esther got in her car and disappeared for several hours. Mal didn't go to work. He shut himself away in the library or paced the grounds in a furious fashion. He was drinking too much and his face looked grey. Lita was filled with a sense of foreboding. It was as if a loose end had been pulled and everything was gradually unravelling.

In order to escape from the stifling atmosphere of the house, Lita walked down to the village. It was one of those close, humid mornings, the air thick and heavy. The clouds were low and in the distance she could hear rumbles of thunder. By the time she reached the shops, big drops of rain were starting to fall and she hurried for shelter before she got caught in a downpour.

The café with the courtyard was the nearest place. Lita went inside, ordered a coffee and found a free table by the window. She'd barely sat down when the door opened and Theresa came in.

'Hi,' she said, pulling out a chair. 'I thought it was you. You okay? How's things?'

'All right, thanks.' Lita wondered why that response immediately sprang to her lips. British politeness, she supposed, but it was about as far from the truth as it could possibly be. 'You?'

'Not bad. I just dropped Sam off with my mum. I've got a shift at the pub at twelve.' Theresa inclined her head and stared at Lita. 'I've heard things are a bit . . . well, less than peaceful over at the house.'

Lita was no longer surprised by how much the villagers knew about the Fury household. Gossip travelled fast in small communities. 'You could say that.'

Theresa leaned forward, lowering her voice so no one at the surrounding tables could hear. 'What's Esther playing at?'

Lita shrugged. 'I don't have a clue.'

'Of course you do.'

Lita gazed back at her. She didn't want Theresa to think she was holding out, but didn't want to add to the gossip either. 'They're just arguing all the time.'

'Well of course they are. I mean, shit, she's off shagging someone else and—'

'What?'

'Oh, come on. You must have realised. Why else do you think they're at each other's throats? Everyone knows. She's not exactly being discreet. It's humiliating for him, isn't it?'

Lita was shocked, still trying to digest the revelation. She hadn't guessed, not for a second, that this was the cause of the trouble. Now she thought about it, it all made sense: the rowing, the anger, Esther's frequent disappearances. Suddenly a cold wave of suspicion washed over her. A series of images flashed into her head: Esther and Jude sitting together at lunch, the way she whispered in his ear, the way he looked at her. And then there had been Anna Leighton's insinuations. *Are you sure it's just the script she likes?* 'Who . . . who is it?' she stammered. 'Who's she seeing? Do you know?'

Theresa shook her head. 'I've no idea. I thought you might—'

'No,' Lita said quickly. 'I don't. I haven't heard any names. I didn't even . . . No, I don't know.'

'Beats me why the two of them even stay together. It's hardly a marriage made in heaven, is it?' Theresa glanced at her watch, sighed and stood up. 'I'd better go or I'll be late for my shift. Catch you later, yeah?'

'Yeah,' Lita said, forcing a smile.

The waitress turned up with her coffee. Lita's hand shook as she lifted the cup to her lips. All she could think about was Jude and Esther. Could it be true? Was that why Jude had bailed on her? The more she thought about it, the sicker she felt. Esther might be older than him but so what? She was beautiful and glamorous and a part of that world Jude was so entranced by.

It had grown dark outside and the rain was lashing down into the courtyard. Lightning forked across the sky, closely followed by a loud clap of thunder. Lita flinched. She knew she had no rights to Jude's affections, that no promises had been made, but she still felt like her heart was breaking. And what about Mal? She was the one who'd introduced Jude to Esther, and now . . .

Lita took a few deep breaths and tried to rein in her emotions. She was jumping to conclusions that could be completely false. Esther could be having an affair with anyone or no one. Jude could be on the Mansfield, working on his script. None of the bad stuff was necessarily true. She drank some more coffee and stared out at the rain.

It was another fifteen minutes before the storm passed over. Lita paid the bill and left. She walked slowly back along the lane, dragging her feet, reluctant to get home any sooner than she had to. The ground was covered with puddles, the hedgerows drenched in rain. She plodded on with her head bowed, hoping that her worst fears weren't about to become reality.

Lita went through the side gate and along the drive. She was just rounding the bend when she heard raised voices carried on the sluggish air. She thought she caught the name 'Teddy' but couldn't be certain. A few seconds later, when she had a clear view of the entrance to the house, she could see Mal and Esther standing outside the front door. The two of them were in a fight, yelling at each other, their faces twisted and full of rage. Mrs Gough hovered in the background, a silent witness to it all.

'I've had enough. Don't you get it?' Esther was shouting. 'I'm not doing this any more.'

'*You've* had enough. Jesus, that's rich. How can you even—'

'Just stop it, Mal! Stop it! It's over!'

'You're not going!'

'For God's sake!'

Lita was walking forward although she was barely aware of it. Her gaze was fixed on the battle taking place in front

426

of her. Esther turned away and made an attempt to go down the steps, but Mal grabbed hold of her. There was a brief struggle, more shouting, a flailing of arms and then . . . Lita's eyes filled with horror as one moment Esther was at the top of the steps and the next she was tumbling down them.

It all happened so fast, she could barely take it in. And then there was a pause as though time had slowed down, followed by a dreadful silence. Esther lay motionless, strangely twisted, with one arm thrown out by her side. And then suddenly everything started moving again. Mrs Gough let out a small high-pitched scream. Mal launched himself down the steps.

Lita broke into a run. She heard Mal shout for an ambulance and saw Mrs Gough rush back inside. By the time she reached him, Mal was crouched down beside his wife, his face ashen, his lips moving but no sound coming out. For a second, Lita thought she was dead – she had a cold flashback to her mother lying on the grass outside Carlton House – but then saw the shallow movements of Esther's chest. Not conscious, though, and an injury to her head was leaking blood.

'Don't try and move her,' Lita said, recalling her first-aid classes at school. 'Keep her still.' She knelt down beside Mal who finally found his voice.

'Esther,' he said. 'Open your eyes. Talk to me.'

But Esther didn't open her eyes.

'Christ,' he murmured. He covered his face with his hands and groaned. 'What have I done? Jesus, what have I done?'

'She'll be all right,' Lita said, even though she knew the words were empty. Esther looked about as far from all right as a person could be. But she had to say something and didn't want to cause panic. She could smell the booze on him, knew he'd been drinking. Her gaze slid across the drive to where one of Esther's shoes was lying, and then on to the two suitcases that were standing by the boot of the red MG.

People seemed to appear from nowhere, gardeners and cleaners, even Mrs Docherty who had come up from the basement. They stood around, not sure what to do. Mrs Gough had come back and she stayed close to Esther, her teeth bared like a tiger defending her cub. She glared at Mal, her hatred palpable, a thin hiss escaping from between her lips.

It felt like a long time before the ambulance arrived. Lita heard the siren in the distance, the ominous noise that always made her stomach lurch. And this time there was good reason for it. Was Esther slipping away? Her face was pale, almost translucent. She hadn't moved or made a sound since the fall.

The police followed in the wake of the ambulance, and while the medics dealt with Esther, Mrs Gough talked to the cops. It was obvious what she was doing – laying blame where she thought it should be laid. The housekeeper's loyalties were not divided; it was only Esther she cared about.

'He pushed her. I saw it. It was his fault. He pushed her down those steps!'

Lita didn't like what she was saying – surely it had been an accident? – but she didn't get the chance to interject. Mal was trying to get in the ambulance with Esther and one of the officers was barring his path.

'I don't think so, sir.'

'I have to go with her.'

'I'm afraid that won't be possible.'

'Get out of my way!'

And Lita, seeing that he was about to lose his temper, quickly stepped in before he did something else he'd regret. She took his arm and gently tried to pull him aside. 'Leave it, Mal. Come on. Mrs Gough can go to the hospital with her. She won't be on her own. We can follow on behind.'

But Mal wasn't having any of it. The mixture of shock and guilt and alcohol proved to be a lethal combination. Freeing himself from her grasp, he attempted to push past the constable. 'Move! That's my wife. I'm going with her.'

There was an ungainly scuffle that was only ever going to end one way. Thirty seconds later Mal had been handcuffed and was sitting in the back of a panda car. The only place he was going now was the police station. As the ambulance pulled away, Lita prayed that Esther would survive. She had to. She must. If she didn't, Mal's life was about to come crashing down around his ears. Her gaze flicked towards the suitcases still standing on the drive. Lita sucked in a breath. Perhaps it was too late. Perhaps the crashing had already happened.

51

Lita kept eye contact with the constable, determined not to look shifty or evasive. She had told the truth when she'd said she was sure it was an accident, but was prepared to lie when it came to the details. Although it had been a long time since she'd last had to talk to the police, she'd lost none of her natural suspicion. On the Mansfield the cops had been the enemy, and she still didn't trust them.

PC Rowland was sitting at the kitchen table with his notebook. 'But you were quite a distance away. How could you see what happened?'

'Not that far,' Lita replied. 'I was on the drive. I could see quite clearly.'

'And they were arguing?'

'Yes. At the top of the steps.'

'And then what?'

Lita phrased her answer carefully. 'Mal had hold of her arm. Esther kind of twisted away, trying to shake him off, and then ... then she lost her balance and fell down the steps.'

'You're quite sure she wasn't pushed?'

'Quite sure,' Lita said firmly.

'Only Mrs Gough was standing right beside them and she thinks otherwise.'

Lita kept her eyes on him. 'Well, maybe she was *too* close. Sometimes you can't see the wood for the trees, can you? It was all quite fast, but I know what I saw. It was an accident, pure and simple. Mal would never do anything to deliberately hurt Esther.'

'Even if she was leaving him?'

'I wasn't aware that she was.'

'You didn't notice the cases on the drive?'

'There was nothing unusual about that. She often goes away for work.'

The officer wasn't writing anything down. He tapped the pen against the notepad but didn't appear to think that anything she said was important enough to record. 'Mrs Gough says the marriage was over, that Esther Fury was leaving her husband.'

'I don't know about that.'

'Did Mr and Mrs Fury argue a lot?'

Lita inclined her head and gazed at the constable. She could have told him about the recent rows, the simmering tension, but of course she didn't. 'No more than most married couples, I should imagine.' And then before he could interrogate her any further she quickly asked, 'So what's going to happen to Mal?'

'That depends.'

'On what?'

'On what Esther Fury says when she comes round – *if* she comes round. And if we decide to charge him with assaulting a police officer.'

'You won't do that, will you? I mean, he was just upset. All he wanted was to go in the ambulance with her. I know he shouldn't have lashed out, it was stupid, but it was just the heat of the moment.'

'A lot of things can happen in the heat of the moment.'

Lita knew he was referring to Esther's fall, and shook her head. 'He's not a violent man. He's not. Ask anyone in the house, they'll tell you. Ask Mrs Docherty.'

Mrs Docherty, who had been listening to the exchange while she chopped vegetables for a meal that might never be eaten, quickly agreed. 'Not Mr Fury,' she said. 'He's not got a mean bone in his body. And when you think of all he's had to put up with over the years ...'

The constable's eyebrows shifted up. 'Put up with?'

A red flush swept across Mrs Docherty's face as she realised how this might have sounded. 'With the baby and all,' she added smartly. 'With little Kay going missing like that.'

'Yes, it must have been a strain,' he said. 'I suppose—'

Lita jumped to her feet, deciding to put an end to the interview before the policeman began probing even further into Mal and Esther's relationship. 'Well, if there's nothing else ...'

PC Rowland didn't stand up immediately. His gaze drifted between her and Mrs Docherty for a few seconds, his eyes narrow and suspicious. 'We might need you to come down to the station and make a formal statement. I'll let you know.'

'That's fine,' Lita said.

She led him back upstairs and through the hall. The two suitcases had been brought in and were sitting at the base of the stairs. She found herself wondering if someone, somewhere, was waiting for Esther to arrive. Maybe it was Jude. Maybe he was in his flat or a fancy hotel room with champagne on ice and . . . She blinked hard trying to shake the image from her head. No, she couldn't bear to think about it.

When they reached the front door, the constable stopped again and peered along the drive. 'One last thing: perhaps you could point out exactly where you were when the incident took place.'

Lita followed his line of vision. Would Mrs Gough remember where she'd been? She didn't think so. The housekeeper had been too distracted by what was going on between Mal and Esther. Accordingly, she moved her position about ten yards closer to the house. 'By the rhododendrons,' she lied. 'You see, just past the lamp. I was on my way back from the village and it looked like it was going to rain again so I was walking quickly.'

He stared silently along the drive as if trying to mentally assess how clear a view she would have had from this point.

She opened her mouth to add a little extra detail but then thought better of it. It was all too easy to fill a silence with a big mistake.

Eventually he turned to her and nodded. 'Okay. We'll be in touch.'

Lita went inside, closed the door and hurried back down to the basement. Everything had happened so fast, it was only just starting to sink in. What if Esther never came round? Mal could be looking at a manslaughter charge. That's all it took, one random action and everything was changed for ever.

Mrs Docherty stopped her preparations and wiped her hands on her apron. 'I knew something was brewing soon as I saw them at breakfast, but this . . . Do you think Mrs Fury will be all right? She didn't look good, not good at all.'

'Did you know she was leaving?'

'She'd have come back. She always does.'

Lita wondered how many times Esther had walked out before. Being away at school for most of the year she hadn't always been aware of what was going on in the house. She had, however, known that the Furys' relationship was a complicated one, brittle and fragile and only held together by the dark legacy of Kay's abduction.

'Do you think I should call the hospital, try and find out what's happening?'

Mrs Docherty poured out two mugs of tea and passed one over to her. 'It's a bit soon yet, love. She'll have only just got there. Oh, it's a dreadful business, isn't it? What if . . . ? Well, we have to stay positive and hope for the best. That's all we can do.'

Lita was too restless, too anxious, to stay still. She walked around the kitchen while she drank the tea. She hoped Mal had sobered up enough to start thinking clearly. With a bit of luck – and a show of contrition – he might escape with a caution when it came to the assault on the police officer. But that was the least of his problems. If Esther didn't survive . . .

'Can't you stand still for a minute?' Mrs Docherty said. 'You're shredding my nerves pacing up and down like that.'

'Sorry. I just need to be *doing* something.' She stopped walking and leaned against the side of the table. 'He didn't mean to hurt Esther. It was an accident.'

'Of course it was.'

'But that's not what Mrs Gough is saying.'

'Yes, well, Mrs Gough must have got it wrong. Anyway, it'll be Esther they listen to, not her.'

Lita wondered how much of the incident Esther would even recall. Head injuries were strange things. And even if she did remember, she might prefer to tell a different version of events. A niggling doubt had entered Lita's mind. The more she thought about it the less sure she was about what she'd actually seen, although she'd never admit this to anyone. In her experience a secret shared was a secret that was common knowledge within twenty-four hours.

She looked at her watch – it was only one o'clock – and knew that the next few hours would pass slowly. There was a question she wanted to ask Mrs Docherty but was afraid of hearing the answer. It was on the tip of her tongue but still she hesitated. Eventually she took a deep breath and asked as casually as she could, 'Do you know where Esther was going?'

'I've no idea, love, no idea at all.'

'Has she been seeing someone else?'

Mrs Docherty stared at her for a moment over the rim of her mug before her gaze slid away. 'It's not for me to say.'

Lita could see how uncomfortable she looked, but was that because she knew who Esther had been seeing or because she didn't want it known that she listened to gossip about Esther's private life? Mrs Gough was always down here, whispering in her ear, but maybe she wouldn't have shared this particular piece of information.

When it became obvious that Mrs Docherty's lips were firmly sealed, Lita finished her tea and went upstairs. For a while she roamed from room to room, unable to stay still. She walked out of the front door and looked up the drive, hoping to see a taxi round the bend, a taxi with Mal in the passenger seat. But it was way too early for that. The law would keep him down the station for a good bit longer yet, maybe even until after they had talked to Esther. That could be hours, days even.

She went back inside and climbed the stairs to her bedroom where she retrieved the slip of paper with Jude's number on it. She could call and tell him what happened, and from his response – if he was there – she should be able to figure out the truth. But maybe now wasn't the time for that. She dithered, unable to make up her mind. She sat down on the bed and stood up again. She went over to the window and looked outside. She gazed down at the piece of paper.

Eventually, frustrated by her own indecision, she marched down to the hall and snatched up the phone. Doing something was better than nothing, whatever the outcome. Her hand shook a little as she pressed the receiver against her ear. She dialled the number and listened to it ring – but just like before, Jude didn't answer. She could imagine the phone ringing in the room with the green corduroy sofa. She could see the films stacked up on the shelves, the makeshift screen hung on the wall. She sighed down the line. She let it ring for a while longer before giving up. All she could do was try again later.

Over the next few hours, Lita called the number several times but nothing changed. She tried the hospital and was told, rather oddly she thought, that no information could currently be given out about Esther Fury.

'I just want to know if she's all right. I'm Mr and Mrs Fury's ward, Lita Bruce. Surely you can tell me something? We're all very worried about her.'

But the woman on reception was adamant. 'Sorry.'

Lita went down to the kitchen and relayed this latest development to Mrs Docherty. 'What do you think it means? Why won't they tell me anything?' She had a horrible, sickening feeling that Esther might be dead and that the hospital weren't willing to convey this information over the phone. 'You don't think ... What if it's bad news?'

'We'll have to wait for Mrs Gough. There's nothing else we can do. Try not to worry, love. It might just be that they're concerned about the papers. You know what those reporters are like, always poking their noses into other people's business. I mean, you could be anyone, couldn't you? Just because you say you're Lita Bruce doesn't mean you are. Perhaps they're being cautious.'

Lita could see the logic to this, although she wasn't completely reassured. She spent the rest of the afternoon in a state of trepidation, pacing the house while she waited for news on both Esther and Mal. She must have covered a couple of miles by the time Mrs Gough finally returned at ten past six.

The housekeeper came down to the kitchen full of puffed-up self-importance. She didn't even acknowledge Lita, not so much as a glance, completely ignoring her as though she was invisible. Her news was delivered to Mrs Docherty and Mrs Docherty alone. Before proceeding she touched her brow and sighed like some B-movie actress making the most of a cameo role.

'Well, you'll be glad to hear that Mrs Fury has come through the worst. She's not out of the woods yet, of course, but the doctors are pleased with her progress. She's conscious, which is the main thing. Her arm is broken but that will mend in time. The head injury was the biggest worry; they're going to keep her in while they monitor the situation, but there doesn't seem to be too much to worry about.'

Mrs Docherty clapped her hands and smiled. 'That's such good news! What a relief!' She fussed around Mrs Gough, taking her coat, pouring her a cup of tea and settling her in a chair at the table. 'Sit down, sit down. You must be exhausted.'

Mrs Gough eased off her shoes. 'It has been a long day. There's no denying it.'

'Have the police talked to Esther?' Lita asked.

Mrs Gough finally looked at her. She pursed her lips in that familiar fashion. 'Yes, they most certainly have.'

Lita waited but she didn't elaborate. 'So what's happening? Mal isn't back from the police station yet. He's been down there for hours.'

'I don't think he'll be back any time soon.'

Lita exchanged a quick worried glance with Mrs Docherty. 'What do you mean? It was an accident. He didn't mean to hurt her.'

Mrs Gough's expression was almost smug. She knew something the rest of them didn't and wasn't going to rush to break the news.

'They're not going to charge him, are they?' Mrs Docherty asked.

'I should imagine he's already been charged by now.'

Lita sucked in a breath. 'But that's not right. He didn't do it. He didn't push her.'

Mrs Gough sat back, savouring her time in the spotlight. 'I'd say that's the least of his worries at the moment.'

Lita's face grew pale. 'What do you mean?' She stared at the housekeeper, a feeling of dread starting to creep over her. 'What is it? What's going on?'

Mrs Gough left a dramatic pause, slightly lifting her chin before she made the big announcement. 'Mrs Fury has accused him of murder,' she said. 'The murder of Teddy Heath.'

52

There was a cold, stunned silence in the kitchen. Lita opened and closed her mouth like a fish. Her head was spinning as she tried to make sense of what Mrs Gough was telling them. 'Teddy Heath?' she repeated hoarsely. 'Teddy Heath?'

The housekeeper gave a grim smile. 'Indeed.'

Mrs Docherty shook her head. 'Murder? Mr Fury hasn't *murdered* anyone. You've got it wrong. You must have. You've got the wrong end of the stick.'

Mrs Gough's expression tightened at what she probably perceived as an attack on her integrity. 'I was there, Mrs Docherty, sitting right beside her. I heard exactly what she said. It's a secret that she's had to keep for way too long and now ... well, after what happened today she's not prepared to keep quiet about it any more.'

'But murder?' Mrs Docherty said, horrified. 'And who on earth is this Heath person?'

It was a question that Lita didn't need to ask. It wasn't that long since Nick Trent had been asking about him. The man her mother had talked about, fretted about, the man who had allegedly been following her. And the same Teddy – it had to be, didn't it? – who Mal and Esther had been arguing over.

Mrs Gough lifted and dropped her shoulders. 'Just someone the Furys knew. It was way back, years ago, before we came to work here.'

'But why would ... why ... I don't ...' Mrs Docherty spluttered. 'Mr Fury? He'd never do a thing like that.'

'I'm just saying it like I heard it. And there's no point asking me anything else because that's all I know.'

Lita thought this highly unlikely, but decided it was pointless to press her. Instead she left the kitchen and hurried upstairs with her knees shaking and her heart drumming in her chest. She had spent the afternoon stressing over what Esther would say to the police, but had never in a thousand years expected this. It was mad, crazy, an accusation so serious it was impossible to take in properly.

In the library she dug out Mal's address book from the small mahogany bureau and flicked through the pages until she came to an entry for a Lincoln's Inn solicitor called Paul Considine. She dialled the number, hardly expecting anyone to pick up at this time of day, and was surprised when a woman answered. She asked for Mr Considine but was told he wasn't available. Lita explained who she was and asked if he could call her back.

'Of course, but it probably won't be until tomorrow now.'

'Do you know if Mr Considine is in Kent at the moment? Is he with Mal . . . with Mr Fury?'

But the woman wouldn't say. 'I'll let him know you called.'

Aware that this was the best she was going to get, Lita thanked her and hung up. If Mal was being questioned in connection with a murder, then his lawyer had to be with him. She thought about going to the police station – maybe Considine was still there – but had no way of knowing if he would talk to her even if he was.

Lita had another idea. She rushed up the stairs to her bedroom and grabbed her jeans, relieved that she hadn't got around to chucking away the letter Nick Trent had sent. She pulled it from the back pocket and smoothed it out. Then it was back downstairs to the hall where she tapped out a beat on the table while she listened to the ringing at the other end. She had almost given up when the phone was eventually answered.

'Hello?'

'Is that Nick Trent? It's Lita, Lita Bruce.'

'Oh,' he said, sounding surprised. 'I didn't think you'd call. Thanks. I just wanted to apologise for—'

'Yes, yes,' Lita interrupted impatiently. 'I need to ask you something. What do you know about Teddy Heath?'

'Not much. Only that he's an actor and he was friends with the Furys. Why?'

'Is he still alive?'

'I've no idea.'

'Can you find out?'

'I've been trying, but no luck to date. He seems to have disappeared. I think I mentioned it to you.'

Lita felt her stomach lurch. Of course he had. She remembered now. She'd been hoping that Esther's damning accusation was something she'd made up after her fight with Mal, a wild impetuous act of revenge – and about as far from the truth as a lie could be. Now the first glimmer of doubt crept into her mind. 'Disappeared,' she repeated blankly.

'What's going on? Why do you want to know about Teddy?'

Lita wasn't sure how much to reveal. She didn't trust the guy, but he might be her only hope. He knew stuff about the past, perhaps more than he was telling. A few seconds passed while she tried to make up her mind.

'Hello?' he said. 'Are you still there?'

Lita decided to take a chance. 'Look, something's happened. I don't want to go into it over the phone. Can you come here tomorrow?'

'Yes, I can do that. What time?'

'About ten? No, hold on, we'd better make it a bit later.' She was hoping Considine would ring in the morning and didn't want to miss him. 'Let's say midday. And don't come to the house. I'll meet you down in the village. There's a café there with a courtyard. It's near the pub. Do you know it?'

'I'll find it.'

'Okay, I'll see you there at twelve.'

Lita said goodbye and hung up. She stood for a while gazing along the hallway, wondering if she'd done the right thing. But she had nothing to lose. If it turned out that Esther was lying, she could always ring and cancel the appointment. But if she was sticking to her story, Lita would need all the information she could get to help clear Mal's name. He was innocent. He had to be. There was no way he was a murderer.

53

Lita had a restless night's sleep, her dreams full of panic and dread. In them she was trying to run but her legs wouldn't move properly. She was dragging herself along a street in Kellston, desperate to get somewhere although she didn't know exactly where that somewhere was. It was winter, cold and dark, and the rain was lashing down. Jude was waiting for her – she was sure he was – but she wasn't going to get to him on time.

She woke at the crack of dawn, feeling as refreshed as a woman who had been on a treadmill all night. For a while she lay and listened to the chorus of the birds. Haphazard thoughts tumbled through her mind, one leading to another but none of them making a great deal of sense. Eventually a thin bright light began to stream through the gap in the curtains and she knew it was going to be sunny. Yet there would be nothing bright, she suspected, about the day that lay ahead.

Later, hopefully, she would find out what was happening with Mal. Perhaps Esther had already thought better of what she'd told the police and retracted her statement. Or was that just wishful thinking? No matter how hard she tried, Lita could not cast Mal in the role of a murderer. He had always been kind to her, always patient. She had never even seen him lose his temper before yesterday. And what man wouldn't get angry, wouldn't get upset, when he discovered his wife was leaving him?

Immediately she thought of Jude. If he was Esther's lover, surely he'd have rung the house when she hadn't turned up, trying to find out where she was and what was going on. Or maybe he'd presumed she'd had a change of heart and been too proud to go chasing after her. And then another idea entered her head: it was perfectly possible that Esther had got Mrs Gough to call him while she was at the hospital.

Lita got up, had a wash, brushed her teeth and slowly got dressed. She put on her old faded jeans and a black T-shirt, ran a comb through her hair, tied it back in a ponytail and tried to prepare herself for whatever was coming next.

The atmosphere in the kitchen was grim. Mrs Docherty was unusually quiet, shuffling around with her eyes downcast, shifting dishes from one place to another before moving them back again. She seemed at a loss as to what to do or say, and Lita understood how she felt. It was as though the house had undergone a fundamental change. Everything was weird and wrong, and nothing was as it should be.

Lita grabbed some toast and went outside to eat it on the

back step. It was probably too early for Considine to ring but she didn't want to stray too far in case she missed the call. There was no sign of Mrs Gough so presumably she'd returned to the hospital. How long would it be before Esther came home? *If* she came home. But if Mal wasn't here, there was no reason for her to stay away.

The next few hours dragged by. Lita kept looking at her watch as if by sheer force of will she could make the phone start ringing. She roamed around the library, taking books off the shelves, flicking through them and putting them back. She worried about Mal – a night in a police cell can't have been pleasant – and wondered how he was coping. Being falsely accused was a terrible thing.

It was exactly 9.32 when the phone finally sprang into life. Lita rushed out of the library and snatched up the receiver.

'Hello? Yes?'

'Is that Lita?'

'Yes, yes it is.'

'This is Paul Considine. Apologies for the delay in getting back. I wanted to see Mr Fury again before I spoke to you.'

The lawyer had a soft, lilting Scottish accent that under different circumstances might have sounded reassuring, but she heard something in its tone that sent a chill down her spine. 'Is he all right? God, no, of course he isn't. What's going on? Can you say? Is it true that ... Mrs Gough claims he's going to be charged with the murder of Teddy Heath, that Esther has ... I don't understand. She came back from the hospital last night and ...' Then, realising she wasn't giving him time to speak, she sucked in a breath and said,

'Sorry, sorry. I'm not making any sense. I'm just ... my head's all over the place.'

'That's all right. But I'm afraid the news isn't good.'

Lita pressed the receiver against her ear. She swallowed hard, trying to stay calm, trying to prepare herself. 'Okay. Just tell me.'

As she listened to what Paul Considine had to say, she felt the hope rush from her lungs and the ground shift beneath her. She didn't interrupt, didn't ask any questions. It was all she could do to remain on her feet. His words flowed over and around her like some terrible tsunami.

54

Mal Fury lay back on the hard, narrow bunk, put his hands behind his head and gazed up at the ceiling. The police cell was small and bare, but he wouldn't be here for long. Soon they'd be taking him to the magistrates' court and from there, after he had entered his plea, to a London jail where he would be put in another cell probably not that different to this one. For now there was little else he could do but accept it.

Twenty-four hours was all it had taken to rip his life apart. He could have denied the charge, of course, but Esther knew too much. Her betrayal didn't come as any great shock. What was more surprising, perhaps, was that she'd kept her mouth shut for all these years. But now he understood that she'd simply been waiting for the right time, for the moment she could use the revelation to her own advantage. And he had played right into her hands.

Mal smiled wryly. It didn't pay to underestimate a woman

like Esther. When she wanted something, nothing would stop her. She had played out the scene to perfection, drawing on all her acting abilities. And made damn sure there was a witness too. What she couldn't have anticipated was that she'd fall so badly, but even that had turned out to her advantage. Now she could paint him as a cruel and violent man, the kind of husband who wouldn't think twice about throwing his wife down a flight of steps.

Mal felt less afraid than he probably should, although in truth he was still trying to get his head round it all. One minute he'd been in the frame for assault – well, two charges of assault if he counted the one against the officer who had tried to stop him getting in the ambulance – and the next he'd been staring down the barrel of a life sentence.

DI Stone had been one of the detectives who'd interviewed him, an ageing, wily cop who had seen it all and heard it all, and probably wished he hadn't. He'd interspersed his questions with soft wistful sighs, as though he harboured a quiet despair at the depths to which so many human beings sank.

'Tell me about Teddy Heath. When did you first meet him?'

Mal had thought about it. 'It was before Kay was born. Three years? Four? Maybe longer. I don't remember exactly. He was an actor of sorts. He didn't get much work, bit parts mainly, but he liked to hang out with the crowd. I suppose he was quite charming in a drunken, louche kind of way.'

'And your wife? How did she feel about Teddy?'

'Oh, you already know the answer to that question. They

450

had a brief affair, nothing serious. She soon got bored. As it happens, Esther has a very low boredom threshold. Teddy wasn't the first and he wasn't the last.'

'And how did that make you feel?'

'How do you think? But I'd learned to live with it by then. They came and went. We survived – the marriage survived. That's how it was. I don't expect you to understand. Why should you? I suppose our relationship isn't what you'd call conventional.'

'Some people might think that you killed Teddy Heath because he had an affair with your wife.'

Mal gave a dry smile. 'If I'd murdered every man my wife had ever slept with, Inspector, you'd be looking at a serial killer.'

DI Stone hadn't smiled back. He'd stared at him, a slow careful scrutiny while he weighed up the truth – or otherwise – of what Mal was saying. 'So when was the last time you saw Teddy? I mean, the last time before you bumped into him again in London.'

'I don't recall exactly. A year, eighteen months before Kay came along? He wasn't her father if that's what you're thinking. No, he was well gone by then. There were rumours he was working in Spain, Almeria, but who knows? The acting business is full of rumour and gossip.'

The next part of the interview had gone pretty much along the same lines as his conversation with Nick Trent, with Stone asking whether he'd ever suspected Teddy after Kay's abduction and Mal saying that it had never crossed his mind. 'Teddy wasn't an aggressive sort of person. He might

451

not have been what you'd call moral but even when he was drunk – which was most of the time – he was still good-natured. I got the impression he never planned anything, that he was one of those men who just drift through life.'

'So take me through what happened that day in London. This was about two years after Kay was taken, is that right?'

'Yes, 1960. It was November, early evening, about half past five. I was walking along Shaftesbury Avenue – I'd been to see a client in Covent Garden – when I spotted him. Well, I'd already walked straight past when I suddenly realised who it was. I turned round and called out his name. And that's when it happened. Teddy turned round too, saw me, and then seemed to freeze. He had this look on his face – pure fear, horror – as though he'd just seen a ghost. And then he suddenly took off and sprinted away down the street. That's when I knew.'

'What did you know, Mr Fury?'

'That he'd had something to do with Kay's abduction.'

DI Stone raised his eyebrows. 'That's quite a leap, don't you think? I mean, couldn't he have wanted to avoid you for a different reason? Like the fact he'd been sleeping with your wife, for instance?'

'No, I'd seen him plenty of times after his affair with Esther ended. If I'd been going to confront him about it, I'd have done it long ago. This was something else. Call it a gut feeling, if you like, but no one reacts that way unless they're seriously scared.'

'So you went after him?'

'No, not straight away. It was too late to try and catch up.

He was out of sight by then. But I knew he'd need a drink after what had just happened. Teddy always needed a drink. So I decided to head into Soho and see if I could track him down. I figured it wasn't that far away and was the kind of place he might feel safe.'

'And you found him?'

'Not for hours. I must have checked out every pub and bar before I finally came across him in a seedy little dive at the bottom of Berwick Street. It was late by then, almost closing time. He didn't see me enter the bar so I went back outside and waited for him there. When he came out I followed him to his flat. I kept my distance but he was too drunk by then to be cautious. It was Lexington Street, about halfway along. He had a place above a shop, a barber's.'

Mal had paused to drink some water. His mouth was dry and he had the start of a hangover headache. He'd spent years trying to forget what had happened next, to delete the memory from his brain, but now it was all flooding back.

'And then?' DI Stone prompted.

'I caught up with him just as he had the key in the lock. He tried to bolt again but I was ready this time. I pushed him through the door and up the stairs. Two flights. He was frightened. I could see that. Even with the booze inside him. I don't know what I said exactly, something about having to know what happened to Kay. He tried to make out he didn't understand, but his heart wasn't really in it. He knew he'd blown it the minute he did a runner. That's the irony, I suppose: if he hadn't lost his nerve when we bumped into each other, I'd never have suspected him.'

Mal lifted the plastic cup and drank some more water before he continued. 'We went into the flat – it was filthy, a hovel – and that's when he dropped the innocent act. He knew there was no point in pretending any more. He said it was all down to Esther, that he'd taken Kay to punish her, so she'd know how it felt to lose someone you loved. He was angry, bitter about how she'd treated him. It all came pouring out in a drunken tirade. I didn't believe him, not entirely; I still think it was more about the money. He said he'd never meant to kill Cathy Kershaw, it had been an accident, but after that he'd been too afraid to go through with the ransom demand.'

DI Stone nodded. 'Go on.'

'All I wanted to know was whether my daughter was still alive. That was the only thing that mattered. I didn't want to hear his self-pitying crap. But then he turned all sly on me, said if I laid a finger on him or went to the law I'd never find out the truth, that he'd deny everything and I'd never see Kay again. He said she was safe, that she was living some-where I'd never find her. He said we could make a deal, come to an "arrangement", that if I paid him the reward money he'd tell me where she was.'

'Did you believe him?'

'I wanted to. At least I wanted to believe she wasn't dead. But I didn't trust him. And I was angry, at my wits' end. It felt like he was playing games with me, with my daughter's life and I just … I snapped, I suppose, and grabbed hold of him. I punched him, once, a couple of times perhaps – I'm not sure – and he staggered back and fell on the floor.

I think I was shouting at him, swearing. Then he started clutching his chest. I thought he was faking it, just trying it on but then his eyes rolled back and . . .' Mal shook his head. 'He must have had a heart attack. I didn't mean to kill him, I just—'

'There's no proof that you did kill him,' Considine interrupted. He looked across the table at DI Stone. 'Teddy Heath could have had a heart attack at any time. He was already sick, and he drank and smoked excessively. While it might be true that my client exacerbated the situation, in no way can it be proved that Heath died as a direct consequence of his actions that night. In fact, he called an ambulance and did all he could to try and revive the man. The *last* thing he wanted was to kill Teddy Heath – Teddy was the only person who knew of his daughter's whereabouts.'

Mal came back to the present, blinked a couple of times and continued to gaze up at the ceiling and the web of cracks running across the plaster. He had agreed in the end to plead guilty to involuntary manslaughter. Considine had recommended this, saying that if he got a sympathetic judge prepared to take into account the mitigating circumstances, he might get a suspended sentence. If he pleaded not guilty, the case would be in the hands of the jury and they might, if he was unlucky, decide that he had used excessive force in trying to persuade Teddy to come clean.

Parts of that night were not entirely clear to Mal. Had he waited for the police and the ambulance to arrive he would probably have been in a better position to explain and defend his actions, but instead he'd panicked. There had been no phone in the flat and he'd had to run down the street to find one. By the time he'd finished making the anonymous call, he'd known he wasn't going back.

This had been his first mistake, and the second had been his confession to Esther. He had still been in shock, of course, by the time he got home. Dazed and shaken, he hadn't thought twice about telling her everything. For the next few days they had waited for the knock on the door, for the police to make the connection between them and Teddy Heath – but it had never happened.

It was Mal who'd spotted the piece in the *Evening News*, the story about a man called Harry Taylor found dead in suspicious circumstances at his flat in Soho. That was when he realised Teddy had been using a pseudonym, reversing his initials, and that this fake identity meant the police didn't know who the victim actually was. And that was how it had stayed until now.

Mal felt no remorse over Teddy Heath's death, only regret. That fatal heart attack had robbed them of what might have been their only opportunity of discovering the truth. Kay was still out there somewhere, alive or dead. This was why Esther had stayed for so long. Guilt had been the third party in their marriage for all these years – her guilt for sleeping with Teddy in the first place, his for blowing the one chance of finding their daughter. Secrecy and lies had been the glue holding them together. But not any more. Esther had drawn a line and was finally moving on. She had turned her back on him. She had thrown him to the dogs.

55

Lita was still trying to absorb everything Paul Considine had told her. None of it felt quite real, more like a far-fetched drama on the TV than something that was happening in real life. That Mal had lived with such a terrible secret for so long filled her with surprise and sadness. He must have always been looking over his shoulder, always waiting for the law to catch up with him. Sixteen years of fear and uncertainty.

She neither judged nor blamed him for what had taken place that night in Soho. Who wouldn't have done the same in his shoes? Esther, however, was a different matter. Mal's actions were understandable, but hers felt cold and vengeful. She hadn't just chosen to leave him but to try and destroy him in the process. Lita wondered if this was a knee-jerk reaction, a response to the event of yesterday, or if she had planned it all along.

She was pondering on this – and leaning towards the latter option – when Mrs Gough walked into the library.

Lita was surprised to see her, thinking she was still at the hospital. The housekeeper approached with a cold expression on her face. Her voice was tight and clipped, authoritarian. 'According to the doctors, Mrs Fury will be discharged within the week. She'll be returning here, to the house, where she can be properly taken care of.'

'I see.'

'Do you?' Mrs Gough asked. 'I hope so. Only with the current situation being as it is, Mrs Fury would prefer that you weren't here on her return.'

Lita stared at her, not sure if she entirely understood. 'Not here? You mean—'

'What I mean is that you can't live here any more. It simply isn't acceptable. You were always Mr Fury's responsibility and now that he's ... Well, it isn't up to her to look after you.'

Lita was dumbfounded. 'She's kicking me out? She can't do that. This is my home.'

'You're eighteen now. It's time to stand on your own two feet.'

A thin, brittle laugh escaped from Lita's lips. 'And where am I supposed to go? I haven't got any family, for God's sake. I haven't got any money.'

Mrs Gough reached into her pocket, took out an envelope and passed it over. 'There's a hundred pounds in here. I think Mrs Fury has been more than generous. It should be enough to tide you over until you find a job.'

'So you're just going to throw me out on the street?' Lita was tempted to hurl the money back in her face, but practicality overcame what would only be an empty gesture. Pride was all very well but it didn't put food on the table. 'Mal isn't going to be happy.'

'I'm sure Mr Fury has more important things on his mind at the moment.'

Lita knew this was true, and that it was pointless to argue. Although she could have dug in her heels, refused to leave, she knew the atmosphere would be intolerable once Esther returned. And who wanted to stay where they weren't wanted? It could be months, even years, before Mal was back. 'Fine,' she said. 'I'll go. I'll go today.'

'No one's saying that you have to go straight away. You can take a few days to make some arrangements.'

'That won't be necessary.'

Lita stormed out of the library and up the stairs, wondering what those arrangements could possibly be. It wasn't as if she had any relatives or close friends. There was Theresa of course, but she lived with her husband and son in a small two-up, two-down cottage that was cramped enough without an additional person in it. And it wouldn't be long before the new baby arrived. Although Theresa would never turn her away, she knew it wasn't fair to ask.

Lita went into her bedroom and sat down on the bed. The more she thought about it, the less she wanted to stay in the village. There'd be gossip. There'd be whispering and pointing. She'd be the girl who'd been thrown out of the big house – and Mrs Gough wouldn't be slow to start some rumours as to why that was. Maybe she'd even bring up the business of the button.

Lita winced, jumped up, went over to the wardrobe and opened the doors. Having decided she was better off away from West Henby, she could only think of one other place to go. It would have to be London. And there were advantages in heading for the big city: one was that she should be able to find work, the other that she'd be able to visit Mal more easily. Considine had said he'd probably be remanded to Wandsworth or the Scrubs.

Suddenly she remembered her appointment with Nick Trent. He lived in the city, didn't he? Yes, the number she'd called had definitely had a London code. And if he'd give her a lift, that would save money on the train fare. She looked at her watch: half eleven. Half an hour to get packed and get down to the village.

She reached into the wardrobe and pulled out the smaller of the two suitcases. It was better to travel light; she didn't want to be lugging anything heavy around. Quickly she rifled through the hangers, dismissing most of the clothes, taking only those she was sure she would use. She moved on to the chest of drawers, packing T-shirts and underwear. From there she hurried to the bathroom where she swept up a towel, toothbrush, toothpaste, soap, shampoo and conditioner. What about jewellery? She could take the ruby necklace but what if it got stolen? No, she would leave it behind where it was safe. The last two items she placed in the case were the book of fairy tales and the small seashell box. Neither of these was exactly essential but she didn't trust Mrs Gough to take care of them in her absence.

Finally, Lita picked up the envelope from where she'd

dropped it on the bed. She was still reluctant to take the money, to take *anything* from Esther, but couldn't afford to be precious about it. When she got a job, the first thing she'd do was pay back every penny. Having resolved on this, she sighed and slipped the envelope into her shoulder bag.

By now it was getting on for ten to twelve. She stood for a moment staring at the peacocks on the wall wondering when or if she'd ever see them again. This had been her home, when she hadn't been at school, for the past five years. She felt a tightening in her chest as she wondered what lay ahead. It was scary to be starting again, to be heading out into the unknown without the protection of Mal. But now wasn't the time to be losing her nerve. She swallowed hard, stood up straight and pushed back her shoulders.

'You can do it,' she murmured. 'You can do it, Lita Bruce.'

Then she left the room and didn't look back.

56

Nick Trent was on his second cup of coffee and pretty sure he'd been stood up when he finally saw Lita outside the café window. Without smiling, she beckoned him outside. It was only when he stepped through the door that he noticed the suitcase at her feet.

'I need a lift,' she said. 'Can you take me to London?'

'Hello, Nick,' he said. 'How are you? I'm fine, thanks. Lovely day, isn't it?'

Lita, who wasn't in the mood for his dry wit or sarcasm or whatever it was, pulled a face. 'It doesn't matter if you can't. I can get the train.'

'No, it's not a problem. Do you want to go right now or would you like a coffee first?'

'I'd rather just go.' And then, in a slightly more concilia-tory tone, she added, 'Thanks. If you don't mind.'

'Okay. Give me two minutes.' Nick went back inside to pay the bill, wondering what was going on. This was a change of plan but that wasn't necessarily a bad thing; it meant he'd have over an hour to talk to her on the journey home, longer perhaps than she'd have given him under normal circumstances.

By the time he got outside again she'd already walked along the road to where his car was parked. As he strolled towards her, he noticed the nervy, anxious way she shifted from foot to foot. Someone was in a hurry. He unlocked the passenger door and watched her get in before taking her case and placing it in the boot.

Nick got in the car and put on his seat belt. He glanced at her but she didn't look back. She sat staring straight ahead with her hands clenched tightly in her lap. He didn't say anything. She looked worried, scared even, and he didn't want to spook her. She gave the impression of a small wild animal, cornered and afraid, the type who might bite off your fingers if you got too close or made any sudden movements. It was best to take things slowly. There was plenty of time to get to the bottom of it all.

Nick leaned forward, switched on the engine and pulled away from the kerb. He thought she relaxed a little but couldn't be sure. Maybe it was just his imagination. It was an effort to keep his curiosity in check, but he managed it until they'd cleared the village boundaries and gone a couple of miles beyond. As they wound through the country lanes, he asked as casually as he could, 'So, are you going to tell me what's going on?'

She didn't answer straight away. As if she hadn't even heard, she continued to gaze through the windscreen at the trees and hedgerows. Well, maybe she was looking but he wasn't convinced she was actually seeing anything. And then, just as he was starting to think it was going to be a very quiet journey, she came out with it.

'Mal's been arrested,' she said. 'He's been charged with killing Teddy Heath.'

'What?' Nick was so startled he took his eyes off the road and almost ran into the grass verge. Quickly he straightened out the car again. 'Are you serious?'

'It's hardly something to joke about.'

'No, no of course it isn't. But Teddy Heath? Mal? Christ, I didn't see that coming.'

Lita hesitated, but eventually told him what had happened, the words recited in a dull monotone as if this was the only way she could deal with telling the story. She explained about the rows, the bad atmosphere and how Mal and Esther had argued at the top of the steps. She told him about Mal being taken into custody, Esther's accusation and Mal's subsequent confession. 'So you were right, I suppose, to be interested in him. In Teddy Heath, I mean.'

There was, he thought, a hint of accusation in what she said – as if his talk with Mal Fury had set in motion a chain of events that had eventually culminated in the man's arrest – but he let it slide. He was too busy trying to figure out how this all fitted in with his uncle's investigation and his death in the hit-and-run.

'When did it happen? What year? Do you know?'

'A couple of years after Kay disappeared.'

Which made it 1960, the same year Stanley had been

employed by Mal. Employed but kept in the dark, because the one useful lead – Teddy – was already dead, and Mal Fury couldn't share that information without implicating himself in the killing. So Stanley had been taken on simply in the hope that someone would eventually come forward with the child. He'd been paid to sift out the crooks and the crazies and the timewasters, but not to solve the mystery of Kay's disappearance. Yet somehow, all those years later, Stanley had almost done exactly that, stumbling on to the name Teddy Heath, making a connection and knowing that it meant something.

'What are you thinking?' Lita asked.

'Stanley made a phone call to Mal on the day he died. Maybe it was to do with Teddy Heath. That would have come as quite a shock, wouldn't it? All those years having gone by and then—'

Lita turned her face to him, her eyes flashing with anger. 'What are you saying – that Mal killed him too? Is that what you think?'

'No, of course not,' Nick said, although in fact that was exactly what was in his mind. Mal Fury would have had a lot to lose if the truth came out. 'I was just . . . I don't know, thinking aloud. I didn't mean anything by it.'

'Why say it then?'

'Sorry,' he murmured, wanting to placate her. 'Anyway Mal told me that he didn't take the call, that he didn't speak to Stanley that day, so he wouldn't have had a motive.'

'Except you don't believe him.'

This was true too, but Nick shook his head. 'Of course I

do.' Obviously Lita was fond of Mal and would never want to think the worst. It was one thing being responsible for a heart attack, quite another ploughing someone down in cold blood. He quickly changed the subject. 'So why are you leaving?'

'Esther's coming back soon. She doesn't want me there.'

'She can't just chuck you out.'

'I'd rather not be in the house with her, not without Mal. It's better this way.'

'Better for whom?'

Lita gave a shrug. 'We've never really got on.'

Nick wondered what kind of a person Esther Fury was. He'd only met her briefly at the party but she had struck him as one of those beautiful women who are strong-willed and manipulative and utterly selfish. What had given him that impression? It had been partly coloured, perhaps, by his natural prejudice when it came to the glitterati, but was mainly down to that scene in the garden where she'd used him to separate Lita from her friend. And then, of course, there was his uncle's opinion. Although Stanley had never directly criticised her in his reports, it hadn't been too difficult to read between the lines.

'Who was Esther leaving him for?'

Lita flinched, a tiny movement that she tried to cover up by fiddling with her seat belt. 'I don't know. Maybe no one.'

Nick snorted. 'Oh, there's always someone. Women like Esther never just leave, not unless they have somewhere better to go.'

Lita gave him an odd look. She was quiet for a while as

if thinking this through, but if she came to a conclusion she didn't share it with him. The silence remained until he started up the conversation again.

'I found out something interesting about Billy Martin.' Perhaps his idea of interesting was different to hers because she didn't ask what, but just gave him a distracted glance and focused her attention on the road again. He carried on, regardless. 'I went through Stanley's address book, looking for his old police contacts and came across this guy called Donal Stewart. He's a DS working out of West End Central. It seems Stanley called him about Billy, and Stewart did a search. Turns out Billy was in jail at the time of Kay's abduction; he was in the Scrubs and didn't get out until '63.'

Lita must have been listening after all because she wrinkled her nose and said, 'I don't get it.'

'That's because we haven't got to the good part yet. On the day he died, Stanley called Stewart again, only this time he was asking about Teddy Heath. And guess what? Teddy served a short stretch in the Scrubs too, six months for theft. He was there at the same time as Billy.'

'You think they knew each other?'

'It's a theory. I can't prove it, of course, but it's possible. Prisons are big places but they might have met. Teddy was a drunk and there's always booze in jail if you know where to find it. And the trouble with drunks is that they can't keep their mouths shut. Maybe he told Billy about the kidnap or maybe Billy heard it from someone else. Either way, it must have stuck in Billy's head and when he turned up on Angela's doorstep to find she had a child she couldn't or *wouldn't* explain he may have wondered if you were the missing Fury child.'

Lita didn't look impressed. 'Wouldn't that have been a bit of a coincidence?'

'Like I said, it's just a theory.' Nick scratched his chin and put his hand back on the wheel. 'Maybe he never thought that at all but just said it to try and find out where you really came from. He wouldn't have liked not knowing. Stanley talked to a guy called Calvin Cross – an old boyfriend of your mum's . . . of Angela's . . . and he reckoned Billy was a nasty bit of work, a real control freak.'

'But she must have known I wasn't Kay Fury.'

'Must she?'

Lita gave him a sidelong glance. 'What do you mean?'

'Unless she was there at your birth, she couldn't have been a hundred per cent sure of anything. I think Billy might have started putting ideas in her head, questioning what she believed to be true. It would explain why she had a fear of Mal Fury. What if he found her and took you away? That must have been a pretty scary thought for her.'

Lita's eyes grew sad and solemn as though she was remembering past times – times that were not entirely happy. 'But what was in it for him, for Billy?'

'Who knows? Just the fun of it, perhaps. It gave him a hold over her. If she didn't do what he wanted, he'd pick up the phone and tell Mal Fury where she was. She wouldn't have wanted that even if she could prove you weren't his. It would have meant the truth coming out. It would have meant you finding out that she wasn't actually your mother.'

'That's evil,' she said.

'It's that all right.' Nick had been talking to lots of people since his last meeting with Lita. He'd been retracing Stanley's steps, repeating conversations, going over old ground in the hope of unearthing something new. And eventually his persistence had paid off. He now had another theory, but not one he was currently prepared to share with Lita. He thought he knew who her real mother was.

57

Lita didn't like the Blackwall Tunnel. It felt like a never-ending corridor of gloom; grey and bleak with the walls pressing in on her. She half closed her eyes so she wouldn't need to see it clearly. Her head was full of too many things for her to concentrate on any one of them: her mother, Billy Martin's sick machinations, Mal's imprisonment, the death of Teddy Heath, and the fact that she was homeless and had nowhere to go. The latter of these was brought to the forefront when Nick asked her where she'd like to be dropped off.

As yet, Lita hadn't really thought this through. She tried to think of somewhere, anywhere.

'Lita?'

'Huh?' she said, playing for time as if she hadn't heard the question.

'I was just asking where you'd like to go.'

Lita had to make a quick decision. She only knew two

parts of London well and one of these was the Hatton Garden area – completely out of the question – and the other was Kellston. It was better, surely, to choose somewhere familiar. It wasn't ideal but it would do for now; she could always move on once her head was less frazzled.

'Oh, right, yes. Could you drop me off in Kellston?'

Nick seemed surprised. 'Are you sure?'

'Yes. I've got friends there.' It only occurred to her, as she said this, that what she actually had were enemies. Brenda Cecil and her sons would still be harbouring a grudge. Tony would be out of prison by now and she doubted his time inside had done much, if anything, to alter his feelings towards her. But it was too late to change her mind. With any luck they wouldn't even recognise her after five years. 'The station will be fine. I can ring them from there.'

'They're not expecting you then?'

Lita thought she detected a hint of scepticism in his voice and said firmly, 'Of course they are. I just wasn't sure what time I'd arrive.'

Nick's eyebrows shifted up a fraction but he didn't pursue it.

Ten minutes later they were out of the tunnel and in the East End of London. It wouldn't be long now before they got to Kellston. Gradually the streets became more familiar until Lita felt a lurch in her stomach. She saw the three tall towers in the distance and knew she was on home ground. The sudden swelling of emotion took her by surprise and she swallowed hard, turning her face away so Nick couldn't see it.

There was nowhere to stop outside the station and instead he pulled into the car park of the Fox. He kept the engine idling while he jumped out and retrieved her suitcase from the boot. Lita followed him, reaching out a hand to take the case.

'Thanks for the lift,' she said.

'Are you sure you'll be okay?'

Lita forced a smile. 'Why shouldn't I be?'

'You've got my number. You'll stay in touch, yeah?'

'Yes, I will.'

But still he didn't go. Instead he said, 'I'll tell you what, why don't we meet up here on Saturday? We can have a catch-up. How about seven o'clock?'

'Seven,' she repeated. 'Fine. Okay. I'll see you then.'

'You won't forget?'

Lita shook her head. 'Bye then.'

'Bye.'

Before he could think of anything else, Lita started walking towards the station. She was aware of the car door shutting and the car moving off. She waved as he went past, trying to keep the smile on her lips. It was only when he'd gone through the traffic lights on the corner that she stopped and put the case down again.

Lita wondered why she'd lied, pretending to have somewhere to stay when she didn't. It was partly pride – she didn't want his pity or his help – but mainly because she didn't trust him. Mal was in enough trouble without being implicated in Stanley Parrish's death as well. The corners of her mouth turned down. Would she turn up on Saturday?

She hadn't decided yet. Maybe not, but then again . . . There was an old saying, wasn't there, about keeping your friends close and your enemies closer?

Lita sighed and turned her attention to the matter in hand. Station Road was lined with boarding houses and B&Bs and she reckoned she could find some cheap accommodation, especially if she headed for the less desirable area up by Albert Road. Accordingly, she turned round, picked up the case and started walking in the opposite direction to the station.

It was hot and despite her economical packing the suitcase seemed to get heavier with every step she took. She could feel the ache in her arm and a prickle of sweat on her forehead. Once she had booked into a room, her next task was to find a job. Anything would do, although she wasn't exactly qualified for much. Ideally she'd like to work in a jewellery shop, but without a reference the chances were slim. She thought of the job she'd been supposed to be starting at Fury's in September, and sighed again. It was unlikely to happen now. With Mal locked up she wasn't even sure if the business would keep running.

Lita plodded on. The large redbrick Victorian houses grew shabbier the further she got from the station. Most of them had a cardboard sign stuck in a bottom window with the word VACANCIES scrawled on it. She stared at each one as she passed, trying to figure out from its appearance – the state of the paintwork, the colour of the net curtains – which was likely to be the cheapest. She would need to be frugal if she was to make Esther's money last.

Lita was still trying to make up her mind when she came to a short row of shops squashed between the houses. A tallish woman emerged from a newsagent's holding a bottle of milk in one hand and a pack of cigarettes in the other. She was in her late forties with dyed blonde hair, and was wearing a white leather miniskirt, a skimpy white top and a lot of make-up. There was something familiar about her but it took a moment for the penny to drop. Lita's mouth widened into its first genuine smile of the day.

'Stella!'

The woman turned a blank face towards her, her scarlet lips parting slightly.

'It's me,' Lita said. 'Don't you remember? It's—'

Stella suddenly let out a squawk. 'Oh my God! Lolly! It's little Lolly!' She tottered a few steps in her high heels before wrapping her skinny arms round Lita and giving her a mighty hug. Lita could feel the cold chill of the milk bottle on her back, but the warmth of the greeting more than made up for it.

Stella leaned back and gazed at her. 'I can't believe it's you. I really can't. What are you doing here, love? Look at you! All grown up! God, it's been years.'

Lita laughed and some of the tension slipped from her body. 'Five,' she said. 'How have you been?'

'Oh, you know me. I always get by. I asked that Brenda Cecil about you but she wouldn't tell me nothin', just that you'd gone off to live with someone else. She doesn't open her gob without a lie coming out of it so I didn't know what to believe. I thought she might have put you into care.'

Lita's smile faltered a little on hearing Brenda's name. 'She's still here then?'

'Christ, yeah. The only way she'll be leaving that shop is when they carry her out in a box. But enough about that old cow. Tell me about you. How have you been? What have you been doing?' Before Lita had a chance to answer, Stella's gaze slid down and alighted on the suitcase. 'You planning on staying a while, hon?'

'For now. It's a long story, but I need somewhere cheap to stay. Do you know anywhere that isn't too pricy?'

Stella shoved the cigarettes in her bag and linked her free arm through Lita's. 'Come with me,' she said. 'We'll have a brew while I think about it.'

The house on Albert Road hadn't changed much since Lita had visited as a thirteen-year-old. The kitchen still had paint peeling from the walls and still smelled of stale cigarette smoke and weed. The door to the small back yard was open but there wasn't a breeze. She sat at the table while Stella put the kettle on and washed out a couple of mugs.

'You've had some problems then, the place you've been living?'

Lita didn't want to go into it all. The story was too long and even the thought of explaining made her feel tired. 'You could say that.'

Stella looked over her shoulder and smiled. 'Well, these things happen; it's not the end of the world. You're back where you belong now. We'll soon get you fixed up.'

Lita nodded, smiling too. In truth, she had never been entirely sure where she belonged, but it felt comforting to be in the kitchen, to be back in the place where she had once found a temporary escape from her misery. 'You always were good to me. Kind, you know? I never forgot. I'm sorry I didn't have the chance to say goodbye.'

'You don't have to worry about that.' Stella flapped a hand dismissively. 'You were only a kid. Anyhow, you must have had more important things on your mind than us lot.'

'I used to like coming here.'

'This old dump? I can't think why. All we ever do is sit around and gossip.'

Lita knew it was because they'd taken an interest, paid her some attention, but wasn't sure how to put into words without coming across as sad and needy. 'I've got a lot to catch up on then. You'll have to tell me *everything*.'

'How long have you got?' Stella put the mugs of tea down on the table and pulled out a chair. 'You heard about Joe Quinn, did you?'

'Only recently.'

Stella lit a cigarette, inhaled and blew the smoke out through her nose. 'I know you shouldn't speak ill of the dead and all, but he was one nasty bastard. Deserved everything he got if you ask me. Terry's got his faults – ain't they all? – but at least he treats us decent. You can talk to him, straightforward like, without him going off on one.'

It was a long time since Lita had thought about Terry Street. She remembered him coming to Brenda's on the day he organised the alibi for Tony, standing at the back door with his dark hair slicked down by the rain. 'He's still around then?'

'Stepped straight into Joe's shoes, didn't he? He even bought the Fox. Got it for a snip, mind, after Joe's boys went down. That wife of Tommy's couldn't wait to get rid.'

Lita, recalling the errands she'd used to run, wondered if Terry had any jobs going now. She wouldn't be much use to him in her former position – she was too old to run around unnoticed like she used to – but maybe there was something else. In the pub, for instance. It couldn't be that hard to pull a pint. But would he even take her on? She took a sip of tea, frowning while she thought about it.

Stella must have mistaken her worried expression for concern about something else, because she suddenly reached out and laid her hand across Lita's. 'Are you in trouble, love? Is that it? Only if you are, you can tell me. You can tell me anything.'

'I'll be okay.'

'We all make mistakes. You're not the first and you won't be the last. And it's always the woman, of course, who's left to pick up the pieces. But don't you worry about it. You've got choices, you know.'

It was a moment before Lita realised what kind of trouble she meant. 'God, no. I'm not ... I'm not pregnant.' And then, because she thought Stella deserved some kind of an explanation she quickly added, 'I just can't go back to where I was living. Not at the moment. It's all gone wrong.' Recent events tumbled through her mind and she felt her lower lip start to tremble. 'I can't go back. I can't.'

'And no one's saying you have to, hon.' Stella patted her hand. 'Don't go getting upset. You don't have to do anything you don't want to. Look, why don't you stay here for a while, just until you get yourself sorted? There's an empty room up top. It's nothin' much but it's a roof over your head.'

Lita felt relief wash over her. 'Really? Do you mean it?' Suddenly, she didn't feel quite so alone. 'Thank you so much.'

'You won't be thanking me when you've seen it, love.'

'I don't care what it's like.'

Stella stood up and laughed. 'Famous last words. Come on, grab that case of yours and we'll get you settled in.'

The room was up three flights of stairs, under the eaves at the very top of the house. The slant of the roof took up a third of the space and the rest was filled with a bare single mattress, a rickety looking chest of drawers and an old armchair with stuffing oozing out of the arms. There was a stained beige carpet on the floor, and a bare bulb hanging from the ceiling. Dust lay everywhere, a thick unmoving blanket. It was a far cry from the room with the peacocks, but Lita didn't care. For her, at this moment, it was sanctuary.

'See what I mean?' Stella said. 'It ain't exactly the Ritz.'

Lita dropped the case on the floor. 'It's fine, really it is.' She went over to the window and looked out. Albert Road was quiet with only a few cars cruising by. There was a crack in the pane of glass running from the top right hand corner to the centre where it suddenly stopped as though it had run out of steam. A thin pair of curtains hung either side, slightly lopsided from where they'd come adrift from the rings on the rail.

'I'll sort you some sheets and stuff, and you can use the bathroom downstairs.'

Lita turned and smiled. 'Thanks.'

'No need to thank me, hon. Like I said, it ain't what you'd call five star. Still, so long as you're okay with it.'

They went back downstairs where the kitchen table was now occupied by two other women. Lita recognised one of them straight away, but the other was a stranger.

'Hey, Jackie,' Stella said. 'Look who I bumped into!'

Jackie stared hard at Lita, clearly trying to place her without having much success.

Stella gave up waiting and announced, 'It's Lolly, little Lolly! Don't you remember? I was just walking down the street and . . . Can you believe it after all these years?'

'Hi,' Lita said.

Jackie, who had never been especially friendly back in the day, hadn't mellowed with age. She gave a low grunt as if Lita's presence was of no more interest to her than a speck of dust in the air. 'Oh, right.'

Stella turned her attention to the other woman. 'Maureen, this is Lolly. She's going to be staying for a while.'

Maureen nodded and smiled. 'Hello, hon. Nice to meet you.'

'What do you mean, *staying*?' Jackie asked, her indifference instantly switching to something more aggressive. 'Why haven't I been told about this?'

'I've just told you,' Stella said. 'What's your problem? The room at the top's empty, no one's used it for ages, and she has nowhere to go so . . . It ain't doing no harm, is it? What difference does it make?'

Jackie's cold gaze flicked from Stella to Lita and back again. 'It's not a bloody hotel. She can't stay here for nothin'.'

'I don't mind paying,' Lita said. The last thing she'd wanted was to start a row. 'I really don't. Whatever you think is fair.'

Stella shook her head. 'You don't have to, love. It's not as though you'll be taking up a space someone else could be using. It's a shitty little room but you're welcome to it for as long as you need.'

'Terry won't like that,' Jackie said.

'I'll sort it with Terry.'

'You do that.' Jackie stood up, threw Lita a filthy look and then walked out of the kitchen, slamming the door behind her.

'Don't take any notice,' Stella said. 'She's always got the hump about something. It ain't personal.'

Except Lita was pretty sure it was. Jackie had never liked her. As a kid, she hadn't thought too much about her hostility but now she was starting to wonder if there was more to it. While the other women had always welcomed her, fussed over her, Jackie had done the very opposite. But why? She thought about it for a moment and then pushed the question to the back of her mind. She had more important things to worry about.

58

Over the next few days, Lita kept busy. She bought the *Evening Standard*, the *Evening News* and a couple of local papers, scouring the columns at the back for any suitable job vacancies. But every number she rang drew a blank. She was either too young and didn't have enough experience or the position was already taken. Her spirits dropped after every rejection. At this rate she'd never find anything.

A call to Considine's office established that Mal had been remanded to Wandsworth. She found the address in the phone book and wrote him a letter asking how he was and saying she was fine and staying with a friend in London for a while. She didn't mention that Esther had thrown her out. He had enough to deal with. She hoped he wasn't familiar with Kellston and wouldn't recognise Albert Road as being right in the middle of the red-light district.

Grateful for her free room in the house, Lita did her best to make herself useful. In the mornings she got up and

481

cleaned the main reception area where the punters waited, emptying the ashtrays and the bins, clearing away the rubbish left behind. She cleaned the kitchen too, although no amount of air freshener could eliminate that pervading smell of dope.

She had quickly worked out how the house operated. There were rooms on the ground and first floors for 'business' and other private bedrooms on the second floor for the girls who lived in. At the moment this was only Stella, Maureen and Jackie. Other girls came and went, depending on how busy they were. Lita tried not to think too much about what went on behind closed doors. She had learned long ago that for some sex was only a commodity, something to be bought and sold, a business deal that had nothing to do with love or affection.

Lita kept out of the way when the punters were around, retreating to the kitchen or her room under the eaves. She had scrubbed the latter from top to bottom, straightened out the curtains and covered the bare bulb with a cheap lampshade bought from the market. It was spartan but serviceable, somewhere to sleep until she found a place of her own. But of course this couldn't happen until she got a job.

Although she'd originally intended to search out Terry Street and ask him if he knew of anything, she'd been put off by Jackie's comments. Perhaps it wouldn't be wise to draw attention to herself while she was living for free in the house. What if Terry got the hump and threw her out? They'd been friendly once but that was years ago. He probably wouldn't even remember her.

Lita didn't dwell on this, determined to stay optimistic. As she walked up the high street she studied the shop windows in the hope she might come across one advertising a vacancy. She wasn't fussy; anything would do: she could work on a till, sell shoes, make sandwiches. On passing Connolly's she glanced inside and saw that it was full of teenagers. It took her back to her youth. For a second she almost expected to see a younger version of Jude, to see Amy Wiltshire flicking back her long fair hair, but the only familiar face was Maeve Riley's.

Lita moved on. When she drew close to the pawnbroker's she crossed over to the other side of the road. It was unlikely that Brenda would spot her but she wasn't taking any chances. There was no point looking for trouble. She gave a single glance over her shoulder, her gaze lifting towards the window of the bedroom on the top floor – FJ's room, although it had been hers for a while. She recalled the five one-pound notes she had hidden in the mattress – money earmarked for her mother's headstone – and later taken to West Henby. She never had spent it. The notes were still wrapped up in a sock at the back of a drawer. She gave a soft curse, wishing she'd remembered earlier and brought them with her.

By the time she reached the end of the high street she wasn't any better off than when she'd started. Not even the sniff of a job. She crossed back over and stood on the corner of Mansfield Road. Straight ahead were the three tall towers of the estate. She felt simultaneously drawn and repulsed by them. It was where Jude might be at this very moment, but it was also where her mum had died.

Lita screwed up her face as she rolled the word over her tongue. *Mum*. She wondered if Angela would have ever come clean. And now that she was dead, maybe the truth had died with her. She wasn't sure if this mattered or not. Did she want to know who her real mother was – someone who had given her up, given her away – or was she better off remaining in ignorance? Sometimes the truth wasn't all it was cracked up to be.

Now that she was so close to the estate, she thought she may as well see if Jude was in. There was a phone box near the gate to the main entrance but she walked straight past. If she called first it would give him the opportunity to make an excuse as to why he couldn't see her. Maybe he'd say he was ill or busy working. She still harboured doubts about his motives for turning up in West Henby. The visit had, she suspected, been more to do with promoting his screenplay than any real desire to renew their friendship.

And if that was the case, then why was she bothering?

Lita didn't have an answer. All she knew was that she wasn't prepared to give up on him, not until she had to. She'd already lost her mum, Mal, her home, her future; surely she deserved a break. God couldn't begrudge her one small bit of happiness in her life.

She strode along the main path to Haslow House, trying not to think too much about the past. She didn't look up at Carlton, didn't even glance in that direction. The lobby hadn't changed since the last time she was there. There was still litter strewn across the floor – fag ends, tin cans, empty crisp packets – and it had the same smell of dope as the kitchen in Albert Road.

She took the lift up to the twelfth floor and hurried along the corridor before she lost her nerve. She raised her hand and rapped on the door with her knuckles, three hard knocks with nothing tentative about them.

Jude answered almost immediately. He opened the door and stared at her. 'Lolly! What are you doing here?'

No smile, she noticed. No light of pleasant surprise in his eyes. 'Hi,' she said, as casually as she could manage. 'I'm in London for a while, staying with a friend. I thought I'd drop by, just on the off chance.'

He hesitated, long enough for her to notice, before standing aside to let her in. 'You should have called.'

'Sorry. I tried the box on the corner but it's out of order. Am I interrupting? I won't stay long.'

'It's okay,' he said, although not with any enthusiasm. 'I can take a break for five minutes. Do you want a coke?'

'Thanks.'

While Jude went to the kitchen, Lita glanced round the living room she had once known so well. Changes had been made. The old corduroy sofa was gone, replaced by one in mock brown leather. The room had never been cluttered but now it was bordering on the minimalist, the only other furniture being a table and chair by the window. There was a typewriter on the table and a heap of paper. All that had remained the same was the films stacked up on the shelves – although there were many more of them now, as though they had bred and multiplied in her absence.

Jude came back with two bottles of Coke and passed one over to her. 'Here.'

'Thanks,' she said again. 'So are you feeling better now?'

'What?'

'You said you were ill. Flu was it?'

Jude sat down on the chair by the table. He was wearing shorts and a grey T-shirt, and his feet were bare. He shrugged. 'It was just some kind of bug, a twenty-four-hour thing.'

'Oh, right.' She sat on the sofa, feeling that awkwardness that comes when you sense you're not welcome, that someone is simply putting up with you. 'So how's your dad?'

'He doesn't live here any more. He's shacked up with some tart on the Isle of Dogs.'

Lita had never liked the way he talked about girls, about women. She took a swig from the bottle and stared at him. For once she decided to challenge his views. 'What makes her a tart, exactly?'

'Same thing that makes any woman a tart,' he said dismissively. 'Anyway, good luck to him. He'll need it.' Jude turned slightly, his gaze straying towards the heap of paper on the table as if he couldn't wait to get back to work. 'I heard what happened with the Furys. Is that why you've left?'

Her suspicions about him and Esther jumped back into her head. 'How do you know about that?'

'It was in the papers,' he said. 'You'll be taking his side, I suppose.'

'It was an accident.'

'Which part of it? Throwing Esther down the steps or killing Teddy Heath?'

Lita frowned. 'She fell down the steps; she wasn't pushed. And Mal didn't kill him, not deliberately. The guy had a heart attack.'

'A heart attack brought on by Mal having his hands around his throat. How can you defend him after everything he's done?'

'All he's ever done is try to find his daughter. That's not a crime, is it?'

Jude shook his head, his mouth growing sulky. 'I knew you'd be like this.'

'Like what?'

'Making excuses for him. I saw the way he treated her. He can't stand anyone else being around. I mean, shit, if he had his way, he'd lock all the doors and put a bloody moat around the house.'

Lita felt the blood rise into her face. 'You don't have a clue what you're talking about. The place is always full of people. And you've only been there twice.'

'Often enough to see what's he like.'

'That's crap and you know it! You've only heard *her* side of things. You're just believing what you want to believe.'

'And you're not?'

Lita felt like he was deliberately goading her, trying to create a row from which there could be no going back. 'Why are you doing this?'

'Doing what?'

'This. Everything. Getting involved. It's got nothing to do with you.'

'Sometimes you have to take a stand, to decide where your loyalties lie. I can't support Mal Fury so . . .'

'So you don't want anything to do with me either.'

Jude pulled a face but didn't deny it. 'It could be awkward.'

Lita was stung to the core. That his loyalties didn't lie with her shouldn't have come as any great surprise – it was hardly the first time he'd pushed her aside for something better – but the fact he was so blatant about it showed him in his true colours. The retort sprang to her lips before she had time to think about it. 'Is that damn screenplay really so important to you? Or is this just about Esther? She doesn't care about you. Jude. She's only using you.'

'Maybe she is. Why should I care?'

Lita shook her head, put the coke bottle down on the floor and stood up. 'No, you don't care about anyone but yourself.'

Jude rose to his feet and accompanied her to the narrow hall. 'I know what you're thinking,' he said. 'That I should be grateful to you, right? For what you did all those years ago. And I am, really I am. But it doesn't mean I have to be beholden to you for the rest of my life. You made a choice to do what you did. No one forced you. It doesn't mean we have to be best buddies until the end of time.'

Lita stopped and stared at him. 'Did I ever ask for that? You were the one who came to West Henby, remember? You sought me out, not the other way round.' She waited for an answer but all she got was a nonchalant shrug. Reaching out, she opened the front door and stepped into the corridor. She was angry and upset, as much at herself as at him. Would she never learn? She just kept making the same mistake. 'You're a sad person, Jude Rule.'

'Don't be mad at me,' he said.

Lita didn't reply. She wasn't going to waste her breath on him. She pushed back her shoulders and walked off towards the lifts without a backward glance. She heard the door close behind her and knew that it had closed for ever.

59

Lita was too impatient to wait for the lift. She wanted to get away from Jude and from the estate. She jogged down the steps with her jaw clenched and her pride in tatters. 'Bloody fool,' she muttered. 'Moron, idiot, ass.' Sunlight streamed through the windows striping the grey stone. She passed from light to shade, from light to shade, as she descended the twelve floors. When she finally reached ground level her lungs were pumping and she slowed to a trot to get her breath back.

Leaving the lobby, her intention was to head straight back to Albert Road and up to the room under the eaves. She needed a quiet place to hide, somewhere she could lick her wounds in private. Jude had plunged a knife into her heart and this time there would be no second chances. So far as she was concerned, he was out of her life for good.

Lita still wasn't sure what was going on between him and Esther. Was he motivated by business or pleasure? Maybe it was both. Anyway, it was of no concern to her. From now on, Jude Rule no longer existed. It was over, finished – whatever 'it' had been – and all that remained was a bad taste in her mouth.

She was almost at the gate when she saw the black guy sitting on the wall with his face raised to the sun. He was wearing big aviator sunglasses but she knew him instantly. *Joseph.* She gave a start, in two minds whether to talk to him or not. It would be cowardly not to – she still felt guilty over what had happened – but she was tempted to walk on past. It would be easier that way, and she'd had enough of hard this morning.

Lita had already walked through the gate when she stopped in her tracks and glanced over her shoulder. Joseph hadn't moved or shown any sign of recognition. She was free to keep going, but something stopped her. A little voice whispered in her ear: *Do the right thing.* It was time, perhaps, to stop running away from the past.

She turned and walked back to him. 'Joseph?'

Slowly he lowered his face and stared at her. It was a long scrutinising look, taking her in, feature by feature. Eventually his mouth slid into a smile. He laughed, showing a gold tooth at the front of his mouth. 'Lollipop,' he said. 'Ain't seen you around in a while.'

'I wasn't sure you'd know me.'

'What, my favourite delivery girl? I'd never forget you, babe.'

Lita sat down beside him on the wall and squinted into the sun. 'So how have you been?'

'Been better, been worse. No point complaining. Ain't gonna change nothin'. Just got to keep going, right?'

'I guess.'

'You back living here?'

Lita shook her head. 'Not on the estate. I'm staying with a friend.'

Joseph gave her another searching look. At least she presumed that was what he was doing; she couldn't really tell through the sunglasses. 'Someone piss you off, babe?' he asked. 'You don't look too happy if you don't mind me saying.'

'Yeah, someone did. But it doesn't matter. I won't be seeing him again.'

'I thought so. I might only have one eye but I still know a pissed-off lady when I see one.'

Lita flinched as he mentioned his eye and instantly knew that she couldn't keep the truth from him. 'It's my fault,' she blurted out. 'What happened to you, with Tony Cecil, I mean.' And then it all spilled out, everything about the night he had been attacked, how she'd overheard the exchange in the yard between Tony and his mates, how she'd known about their plans but done nothing. She didn't pause for breath until she'd finished, and then she took in a large gulp of air like a drowning swimmer desperate for oxygen.

'Shit, it weren't your fault. Don't be crazy. What could you have done about it?'

'Told someone? Rung the police?'

'It wouldn't have made no difference. By the time they got here, it would have all been over.' Joseph gave her elbow a

492

nudge. 'You been carrying that around all these years? You got to put it out of your mind. You ain't got nothin' to feel bad about.'

Lita was relieved he didn't blame her, even if she couldn't quite stop blaming herself. At the age of thirteen she'd known the difference between right and wrong. She'd been too afraid to do anything, but fear was no excuse for cowardice.

Joseph leaned forward, took a pouch from his shirt pocket and began to build a cigarette. She watched his fingers as they laid out a pinch of tobacco before he deftly rolled the paper into a perfect cylinder. He put the cigarette to his lips and lit it. 'What you got to understand,' he said, 'is that if it hadn't been that night it would have been the next, or the one after that. It was going to happen, no matter what.'

'But why you? Tony was convinced it was Jude Rule until that point.'

''Cept you gave the guy an alibi.'

Lita glanced away. Joseph knew that alibi was fake – she'd been in the tunnel with him when she was supposed to be watching *Sunset Boulevard* – and didn't know what to say.

'Once Tony figured Rule was out of the frame, he had to pick on someone else. He had to be seen to be taking revenge on the murdering fucker who'd killed his girl-friend. It was a matter of "respect", of reputation. Anyone would have done, but the fact the filth had pulled me in over Amy gave him the excuse he needed. No smoke without fire and all that.'

'Did they give you a bad time, the cops?'

Joseph gave a low laugh. 'No worse than usual. If they could have pinned it on me, they would – some black dope-dealing scumbag who hangs out on the estate – but I ain't got no form for violence and they sure as hell couldn't find no evidence of murder.'

'It doesn't stop people talking though, does it?'

'People can say what they like.' He touched his chest with his palm. 'It's what's in here that counts. I know the truth and that's all that matters.'

'So who do you reckon killed Amy? Do you think it was Tony?'

Joseph dragged on his cigarette, and gave her a sidelong glance. 'Can't have done, can he? He had an alibi.'

Lita hesitated before speaking again. 'But what if ... I mean, what if the alibi was false?'

'Course it was false, babe. Terry fixed it for him, didn't he?'

She looked at him, surprised. 'You knew that?'

Joseph grinned. 'I know everything that goes on around here.'

'So Tony could have done it. If he lied about where he was—'

'He didn't kill her.'

'How can you be sure?'

'Because I know where he really was that afternoon.' Joseph's mouth twitched at the corners. 'He went where he always went when his uncle cleared off early – to a certain gentleman's club in Stoke Newington.'

'I don't understand. If he was at a club then why didn't he just say?'

"Cause this ain't the sort of club you want people to know about.'

Lita frowned. 'Why not?'

'Let's just say it's ain't the kind of place you'll find any ladies. Men only, if you get my drift.'

'You mean . . . But Tony isn't like that. He had girlfriends. He was going out with Amy.'

Joseph gave her a look. 'Sure he was. Had to look the part, right? Didn't want people guessing he'd rather play with the boys than the girls. Man has a reputation to uphold.'

'Oh.'

'Don't mean he ain't still one nasty sonofabitch, though.'

Lita pushed aside her ponytail and scratched the back of her neck where the sun was prickling her skin. 'No, he's that all right.' Despite the heat, a chill was starting to sink into her. For all these years she'd believed that Tony had to be responsible for Amy's death but now . . . If he wasn't guilty, then who was? Only one name sprang to mind.

'You okay, babe?'

Lita nodded and stood up. Her legs didn't feel entirely steady. 'I've got to go. It's been good to see you again. You take care, yeah?'

'You know where I am. Don't be a stranger.'

'I won't.' She said her goodbyes and headed for the gate. As she walked towards the high street she thought about the alibi she'd given Jude. Had she inadvertently protected a killer, lied and schemed to cover up a murder? The idea made her sick to her stomach.

60

As Lita opened the front door she could hear raised voices coming from the kitchen. She would have gone on upstairs, kept out of the way, if she hadn't heard her own name mentioned. At this point natural curiosity took over. She tiptoed through the hall even though she didn't need to bother – Stella and Jackie were arguing so loudly they wouldn't have noticed if the Coldstream Guards were marching through the house.

'Just get over it, can't you? She's not doing any harm. What's with all the aggro?'

'I don't want her here. How many times do I have to fuckin' tell you? It's my house too. I've a right to decide who lives in it.'

'Not when you're behaving like a stupid cow. Give me one good reason why I should chuck her out. C'mon, I'm waiting.'

'She's only here to cause trouble. Can't you see that? The sooner we get shut of her the better.'

'What the hell kind of trouble can Lolly cause? She's just a kid for God's sake, a kid who needs a roof over her head. Since when did you become so bleedin' hard-hearted? What's she ever done to you?'

Lita was almost at the kitchen door by now. She'd like the answer to that question too. And why was it that people were always going on about her causing trouble? It was an accusation that followed her round, like a grim shadow tugging at her heels. First there had been Brenda and Freddy, Tony and FJ, then Mrs Gough and Esther, and now it was Jackie. Everywhere she went it was the same. Which made her wonder if the fault lay in herself, that maybe there was something bad in her, something rotten.

Lita was so distracted by this thought that she banged into a small table set against the wall. The noise was enough to alert the two women and they immediately fell silent. With little choice other than to brazen it out, she stepped forward and showed herself.

'Don't stop on my account.'

Jackie's face was pink, but not with embarrassment. There was rage in her eyes and her mouth was twisted. Lita was taken aback. How could she be the cause of so much negative emotion in a woman she hardly knew? There had to be a reason but she couldn't figure it out.

'It's somethin' and nothin',' Stella said, trying to smooth over an awkward situation.

Jackie's nostrils flared. 'In *your* opinion.'

'Which was as good as yours last time I checked.'

'Go to hell!' And with that Jackie stomped out of the

kitchen, pushing past Lita on her way. 'You can both go to hell!'

Stella rolled her eyes. 'She's just having a bad day, hon. Time of the month.'

'Why does she hate me so much?'

'Oh, she doesn't, not really.'

'Maybe it would be better if I did go.'

'You're not going anywhere,' Stella said stubbornly. 'Not until you're good and ready.'

Lita thought that she was pretty much ready now – she'd had enough of living in war zones – but didn't want to appear ungrateful. Stella had fought her corner and that was no small thing. 'Well, it shouldn't be too long. As soon as I get a job . . .'

'There's no rush, sweetheart, no rush at all. Just forget about it. Do you fancy a brew?'

'No, thanks. I've got to go somewhere. I'll see you later.'

As Lita passed the reception area she saw Jackie perched on the edge of one of the sofas with the phone pressed against her ear. There was a sense of urgency about the way she spoke, quickly in a low voice, almost whispering, her whole body tensed. What was going on? It was time, perhaps, to confront her head on. But not right now. She had something to do and it couldn't wait.

It was always a trial negotiating Albert Road. No matter how quickly she walked, her gaze focused dead ahead, the kerb-crawlers wouldn't leave her alone. They wound down their windows and called out. They cruised along beside her, coarse and vile, their voices demanding what she wasn't prepared to give. Ignoring them made no difference; they persisted until she turned the corner.

Lita walked as fast as she could without breaking into a run. It was a relief to finally reach Station Road and shake off her pursuers. Although she was free of them, their lewd suggestions still echoed in her mind. Like she was a piece of meat, an object, a *thing*.

She crossed over and headed for the Fox. The plus side to Jackie's outburst was that it had put Jude temporarily out of her mind. But now what Joseph had said came back to haunt her. Had she made a terrible mistake? Jesus, she hoped not. She'd spent all these years clinging to the belief that Tony Cecil was guilty and the knowledge that he couldn't be was a truth that sat uneasily with her.

Lita pushed open the door to the pub and stepped inside. It wasn't too busy and she spotted Terry straight away. He looked the same and yet different: the familiar Terry but older and with a new air of authority. He was sitting at a table to her left with the big guy, Vinnie Keane. She didn't pause but walked straight over and stood in front of him.

'Hello, Terry.'

He looked up and grinned. 'Ah, if it isn't my old friend, Lolly Bruce. About time too.'

Lita was surprised he even recognised her. She frowned and smiled at the same time. 'What do you mean?'

'How long have you been back now? Three days, four, and I haven't seen hide nor hair of you. I was starting to think you'd forgotten all about your old mate.'

'How did you ...' But she didn't bother to finish the

question. Jackie had probably filled him in on her un-expected arrival at the house in Albert Road. Or maybe Stella had got there first, although if she had she hadn't mentioned it. 'Sorry. Still, I'm here now.'

Terry patted the empty chair beside him. 'Better late than never. Here, grab a pew. Let me get you a drink.'

'I'll just have an orange juice, thanks.'

Vinnie immediately got up to go to the bar. 'Same again, guv?'

Terry nodded. Then he turned to Lita and asked, 'So what brings you back to Kellston? I heard you were living in Kent.'

'Who told you that? Oh, Brenda, I suppose.'

'You get sick of all those nice green fields?'

'Something like that.'

'That's because you're a city girl, sweetheart, born and bred. You don't belong in the country. All them cows and sheep are enough to send anyone crazy after a while. When all's said and done it just ain't natural.'

Lita laughed, surprised by how comfortable she felt with him. He might look the part of the East End gangster with his smart suit and cool eyes, but underneath the veneer she could still see the original Terry. 'As opposed to the dirt and the noise and the never-ending hassle?'

'Yeah, lovely ain't it?'

'Is it true that you own this place now?'

'You like it?'

It was the first time Lita had ever been inside. As a youngster she'd loitered by the side door, ferrying messages between Joe Quinn and Brenda, but had never once crossed the threshold. She looked around. The pub had an old-fashioned air to it, but in a good way. There was a polished wood floor, an open fireplace and lots of nooks and crannies. The sturdy benches and chairs were covered with a dark red velvety material. The long mirror behind the bar gleamed, and she realised on staring at the reflection that from where he was sitting Terry could keep an eye on almost every part of the main room. 'It's nice,' she said. 'It feels very ... welcoming.'

'I like that,' he said, nodding. 'Welcoming, huh? I reckon that's what a pub should be.'

Vinnie came back with the drinks, and sat on the other side of Terry. He was a huge, intimidating bear of a man, probably in his late thirties or a bit older, and had one of those faces it was impossible to read. She'd have preferred to speak to Terry in private but could hardly ask the guy to leave. She sipped on her orange juice and said, 'I hope you don't mind me staying with Stella. It won't be for long, just until I get a place of my own.'

'Why should I mind? Ain't no skin off my nose.'

'Thanks.'

'Just watch yourself, that's all.'

'Who should I be more worried about – the punters or Jackie?'

Terry grinned at her bluntness. 'Both.'

'I don't know what her problem is. Do you?'

'You'll have to ask her that. If there's one thing I've learned in life, it's never to get involved in women's arguments.

Believe me, it don't ever end well. I prefer to keep me balls attached to my body, if you'll pardon the language.'

Lita, accepting that he wasn't going to tell her even if he did know anything, moved swiftly on. 'I was wondering if you had any jobs going? Maybe here, behind the bar?'

'You ever worked in a pub before?'

Lita shook her head. 'I'm a fast learner. I reckon I could pick it up.'

'Well, there's nothin' at the moment, but I'll bear you in mind if anyone leaves.'

'What about something else?'

'What have you got in mind?'

Lita shrugged, unwilling to give up. 'Whatever. I've worked in a jewellery store. I'm no expert but I know a bit about watches and precious stones and the rest.'

Terry raised his eyebrows in a sceptical arch.

'Really,' she said.

But Terry seemed more amused than impressed by her claims. He put his hand in his inside jacket pocket, pulled out a ring and passed it over to her. 'What do you make of this, then?'

Lita held the sparkling ring in her palm. On first sight the stone looked like a large circular diamond – about 0.90 carats – set in platinum, but she wasn't fooled by appearances. Mal had always said she had a good eye. He'd talked her through all the techniques of telling a genuine stone from a fake, and she'd listened carefully, wanting to please him. In some cases, like this one, it was simple; in others, there was more work involved.

'So?' Terry said.

Lita checked the 'diamond' for flaws, holding it up to the light. Then she put the stone close to her mouth and breathed lightly on it. Immediately a thin mist appeared on the surface. She laughed and handed it back. 'I hope you didn't pay too much. That flashy stone's never seen a mine in its life.'

Terry dropped the ring back in his pocket. 'Lucky guess,' he said.

'Nothing lucky about it. Want to try me with another?'

'Like I'm carrying round the bleedin' Crown Jewels!'

Vinnie leaned forward, looked at Lita and spoke for the first time. He had a deep bass voice that seemed to travel from the depths of his chest. 'How did you know?'

Lita tapped the side of her nose and smiled. 'Trade secret,' she said. 'But if you ever need anything valued, just ask.'

'I've got people to do that,' Terry said.

'What, like Brenda? I bet she's never given you a fair price in the past ten years.'

Lita was surprised by the confident way she was talking, as if she was an expert when it came to fencing stolen goods. But now that she'd started she was determined to keep up the act. It was desperation that spurred her on; if she couldn't make some cash, her choices in the future were going to get smaller and smaller. She had to find the means to survive and if that meant working on the wrong side of the law, so be it. 'You'd be better off selling straight to a jeweller.'

'And getting myself nicked in the process? I think I'll pass if you don't mind, love.'

'Obviously you have to stay away from the London stores – they've all got lists of stolen gear – but there's less chance of that in other places, Surrey or Buckinghamshire, counties with money. I reckon the right person could shift the better pieces for twice what Brenda gives you.'

Terry folded his arms across his chest and gazed at her. 'You reckon, do you?'

Lita looked straight back into his eyes. 'I do.'

'And that right person would be . . . ?'

'Someone who looks the part, who speaks with the right accent. Someone they'd never suspect of doing anything illegal.' She paused and then added, 'Someone you can trust.'

Terry laughed, showing a row of perfect white teeth. 'How old are you, Lolly?'

'Eighteen,' she said. She could have added that everyone called her Lita now, but she didn't. Somehow it would feel like an affectation, as though she was saying that her old name wasn't good enough for her any more. Lita was Esther's invention, a diminutive that belonged to Kent, to a big house in the country and a lake that shimmered in the midday sun. Here on the dirty streets of Kellston she would always be Lolly.

'I'll think about it, okay?'

But Lita suspected he was only humouring her. And who could blame him? She smiled anyway. 'Don't think too long or I might get snapped up by someone else.'

Terry grinned back at her. 'I'll bear it in mind.'

Lita finished her orange juice, put the empty glass on the table and stood up. 'Thanks for the drink. It was good to see you again.'

'You too. Take care, Lolly.'

Before she left to resume her job hunting, Lita went to the Ladies. Here she sat and peed and wondered how long it would be before her money ran out. A few weeks? A month? She was living frugally but she still had to eat. And she couldn't stay in Albert Road for ever.

She flushed the loo and washed her hands at the basin. Her gaze slipped to the gold Cartier watch on her wrist, a present from Mal. If she was desperate, she could sell it, although she baulked at the idea. It wasn't only beautiful, but it had sentimental value too.

Lita dried her hands, sighing as she thought of Mal. He could be locked up for months before the case went to trial. And what then? She didn't want to dwell on what kind of sentence he might get. Hopefully, he would send her a visiting order soon. She wanted to see him again, to let him know that she hadn't turned her back. He'd been there for her and she would do the same for him.

Lita was still thinking about Mal as she walked out of the Ladies into the narrow corridor leading back to the main part of the pub. She had only gone a short distance when she sensed rather than heard that someone was behind her. Glancing casually over her shoulder, all she saw was a fast blur of movement before a hand was clamped over her mouth. Suddenly she was being hauled back and round a corner, her heels dragging on the floor. She had barely acknowledged what was happening to her when she was abruptly manhandled into an upright position, spun around and slammed against the wall. A tremor ran down her spine, making her legs shake.

It was only then, as he stood in front of her, that she saw her assailant clearly for the first time. Panic welled, sheer black fright that made her heart thump uncontrollably. Tony Cecil loomed over her, his features contorted with rage. He put a hand to her throat, pushed his face into hers and hissed, 'Make a sound you bitch, and you're dead!'

Lita didn't think she could make a sound even if she tried. Her throat was closing up from the pressure of his fingers, a strange wheezing noise emanating from her chest.

'Do you hear what I'm saying? Do you?'

She made a valiant attempt at a nod, a gesture to confirm she understood. And only then, finally, slowly, did he begin to loosen his hold. She felt the air rush back into her lungs, a sudden rush of oxygen that made her feel light-headed.

'Welcome back, Lolly Bruce. I've been waiting fuckin' years for this!'

Staring into his eyes, Lita saw his dilated pupils and knew that he was high on some shit or other – a revelation that only added to her terror. He was out of control, beyond rational thought or logic, indifferent to the consequences of his actions.

'It's payback time,' he whispered.

She could smell the beer on his breath and another more chemical odour. There was spittle at the corners of his mouth. She didn't even try to move, didn't do anything that might provoke him – his hand was still resting at the base of her throat – but her mind, driven by fear, had gone into overdrive. What now? She had to do something? Do what? She had to *think*.

'You're still the same little bitch you always were. A grass! And you know what happens to filthy grasses, don't you?'

Lita knew it was pointless to try and protest her innocence; it would only wind him up even more. She glanced frantically to her left – ten feet of space to the emergency exit – and to her right where the short corridor formed a right angle with the one where she'd been grabbed. What were the chances of someone coming along? Just about zero, she reckoned, unless the bloody pub was burning down.

Tony gave a mocking laugh. 'No one's coming to save you, babe. Nobody gives a shit.'

She heard the noise, an ominous click, before she saw the glitter of the blade. Cold steel pressed against her throat. She flinched and his evil grin grew wider. He could cut her throat from ear to ear, slice straight through the jugulars and leave her to bleed to death. *Think.*

'Say your prayers, Lolly Bruce. It's time to say hello to your crazy mum again.'

Perhaps it was the callous mention of her mother that sparked off the anger deep inside her. It didn't replace the fear but grew alongside it, a swelling of resentment, a fury against all the people who had pushed her around, bullied and tormented her. She could die like she had lived – with her head bowed, with dull acceptance – or she could go out fighting. Lita ran her tongue along her dry lips. Her voice was a thin croak.

'If you kill me, you'll never know.'

Tony Cecil stared at her, his mad eyes showing a glimmer of confusion. 'What won't I fuckin' know?'

She breathed in, careful not to move too much. 'Who murdered Amy.'

The words seemed to throw him off balance for a moment, but he quickly recovered. 'Your stinkin' pervert boyfriend, right?' Angrily, he pushed the sharp blade into her throat, piercing the flesh. 'Right?'

Lita gasped as she felt the blood slide down her neck. She felt no pain – adrenalin was pumping through her body – but she knew he wouldn't stop there. Next time the cut would be deeper. Next time he would finish what he'd started. 'It wasn't him! And it wasn't Joseph either.'

'You're a fuckin' liar!'

'I saw him. I saw him on the Mansfield that day.'

'Who the fuck are you talking about?'

Lita's eyes slid left and right again. If she could just break his hold for a few seconds, she might be able to make it to the fire doors. But what if the damn things were locked? What if the steel bar didn't work, wouldn't release? She'd be trapped, back to square one with nowhere to go. No, she was better off heading for the corridor with the Ladies. She could scream, shout, create some noise. Surely someone would hear?

'I can't . . . can't breathe,' she said, forcing a rattling choke from the back of her throat. She half-closed her eyes and tried to make her body go limp. As if she wasn't a threat. As if she was too weak to do anything even if she wanted to. Her senses suddenly seemed extra sharp, as though she could see and smell everything more clearly. Her heart, beating twice as fast as it should, felt like it might explode.

And now he wasn't sure what to do next. His drug-fuelled

brain was struggling with the options. He wanted to carry on hurting her, but he also wanted to know what she knew. It was the latter that won out. He drew back, not far but just enough to give her that window of opportunity. And she didn't waste it. As soon as she felt him release his grip she sprang back to life, ducked under his arm and sprinted along the corridor.

Surprise had given her a couple of seconds' advantage, but he was faster and stronger than she was. As she turned the corner, she could hear his footsteps crashing behind her, hear the curses spilling from his mouth. She wasn't going to make it into the safety of the main part of the pub. He would catch her, grab her, drag her back. And this time he wouldn't make the same mistake.

In her frantic attempt to get away, she didn't even open her mouth to scream. She was using every bit of energy she had left just to try and outrun him. But it wasn't going to happen. He was almost on her again, so close she could feel the movement of air between them. Desperate for a weapon, anything she could use to defend herself, she spotted a fire extinguisher and in one last mad gamble swept it up and turned to face him. It was heavier than she'd expected, a dense weight in her arms.

Tony Cecil stopped in his tracks. His teeth were bared, his cheeks scarlet with rage. As he prepared to pounce, Lita did the only thing she could – she turned slightly to one side and, using every bit of strength she had left, hurled the fire extinguisher straight towards him. He tried to dodge out of the way but his reactions were too slow. She missed where she was aiming – right for the centre of his body – and it landed instead on his foot.

Tony let out a howl and dropped to his knees. The knife skittered across the floor. He clutched at his toes, hunched over, rocking back and forth. Lita didn't hang around to see any more. She turned to get away, but as she did found her path blocked by someone else. Any relief she'd been feeling was instantly replaced with horror. Her immediate thought was FJ, that Tony hadn't been alone, and she quickly raised her fists to protect herself.

'Hey,' a familiar voice said, firmly taking hold of her wrists. 'That's no way to treat an old mate.'

Lita's eyes focused on the face of Terry Street. She didn't think she'd ever been happier to see anyone in her entire life. Her lips tried for a smile but didn't quite make it. 'Sorry,' she murmured. He let go of her wrists and her arms fell limply back to her side.

Terry took her chin in his hand and tilted it up to check out her neck. He gave a nod. 'You'll live. It looks worse than is.'

Then he walked over to Tony and glared down at him. 'Stop yer fuckin' bawling. It's hurting my ears.'

'She's broken it, man, she's fuckin' broken it.'

'You got what you deserved, you lousy piece of shit.'

Tony looked up, his face now white as a sheet.

Terry's voice was cold and menacing. 'You touch her again – *anyone* touches her – and you'll have me to answer to. You get it?' When Tony said nothing, he prodded the injured foot with the toe of his shoe. 'You get it, shithead?'

Tony yelped with pain, but eventually gave the required nod.

'Don't forget. 'Cause I know everything about you, every sordid little detail. You cross me again and you'll fuckin' regret it.' He didn't wait for a response, but walked back to Lita, bending to scoop up the knife on his way. 'Let's get you sorted,' he said.

Lita's hand fluttered to her neck and she saw the blood on her fingertips. There were all sorts of things she might have said, could have said, but what came out of her mouth was utterly mundane. 'Sorry about your fire extinguisher.'

'Yeah, try and take a bit more care in the future. Those things don't come cheap, you know.'

61

Yesterday, Nick Trent couldn't have said that he was a hundred per cent certain, that he didn't have a single doubt, but he'd been sure enough to follow up, to make the call and arrange to see her again. What had given her away? It was the nerves, he thought, the inexplicable anxiety. He had taken her by surprise, caught her off guard, like a knock on the door in the middle of the night.

Now, as they sat by side on the wooden bench on the green, he knew he was about to hear the truth. She had held out for a while, feigning ignorance, batting away his questions with well-worn lies until he had played his trump card.

'You won't mind doing the blood test, then?'

'What blood test?'

Nick had no idea if what he'd said next was true or not. Although he'd heard there had been advances, he wasn't familiar with the details. 'It's new. Much more accurate than the old one. Just to eliminate you, so to speak, to show that you can't be Lita's … Lolly's biological mother.'

He'd heard the breath catch in her throat. 'Of course I'm not! Why would you think that?' And although she must have aimed for indignant, it came out sounding shrill and defensive. 'No, I'm not taking any test.' She'd rubbed at her bare arm, glanced at him, given a rueful smile. 'Can't stand needles, me.'

'Me neither,' Nick had left a brief silence before saying very softly, 'It's time to stop all this. It's going to come out. You know it is. She's yours, isn't she?'

The woman had opened her mouth as if to protest, but then a wretched weariness had come over her. She'd covered her eyes for a moment as if her blindness might make it all go away. When she lowered her hands, there was fear on her face. 'You can't tell anyone! The old man's going to kill me if he finds out.'

Nick wasn't prepared to make any promises he couldn't keep. 'How did it happen?'

It was a good minute now, maybe longer, since he'd asked the question, but he didn't press her. The genie was out of the bottle and she'd answer in her own good time. While he waited he stared out across the green, taking in the parched grass and the sunbathers. A dog sniffed at the base of a tree.

Maeve Riley began slowly, tentatively, as if reaching for the right words. 'It was while the old man was away, wasn't it? Halfway through a three-stretch at the Scrubs. And he's not what you'd call the forgiving sort. I wanted to get rid, but Angela said it was too risky, that half the time women

513

bled to death. It wasn't legal then, of course, you just had to take your chances.'

She sighed into the still summer air, her hands twisting in her lap. 'I should never have let her talk me out of it. It would have been done then, wouldn't it, over with one way or the other? But she talked me round, said I could go up to my sister's in Glasgow for the last few months, tell my Mick that she was sick and needed looking after. That way he'd never guess. And then after the baby was born . . . well, she'd take it on, wouldn't she? Angela. She'd always wanted a kid but she couldn't have one of her own.'

Nick nodded, starting to get the picture. 'I take it the deal was that she wouldn't come back to Kellston?'

Maeve flinched at the word 'deal'. 'Manchester. That's where she said she was going, reckoned she had friends there.'

'And it all went smoothly?'

'Smooth enough until five years down the line when she suddenly appeared again.'

'That must have been a shock.'

'She was acting strange too, not like the old Angela. Always looking over her shoulder, if you know what I mean. And she said there were voices in her head telling her what to do, voices that had told her to come back to Kellston. I took her to the doc straight off and he put her on some pills. She was all right for a while after that. Things settled down and I got her a job at the Fox.'

'You must have been worried.'

Maeve shot him a sidelong glance. 'Course I was worried. You don't know my Mick. He'd have lost the plot if he'd ever found out. But she swore, swore on her life, that she'd never tell.'

'Who was Lolly's dad?'

The sudden change of tack took her unawares. 'No one,' she said sharply. 'Least no one worth remembering. I can't tell you his name so don't bother asking. And when I say can't, I mean can't and not won't. It was just a drunken mistake. I'd never met him before and I wouldn't know him if he walked straight past us now.'

'Okay.' Nick was still trying to absorb the fact that, with a little help from Sheila Barstow, he'd actually discovered who Lolly's mother was, but he felt no sense of triumph. There were no winners in this tragic story. And although he'd succeeded where his uncle hadn't, this hadn't been down to any great detecting skills. Stanley had mistaken Maeve's anxiety for a fear of Joe Quinn, and he'd have probably done the same in his position. 'It must have hard for you though, seeing Lolly around all the time, knowing she was really yours.'

'She was never mine,' Maeve snapped. 'Angela was her mother.'

Nick moved swiftly on. 'And then Billy Martin turned up. I guess that's when things got really complicated. I mean, he knew Angela couldn't have kids, didn't he? He must have asked a lot of awkward questions.'

'That man ...' Maeve spoke through gritted teeth, as though even the mention of his name caused her pain. 'He just wouldn't stop. He was at her all the time, pushing and pushing. She told him Lolly was adopted but he didn't believe her; she didn't have any legal papers, didn't have any proof at all. And Billy couldn't stand her holding out on him. He was a nasty piece of work, a control freak, the sort of man who isn't happy unless he's making someone else's life a misery. Ruining her life once wasn't good enough for the bastard; he had to start all over again.'

'Why didn't she just go somewhere else, get away from him?'

'I kept telling to leave, but she wouldn't. She said that would only make it worse, that he'd come after her, track her down, and then he'd be angry, and when Billy was angry . . . well, you can guess the rest.'

'So how did the whole Fury business come about?'

Maeve lifted a hand to her mouth and chewed on a nail. 'It was just another way of tormenting her. When she wouldn't tell him where Lolly had come from, he started joking that she must be Kay Fury, the missing baby. Everyone knew about that; it was all over the papers. But nothing ever stopped as a joke with Billy. This was around the same time he flushed her pills down the toilet, told her she didn't need them, claimed he was doing it for her own good.'

'And that's when she began getting ill again?'

Maeve nodded. 'She started getting confused about things, and the more confused she got the more Billy took advantage. He said Mal Fury and his wife had spies everywhere, people feeding back information about children who might not belong to the parents they were with. He said he'd protect her, keep them away, but that if she ever left he'd pick up the phone and she'd never see the kid again. It was just a sick game for him, a way of playing with her head.'

'But she knew Lolly wasn't Kay Fury so why should she be worried?'

'Because she started having doubts. She began to wonder if she really did know. She came round to see me, asked if I'd ever actually been pregnant. She hadn't seen me in those last few months, not while I'd been up in Glasgow, and she wasn't there at the birth. She only saw Lolly for the first time when she was a few weeks old.' Maeve released a sigh of frustration. 'There was no telling her. She had this idea that Joe Quinn had organised the kidnap and that when it all went wrong he'd given me the baby to get rid of. I told her it didn't make any sense, that even if Joe had done it – which he hadn't – he wouldn't have known in advance what was going to happen. Why would he make plans to offload the baby if he was hoping to get a ransom for returning her?'

'And what did Angela say?'

'She couldn't think it through properly. One minute she was saying that maybe Joe had never planned on returning her, that he was just going to take the money, and the next suggesting that I'd double-crossed him, told him the baby was dead and passed Kay over to her instead. I even went to the library and got a copy of a newspaper article, one that had a picture of Kay, but she said it was fake, that I was just trying to fool her.'

'Billy did a good job screwing with her head.'

'Oh, it didn't stop there. He even produced a button he claimed had come off Kay Fury's cardigan during the kidnap. It was nonsense, of course – he must have checked out the pictures in the paper too – but by this time she was too confused to know what day of the week it was, never mind remember what buttons had been on the clothes Lolly had been wearing when I passed her over. But he kept pressing her saying, 'It's the same, isn't it?' I asked her how the hell Billy could have got hold of something like that, but she just shrugged and said that he 'knew people.'

'And then Billy suddenly disappeared. What do you think happened there?'

'Happened?' she echoed.

Nick didn't elaborate. She knew exactly what he meant.

Maeve's thin shoulders shifted up and down. 'He just took off, didn't? Maybe he got bored. Maybe he found some other poor cow to torment. Who knows? Who cares? She should have been glad to see the back of him.'

'Except she wasn't. Billy had convinced her he was keeping her safe, protecting her from the Furys. And now she didn't feel safe any more. She reckoned Joe was behind it, didn't she?'

'Only because of what Billy had been telling her.'

And Nick wondered what Maeve had been telling Joe about Billy: something inflammatory, some lie to get the old gangster pissed off enough to dispose of a lowlife no one but Angela would miss. That he was a grass, perhaps – or that he'd been badmouthing Joe behind his back. From what he'd heard, Joe Quinn's fuse had been a short one.

'It must have been a worry for you, all this.'

Maeve turned a pair of suspicious eyes on him. 'I was worried for *her*.'

'Is that why you got her fired from the pub?'

The direct question made her wince. Her hands began their restless dance again. 'That was Joe's doing, not mine.'

'But you were the one who put the idea in his head. You must have been scared that she'd let something slip, that the truth about Lolly might finally come out.'

Maeve didn't deny it. Her eyes narrowed and her voice turned ugly and peevish. 'I just wanted her to go away, for God's sake. I'd had enough of it all. I thought . . . I thought if she didn't have a job, if Billy wasn't around any more, then she might go back to Manchester. She was asking weird questions in the pub, saying crazy stuff. It was only a matter of time before someone put two and two together. I didn't have a choice. I told Joe he should let her go before she scared off all the customers.'

Nick guessed she'd said a damn sight more than that, but kept his suspicions to himself. 'But she didn't leave.'

'No.'

'That can't have been easy for you.'

'I just stayed out of her way, avoided her.'

'For eight years?'

'What else could I do?'

Nick saw the agitation in her again, knew that she was hiding something. 'But you talked to her before she died.' It was a shot in the dark, but he knew he'd hit pay dirt. Her whole body stiffened, the blood draining from her face. She looked as pale as a body laid out in the morgue.

'It-it wasn't my fault,' she stammered. 'You can't blame me. I only wanted her to go away, to get out of Kellston. That's all I ever wanted.'

'What did you say to her?'

'She grabbed hold of me on the high street and wouldn't let go. She was gabbling, talking nonsense, going on about spies and Billy and some Teddy guy he'd met in jail, and how she was being followed. I couldn't take any more. I'd had enough. I mean, I had my kids with me. It wasn't right. She was scaring them.'

Nick squinted into the sun, almost afraid of what was coming next. He held his breath and waited for the revelation.

Maeve wrapped her arms around her chest, shivering as though it was the middle of winter rather than a hot summer's day. 'I told her she should go home, pack up her stuff, take Lolly and get out of Kellston as fast as she could. I said it was true about the kidnap, that Lolly wasn't my baby. I said Mal Fury had been in the pub looking for her.'

'What?'

'It wasn't my fault,' she insisted again. 'How was I to know she'd do a thing like that?'

Nick slowly turned his face to look at her. She wouldn't meet his gaze. He felt disgust and contempt and something he couldn't quite describe – a kind of pity, perhaps, for all the dreadful mistakes that human beings made.

62

It was two weeks now since Lita had learned the truth about her birth mother. It still hadn't quite sunk in. *Maeve Riley*? When Nick Trent had broken the news, she'd shaken her head, laughed, said he'd got it all wrong. Not Maeve, it couldn't be. She was the woman who worked at the caff, the friend her mum had fallen out with, not . . . But the words had dried on her lips as the story unfolded.

At first, bombarded by emotions – anger, bitterness, resentment – she had withdrawn into herself. How to make sense of it? She didn't think she could. It was hard not to dwell on the fact she'd been unwanted, 'a mistake', something to be flushed away at the first opportunity.

'You can't think like that,' Stella had argued. 'She was young and scared, knocked up by a man who wasn't her husband. That Mick, he's got a temper on him. Jackie says—'

'She's known all along, hasn't she? That's why she didn't want me here.'

'She and Maeve go way back. They grew up together. She was just looking out for her in her own stupid way.'

'By being vile to me?'

'She thought you'd come here to cause trouble, to start digging up the past. That guy Trent was sniffing around, asking Maeve about Angela, and then you showed up too and ... I don't know, love. What can I say? When people have secrets, they want them to stay that way.'

Lita thought about secrets as she gazed across the table at Mal. They had been his undoing too. Did the damn things ever stay buried? The visiting room was crowded, with all of the tables taken. Voices, male and female, wrapped around each other, kids shouted and babies cried. She was glad of the noise because it made talking easier, their conversation less likely to be overheard above the surrounding din.

She studied his face, looking for signs of fear or despair, but he appeared surprisingly calm. Perhaps it was a relief to shed that burden, to stop living in dread of the truth coming out. Having just finished her revelations about Maeve, she shrugged and said, 'But you don't want to hear all this. Tell me what's going on with you. What's it like here? Can you bear it? Is it too awful?'

Mal placed his elbows on the table and smiled. 'No, don't stop. I want to hear the rest. There's nothing interesting to say about prison. It is what it is. You don't have to worry about me. Have you talked to Maeve yet or would you rather not?'

'I wasn't going to. I couldn't see the point, but then I thought ... I'm not sure what I thought.' Lita played with the plastic cup, turning it around in her fingers. An inch of cold tea sloshed around in the bottom. 'We met in a café in Shoreditch. The very first words out of her mouth were, "Are you going to tell my Mick?" I despised her for that, for not even pretending to care about anyone but herself.'

'She was scared. People behave badly when they feel threatened – or guilty.'

Lita wondered if he was talking as much about himself as Maeve. She remembered how angry she'd felt when she'd heard Maeve's question, and how this had been quickly followed by another more corrosive emotion. She'd felt *powerful* too, knowing how much damage she could inflict, knowing that just by telling the truth to the world she could rip this woman's life apart. And why shouldn't she? Why should Maeve be allowed to get away with what she'd done? 'I wanted to hurt her. Is that terrible? I wanted to make her suffer.'

'But you haven't,' Mal said. 'And you won't.'

Lita shrugged, knowing he was right. When push came to shove, she didn't have the heart for it. 'Well, it wouldn't make any difference, would it? Not really. It wouldn't bring Mum back. It wouldn't change anything that's happened.' She glanced around the room, looked back at Mal. 'It was tempting though.'

He smiled. 'I can imagine.'

'And I'm glad I met her. I wanted to see her face to face and make sure ... I wanted to be certain there was nothing there between us, no weird connection or anything, and there wasn't. So much for biology!' As soon as she said it, she wished he hadn't. Mal still didn't know the fate of his own daughter, whether she was dead or alive – and maybe he never would. 'I suppose it's different for everyone.'

They were quiet for a while, two people trying to come to terms with their respective pasts. It was Mal who broke the silence. 'Angela must have loved you. I'm not saying that what she did was right, but she must have wanted you enough to be prepared to live a lie. I understand how hard that is, what it means to be always looking over your shoulder. She must have lived with the fear of losing you every single day.'

'I know.'

Lita thought about the tin box Maeve had passed over in the café, perhaps the only decent thing the woman had ever done. She had stolen it, using the spare key Angela had given her before they'd fallen out, to gain access to the flat. Inside the box were all the items Lita remembered: the beads, the brooch, the pink ribbon, the cinema tickets and the hair grips. Small unimportant things, except they weren't unimportant to her. They were all she had left of her mother. The letters had gone, of course, destroyed by Maeve – incriminating letters written from Glasgow that said too much about their plans.

Mal cut across her thoughts. 'Can I ask you something? Why did you leave home? Did Esther make you?'

'It wouldn't have worked out,' she said, avoiding a direct answer. 'Can you imagine me and Esther living there together? Anyway, I fancied a change. I like living in London.'

Mal inclined his head while he read between the lines. 'You'll need some money. I'll talk to Considine, get a monthly payment organised.'

Lita knew she should jump at the opportunity to solve her financial problems. She could get her own flat, pay the bills and never have to worry about where the next meal was coming from – so why was she hesitating? Because taking the cash would be the easy option. She knew it was time to make her own way, her own decisions, to start standing on her own two feet as Mrs Gough had so succinctly put it. 'Thanks, but I'm okay. I've got a job lined up, nothing special but it'll tide me over.'

'I've let you down. I'm sorry.'

'You haven't let me down.'

'I promised you a job at Fury's, didn't I? Things aren't looking too good on that front. I'll probably have to cut my losses and close the place – people don't like doing business with murderers – but I could ask around, try and get someone else to take you on.'

'There's no need,' Lita said. 'Don't worry about it. Please. You've done enough. You took me in when Brenda didn't want me any more. You've taken care of me for the past five years.' She almost added that he'd been like a father to her, but thought of Kay and bit her lip. 'I don't even know why you did all that.'

Mal gave a soft laugh. 'To salve my conscience, to have someone young around the house, to do the right thing for once? Take your pick. None of them are what you'd call selfless.'

'Nobody's selfless,' she said. 'Well, hardly anyone.'

Mal frowned as he looked across the table, noticing something for the first time. He leaned forward and peered at her. 'What happened to your neck?' he asked, touching the mirror spot on his own throat.

Lita's hand lifted to where the blade of Tony's knife had sliced through her skin. It was healed up now with only a short pink scar to remind her of the terror of that afternoon. 'It's nothing, just a scratch.'

The lines between his eyes grew deeper, but perhaps there was something in her tone, her expression, which made him think twice about challenging her explanation. 'What's it like where you're living?'

'Much the same as it always was. Kellston doesn't change much.' She pushed the plastic cup away, drew it back again, knowing that their time was running out. The atmosphere in the room had altered, a subtle shift, a sense of drawing in as people prepared themselves for separation. In a few minutes she'd have to leave. Already some of the visitors were scraping back their chairs, standing up and saying their goodbyes.

'Will you come again?' Mal asked.

Lita looked at him and nodded.

'You don't have to.'

'I want to.'

She let her hand rest on his for a moment. Sometimes the people you loved looked after you, and sometimes you looked after them. That's just the way it was.

Epilogue

Six months later

Lolly's flat was small and beige and often smelled of curry from the takeaway downstairs, but she still loved it. For the very first time she had a place of her own and nothing could beat the feeling. When she closed the door, there was no one to answer to but herself. She could do what she liked when she liked. She could walk around stark naked if she wanted to. She could shut out the rest of the world and forget about it.

On the table by the window was a box of broken watches. When she wasn't working for Terry, she would spend her time repairing them, carefully restoring the pieces to their former glory before flogging them on a stall she had on Camden Market. The watches came from all over the place, second-hand and charity shops, auction houses, pawn-brokers and from an ad she ran in the local paper. It was surprising how cheaply she could pick them up, even the big names like Omega and Breitling and Rolex.

There was some profit to be made, but the work was time-consuming. It was the jobs she did for Terry that brought in the bigger bucks, valuing jewellery and sometimes selling it on. Despite her age, he'd given her a chance and she didn't think she'd disappointed. Once a month or so, she'd get dressed up to the nines and Vinnie would drive her out to some fancy jeweller's in the country where she'd put on her best cut-glass accent and spin them a yarn about her grandmother dying and leaving her some rings. The first time she'd done it, she'd been terrified of being caught, sure that they'd see straight through her. But maybe they'd mistaken her nerves for grief because she'd walked out of the shop with six hundred quid in her pocket.

Lolly didn't intend to do this indefinitely – everyone's luck ran out at some point – but for now it provided a much-needed boost to her income. It was a means to an end, a way of keeping afloat. In truth, she didn't much care that she was breaking the law. Her sense of what was right and wrong had started to blur around the edges. Some people had so much and others so little and often that was decided by pure chance, an accident of birth. She had experienced both sides, rich and poor, and although she didn't miss the lavish surroundings of the Fury house, she was determined never to go without again.

Every fortnight Lolly travelled to Wandsworth to visit Mal. The judge had not been too harsh on him – a three-year sentence of which he'd only serve half – and already he was making plans for when he was released. There, in the visiting room, she became Lita again, a different girl to the one who did business with Terry Street and hung out with the whores on Albert Road. It was odd, she thought, like having a split personality.

Although she kept in touch with Theresa and Mrs Docherty – duly passing on any juicy gossip to Mal – she wondered if she'd ever see them again. Sometimes the beautiful house with the shimmering lake seemed a distant memory, something so far away it might almost be a dream. She inhabited a different world now, one without peacocks and plump white towels.

Lolly picked up the seashell box from the table. Inside was the Fanta cap she'd saved from all those years ago, a reminder of Jude Rule. She hadn't seen him since the trial, since he'd turned up at the courtroom to support Esther. They hadn't spoken. There was nothing left to say. She was still haunted by the awful suspicion that he had murdered Amy Wiltshire and she had helped him get away with it. Would the truth ever come out? Only time would tell.

She went over to the window and opened it. A cold blast of winter air rushed into the room and made her hair fly horizontal. After checking that the coast was clear, she pulled back her arm and hurled the cap as far as she could. It caught on the wind for a second before arcing down into the road, bouncing twice and rolling into the gutter. She slammed shut the window with a grunt of satisfaction.

The next item she picked out of the box was Stanley Parrish's business card. It reminded her of Nick and she wondered when she'd see him again. He had a habit of turning up out of the blue, acting as though they were friends, although she couldn't quite recall when she'd agreed to this. She both liked and disliked him, found him simultaneously annoying and intriguing, and these were contradictions she hadn't quite come to terms with. She didn't have the heart to throw the card away and carefully placed it back where it had been.

Finally she took out the black and white photo taken in the Woolworths booth. A scrawny kid stared at the camera with startled eyes and a sad mouth. 'Look at you,' she murmured, feeling an odd combination of pity and pride. Eventually she smiled. She'd survived, hadn't she? That was no small thing. Against all the odds, she'd found her way.

Nick Trent had plans. The first of these was to go home and have a long hot bath. The second was to get a less tedious job. He'd been on the tail of an adulterous husband for the past four hours and felt like his bones were turning to ice. The heating in his car didn't work and his teeth were chattering. He'd been hired by the private investigators Marshall & Marshall, two ex-cop brothers who sat on their fat arses all day and delegated all the crap assignments to new recruits like him.

Nick glanced at the clock on the dashboard for the umpteenth time before his gaze returned to the modern detached house. He hoped the guy wasn't planning a sleepover. Unlikely as he was married, but you never could tell: the lying sod probably had a ready-made list of excuses as to why he couldn't make it home.

In order to oil the cogs of his rapidly freezing brain,

Nick started going over the Fury case again. It still bugged him that he couldn't prove his uncle had been deliberately killed. Had Mal Fury been involved? That had been his original theory. Now he had another, although this wasn't one he could prove either. He reckoned Stanley, following up on the Teddy Heath lead, had gone back to the café to ask Maeve more questions. Maybe something he'd said had spooked her, making her think he knew more than he did. Maybe Jackie had been there when it happened. Maybe the two women had conspired to get him down to Albert Road, and maybe Joe Quinn had been tipped the wink that Stanley Parrish was asking questions about Billy Martin again, even threatening to go to the law.

'That's a shit-lot of maybes,' Nick said out loud.

But he thought the truth was buried in there somewhere. Perhaps not exactly in the form he had it, but something similar, a variation on the theme. However, no one was going to confirm his suspicions. Neither Maeve nor Jackie were about to implicate themselves in a cold-blooded murder.

Whenever Nick thought about Stanley, it wasn't long before Lita Bruce sprang into his head. She wasn't his responsibility and yet in an odd kind of way he did feel responsible for her. Like an obligation he'd inherited from his uncle. Except that made it sound like a duty, which wasn't what he meant at all. Far from it. He liked the girl, even though she could be impossible, stubborn and defensive, a tangled mass of contradictions. Or maybe that was why he liked her. She was tough and vulnerable, sassy and naive. She was different.

*

Mal Fury lay stretched out on the bed with his hands behind his head. Even in the dead of night, prison was never quiet. The potential silence was like an empty vessel into which every man's pain was poured, a jet-black liquid of rage and regret and frustration. Fists pummelled against locked doors, the sound echoing along the empty corridors. Curses travelled through the thick walls. Awake or asleep, the men still called out, a never-ending cry of hopelessness.

But Mal knew now that he could survive this. He could endure the claustrophobia, the routine, the perpetual air of menace. The trick was to keep your head down and make yourself useful. He wrote letters for the illiterate to wives and girlfriends, read out the replies and listened to their problems. He helped with legal queries, translating jargon into plain English whilst clearing a way through the tortuous maze of parole boards and appeals.

And then there was Lita. Her visits kept him going, gave him something to look forward to. He remembered the girl she had been – a lost soul – and thought of how she was now, strong and independent and fiercely loyal. Not that any of that was down to him. She had forged her own path and always would. She was the kind of young woman he would have wanted Kay to become, a daughter to be proud of.

Sometimes, when he closed his eyes, he would see Teddy Heath's sly face, goading him, taunting him about the kidnap. He had lied about the bastard's motives. It had only ever been the money, nothing else. By persuading Esther that Teddy had acted out of revenge, payback for being used and discarded, he had laid a burden of guilt from which she could never be free. Her casual infidelity had cost them their daughter. He had never felt bad about doing this. Why should he? Guilt was a great leveller. She had always had the upper hand, always been loved more than she had loved.

Mal knew their relationship was toxic but it was, ironically, his connection to Esther that did most to secure him a position within these walls and keep him relatively safe. Even in jail, there was a fascination with celebrity. It gave him a peculiar status, which he was careful not to abuse.

'Esther,' he whispered.

Her name hung from his lip in the cold night air, a stalactite of love and hate, of agony and despair. Even after everything that had happened, he was not prepared to relinquish her yet. They were bound together, joined by secrets and lies. He had heard that she was back with Claud Leighton, but it wouldn't last. Nothing ever did with her. In time she would return to him. Their whole marriage had been a drama and this was just another act.

It was seeing the story in the newspaper that brought it all flooding back: Mal Fury being up in court for manslaughter. Hazel's mouth had fallen open. Somehow, after all these years, she'd been convinced it was finished, over with, a nightmare she'd buried long ago. There was an old photo of Teddy smiling for the camera. She'd never seen that picture before. It made her stomach flip.

Everyone has a first love and hers was Teddy Heath. She'd forgiven him everything: his drunkenness, his infidelity, even the habit he had of disappearing for weeks on end. She shouldn't have put up with it but she'd been too young to know any better. Infatuated, that was the word. She would have walked over hot coals if he'd asked her too.

In the event, he'd asked her to do much worse. She could have refused, but he'd always been able to twist her round his little finger. And it was foolproof, he'd insisted, no way it could go wrong. And after, when it *had* all gone wrong, she'd been the one left to pick up the pieces.

'You've got to help,' he'd pleaded. 'Leave her somewhere, anywhere she'll be found.'

And Hazel would have done exactly that, dumped the baby on the church doorstep or down by the library, if he hadn't scarpered, taking off in the middle of the night without so much as a goodbye note. She'd waited and waited but he hadn't come back. Of course she could have still gone ahead, but she didn't see why she should take the risk. What if someone saw her? She'd have been the one who paid the price for Teddy's crime.

An accessory, that's what the law would have called her. At the very least she would have been done for aiding and abetting. And who wants to spend the best years of their life in jail? She was scared, that's the truth. And the longer it went on, the more terrified she became. In the end, she had made her own choice and whether it was right or wrong was irrelevant now.

She didn't feel any guilt over Esther Gray. Why should she? How much guilt had Esther felt when she was screwing Teddy behind her husband's back? The bitch hadn't thought twice about it. You reap what you sow, as they say. What goes around comes around. Anyway, there was no turning back time. What was done was done and couldn't be changed. There was no point dwelling on it.

When she looked at her daughter, she saw a strong, capable girl with a good future ahead of her. What she didn't know couldn't hurt. The past was the past. It didn't need digging up and raking over. Why ruin another life? There had been enough damage already. Better to let sleeping dogs lie.

It was freezing in Kellston cemetery, but still and peaceful too. Lolly walked between the graves with one hand deep in her pocket, the other clutching a bowl of blue hyacinths. Her feelings towards Angela had changed a lot in the past six months and she was starting to understand how love wasn't always straightforward, how it could twist and turn like a plant searching for the sun.

It pained her to think of how much her mother had suffered, of how the fragile edifice of everything she'd built had slowly crumbled away as the illness ate away at her. Perhaps she would have got better if Billy Martin hadn't turned up. Perhaps she would never have jumped if she hadn't talked to Maeve that day.

Lolly was sure it hadn't just been fear that had made her take that fateful leap. It would have torn her mum apart to think she had been the cause of someone else's pain, that she had stolen a baby who was loved and cherished. And she wouldn't have run, not in a hundred years. Her conscience wouldn't have allowed it. Faced with a future without her child, she had chosen death instead.

Lolly came to the place where her mother's ashes had been interred. She stopped and gazed down at the new white headstone with its marble sheen and its angels and doves. It had taken five years but she had finally done it. People always said that life wasn't a fairy tale, but in many ways it was – a battle between good and evil, a struggle out of darkness towards the light. It was just the happy ending that didn't always quite come off.

Angela Bruce
Beloved mother of Lolly
Rest in peace

If you enjoyed *Survivor*
read on for an exclusive extract
from Roberta Kray's new novel,

DECEIVED

Out November 2018

PROLOGUE

1937

She lifted the long mink coat from the bag on the floor and held it up in front of her before slipping it around her shoulders. As she stared at her reflection in the mirror, she imagined she looked like one of those rich Mayfair ladies, the sort who took afternoon tea at the Ritz and treated the waiters with polite disdain. She turned to the left and the right, viewing the effect. Yes, if she kept her mouth shut she could easily pass for a woman of substance.

She stroked the soft mink, wishing she could keep it, but fancy furs didn't pay the bills or put food on the table. Anyway, the coats were too hot to hold on to. As soon as Lennie Hull found out they were missing, he'd do his nut. To thieve off a thief was a risky business at the best of times, but when that thief was Hull you were just asking for trouble. Ivor didn't care – said the cheating bastard owed him – but that wouldn't count for much when his legs were being broken.

She flinched at the thought of it.

Still, they'd be away soon, out of here and out of London. She glanced down towards the five bags full of ermine, sable and mink. They'd bring in a pretty penny once they found the right buyer. Her gaze lifted to the clock on the mantelpiece. Half an hour Ivor had said, and it was way past that. How long did it take to buy petrol?

'Come on, come on,' she muttered.

Nerves were starting to get the better of her. She lifted a hand to her mouth and chewed on her nails. The seconds ticked by slowly. The sky was darkening, the low clouds full of rain. That song, *Stormy Weather,* crept into her head. 'Don't know why there's no sun up in the sky . . . ' she crooned. She lit a cigarette and paced from one side of the room to the other. Had something gone wrong? No, she just had the jitters.

It would be fine once Ivor got back. She had never known a man like him before: smart and witty and fearless. Just the thought of him took her breath away. She'd grown up surrounded by villains, most of them with big ideas and cotton wool between their ears, but he was a world apart. He had a talent, a skill that none of them possessed. There wasn't a lock he couldn't open in England – maybe the whole world – or a safe either. All of which meant he'd never be out of work. It was the kind of work, however, that came with risks. The East End was full of copper's snouts, lowlifes who'd grass you up for the price of a pint. And who wanted to spend years in the slammer with nothing to look forward to than more of the same? It was a mug's game and he knew it.

Ivor had no respect for the law, for authority, but he wasn't a fool. 'The system always wins out in the end,' he said. If it wasn't a bent copper planting evidence, it was some loose-mouthed idiot bragging about a job in the boozer. He was forever looking over his shoulder, forever waiting for the knock on the door. And even though he'd grown up in Kellston, he didn't really fit in. He wasn't one of the boys. He was different and people round here didn't like different.

'It's time to make a move, love. Time for pastures new.'

And she hadn't disagreed with him. She'd be glad to see the back of this place although she'd miss her friends. Still, it would be an adventure. And who cared where they lived so long as they were together? The cash from the furs would give them a fresh start, a chance to get established. She stubbed out her ciggie and went back to the window. She wondered what it would be like up North. She had never been further than Epping in her life.

Her gaze strayed to the clock again – ten to ten. They'd intended to leave at the crack of dawn but that plan had gone for a burton when Ivor climbed into the Humber and discovered some tealeaf had emptied the petrol tank in the middle of the night. With the local garage closed until nine, they'd had no choice but to sit it out until opening time. Of course he could have gone and done some siphoning of his own, but that was always risky. Getting nicked was the last thing he needed.

She peered out of the window again. Where was he? It was then she saw the motor, a dark saloon, turn the corner and start travelling slowly down the road as though the driver was counting off the numbers on the houses. Her whole body froze. For a moment she stood rooted to the spot. She knew who it was and why they were coming. The name rose to her lips and hung there in an agony of disbelief.

Lennie Hull.

How had he found out? The furs weren't due to be moved from the warehouse until tomorrow. And how had he guessed that Ivor had nicked them? But none of that was important now. Jesus, they were for it! She had to scarper and fast. They'd be here in a minute and one flimsy front door wasn't going to hold them for long.

Finally the adrenalin kicked in. Shrugging off the mink she legged it to the kitchen, pulled back the bolts and threw open the door. She rushed through the backyard and along the long, narrow, weed-filled alley that ran behind the terrace. Should she duck into one of the neighbours' yards and hide in the lavvy? No, it was too risky. Hull and his goons would search every square inch until they found her.

She ploughed on until the alley eventually turned and re-joined the road further up. Here she stopped, knowing that the moment she stepped out they would be able to see her. She could wait until they forced their way into the house, but what if they decided to come round the back instead? She'd either have to make a run for it or double back and if she did the latter she'd be trapped with nowhere to go. No, her only option was to walk out as if nothing was wrong, to act normal like she was just an innocent woman on her way somewhere. She took a deep breath. *Hold your nerve, girl.*

She saw the motor out of the corner of her eye as she turned the corner, but didn't stare. It was parked in front of the house, the occupants in the process of getting out. Four of them, maybe five: big fellas suited and booted. They were about twenty yards away, far enough perhaps for them not to recognise her. She set off in the opposite direction, spine straight, head up, heels click-clacking on the pavement. Not too fast, not too slow. *Don't look back.*

She might have got away with it if she'd taken her own advice. Past the first lamppost and then the second, trying to stay calm even though her head was exploding, but she just couldn't resist that quick glance over her shoulder. Big mistake. Hull and the others were at the front door giving it a hammer, but the driver was leaning against the saloon with his arms folded across his chest and his gaze focused right on her.

Blind panic engulfed her body as their eyes met. She made a split second decision, and it was a bad one. Reason went out of the window. Before her instincts could engage with her brain, she took off. Almost immediately she stumbled and knew she'd have to ditch the heels. Quickly she kicked off her shoes and started to run again.

From behind she heard a shout 'Oi!' And then the sound of the saloon doors banging shut.

She was dead. She knew it. She ran as fast as her legs would carry her, her stockinged feet slapping against the cold pavement. But it wasn't fast enough. She could hear the motor getting closer. Her face was twisted, wet with tears, as she hurtled forward intent on only one thing – if she could just reach the cemetery she might be able to give them the slip, to hunker down and hide among the tombstones.

She had to get off the main road before they caught up with her. Out here she was a sitting duck. Which way now? She knew Kellston like the back of her hand but her mental map was being ripped apart by fear. There was a network of alleyways criss-crossing the district but if she chose the wrong one she could finish up in a dead end, trapped like an animal. Was it the next right? She thought it was. She prayed it was. Anyway, she had no choice. She dived across the road and sprinted into the gloom.

She heard the squeal of brakes as the motor pulled up. This time she didn't look back and kept on running. Her heart was pounding, the breath bursting from her lungs. The alley twisted and turned, the high brick walls looming over her. On the ground there was hard soil and sharp stones that dug into the soles of her feet, but she didn't slow down. On and on until she finally found what she was looking for.

The gate was ancient and rusty, hanging off a single hinge. She pushed it just far enough for her to squeeze by and then launched herself into the undergrowth. There had been a path here once but now it was overgrown, a mass of brambles and stinging nettles. As she stumbled through them, thrashing her arms, she could hear the heavy thud of footsteps back in the alley.

She was exhausted, but terror spurred her on. Here, in the older part of the cemetery, she should be able to find somewhere to hide. Eventually she emerged into clearer territory, full of long grass and weeds but easier to negotiate. She flew past weathered graves, granite towers and grey stone angels until she reached a dark place overhung by trees. A row of mausoleums, like an avenue of small abandoned houses, lay ahead. She got as far as the fifth before her legs gave way and she slumped to the ground.

Even as her backside hit the earth, she heard the male voices travelling through the air. Sick panic rose into her throat. Crawling on her hands and knees, she dragged herself round to the back of the tomb, curled up and tried to make her body as small as possible. It was then that the pain made contact with her brain. Her stockings were torn and her legs, arms and feet were covered in scratches and bright red welts from where she'd been stung.

She whimpered and quickly clamped her hand across her mouth. If they heard her, she was done for. She held her panting breath, pressed her cheek against the cool brick and listened. Now the voices were coming from different directions as the men spread out searching for her. How many? Two, three? She reckoned Hull and at least one of the others would have stayed behind to retrieve the furs – and wait for Ivor.

Ivor, Ivor. She repeated his name in her head like a mantra. When he got home, he'd be walking straight into an ambush. There wouldn't even be the saloon parked outside as a warning. Perhaps they'd grabbed him already. She shivered. Her heart thudded in her chest. Hull would make an example of Ivor, of them both.

She closed her eyes and prayed: *Please God, keep him safe. Please God, don't let them find me.*

It was starting to rain. The water pattered against the leaves and made a pocking sound as it dripped off the roof of the tomb. She stayed tightly curled, rigid with fear. Her teeth began to chatter. She clamped shut her jaw, scared the noise would betray her. Footsteps drew nearer. She heard the boots, heavy on the earth, and the sound of snapping twigs. The smell of cigarette smoke floated in the air.

This is it, she thought. This is the end.

The steps advanced, closer and closer, until her pursuer was only a few yards away. And then he stopped. There was a long silence as though he was trying to do decide what to do next. Or maybe he was just listening. She held her breath. All that separated them was the square brick tomb. If he decided to check round the back, it would all be over.

She pressed herself closer to the wall, wishing she could pass right through it into the darkness on the other side. The dead felt no fear, no horror. All she wanted was to be safe again. Time passed as slowly as it had in the house. Then there had been anticipation; now there was only dread.

The man remained for what felt like an eternity. Then, like a miracle, he began to walk away. She heard his steps receding, growing fainter, but she stayed completely still. Maybe he was just toying with her, playing a game. Maybe it was a trap so she would show herself. She wasn't going to fall for that one. No mistakes. No sudden stupid movements. Patience.

And so she waited ... and waited. The cold and damp crept into her bones. She thought about which exit to head for. There were three in all, including the old gate she had used. Best to stay clear of that. So one of the others. But where could she go from there? Not back to the house, that was for sure; there'd be a welcome committee installed in the living room.

With no money and no shoes on her feet, she needed somewhere close by and someone she could trust. Her friend Amy was her best bet. She had a flat on the high street, above the baker's. Yes, that was the place to go. Which meant she had to circle round the cemetery to the main entrance, but not until she was certain the coast was clear.

Carefully she stretched out one leg and then the other. How long had she been here? Over an hour, she thought. Her joints were stiff and aching. She concentrated hard, listening for any unwanted sounds. There were none. No voices. No footsteps. Surely they must have given up by now.

If it had been warmer, and dryer, she would have stayed where she was for even longer. But the cold was starting to get to her. She was shivering and soaked through. Much more of this and she'd end up with pneumonia. She hauled herself upright and tip-toed round the side of the tomb to peek along the narrow path. Empty. But she couldn't see far. Someone could be hiding in the trees.

She had to make a move at some point, but fear made her legs leaden. Her intention was to sneak through the darker parts of the cemetery, keeping off the main thoroughfares until she reached the perimeter wall. From there she could edge round to the main gate. She thought this over. All things considered it wasn't much of a plan, but it was all she'd got.

Her heart was in her mouth as she set off. Her feet, cut and sore, made every step a painful one. She tried to stay in the shelter of the trees and bushes, keeping her eyes peeled for Hull's men. Her ears strained to hear the slightest sound. She moved slowly, taking care where she trod. She sniffed the air, paused and went on. As she passed between the old graves, her gaze skimmed over the names of the dead, the young and the old, the husbands and wives, the mums and dads.

Ivor was in her thoughts. There was still a chance he'd got away. Maybe he'd realised something was wrong as he approached the house. All she could do was hope. He'd have to make himself scarce, lie low until the heat was off. But he'd come back for her. She was sure of it.

The wall was within spitting distance when it happened. She heard the tiniest of noises behind her, no more than a shifting in the air. As she whirled around, her worst nightmare became reality. The man was rising up from behind a pink granite tombstone, his face scarred and brutish, his mouth stretched into a devil's grin. He had a shooter in his hand and it was pointed straight at her.

'You took yer time, doll. I was starting to think you were never coming. Been freezing my bollocks off here.'

She backed away from him, but only as far as the wall. A thin whimpering sound escaped from her lips. It was too late for regrets, but they still tumbled through her head: if only she'd stayed where she was, if only that petrol hadn't got nicked, if only Ivor had stayed well away from those bloody furs . . .

'What's the matter, darlin',' he mocked. 'Cat got your tongue?'

With nothing left to lose, she raised her chin and stared him defiantly in the eyes. 'Go on, then. If you're going to shoot me, you may as well get it over and done with.'

'I ain't gonna shoot you,' he said. 'Not here at least. Wouldn't want to disturb these poor souls, now would we?' He glanced round at the graves and sniggered at his own joke. 'Nah, you and me are going take a little walk, all nice and calm like. You'll go first and I'll be right behind.' He gestured with the gun. 'Get going, then. Towards the gate. And don't do anything stupid. We pass anyone, you keep yer gob shut, right?'

She nodded.

'So what are you waiting for?'

She walked slowly, unsteadily, her legs like jelly. Her guts were churning over, bile rising into her throat. 'Where are we going?'

'Where do you think?'

'To see Hull,' she said, her voice quivering with fear.

'*Mr* Hull to you, darlin'. And he ain't best pleased with you and your fella. I can tell you that for nothing.'

She could have pleaded with him to let her go, begged and grovelled, but she knew it was pointless. She plodded on, one painful step after another. If she'd had the strength she would have made a run for it – a bullet in the back was better than the long lingering punishment Hull would have in store for her. She bowed her head but didn't bother to pray. She was beyond hope or faith. God had abandoned her. She was on her own.